Ombra by Margaret Oliphant

Margaret Oliphant Wilson was born on April 4th, 1828 to Francis W. Wilson, a clerk, and Margaret Oliphant, at Wallyford, near Musselburgh, East Lothian.

Her youth was spent in establishing a writing style and by 1849 she had her first novel published: Passages in the Life of Mrs. Margaret Maitland.

Two years later, in 1851 Caleb Field was published and also an invitation to contribute to Blackwood's Magazine; the beginning of a life time business relationship.

In May 1852, Margaret married her cousin, Frank Wilson Oliphant. Their marriage produced six children but, tragically, three died in infancy. When her husband developed signs of the dreaded consumption (tuberculosis) they moved to Florence, and then to Rome where, sadly, he died.

Margaret was naturally devastated but was also now left without support and only her income from writing to support the family. She returned to England and took up the burden of supporting her three remaining children by her literary activity.

Her incredible and prolific work rate increased both her commercial reputation and the size of her reading audience. Tragedy struck again in January 1864 when her only remaining daughter Maggie died.

In 1866 she settled at Windsor to be closer to her sons, who were being educated at near-by Eton School.

For more than thirty years she pursued a varied literary career but family life continued to bring problems. Cyril Francis, her eldest son, died in 1890. The younger son, Francis, who she nicknamed 'Cecco', died in 1894.

With the last of her children now lost to her, she had little further interest in life. Her health steadily and inexorably declined.

Margaret Oliphant Wilson Oliphant died at the age of 69 in Wimbledon on 20th June 1897. She is buried in Eton beside her sons.

Index of Contents

CHAPTER I

Katherine Courtenay was an only child, and a great heiress; and both her parents had died before she was able to form any clear idea of them. She was brought up in total ignorance of the natural life of childhood—that world hemmed in by the dear faces of father and mother, brother and sister, which forms to most girls the introductory chapter into life. She never knew it. She lived in Langton-Courtenay—with her nurse first, and then with her governess, the centre of a throng of servants, in the immense desolate house. Even in these relationships the lonely child did not find the motherhood which lonely children so often find in the care of some pitying, tender-hearted stranger. Her guardian, who was her father's uncle, an old man of the world, was one of those who distrust old servants, and accept from their inferiors nothing more than can be paid for. He had made up his mind from the beginning that little Kate should not be eaten up by locusts, as he said—that she should have no kind of retainers about her, flattering her vanity with unnecessary affection and ostentatious zeal; but only honest servants (as honest, he would add, as they ever are), who expected nothing but the day's wages for the day's work. To procure this, he allowed no one to remain long with his ward. Her nurse was changed half a dozen times during the period in which she required such a guardian; and her governess had shared the same fate. She had never been allowed to attach herself to one more than another. When any signs of feeling made themselves apparent, Mr. Courtenay sent forth his remorseless decree. 'Kate shall never be any woman's slave, nor any old servant's victim, if I can help it,' he said. He would have liked, had that been practicable, to turn her into a public school, and let her 'find her level,' as boys do; but as that was not practicable, he made sure, at least, that no sentimental influences should impair his nursling's independence and vigour. Thus the alleviations which natural sympathy and pity might have given her, were lost to Kate. Her attendants were afraid to love her; her often-changed instructresses had to shut their hearts against the appeal of compassion, as well as the appeal made by the girl's natural attractiveness. She had to be to them as princesses are but rarely to their teachers and companions—a half-mistress, half-pupil. An act of utter self-renunciation was required of them before ever they set foot in Langton-Courtenay. Mr. Courtenay himself made the engagement, and prescribed its terms. He paid very liberally; and he veiled his insolence under the garb of perfect politeness. 'I do not wish Miss Courtenay to make any friends out of her own class,' he would say. 'I shall do my utmost to make the temporary connection between my niece and you advantageous to yourself, Miss —. But I must exact, on the other side, that there shall be no sentimental bonds formed, no everlasting friendships, no false relationship. I have seen the harm of such things, and suffered from it. Therefore, if these should be your ideas—'

'You wanted a governess, I heard, and I applied for the situation—I never thought of anything more,' said quickly, with some offence, the irritated applicant.

'Precisely,' said Mr. Courtenay. 'With this understanding everything may be decided at once. I am happy to have met with a lady who understands my meaning.' And thus the bargain would be made. But, as it is natural to suppose, the ladies who were willing to take service under these terms, were by no means the highest of their class. Sometimes it would happen that Mr. Courtenay received a sharp rebuff in these preliminary negotiations. 'I trust, of course, that I shall grow fond of my pupil, and she of me,' said one stouter-hearted woman, for example. And the old Squire made her a sarcastic bow.

'Quite unnecessary—wholly unnecessary, I assure you,' he said.

'Then there is nothing more to be said about it,' was the reply; and this applicant—whose testimonials were so high, and were from such 'good people' (meaning, of course, from a succession of duchesses, countesses, and families of renown), that Mr. Courtenay would, he confessed, have given 'any money' to secure her services—got up with impatience, and made him a curtsey which would, could she have managed it, have been as sarcastic as his bow, but which, as it turned out, was only an agitated and awkward obeisance, tremulous with generous rage: 'such an arrangement would be quite impossible to me.'

And so poor Kate missed a woman who might have been a kind of secondary mother to the forlorn child, and acquired a mercenary dragon instead, who loved nobody, and was incapable of attracting love.

The consequences of this training were not, perhaps, exactly such as might have been expected. Kate's high spirits and energetic temper retained a certain ascendancy over her circumstances; her faults were serious and deep-rooted, but on the surface she had a gaieté du cœur—an impulsive power of sympathy and capacity for interesting herself in other people, which could not but be potent for good or evil in her life. It developed, however, in the first place, into a love of interference, and consequently of gossip, which would have alarmed anyone really concerned for her character and happiness. She was kept from loving or from being loved. She was arbitrarily fixed among strangers, surrounded with faces which were never permitted to become familiar, defrauded of all the interests of affection; and her lively mind avenged itself by a determination to know everything and meddle with everything within her reach. Kate at fifteen was not mournful, despondent, or solitary, as might have been looked for; on the contrary, she was the very type of activity, a little inquisitive despot, the greatest gossip and busy-body within a dozen miles of Langton-Courtenay. The tendrils of her nature, which ought to have clung firm and close around some natural prop, trailed all abroad, and caught at everything. Nothing was too paltry for her, and nothing too grand. She had the audacity to interfere in the matter of the lighted candles on the altar, when the new High-Church Rector of Langton first came into power; and she interfered remorselessly to take away Widow Budd's snuff, when it was found out that the reason she assigned for wanting it—the state of her eyes—was a shameful pretence. Kate did not shrink from either of these bold practical assaults upon the liberty of her subjects. She would no doubt have inquired into the Queen's habits, and counselled, if not required some change in them, had that illustrious lady paid a visit to Langton-Courtenay. This was how Nature managed itself for her especial training. She could no more be made unsympathetic, unenergetic, or deprived of her warm interest in the world, than she could be made sixty. But all these good qualities could be turned into evil, and this was what her guardian managed to do. It did not occur to him to watch over her personally during her childhood, and therefore he was unconscious of the exact progress of affairs.

Old Mr. Courtenay was totally unlike the child whom he had undertaken to train. He did not care a straw for his fellow-creatures; they took their way, and he took his, and there was an end of the matter. When any great calamity occurred, he shrugged his shoulders, and comforted himself with the reflection that it must be their own fault. When, on the contrary, there was joy and rejoicing, he took his share of the feast, and reflected, with a smile, that wise men enjoy the banquets which fools make. To put yourself out of the way for anything that might happen, seemed to him the strangest, the most incomprehensible folly. And when he made up his mind to save the young heiress of his house from the locusts, and to keep her free from all connections or associations which might be a drag upon her in future times, he had been honestly unconscious that he was doing wrong to Nature. Love!—what did she want with love?—what was the good of it? Mr. Courtenay himself got on very well without any such frivolous imaginary necessity, and so, of course, would Kate. He was so confident in the wisdom, and even in the naturalness of his system, that he did not even think it worth his while to watch over its progress. Of course it would come all right. Why should he trouble himself about the details?—to keep fast to this principle gave him quite enough trouble. Circumstances, however, had occurred which made it expedient for him to visit Langton-Courtenay when Kate completed her fifteenth year. New people had appeared on the scene, who threatened to be a greater trouble to him, and a greater danger for Kate, than even the governesses; and his sense of duty was strong enough to move him, in thus far, at least, to personal interference on his ward's behalf.

At fifteen Kate Courtenay was the very impersonation of youthful beauty, vigour, and impetuous life. She seemed to dance as she walked, to be eloquent and rhetorical when she spoke, out of the mere exuberance of her being. Her hair, which was full of colour, chestnut-brown, still fell in negligent abundance about her shoulders; not in stiff curls, after the old mode, nor crêpé, according to the new, but in one undulating, careless flow. Though she was still dressed in the sackcloth of the school-room, there was an air of authoritative independence about her, more imposing a great deal than was that garb of complete womanhood, the 'long dress,' to which she looked forward with awe and hope. Her figure was full for her age, yet so light, so well-formed, so free and rapid in movement, that it had all the graceful effect of the most girlish slenderness. Her voice was slightly high-pitched—not soft and low, as is the ideal woman's—and she talked for three people, pouring forth her experiences, her recollections, her questions and remarks, in a flood. It was not quite ladylike, more than one unhappy instructress of Kate's youth had suggested; but there seemed no reason in the world why she should pay any attention to such a suggestion. 'If it is natural for me to talk so, why should I try to talk otherwise? Why should I care what people think? You may, Miss Blank, because they will find fault with you, and take away your pupils, and that sort of thing; but nobody can do anything to me.' This was Kate's vindication of her voice, which rang through all Langton-Courtenay clear as a bell, and sweet enough to hear, but imperative, decisive, high-pitched, and unceasing. When her uncle saw her, his first sensation was one of pleasure. She was waiting for him on the step before the front door, the sunshine surrounding her with a golden halo, made out of the stray golden luminous threads in her hair.

'How do you do, uncle?' she called out to him as soon as he appeared. 'I am so glad you have made up your mind to come at last. It is always a change to have you here, and there are so many things I want to talk of. You have taken the fly from the station, I see, though the carriage went for you half-an-hour ago. That is what I am always telling you, Giles, you are continually half-an-hour too late. Uncle, mind how you get down. That fly-horse is the most vicious thing! She'll go off when you have one foot to the ground, if you don't mind. I told old Mrs. Sayer to sell her, but these people never will do what they are told. I am glad to see you, Uncle Courtenay. How do you do?'

'A little bewildered with my journey, Kate—and to find you a young lady receiving your guests, instead of a shy little girl running off when you were spoken to.'

'Was I ever shy?' said Kate, with unfeigned wonder. 'What a very odd thing! I don't remember it. I thought I had always been as I am now. Tell Mrs. Sayers, Tom, that I have heard something I don't like about one of the people at Glenhouse, and that I am coming to speak to her to-morrow. Uncle, will you have some tea, or wine, or anything, or shall I take you to your room! Dinner is to be at seven. I am so glad you have come to make a change. I hate dinner at two. It suits Miss Blank's digestion, but I am sure I hate it, and now it shall be changed. Don't you think I am quite grown up, Uncle Courtenay? I am as tall as you.'

He was little, dried-up, shrivelled—a small old man; and she a young Diana, with a bloom which had still all the freshness of childhood. Uncle Courtenay felt irritated when she measured her elastic figure beside the stooping form of his old age.

'Yes, yes, yes!' he said, pettishly. 'Grown up, indeed! I should think you were. But stop this stream of talk, for heaven's sake, and moderate your voice, and take me in somewhere. I don't want to have your height discussed among your servants, nor anything else I may have to say.'

'Oh! for that matter, I do not mind who hears me talk,' said Kate. 'Why should I? Nobody, of course, ever interferes with me. Come into the library, uncle. It is nice and cool this hot day. Did you see anyone in the village as you came up? Did you notice if there was anyone at the Rectory? They are curious people at the Rectory, and don't take the trouble to make themselves at all agreeable. Miss Blank thinks it very strange, considering that I am the Lady of the Manor, and have a right to their respect, and ought to be considered and obeyed. Don't you think, uncle—'

'Obeyed!' he said, with a laugh which was half amusement, and half consternation. 'A baby of fifteen is no more the Lady of the Manor than Miss Blank is. You silly child, what do you mean?'

'I am not a child,' said Kate, haughtily. 'I am quite aware of my position. I may not be of age yet, but that does not make much difference. However, if you are tired, uncle, as I think you are by your face, I won't bore you with that, though it is one of my grievances. Should you like to be left alone till dinner? If you would let me advise you, I should say lie down, and have some eau-de-Cologne on a handkerchief, and perhaps a cup of tea. It is the best thing for worry and headache.'

'In heaven's name, how do you know?'

'Perfectly well,' said Kate, calmly. 'I have made people do it a hundred times, and it has always succeeded. Perfect quiet, uncle, and a wet handkerchief on your forehead, and a cup of my special tea. I will tell Giles to bring you one, and a bottle of eau-de-Cologne; and if you don't move till the dressing bell rings, you will find yourself quite refreshed and restored. Why, I have made people do it over and over again, and I have never known it to fail.'

Miss Courtenay, of Langton-Courtenay, had scarcely ever in her life been promoted before to the glories of a late dinner. She had received no visitors, and the house was still under school-room sway, as became her age, consequently this was a great era to Kate. She placed herself at the head of the table, with a pride and delight which neither her cynical old uncle nor her passive governess had the least notion of. The occurrence was trifling to them, but to her its importance was immense. Miss Blank, who was troubled by fears of being in the way—fears which her charge made no effort to enlighten—and whose digestion, besides, was feeble, preferred to have the usual two o'clock dinner, and to leave Kate alone to entertain her uncle. This dinner had been the subject of Kate's thoughts for some days. She had insisted on the production of all the plate which the little household at Langton had been permitted to retain; she had the table decked with a profusion of flowers. She had not yet discretion enough to know that a small table would have been in better taste than the large one, seated at opposite ends of which her guardian and herself were as if miles apart. They could not see each other for the flowers; they could scarcely hear each other for the distance; but Kate was happy. There was a certain grown-up grandeur, even in the discomfort. As for Mr. Courtenay, he was extremely impatient. 'What a fool the girl must be!' he said to himself; and went on to comment bitterly upon the popular fallacy which credits women with intuitive good taste and social sense, at least. When he made a remark upon the long distance that separated them, Kate cheerfully suggested that he should come up beside her. She took away his breath by her boldness; she deafened him with her talk. Behind that veil of flowers which concealed her young, bright figure, she poured forth the monologue of a rural gossip, never pausing to inquire if he knew or cared anything about the objects of it. And of course Mr. Courtenay neither knew nor cared. His own acquaintance with the house of his father had ended long before she was born, before her father had succeeded to the property; and he never had been interested in the common people who formed Kate's world. Then it was very apparent to Kate's uncle that the man who waited (and waited very badly) grinned without concealment at his young mistress's talk; and that Kate herself was not indifferent to the fond of appreciation thus secured to her. It would be impossible to put into words the consternation which filled him as he ate an indifferent dinner, and listened to all this. He had succeeded so far that no one governess nor maid had secured dominion over the mind of the future sovereign of Langton; but at what a cost had he secured it! 'You seem to interest yourself a great deal about all these people,' he said at length.

'Yes, Uncle Courtenay, of course I do. I have nobody else to take an interest in,' said Kate. 'But the people at the Rectory are very disagreeable. If the living should fall vacant in my time, it certainly shall never go to one of them. The second son, Herbert, whom they call Bertie, is going in for the Church, and I suppose they think he will succeed his father; but I am sure he never shall, if that happens in my time. There are two daughters, Edith and Minnie; and I don't think Mrs. Hardwick can be a good manager, for the girls are always so badly dressed; and you know, Uncle Courtenay, it is a very good living. I have felt tempted a dozen times to say, "Why don't you clothe the girls better?" If they had been farmers, or anything of that sort, I should at once—'

'And how do the farmers like your interference, Kate?'

'My interference, Uncle Courtenay! Why, of course one must speak if one sees things going wrong. But to return to the Hardwicks. I did write, you know, about the candles on the altar—'

'Why, Kate, I did not know how universal you were,' said her uncle, half-amused—'theological, too?'

'I don't know about theology; but burning candles in daylight, when there was not a bit of darkness—not a fog, even—what is the good of it? I thought I had a right to let Mr. Hardwick know. It is my parish and my tenantry, and I do not mean to give them up. Isn't the Queen the head of the Church?—then, of course, I am the head of Langton-Courtenay, and it is flat rebellion on the Rector's part. What do you mean, Uncle Courtenay?—are you laughing at me?'

'Why, Kate, your theories take away my breath,' said Mr. Courtenay. 'Don't you think this is going a little too far? You cannot be head of the Church in Langton-Courtenay without interfering with Her Majesty's prerogative. She is over all the country, you know. You don't claim the power of the sword, I hope, as well—'

'What is the power of the sword, uncle? I should claim anything that I thought belonged to me,' cried Kate.

'But you would not hold a court, I hope, and erect a gallows in the courtyard,' said Mr. Courtenay. 'I suppose our ancestor, Sir Bernard had the right, but I would not advise you to claim it, my dear. Kate, now that the man is gone, I must tell you that I think you have been very impertinent to the Rector, and nothing but the fact that you are a baby, and don't know what you're doing—'

'A baby!—and impertinent!—uncle!—I!'

'Yes, you—though you think yourself such a great personage, you must learn to remember that you are a child, my dear. I will make a point of calling on the Rector to-morrow, and I hope he will look over your nonsense. But remember there must be no more of it, Kate.'

'Don't speak to me like that,' she said, half weeping. 'I will not be so spoken to. Uncle, you are only my guardian, and it is I who am the mistress here.'

'You little fool!' he said, under his breath; and then a sudden twinge came over him—a doubt whether he had been as wise as he thought he had been in the training of this girl. He was not the sort of man, so common in the world, to whom cynicism in every other respect is compatible with enthusiasm in respect to himself. He was a universal cynic. He distrusted himself as well as other people, and consequently he did not shut his eyes to the fact that a mistake had been made. While Kate dried her eyes hastily, and tried her best to maintain her dignity, and overcome those temptations towards the hysterical which prevented her from making an immediate reply, her uncle was so candid as to stop short, as it were, in his own course, and review a decision he had just made. He had not known Kate when he made it; now that he saw her in all her force and untamableness, with all those wonderful ideas of her position, and determination to interfere with every one, he could not but think that it might be wise to reconsider the question. What should he do with this unmanageable girl?—good heavens! what could he do with her? Whereas, here was a new influence offering itself, which perhaps might do all that was wanted. Mr. Courtenay pondered while Kate recovered some appearance of calm. She had never (she said to herself) been so spoken to in her life. She did not understand it—she would not submit to it! And when the hot mist of tears dried up from her eyes, Kate looked from behind the flowers at Mr. Courtenay, with her heart beating high for the conflict, and yet felt daunted—she could not tell how—and did not know what to do. She would have liked to rush out of the room, slamming the door behind her; but in that case she would have lost at once her dignity and the strawberries, which are tempting at fifteen. She would not let him see that he had beaten her; and yet—how could she begin the struggle?—what could she say? She sat and peeped at him from behind the vase of flowers which stood in the centre of the table, and was silent for five whole minutes in her bewilderment—perhaps longer than she ever had been silent before in her life. Finally, it was Mr. Courtenay who broke the silence—a fact which of itself gave him a vast advantage over her.

'Kate,' he said, 'I have listened to you for a long time. I want you now to listen to me for a little. You have heard of your aunt Anderson? She is your mother's only sister. She has been—I suppose you know?—for a long time abroad.'

'I don't know anything about her,' said Kate, pouting. This was not entirely true, for she had heard just so much of this unknown relation as a few rare letters received from her could tell—letters which left no particular impression on Kate's mind, except the fact that her correspondent signed herself 'Your affectionate Aunt,' and which had ceased for years. Kate's mother had not been born on the Langton-Courtenay level. She had been the daughter of a solicitor, whose introduction into the up-to-that-moment spotless pedigree of the Courtenays lay very heavy on the heart of the family. Kate knew this fact very well, and it galled her. She might have forgiven her mother, but she felt a visionary grudge against her aunt, and why should she care to know anything about her? This sense of inferiority on the part of her relation kept her silent, as well as the warm and lively force of temper which dissuaded her from showing any interest in a matter suggested by her uncle. If she could but have kept up so philosophical a way of thinking! But the fact was, that no sooner had she answered than her usual curiosity and human interest in her fellow-creatures began to tug at Kate's heart. What was he going to tell her about her aunt Anderson? Who was she? What was she? What manner of woman? Was she poor, and so capable of being made Kate's vassal; or well off, and likely to meet her niece on equal terms? She had to shut up her lips very tight, lest some of these many questions should burst from them. And if Uncle Courtenay had but known his advantage, and kept silent a little, she would have almost gone on her knees to him for further information. But Mr. Courtenay did not understand his advantage, and went on talking.

'Her husband was British Consul somewhere or other in Italy. They have been all over the Continent, in one place and another; but he died a year ago, and now they have come home. She wishes to see you, Kate. I have got a letter from her—with a great deal of nonsense in it—but that by the way. There is a great deal of nonsense in all women's letters! She wants to come here, I suppose; but I don't choose that she should come here.'

'Why, Uncle Courtenay?' said Kate, forgetting her wrath in the excitement of this novelty.

'It is unnecessary to enter into my reasons. When you are of age you can have whom you please; but in the meantime I don't intend that this house should be a centre of meddling and gossip for the whole neighbourhood. So the aunt shan't come. But you can go and visit her for a few weeks, if you choose, Kate.'

'Why shouldn't my aunt come if I wish it?' cried Kate, furious. 'Uncle Courtenay, I tell you again you are only my guardian, and Langton-Courtenay belongs to me!'

'And I reply, my dear, that you are fifteen, and nothing belongs to you,' said the old man, with a smile. 'It is hard to repress so much noble independence, but still that is the truth.'

'You are a tyrant—you are a monster, Uncle Courtenay! I won't submit to it! I will appeal to some one. I will take it into my own hands.'

'The most sensible thing you can do, in the meantime, is to retire to your own room, and try to bring yourself back to common sense,' said Mr. Courtenay, contemptuously. 'Not another word, Kate. Where is your governess, or your nurse, or whoever has charge of you? Little fool! do you think, because you rule over a pack of obsequious servants, that you can manage me.'

'I will not be your slave! I will never, never be your slave!' cried Kate, springing to her feet, and raising her flushed face over the flowers. Her eyes blazed, her little rosy hand was clenched so tight that the soft knuckles were white. Her lips were apart, her breath burned, her soul was on fire. Quite ready for a fight, ready to meet any enemy that might come against her—breathing fire and flame!

'Pho! pho! child, don't be a fool!' said Mr. Courtenay; and he calmly rang the bell, and ordered Giles to remove the wine to a small table which stood in the window, where he removed himself presently, without taking the least notice of her.

Kate stood for a moment, like a young goddess of war, thunder-stricken by the calm of her adversary; and then rushed out, flinging down her napkin, and dragging a corner of the table-cloth, so as to upset the great dish of ruby strawberries which she had not tasted. They fell on the floor like a heavy shower, scattering over all the carpet; and Kate closed the door after her with a thud which ran through the whole house. She paused a moment in the hall, irresolute. Poor untrained, unfriended child, she had no one to go to, to seek comfort from. She knew how Miss Blank would receive her passion; and she was too proud to acknowledge to her maid, Maryanne, how she had been beaten. She caught the broad-brimmed garden-hat which hung in the hall, and a shawl to wrap herself in, and rushed out, a forlorn, solitary young creature, into the noble park that was her own. There was not a child in the village but had some one to fly to when it had received a blow; but Kate had no one—she had to calm herself down, and bear her passion and its consequences alone. She rushed across the park, forgetting even that her uncle Courtenay could see her from the window, and unconscious of the chuckle with which he perceived her discomfiture. 'Little passionate idiot!' he said to himself, as he sipped his wine. But yet perhaps had he known what was to come of it, Mr. Courtenay would not have been quite so contented with himself. He had forgotten all about the feelings and sufferings of her age, if indeed he had ever known them. He did not care a jot for the mortification and painful rage with which he had filled her. 'Serve her right!' he would have said. He was old himself, and far beyond the reach of such tempests; and he had no pity for them. But all the more he thought with a sense of comfort of this Mrs. Anderson, with her plebeian name, and sentimental anxiety about 'the only child of a beloved sister.' The beloved sister herself had not been very welcome in Langton-Courtenay. The Consul's widow should never be allowed to enter here, that was very certain; but, still, use might be made of her to train this ungovernable child.

CHAPTER III

Kate Courtenay rushed across the park in a passion of mortification and childish despair, and fled as fast as her swift feet could carry her to a favourite spot—a little dell, through which the tiniest of brooks ran trickling, so hidden under the trees and copse that even Summer never quite dried it up. There was a little semi-artificial waterfall, just where the brook descended into the depths of this little dell. In Spring it was a wilderness of primroses and violets; and so long as wild flowers would blow, they were always to be found in this sunny nook. The only drawback was that a footpath ran within sight of it, and that the village had an often-contested right of way skirting the bank. Kate had issued arbitrary orders more than once that no one was to be suffered to pass; but the law was too strong for Kate, as it had been for her grandfathers before her; and, on the whole, perhaps the occasional passenger had paid for his intrusion by the additional liveliness he had given to the landscape. It was one of Kate's 'tricks,' her governess once went so far as to say, to take her evening walk here, in order to detect the parties of lovers with whom this footway was a favourite resort. All this, however, was absent from Kate's mind now. She rushed through the trees and bushes, and threw herself on the sunny grass by the brookside; and at fifteen passion is not silent, as it endeavours to be at a more advanced age. Kate did not weep only, but cried, and sobbed, and made a noise, so that some one passing by in the footway on the other side of the bushes was arrested by the sound, and drew near.

It is hard to hear sounds of weeping in a warm Summer evening, when the air is sweet with sounds of pleasure. There is something incongruous in it, which wounds the listener. The passenger in this case was young and tender-hearted, and he was so far like Kate herself, that when he heard sounds of trouble, he felt that he had a right to interfere. He was a clergyman's son, and in the course of training to be a clergyman too. His immediate destination was, as soon as he should be old enough to be ordained, the curacy of Langton-Courtenay, of which his father was Rector. Whether he should eventually succeed his father was of course in the hands of Providence and Miss Courtenay; he had not taken his degree yet, and was at least two years off the time when he could take orders; but still the shadow of his profession was upon him, and, in right of that, Herbert Hardwick felt that it was his business to interfere.

What he saw, when he looked through the screen of trees, was the figure of a girl in a light Summer dress, half seated, half lying on the grass. Her head was bent down between her hands; and even had this not been the case, it is probable Bertie, who had scarcely seen Miss Courtenay, would not have recognised her. Of course, had he taken time to think, he must have known at once that nobody except Kate, or some visitor at the Hall, was likely to be there; but he never took time to think. It was not his way. He stepped at once over the fence, walking through the brushwood, and strode across the brook without pause or hesitation.

'What is the matter?' he said, in his boyish promptitude. 'Have you hurt yourself?—have you lost your way?—what is wrong?'

For a moment she took no notice of him, except to turn her back more completely on him. Herbert had sisters, and he was not so ceremonious to young womankind generally as might otherwise have happened. He laid his hand quite frankly on her shoulder, and knelt down beside her on the grass. 'No,' he said, with a certain authority, 'my poor child, whoever you may be, I can't leave you to cry your eyes out. What is the matter? Look up and tell me. Have you lost yourself? If you will tell me where you have come from, I will take you home. Or have you hurt yourself? Now, pray don't be cross, but answer, and let me know what I can do.'

Kate had almost got her weeping-fit over, and surprise had wakened a new sentiment in her mind. Surprise and curiosity, and the liveliest desire to know whose the voice was, and whose the hand laid so lightly, yet with a certain authority, upon her shoulder. She made a dash with her handkerchief across her face to clear away the tears, and then she suddenly turned round and confronted her comforter. She looked up at him with tears hanging on her eyelashes, and her face wet with them, yet with all the soul of self-will which was natural to her looking out of her eyes.

'Do you know,' she said hastily, 'that you are trespassing? This is private property, and you have no right to be here.'

The answer which Bertie Hardwick made to this was, first, an astonished stare, and then a burst of laughter. The sudden change from sympathy and concern to amusement was so great that it produced an explosion of merriment which he could not restrain. He was a handsome lad of twenty—blue-eyed, with brown hair curling closely about his head, strongly built, and full of life, though not gigantic in his proportions. Even now, though he had heard of the imperious little Lady of the Manor, it did not occur to him to connect her with this stranger. He laughed with perfect heartiness and abandon; she looking on quite gravely and steadily, the while, assisting at the outburst—a fact which did not diminish the amusing character of the scene.

'I came to help you,' he said. 'I hope you will not give information. Nobody will know I have trespassed unless you tell, and that would be ungrateful; for I thought there was something the matter, and came to be of use to you.'

'There is nothing the matter,' said Kate, very gravely, making a photograph of him with the keen, inquisitive eyes, from which, by this time, all tears were gone.

'I am glad to hear it,' he said; and then, with another laugh—'I suppose you are trespassing too. Can I help you over the fence?—or is there anything that I can do?'

'I am not trespassing—I am at home—I am Miss Courtenay,' said Kate, with infinite dignity, rising from the grass. She stood thus looking at him with the air of a queen defending her realm from invasion; she felt, to tell the truth, something like Helen Macgregor, when she starts up suddenly, and demands of the Sassenach how they dare to come into Macgregor's country. But the young man was not impressed; the muscles about his mouth quivered with suppressed laughter and the strenuous effort to keep it down. He made her a bow—the best he could under the circumstances—and stood with the evening sunshine shining upon his uncovered head and crisp curls, a very pleasant object to look upon, in an attitude of respect which was half fun and half mockery, though Kate did not find that out.

'Then I have been mistaken, and there is nothing for it but to apologise, and take myself off,' said Bertie. 'I am very sorry, I am sure. I thought something had gone wrong. To tell the truth I thought you were—crying.'

'I was crying,' said Kate. She did not in the least want him to go. He was company—he was novelty—he was something quite fresh, and already had altogether driven away her passion and her tears. Her heart quite leapt up at this agreeable diversion. 'I was crying, and something had gone very wrong,' she said in a subdued tone, and with a gentle sigh.

'I am very sorry,' said Bertie. 'I don't suppose it is anything in which I could be of use—?'

She looked at him again. 'I think I know who you are,' she said. 'You must be the second son at the Rectory—the one whom they call Bertie. At least I don't know who else you could be.'

'Yes, I am the one they call Bertie,' he said, laughing. 'Herbert Hardwick, at your service. And I did not mean to trespass.'

The laugh rang pleasantly through all the echoes. It was infectious. Kate felt that, but for her dignity, she would like to laugh too. And yet it was a serious matter; and to aid and abet a trespasser, and at the same time 'encourage' the Rectory people, was, she felt, a thing which she ought not to do. But then it had been real concern for herself, the Lady of the Manor, which had been at the bottom of it; and that deserved to be considered on the other side.

'I suppose not,' she said, seriously. 'Indeed, I am very particular about it. I don't see why you should laugh. I should not think of going to walk in your grounds without leave, and why should you in mine? But since you are here, you must not go all that way back. If you like to come with me, I will show you a nearer way. Don't you think it is a very fine park? Were you ever in one like it before?'

'Yes,' said Herbert, calmly, 'a great many. Langton-Courtenay is very nice, but it wants size. The glades are pretty, and the trees are charming, but everything is on a small scale.'

'On a small scale!' Kate cried, half-choking with indignation. This unparalleled presumption took away even her voice.

'Yes, decidedly small. How many acres are there in it? My uncle, Sir Herbert Eldridge, has five hundred acres in his. I am called after him, and I have been a great deal with him, you know. That is why I think your park so small. But it is very pretty!' said Herbert, condescendingly, with a sense of the humour of the situation. As for Kate, she was crushed. She looked up at him first in a blaze of disdain, intending to do battle for her own, but the number of acres in Sir Herbert Eldridge's park made an end of Kate.

'I thought you were going to be a clergyman,' she said.

'So I am, I suppose; but what then?'

'Oh! I thought—I didn't know,' cried Kate. 'I supposed perhaps you were not very well off. But if you have such a rich uncle, with such a beautiful park—'

'I don't know what that has to do with it,' said Bertie, with a mischievous light in his eyes. 'We are not so very poor. We have dinners three or four times a week, and bread and cheese on the other days. A great many people are worse off than that.'

'If you mean to laugh at me,' said Kate, stopping short, with an angry gesture, 'I think you had better turn back again. I am not a person to be made fun of.' And then instantly the water rushed to her eyes, for she was as susceptible as any child is to ridicule. The young man checked himself on the verge of laughter, and apologised.

'I beg your pardon,' he said. 'I did not mean to make myself disagreeable. Besides, I don't think you are quite well. I hope you will let me walk with you as far as the Hall.'

'Oh! no,' said Kate. But the suppressed tears, which had come to her eyes out of rage and indignation, suddenly grew blinding with self-pity, and recollection of her hard fate. 'Oh! you can't think how unhappy I am,' she said, suddenly clasping her hands together—and a big tear came with a rush down her innocent nose, and fell, throwing up a little shower of salt spray from the concussion, upon her ungloved hand. This startled her, and her sense of dignity once more awoke; but she struggled with difficulty against her desire for sympathy. 'I ought not to talk to a stranger,' she said; 'but, oh! you can't think how disagreeable Uncle Courtenay can make himself, though he looks so nice. And Miss Blank does not mind if I were dead and buried! Oh!' This exclamation was called forth by another great blot of dew from her eyes, which once more dashed and broke upon her hand, as a wave does on a rock. Kate looked at it with a silent concern which absorbed her. Her own tears! What was there in the world more touching or more sad?

'I am so sorry,' said Bertie Hardwick, moved by compassion. 'Was that what you were crying for? You should come to the Rectory, to my mother, who always sets everybody right.'

'Your mother would not care to see me,' said Kate, looking at him wistfully. 'She does not like me—she thinks I am your enemy. People should consider, Mr. Bertie—they should consider my position—'

'Yes, you poor little thing,' said Bertie, with the utmost sympathy; 'that is quite true—you have neither father nor mother to keep you right—people ought to make allowance for that.'

To describe Kate's consternation at this speech would be impossible. She a poor little thing!—she without any one to set her right! Was the boy mad? She was so stunned for the moment that she could make no reply—so many new emotions overwhelmed her. To make the discovery that Bertie Hardwick was nice, that he had an uncle with a park larger than the park at Langton-Courtenay; to learn that Langton-Courtenay was 'small,' and that she herself was a poor little thing. 'What next?' Kate asked herself. For all this had come to her knowledge in the course of half an hour. If life was to bring a succession of such surprises, how strange, how very strange it must be!

'And I do wish you knew my mother,' he went on innocently, not having the least idea that Kate's silence arose from the fact that she was dumb with indignation; 'she has the gift of understanding everybody. Isn't it a pity that you should not know us, Miss Courtenay? My little sister Minnie is about your age, I should think.'

'It is not my fault I don't know you,' burst forth Kate; 'it is because you have not behaved properly to me—because your father would not pay any attention. Is it right for a clergyman to set a bad example, and teach people to rebel? He never even took any notice of my letter, though I am the natural head of the parish—'

'You poor child!' cried Bertie; and then he laughed.

Kate could not bear it—this was worse than her Uncle Courtenay. She stood still for a moment, and looked at him with things unspeakable in her eyes; and then she turned round, and rushed off across the green sward to the Hall, leaving him bewildered and amazed in the middle of the park, this time most evidently a trespasser, not even knowing his way back. He called after her, but received no answer; he stood and gazed round him in his consternation. Finally he laughed, though this time it was at himself, thus left in the lurch. But Kate was not aware of that fact. She heard the laugh, and it gave her wings; she fled to her melancholy home, where there was nobody to comfort her, choking with sobs and rage. Oh! how forlorn she was!—oh! how insulted, despised, trodden upon by everybody, she who was the lawful lady of the land! He would go and tell the Rectory girls, and together they would laugh at her. Kate would have sent a thunderbolt on the Rectory, or fire from Heaven, if she could.

CHAPTER IV

Kate rushed upstairs to her own room when she reached the Hall; she was wild with mortification and the sense of downfall. It was the first time she had come into collision with her fellow-creatures of a class equal to her own. Servants and poor people in the village had been impertinent to her ere now; but these were accidents, which Kate treated with the contempt they deserved, and which she could punish by the withdrawal of privileges and presents. She could scold, and did so soundly; and she could punish. But she could neither scold nor punish in the present case. Her Uncle Courtenay would only look at her in that exasperating way, with that cool smile on his face, as if she were a kitten; and this new being, with whom already she felt herself so well acquainted—Bertie would laugh, and be kind, and sorry for her. 'Poor child!—poor little thing!' These were the words he had dared to use. 'Oh!' Kate thought, I would like to kill him! I would like to—' And then she asked herself what would he say at home? and writhed on the bed on which she had thrown herself in inextinguishable shame. They would laugh at her; they would make fun of her. 'Oh! I would like to kill myself,' cried Kate, in her thoughts. She cried her eyes out in the silence of her room. There was no Bertie to come there with sympathetic eyes to ask what she was doing. Miss Blank did not care; neither did any one in the house—not even her own maid, who was always about her, and to whom she would talk for hours together. Kate buried her head in her pillow, and tried to picture to herself the aspect of the Rectory. There would be the mother—who, Bertie said, understood everybody—seated somewhere near the table; and Edith and Minnie in the room—one of them, perhaps, doing worsted-work, one at the piano, or copying music, or drawing, as young ladies do in novels. Now and then, no doubt Mrs. Hardwick would give them little orders; she would say, perhaps, 'Play me one of the Lieder, Minnie,' or 'that little air of Mozart's.' And she would say something about her work to Edith. Involuntarily that picture rose before lonely Kate. She seemed to see them seated there, with the windows open, and sweet scents coming in from the garden. She heard the voices murmuring, and a soft little strain, andante pianissimo, tinkling like the soft flow of a stream through the pleasant place. Oh! how pleasant it must be—even though she did not like the Rectory people, though Mr. Hardwick had been so rebellious, though they did not believe in her (Kate's) natural headship of Church and Slate in Langton-Courtenay.

She sobbed as she lay and dreamed, and developed her new imagination. She had wondered, half angrily, half wistfully, about the Rectory people before, but Bertie seemed to give a certain reality to them. He was the brother of the girl whom Kate had so often inspected with keen eyes, but did not know; and he said 'Mamma' to that unknown Mrs. Hardwick. 'Mamma!' What a curious word it was, when you came to think of it! Not so serious, nor full of meaning as mother was, but soft and caressing—as of some one who would always feel for you, always put her arm round you, say 'dear' to you, ask what was the matter? Miss Blank never asked what was the matter! She took it for granted that Kate was cross, that it was 'her own fault,' or, as the very kindest hypothesis, that she had a headache, which was not in Kate's way.

She lay sobbing, as I have said; but sobbing softly, as her emotion wore itself out, without tears. Her eyes were red, and her temples throbbed a little. She was worn out; she would not rouse herself and go downstairs to tempt another conflict with her uncle, as, had it not been for this last event, she would have felt disposed to do. And yet, poor child, she wanted her tea. Dinner had not been a satisfactory meal, and Kate could not help saying to herself that if Minnie and Edith had been suffering as she was, their mamma would have come to them in the dark, and kissed them, and bathed their hot foreheads, and brought them cups of tea. But there was no one to bring a cup of tea, without being asked, to a girl who had no mother. Kate had but to ring her bell, and she could have had whatever she pleased; but what did that matter? No one came near her, as it happened. The governess and her maid both supposed her to be with her uncle, and it was only when Maryanne came in at nine o'clock to prepare her young mistress's hair-brushes and dressing-gown, that the young mistress was found, to Maryanne's consternation, stretched on her bed, with a face as white as her dress, and eyes surrounded with red rings. And in the dark, of all things in the world, in a place like Langton-Courtenay, where it was well known the Blue Lady walked, and turned folks to stone! At the first glance Maryanne felt certain that the Blue Lady only could be responsible for the condition in which her young mistress was found.

'Oh! miss,' she cried, 'and why didn't you ring the bell?'

'It did not matter,' said Kate, reproachful and proud.

'Lying there all in the dark—and it don't matter! 'Oh! miss, I know as you ain't timorsome like me, but if you was once to see something—'

'Hold your tongue!' said Kate, peremptorily. 'See something! The thing is, in this house, that one never sees anything! One might die, and it never would be known. You don't care enough for one to come and look if one is dead or alive.'

'Oh! miss!'

'Don't say "Oh miss!" to me,' cried Kate, indignantly, 'or pretend—Go and fetch me some tea. That is the only thing you can do. You don't forget your own tea, or anything else you want; but when I am out of sorts, or have a—headache—'

Kate had no headache, except such as her crying had made; but it was the staple malady, the thing that did duty for everything in Miss Blank's vocabulary, and her pupil naturally followed her example, to this extent, at least.

'Have you got a headache, miss? I'll tell Miss Blank—I'll go and fetch the housekeeper.'

'If you do, I will ask Uncle Courtenay to send you away to-morrow!' cried Kate. 'Go and fetch me some tea.'

But the tea which she had to order for herself was very different, she felt sure, from the tea that Edith Hardwick's mother would have carried upstairs to her unasked. It was tea made by Maryanne, who was not very careful if the kettle was boiling, and who had filled a large teapot full of water, in order to get this one cup. It was very hot and very washy, and made Kate angry. She sent away Maryanne in a fit of indignation, and did her own hair for the night, and made herself very uncomfortable. How different it must be with Edith and Minnie! If Kate had only known it, however, Edith and Minnie, had they conducted themselves as she was doing, would have been metaphorically whipped and put to bed.

In the morning she came down with pale cheeks, but no one took any notice. Uncle Courtenay was reading his paper, and had other things to think of; and Miss Blank intended to ask what her pupil had been doing with herself when they should be alone together in the school-room. They ate their meal in a solemn silence, broken only now and then by a remark from Miss Blank, which was scarcely less solemn. Uncle Courtenay took no notice—he read his paper, which veiled him even from his companion's eyes. At last, Miss Blank, having finished her breakfast, made a sign to Kate that it was time to rise; and then Kate took courage.

'Uncle Courtenay,' she said very softly, 'you said you were going to call—at—the Rectory?'

Uncle Courtenay looked at her round the corner of his paper. 'Well,' he said, 'what of that? Of course I shall call at the Rectory—after what you have told me, I have no choice.'

'Then please—may I go with you?' said Kate. She cast down her eyes demurely as she spoke, and consequently did not see the inquiring glance that he cast at her; but she saw, under her eyelashes, that he had laid down his paper; and this evidence of commotion was a comfort to her soul.

'Go with me!' he said. 'Not to give the Rector any further impertinence, I hope?'

Kate's eyes flashed, but she restrained herself. 'I have never been impertinent to any one, uncle. If I mistook what I had a right to, was that my fault? I am willing to make it up, if they are; and I can go alone if I mayn't go with you.'

'Oh! you can go with me if you choose,' said Mr. Courtenay, ungraciously; and then he took up his paper. But he was not so ungracious as he appeared; he was rather glad, on the whole, to have this opportunity of talking to her, and to see that (as he thought) his reproof of the previous night had produced so immediate an effect. He said to himself, cheerfully, 'Come, the child is not so ungovernable after all;' and was pleased, involuntarily, by the success of his operation. He was pleased, too, with her appearance when she was dressed, and ready to accompany him. She was subdued in tone, and less talkative a great deal than she had been the day before. He took it for granted that it was his influence that had done this—'Another proof,' he said to himself, 'how expedient it is to show that you are master, and will stand no nonsense.' He had been so despairing about her the night before, and saw such a vista of troubles before him in the six years of guardianship that remained, that this docility made him at once complacent and triumphant now.

'I don't want to be hard upon you, Kate,' he said; 'but you must recollect that at present, in the eye of the law, you are a child, and have no right to interfere with anything—neither parish, nor estate, nor even house.'

'But it is all mine, Uncle Courtenay.'

'That has nothing to do with it,' said her guardian, promptly. 'The deer in the park have about as much right to meddle as you.'

'Is our park small?' said Kate. 'Do you know Sir Herbert Eldridge, Uncle Courtenay? Where does he live?—and has he a very fine place? I can't believe that there are five hundred acres in his park; and I don't know how many there are in ours. I don't understand measuring one's own places. What does it matter an acre or two? I am sure there is no park so nice as Langton-Courtenay under the sun.'

'What is all this about parks? You take away my breath,' said Mr. Courtenay, in dismay.

'Oh! nothing,' said Kate; 'only that I heard a person say—when I was out last night I met one of the Rectory people, Uncle Courtenay—it is partly for that I want to go—his sister, he says, is the same age as I—'

'His sister!—it was a he, then?' said Mr. Courtenay, with that prompt suspiciousness which is natural to the guardian of an heiress.

'It was Bertie, the second son—of course it was a he. A girl could not have jumped over the fence—one might scramble, you know, but one couldn't jump it with one's petticoats. He told me one or two things—about his family.'

'But why did he jump over the fence? And what do you know about him? Do you talk to everybody that comes in your way—about his family?' cried Mr. Courtenay, with returning dismay.

'Of course I do, Uncle Courtenay,' said Kate, looking full at him. 'You may say I have no right to interfere, but I have always known that Langton was to be mine, and I have always taken an interest in—everybody. Why, it was my duty. What else could I do?'

'I should prefer that you did almost anything else,' said Mr. Courtenay, hastily; and then he stopped short, feeling that it was incautious to betray his reasons, or suggest to the lively imagination of this perverse young woman that there was danger in Bertie Hardwick and his talk. 'The danger's self were lure alone,' he said to himself, and plunged, in his dismay, into another subject. 'Do you remember what I said to you last night about your Aunt Anderson?' he said. 'Shouldn't you like to go and see her, Kate? She has a daughter of your own age, an only child. They have been abroad all their lives, and, I daresay, speak a dozen languages—that sort of people generally do. I think it would be a right thing to visit her—'

'If it would be a right thing to visit her, Uncle Courtenay, it would be still righter to ask her to come here.'

'But that I forbid, my dear,' said the old man.

Then there was a pause. Kate was greatly tempted to lose her temper, but, on the whole, experience taught her that losing one's temper seldom does much good, and she restrained herself. She tried a different mode of attack.

'Uncle Courtenay,' she said, pathetically, 'is it because you don't want any one to love me that nobody is ever allowed to stay here?'

'When you are older, Kate, you will see what I mean,' said Mr. Courtenay. 'I don't wish you to enter the world with any yoke on your neck. I mean you to be free. You will thank me afterwards, when you see how you have been saved from a tribe of locusts—from a household of dependents—'

Kate stopped and gazed at him with a curious, semi-comprehension. She put her head a little on one side, and looked up to him with her bright eyes. 'Dependents!' she said—'dependents, uncle! Miss Blank tells me I have a great number of dependents, but I am sure they don't care for me.'

'They never do,' said Mr. Courtenay—this was, he thought, the one grand experience which he had won from life.

CHAPTER V

Bertie Hardwick was on the lawn in front of the Rectory when the two visitors approached. The Rectory was a pretty, old-fashioned house, large and quaint, with old picturesque wings and gables, and a front much covered with climbing plants. Kate had always been rather proud of it, as one of the ornaments of her estate. She looked at it almost as she looked at the pretty west gate of her park, where the lodge was so commodious and so pleasant, coveted by all the poor people on the estate. It was by Kate's grace and favour that the west lodge was given to one or another, and so would it be with the Rectory. She looked upon the one in much the same light as the other. It would be hard to tell what magnetic chord of sympathies had moved Bertie Hardwick to some knowledge of what his young acquaintance was about to do; but it is certain that he was there, pretending to play croquet with his sisters, and keeping a very keen eye upon the bit of road which was visible through the break in the high laurel hedge. He had been amused, and indeed somewhat touched and interested, in spite of himself, on the previous night; and somehow he had a feeling that she would come. When he caught a glimpse of her, he threw down the croquet mallet, as if it hurt him, and cried out—'Edith, run and tell mamma she is coming. I felt quite sure she would.'

'Who is coming?' cried the two girls.

'Oh, don't chatter and ask questions—rush and tell mamma!' cried Bertie; and he himself, without thinking of it, went forward to open the garden door. It was a trial of Kate's steadiness to meet him thus, but she did so with wide-open eyes and a certain serious courage. 'You saw me at a disadvantage, but I don't mind,' Kate's serious eyes were saying; and as she took the matter very gravely indeed, it was she who had the best of it now. Bertie, in spite of himself, felt confused as he met her look; he grew red, and was ashamed of his own foolish impulse to go and open the door.

'This is Mr. Bertie Hardwick, uncle,' said Kate, gravely; 'and this, Mr. Bertie, is my Uncle Courtenay—whom I told you of,' she added, with a little sigh.

Her Uncle Courtenay—whom she was obliged to obey, and over whom neither her impetuosity nor her melancholy had the least power. She shook her head to herself, as it were, over her sad fate, and by this movement placed once more in great danger the gravity of poor Bertie, who was afraid to laugh or otherwise misconduct himself under the eyes of Mr. Courtenay. He led the visitors into the drawing-room, through the open windows; and it is impossible to tell what a relief it was to him when he saw his mother coming to the rescue. And then they all sat down; Kate as near Mrs. Hardwick as she could manage to establish herself. Kate did not understand the shyness with which Minnie and Edith, half withdrawn on the other side of their mother, looked at her.

'I am not a wild beast,' she said to herself. 'I wonder do they think I will bite?'

'Did you tell them about last night?' she said, turning quickly to Bertie; for Mrs. Hardwick, instead of talking to her, the Lady of the Manor, as Kate felt she ought to have done, gave her attention to Mr. Courtenay instead.

'I told them I had met you, Miss Courtenay,' said Bertie.

'And did they laugh? Did you make fun of me? Why do they look at me so strangely?' cried Kate, growing red; 'I am not a wild beast.'

'You forget that you and my father have quarrelled,' said Bertie; 'and the girls naturally take his side.'

'Oh! is it that?' cried Kate, clearing up a little. She gave a quick glance at him, with a misgiving as to whether he was entirely serious. But Bertie kept his countenance. 'For that matter, I have come to say that I did not mean anything wrong; perhaps I made a mistake. Uncle Courtenay says that, till I am of age, I have no power; and if the Rector pleases—oh! there is the Rector—I ought to speak for myself.'

She rose as Mr. Hardwick came up to her. Her sense of her own importance gave a certain dignity to her young figure, which was springy and stately, like that of a young Diana. She threw back the flood of chestnut hair that streamed over her shoulders, and looked straight at him with her bright, well-opened eyes. Altogether she looked a creature of a different species from Edith and Minnie, who kept close together, looking at her with wonder, and a mixture of admiration and repugnance.

'Isn't it bold of her to speak to papa like that?' Minnie whispered to Edith.

'But she is going to ask his pardon,' Edith whispered back to Minnie. 'Oh! hush, and hear what she says.'

As for Bertie, he looked on with a strange feeling that it was he who had introduced this new figure into the domestic circle, and with a little anxiety of proprietorship hoped that she would make a good impression. She was his novelty, his property—and she was, there could be no doubt, a very great novelty indeed.

'Mr. Hardwick, please,' said Kate, reddening, yet confronting him with her head very erect, and her eyes very open, 'I find that I made a mistake. Uncle Courtenay tells me I had no right at my age to interfere. I shall not be of age for six years, and don't you think it would be best to be friendly—till then? If you are willing, I should be glad. I thought I had a right—but I understand now that it was all a mistake.'

Mr. Hardwick looked round upon the company, questioning and puzzled. He was a tall man, spare, but of a large frame, with deep-set blue eyes looking out of a somewhat brown face. His eyes looked like a bit of sky, which had strayed somehow into that brown, ruddy framework. They were the same colour as his son's, Bertie's; but Bertie's youthful countenance was still white and red, and the contrast was not so great. The Rector's face was very grave when in repose, and its expression had almost daunted Kate; but gradually he caught the joke (which was intended to be so profoundly serious) and lighted up. He had looked at his wife first, with a man's natural instinct, asking an explanation; and perhaps the suppressed laughter in Mrs. Hardwick's eyes was what gave him the clue. He made the little Lady of the Manor a profound bow. 'Let us understand each other, Miss Courtenay,' he said, with mock solemnity—'are we to be friendly only till you come of age? Six years is a long time. But if after that hostilities are to be resumed—'

'When I am of age of course I must do my duty,' said Kate.

She was so serious, standing there in the midst of them, grave as twenty judges, that nobody could venture to laugh. Uncle Courtenay, who was getting impatient, and who had no feeling either of chivalry or admiration for his troublesome ward, uttered a hasty exclamation; but the Rector took her hand, and shook it, with a smile which at once conciliated his two girls, who were looking on.

'That is just the feeling you ought to have,' he said. 'I see we shall be capital friends—I mean for six years; and then whatever you see to be your duty—Is it a bargain? I am delighted to accept these terms.'

'And I am very glad,' said Kate, sedately. She sat down again when he released her hand—giving her head a little shake, as was customary with her, and looked round with a certain majestic composure on the little assembly. As for Bertie, though he could not conceal from himself the fact that his father and mother were much amused, he still felt very proud of his young lady. He went up to her, and stood behind her chair, and made signs to his mother that she was to talk; which Mrs. Hardwick did to such good purpose that Kate, who wanted little encouragement, and to whom a friendly face was sweet, soon stood fully self-revealed to her new acquaintances. They took her out upon the lawn, and instructed her in croquet, and grew familiar with her; and, before half an hour had passed, Minnie and Edith, one on each side, were hanging about her, half in amazement, half in admiration. She was younger than both, for even Minnie, the little one, was sixteen; but then neither of them was a great lady—neither the head and mistress of her own house.

'Isn't it dreadfully dreary for you to live in that great house all by yourself?' said Edith. They were so continually together, and so apt to take up each other's sentiments, one repeating and continuing what the other had said, that they could scarcely get through a question except jointly. So that Minnie now added her voice, running into her sister's. 'It must be so dull, unless your governess is very nice indeed.'

'My governess—Miss Blank?' said Kate. 'I never thought whether she was nice or not. I have had so many. One comes for a year, and then another, and then another. I never could make out why they liked to change so often. Uncle Courtenay thinks it is best.'

'Oh! our governess stayed for years and years,' said Edith; added Minnie, 'We were nearly as fond of her as of mamma.'

'But then I suppose,' said Kate, with a little sigh, 'she was fond of you?'

'Why, of course,' cried the two girls together. 'How could she help it, when she had known us all our lives?'

'You think a great deal of yourselves,' said Kate, with dreary scorn, 'to think people must be fond of you! If you were like me you would know better. I never fancy anything of the kind. If they do what I tell them, that is all I ask. You are very different from me. You have father, and mother, and brothers, and all sorts of things. But I have nobody, except Uncle Courtenay—and I am sure I should be very glad to make you a present of him.'

'Have you not even an aunt?' said Minnie, with big round eyes of wonder. 'Nor a cousin?' said Edith, equally surprised.

'No—that is, oh! yes, I have one of each—Uncle Courtenay was talking of them as we came here—but I never saw them. I don't know anything about them,' said Kate.

'What curious people, not to come to see you!' 'And what a pity you don't know them!' said the sisters.

'And how curiously you talk,' said uncompromising Kate; 'both together. Please, is there only one of you, or are there two of you? I suppose it is talking in the same voice, and being dressed alike.'

'We are considered alike,' said Edith, the eldest, with an air of suppressed offence. As for Minnie, she was too indignant to make any reply.

'And so you are alike,' said Kate; 'and a little like your brother, too; but he speaks for himself. I don't object to people being alike; but I should try very hard to make you talk like two people, not like one, and not always to hang together and dress the same, if you were with me.'

Upon this there was a dead pause. The Rectory girls were good girls, but not quite prepared to stand an assault like this. Minnie, who had a quick temper, and who had been taught that it was indispensable to keep it down, shut her lips tight, and resisted the temptation to be angry. Edith, who was more placid, gazed at the young censor with wonder. What a strange girl!

'Because,' said Kate, endeavouring to be explanatory, 'your voices have just the same sound, and you are just the same height, and your blue frocks are even made the same. Are there so many girls in the world,' she said suddenly, with a pensive appeal to human nature in general, 'that people can afford to throw them away, and make two into one?'

Deep silence followed. Mrs. Hardwick had been called away, and Bertie was talking to the gardener at the other end of the lawn. This was the first unfortunate result of leaving the girls to themselves. They walked on a little, the two sisters falling a step behind in their discomfiture. 'How dare she speak to us so?' Minnie whispered through her teeth. 'Dare!—she is our guest!' said Edith, who had a high sense of decorum. A minute after, Kate perceived that something was amiss. She turned round upon them, and gazed into their faces with serious scrutiny. 'Are you angry?' she said—'have I said anything wrong?'

'Oh! not angry,' said Edith. 'I suppose, since you look surprised, you don't—mean—any harm.'

'I?—mean harm?—Oh! Mr. Bertie,' cried Kate, 'come here quick—quick!—and explain to them. You know me. What have I done to make them angry? One may surely say what one thinks.'

'I don't know that it is good to say all one thinks,' said Edith, who taught in the Sunday-schools, and who was considered very thoughtful and judicious—'at least, when it is likely to hurt other people's feelings.'

'Not when it is true?' said the remorseless Kate.

And then the whole group came to a pause, Bertie standing open-mouthed, most anxious to preserve the peace, but not knowing how. It was the judicious Edith who brought the crisis to a close by acting upon one of the maxims with which she was familiar as a teacher of youth.

'Should you like to walk round the garden?' she said, changing the subject with an adroitness which was very satisfactory to herself, 'or come back into the drawing-room? There is not much to see in our little place, after your beautiful gardens at Langton-Courtenay; but still, if you would like to walk round—or perhaps you would prefer to go in and join mamma?'

'My uncle must be ready to go now,' said Kate, with responsive quickness, and she stalked in before them through the open window. As good luck would have it, Mr. Courtenay was just rising to take his leave. Kate followed him out, much subdued, in one sense, though all in arms in another. The girls were not nearly so nice as she thought they would be—reality was not equal to anticipation—and to think they should have quarrelled with her the very first time for nothing! This was the view of the matter which occurred to Kate.

CHAPTER VI

I cannot undertake to say how it was, but it is certain that Bertie Hardwick met Kate next day, as she took her walk into the village, accompanied by Miss Blank. At the sight of him, that lady's countenance clouded over; but Kate was glad, and the young man took no notice of Miss Blank's looks. As it happened, the conversation between the governess and her pupil had flagged—it often flagged. The conversation between Kate and Miss Blank consisted generally of a host of bewildering questions on the one side, and as few answers as could be managed on the other. Miss Blank no doubt had affairs of her own to think of; and then Kate's questions were of everything in heaven and earth, and might have troubled even a wise counsellor. Mr. Courtenay was still at Langton, but had sent out his niece for her usual walk—a thing by which she felt humiliated—and she had met with a rebuff in the village in consequence of some interference. She was in low spirits, and Miss Blank did not mind. Accordingly, Bertie was a relief and comfort to her, more than can be described.

'Why don't your sisters like me?' said Kate. 'I wonder, Mr. Bertie, why people don't like me? If they would let me, I should like to be friends; but you saw they would not.'

'I don't think—perhaps—that they quite understood—'

'But it is so easy to understand,' said Kate, with a little impatient sigh. She shook her head, and tossed back her shining hair, which made an aureole round her. 'Don't let us speak of it,' she said; 'but you understood from the very first?'

Bertie was pleased, he could not have told why. The fact was, he, too, had been extremely puzzled at first; but now, after three meetings, he felt himself an old friend and privileged interpreter of the strange girl whom his sisters were so indignant with, and who certainly was a more important personage at Langton-Courtenay than any other fifteen-year-old girl in England. Both Mr. Hardwick and Bertie had to some extent made themselves Kate's champions, moved thereto by that strange predisposition to take the side of a feminine stranger (at least, when she is young and pleasant) against the women of their own house, which almost all men are moved by. Women take their father's, their husband's, their brother's side through thick and thin, with a natural certainty that their own must be in the right; but men invariably take it for granted that their own must be wrong. Thus, not only Bertie, who might be moved by other arguments, but even Mr. Hardwick, secretly believed that 'the girls' had taken offence foolishly, and maintained the cause of Kate.

'They have seen nothing out of their own sphere,' their brother said, apologetically—'they don't know much—they are very much petted and spoiled at home.'

'Ah!' said Kate, feeling as if a chilly douche had suddenly been administered in her face. She drew a long, half-sobbing breath, and then she said, with a pathetic tone in her voice, 'Oh! I wonder why people don't like me!'

'You are wrong, Miss Courtenay—I am sure you are wrong,' said Bertie, warmly. 'Not like you!—that must be their stupidity alone. And I can't believe, even, that any one is so stupid. You must be making a mistake.'

'Oh! Mr. Bertie, how can you say so? Why, your sisters!' cried Kate, returning to the charge.

'But it is not that they—don't like you,' said Bertie. 'How could you think it? It is only a misunderstanding—a—a—want of knowing—'

'You are trying to save my feelings,' said Kate; 'but never mind my feelings. No, Mr. Bertie, it is quite true. I do not want to deceive myself—people do not like me.' These words she produced singly, as if they had been so many stones thrown at the world. 'Oh! please don't say anything—perhaps it is my fate; perhaps I am never to be any better. But that is how it is—people don't like me; I am sure I don't know why.'

'Miss Courtenay—' Bertie began, with great earnestness; but just then the man-of-all-work from the Rectory, who was butler, and footman, and valet, and everything combined, made his appearance at the corner, beckoning to him; and as the servant was sent by his father, he had no alternative but to go away. When he was out of sight, Kate, whose eyes had followed him as far as he was visible, breathed forth a gentle sigh, and was going on quietly upon her way, silent, until the mood should seize her to chatter once more, when an event occurred that had never been known till now to happen at Langton—the governess, who was generally blank as her name, opened her mouth and spoke.

'Miss Courtenay,' she said, for she was not even sufficiently interested in her pupil to care to speak to her by her Christian name—'Miss Courtenay, if this sort of thing continues, I shall have to go away.'

Kate, who was not much less startled than Balaam was on a similar occasion, stopped short, and turned round with a face of consternation upon her companion. 'If what continues?' she said.

'This,' said Miss Blank—'this meeting of young men, and walking with them. It is hard enough to have to manage you; but if this goes on, I shall speak to Mr. Courtenay. I never was compromised before, and I don't mean to be so now.'

Kate was so utterly unconscious of the meaning of all this, that she simply stared in dismay. 'Compromised!' she said, with big eyes of astonishment; 'I don't know what you mean. What is it that must not go on? Miss Blank, I hope you have not had a sunstroke, or something that makes people talk without knowing what they say.'

'I will not take any impertinence from you, Miss Courtenay,' said Miss Blank, going red with wrath. 'Ask why people don't like you, indeed!—you should ask me, instead of asking a gentleman, fishing for compliments! I'll tell you why people don't like you. It is because you are always interfering—thrusting yourself into things you have no business with—taking things upon you that no child has a right to meddle with. That is why people hate you—'

'Hate me!' cried Kate, who, for her part, had grown pale with horror.

'Yes; hate you—that is the word. Do you think any one would put up with such a life who could help it? You are an heiress, and people are obliged to mind you; but if you had been a poor girl, you would have known the difference. Nobody would have put up with you then; you would have been beaten, or starved, or done something to. It is only your money that gives you the power to trample others under your feet.'

Kate was appalled by this address. It stupefied her, in the first place, that Miss Blank should have taken the initiative, and launched forth into speech, as it were, on her own account; and the assault took away the girl's breath. She felt as one might feel who had been suddenly saluted with a shower of blows from an utterly unsuspected adversary. She did not know whether to fight or flee. She walked along mechanically by her assailant's side, and gasped for breath. Her eyes grew large and round with wonder. She listened in amaze, not able to believe her ears.

'But I won't be kept quiet any longer,' said Miss Blank—'I will speak. Why should I get myself into trouble for you? I will go to Mr. Courtenay, when we get back, and I will tell him it is impossible to go on like this. It was bad enough before. You were trouble enough from the first day I ever set eyes on you; but I have always said to myself, when that commences, I will go away. My character is above everything, and all the gold in England would not tempt me to stay.'

Kate listened to all this with a bewilderment that took from her the power of speech. What did the woman mean?—was she 'in a passion,' as, indeed, other governesses, to Kate's knowledge, had been; or was she mad? It must be a sunstroke, she decided at last. They had been walking in the sun, and Miss Blank's bonnet was too thin, being made of flimsy tulle. Her brain must be affected. Kate resolved heroically that she would not aggravate the sufferer by any response, but would send for the housekeeper as soon as they got back, and place Miss Blank in her hands. People in her sad condition must not be contradicted. She quickened her steps, discussing with herself whether a dark room and ice to the forehead would be enough, or whether it would be necessary to cut off all her hair, or even shave her head. This pre-occupation about Miss Blank's welfare shielded the girl for some time against the fiery, stinging arrows which were being thrown at her; but this immunity did not last, for the way was long, and Miss Blank, having once broken out, put no further restraint upon herself. It was clear now that her only hope was in laying Kate prostrate, leaving no spirit nor power of resistance in her. By degrees the sharp words began to get admittance at the girl's tingling ears. She was beaten down by the storm of opposition. Was it possible?—could it be true? Did people hate her? Her imagination began to work as these burning missiles flew at her. Miss Blank had been her companion for a year, and hated her! Uncle Courtenay was her own uncle—her nearest relative—and he, too, hated her! The girls at the Rectory, who looked so gentle, had turned against her. Oh! why, why was it? By degrees a profound discouragement seized upon the poor child. Miss Blank was eloquent; she had a flow of words such as had never come to her before. She poured forth torrents of bitterness as she walked, and Kate was beaten down by the storm. By the time they reached home she had forgotten all about the sunstroke, and shaving Miss Blank's head, and thought of nothing but getting free—getting into the silence—being alone. Maryanne put a letter into her hand as she ran upstairs; but what did she care for a letter! Everybody hated her—if it were not that she was an heiress everybody would abandon her—and she had not one friend to go to, no one whom she could ask to help her in all the dreary world. She was too far gone for weeping. She sat down before her dressing-table and looked into the glass with miserable, dilated eyes. 'I am just like other people,' Kate said to herself; 'there is no mark upon me. Cain was marked; but that was because he was a murderer; and I never killed anybody, I never did any harm to anybody, that I know of. I am only just a girl, like other girls. Oh! I suppose I am dreadfully wicked! But then everybody is wicked—the Bible says so; and how am I worse than all the rest? I don't hate any one,' said Kate, aloud, and very slowly. Her poor little mouth quivered, her eyes filled, and right upon the letter on her table there fell one great blob of a tear. This roused her in the midst of her distress. To Kate—as to every human being of her age—it seemed possible that something new, something wonderful might be in any letter. She took it up and tore it open. She was longing for comfort, longing for kindness, as she had never done in her life.

The letter which we are about to transcribe was not a very wise one, perhaps not even altogether to be sworn by as true—but it opened an entire new world to poor Kate.

MY DEAREST UNKNOWN DARLING NIECE,

'You can't remember me, for I have never seen you since you were a tiny, tiny baby in long clothes; and you have had nobody about you to remind you that you had any relations on your mother's side. You have never answered my letters even, dear, though I don't for a moment blame you, or suppose it is your fault. But now that I am in England, darling, we must not allow ourselves to be divided by unfortunate feelings that may exist between different sides of the family. I must see you, my dear only sister's only darling child! I have but one child, too, my Ombra, and she is as anxious as I am. I have written to your guardian, asking if he will let you come and see us. I do not wish to go to your grand house, which was always thought too fine for us, but I must see you, my darling child; and if Mr. Courtenay will not let you come to us, my Ombra and I will come to Langton-Courtenay, to the village, where we shall no doubt find lodgings somewhere—I don't mind how humble they are, so long as I can see you. My heart yearns to take you in my arms, to give you a hundred kisses, my own niece, my dear motherless child. Send me one little word by your own hand, and don't reject the love that is offered you, my dearest Kate. Ombra sends you her dear love, and thinks of you, not as a cousin, but as a sister; and I, who have the best right, long for nothing so much as to be a mother to you! Come to us, my sweet child, if your uncle will let you; but, in the meantime, write to me, that I may know you a little even before we meet. With warmest love, my darling niece, your most affectionate aunt and, if you will let her be so, mother,

'JANE ANDERSON.'

Now poor Kate had only two or three times in her whole life received a letter before. Since, as she said, she had 'grown up,' she had not heard from her aunt, who had written her, she recollected, one or two baby epistles, printed in large letters, in her childhood. Her poor little soul was still convulsed with the first great, open undisguised shock of unkindness, when this other great event came upon her. It was also a shock in its way. It made such a tempest in her being as conflicting winds make out at sea. The one had driven her down to the depths, the other dashed her up, up to a dizzy height. She felt dazed, insensible, proud, triumphant, and happy, all at once. Here was somebody of her own, somebody of her very own—something like the mother at the Rectory. Something new, close, certain—her own!

She dashed the tears from her eyes with a handkerchief, seized upon her letter, her dear letter, and rushed downstairs to the library, where Uncle Courtenay sat in state, the judge, and final tribunal for all appeals.

CHAPTER VII

Mr. Courtenay was in the library at Langton, tranquilly pursuing some part of the business which had brought him thither, when Miss Blank and her charge returned from their walk. His chief object, it is true, in this visit to the house of his fathers, had been to look after his ward; but there had been other business to do—leases to renew, timber to cut down, cottages to build; a multiplicity of small matters, which required his personal attention. These were straightforward, and did not trouble him as the others did; and the fact was that he felt much relieved by the absence of the young feminine problem, which it was so hard upon him, at his age, and with his habits, to be burdened with. He had dismissed her even out of his mind, and was getting through the less difficult matters steadily, with a grateful sense that here at least he had nothing in hand that was beyond his power. It was shady in the Langton library, cool, and very quiet; whereas outside there was one blaze of sunshine, and the day was hot. Mr. Courtenay was comfortable—perhaps for the first time since his arrival. He was satisfied with his present occupation, and for the moment had dismissed his other cares.

This was the pleasant position of affairs when Miss Blank rushed in upon him, with indignation in her countenance. There was something more than indignation—there was the flush of heat produced by her walk, and her unusual outburst of temper, and the dust, and a little dishevelment inseparable from wrath. She scarcely took time to knock at the door. She was a person who had been recommended to him as imperturbable in temper and languid in disposition—the last in the world to make any fuss; consequently he stared upon her now with absolute consternation, and even a little alarm.

'Compose yourself, Miss Blank—take time to speak. Has anything happened to Kate?'

He was quite capable of hearing with composure anything that might have happened to Kate—anything short of positive injury, indeed, which would have freed him of her, would have been tidings of joy.

'I have come to say, sir,' said Miss Blank, 'that there are some things a lady cannot be expected to put up with. I have always felt the time must come when I could not put up with Miss Courtenay. I am not an ill-tempered person, I hope—'

'Quite the reverse, I have always heard,' said Mr. Courtenay, politely, but with a sigh.

'Thank you, sir. I believe I have always been considered to have a good temper; but I have said to myself, since ever I came here, "Miss Courtenay is bad enough now—she is trial enough to any lady's feelings now." I am sorry to have to say it if it hurts your feelings, Mr. Courtenay, but your niece s—she is—it is really almost impossible for a lady who has a respect for herself, and does not wish to be hurried into exhibitions of temper, to say what Miss Kate is.'

'Pray compose yourself, Miss Blank. Take a seat. From my own observation,' said Mr. Courtenay, 'I am aware my niece must be troublesome at times.'

'Troublesome!' said Miss Blank—'at times! That shows, sir, how little you know. About her troublesomeness I can't trust myself to speak; nor is it necessary at the present moment. But I have always said to myself, "When that time comes, I will go at once." And it appears to me, Mr. Courtenay, that though premature, that time has come.'

'What time, for Heaven's sake?' said the perplexed guardian.

'Mr. Courtenay, you know what she is as well as I do. It is not for any personal reason, though I am aware many people think her pretty; but it is not that. She is an heiress, she will have a nice property, and a great deal of money, therefore it is quite natural that it should be premature.'

'Miss Blank, you would do me an infinite favour if you would speak plainly. What is it that is premature?'

Miss Blank had taken a seat, and she had loosed the strings of her bonnet. Her ideas of decorum had indeed been so far overcome by her excitement, that even under Mr. Courtenay's eye she had begun to fan herself with her handkerchief. She made a pause in this occupation, and pressed her handkerchief to her face, as expressive of confusion; and from the other side of this shield she answered, 'Oh! that I should have to speak to a gentleman of such things! If you demand a distinct answer, I must tell you. It is lovers, Mr. Courtenay.'

'Lovers!' he said, involuntarily, with a laugh of relief.

'You may laugh, but it is no laughing matter,' said Miss Blank. 'Oh! if you had known, as I do by experience, what it is to manage girls! Do you know what a girl is, Mr. Courtenay?—the most aggravating, trying, unmanageable, untamable—'

'My dear Miss Blank,' said, Mr. Courtenay, seriously, 'I presume that you were once one of these untamable creatures yourself.'

'Ah!' said the governess, with a long-drawn breath. It had not occurred to her, and, curiously enough, now that it was suggested, the idea seemed rather to flatter her than otherwise. She shook her head; but she was softened. 'Perhaps I should not have said all girls,' she resumed. 'I was very strictly brought up, and never allowed to take such folly into my head. But to return to our subject, Mr. Courtenay. I must beg your attention to this—it has been my principle through life, I have never departed from it yet, and I cannot now—When lovers appear, I have always made it known among my friends—I go.'

'I have no doubt it is an admirable principle,' said Mr. Courtenay. 'But in the present case let us come to particulars. Who are the lovers?'

'One of the young gentlemen at the Rectory,' answered Miss Blank, promptly; and then for the first time she felt that she had produced an effect.

Mr. Courtenay made no reply—he put down his pen, which he had been holding all this time in his hand; his face clouded over; he pushed his paper away from him and puckered his lips and his forehead. This time, without doubt, she had produced an effect.

'I must beg you accordingly, Mr. Courtenay, to accept my resignation,' said Miss Blank. 'I have always kept up a good connection, and never suffered myself to be compromised, and I don't mean to begin now. This day month, sir, if you please—if in the meantime you are suited with another lady in my place—'

'Miss Blank, don't you think this is something like forsaking your post? Is it not ungenerous to desert my niece when she has so much need of your protection? Do you not feel—' Mr. Courtenay had commenced unawares.

'Sir,' said Miss Blank, with dignity, 'when I was engaged, it was specially agreed that this was to be no matter of feelings. I have specially watched over my feelings, that they might not get any way involved. I am sure you must recollect the terms of my engagement as well as I.'

Mr. Courtenay did recollect them, and felt he had made a false step; and then the difficulties of his position rushed upon his bewildered sight. He did not know girls as Miss Blank did, who had spent many a weary year in wrestling with them; but he knew enough to understand that, if a girl in her natural state was hard to manage, a girl with a lover must be worse. And what was he to do if left alone, and unaided, to rule and quiet such an appalling creature? He drew in his lips, and contracted his forehead, until his face was about half its usual size. It gave him a little relief when the idea suddenly struck him that Miss Blank's hypothesis might not be built on sufficient foundation. Women were always thinking of lovers—or, at least, not knowing anything precisely about women, so Mr. Courtenay had heard.

'Let us hope, at least,' he said, 'that your alarming suggestion has been hastily made. Will you tell me what foundation you have for connecting Kate's name with—with anything of the kind? She is only fifteen—she is not old enough.'

'I thought I had said distinctly, Mr. Courtenay, that I considered it to be premature?'

'Yes, yes, certainly—you said so—but—Perhaps, Miss Blank, you will kindly favour me with the facts—'

At this point another hurried knock came to the door. And once more, without waiting for an answer, Kate, all tears and trouble, her face flushed like Miss Blank's, her hair astray, and an open letter in her hand, came rushing into the room. Two agitated female creatures in one hour, rushing into the private sanctuary of the most particular of bachelors! Mr. Courtenay commended her, though she was his nearest relation, to all the infernal gods.

'What is the matter now?' he cried, sharply. 'Why do you burst in uninvited when I am busy? Kate, you seem to be trying every way to irritate and annoy me. What is it now?'

'Uncle,' cried Kate, breathlessly, 'I have just got a letter, and I want to ask you—never mind her!—may I go to my Aunt Anderson's? She is willing to have me, and it will save you heaps of trouble! Oh! please, Uncle Courtenay, please never mind anything else! May I go?'

'May you go—to your Aunt Anderson? Why, here is certainly a new arrangement of the board!' said Mr. Courtenay. He said the last words mockingly, and he fixed his eyes on Kate as if she had been a natural curiosity—which, indeed, in a great degree, she was to him.

'Yes—to my Aunt Anderson. You spoke of her yourself—you know you did. You said she must not come here! and she does not want to come here. I don't think she would come if she was asked! but she says I am to go to her. Uncle Courtenay, in a little while I shall be able to do what I like, and go where I like—'

'Not for six years, my dear,' said Mr. Courtenay, with a smile.

Kate stamped her foot in her passion.

'If I were to write to the Lord Chancellor, I am sure he would let me!' she cried.

'But you are not a ward in Chancery—you are my ward,' said Mr. Courtenay, blandly.

'Then I will run away!' cried Kate, once more stamping her foot. 'I will not stay here. I hate Langton-Courtenay, and everybody that is unkind, and the people who hate me. I tell you I hate them, Uncle Courtenay! I will run away!'

'I don't doubt it, for one,' said Miss Blank, quietly; 'but with whom, Miss Kate, I should like to know? I daresay your plans are all laid.'

Mr. Courtenay did not see the blank stare of surprise with which Kate, all innocent of the meaning which was conveyed to his ear by these words, surveyed her adversary. His own better-instructed mind was moved by it to positive excitement. Even if Miss Blank had been premature in her suggestion, still there could be little doubt that lovers were a danger from which Kate could not be kept absolutely safe. And there were sons at the Rectory, one of whom, a good-looking young fellow of twenty, he had himself seen coming forward with a look of delighted recognition. Danger! Why, it was almost more than danger; it seemed a certainty of evil—if not now, why, then, next year, or the year after! Mr. Courtenay, like most old men of the world, felt an instinctive distrust of, and repugnance to, parsons. And a young parson was proverbially on the outlook for heiresses, and almost considered it a duty to provide for himself by marriage. All this ran through his disturbed mind as these two troublesome feminine personages before him waited each for her answer. 'Confound women! They are more trouble than they are worth, a hundred times over!' the old bachelor said to himself.

CHAPTER VIII

Mr. Courtenay was much too true to his instincts, however, to satisfy these two applicants, or to commit himself by any decision on the spot. He dismissed Miss Blank with the formal courtesy which he employed towards his inferiors, begging her to wait until to-morrow, when he should have reflected upon the problem she had laid before him. And he sent away Kate with much less ceremony, bidding her hold her tongue, and leave the room and leave things alone which she did not understand. He would not listen to the angry response which rose to her lips; and Kate had a melancholy night in consequence, aggravated by the miserable sensation that she had been snubbed in presence of Miss Blank, who was quite ready to take advantage of her discomfiture. When Kate's guardian, however, was left alone to think, it is probable that his own reflections were not delightful. He was not a man apt to take himself to task, nor give way to self-examination, but still it was sufficiently apparent to him that his plan had not succeeded as he had hoped in Kate's case. What he had hoped for had been to produce a quiet, calm girl, who would do what she was told, whose expectations and wishes would be on a subdued scale, and who would be reasonable enough to feel that his judgment was supreme in all matters. Almost all men at one time or another of their lives entertain the idea of 'moulding' a model woman. Mr. Courtenay's ideal was not high—all he wanted was submissiveness, manageableness, quiet manners, and a total absence of the sentimental and emotional. The girl might have been permitted to be clever, to be a good musician, or a good artist, or a great student, if she chose, though such peculiarities always detract more or less from the air of good society which ought to distinguish a lady; but still Mr. Courtenay prided himself upon being tolerant, and he would not have interfered in such a case. But that this ward of his, this representative of his family, should choose to be an individual being with a very strong will and marked characteristics of her own, exasperated the old man of the world. 'Most women have no character at all,' he repeated to himself, raising his eyebrows in wondering appeal to Providence. Had the happy period when that aphorism was true, departed along with all the other manifestations of the age of Gold?—or was it still true, and was it the fault of Providence, to punish him for his sins, that his share of womankind should be so perverse? This was a question which it was difficult to make out; but he was rather inclined to chafe at Providence, which really does interfere so unjustifiably often, when things would go very well if they were left to themselves. The longer he thought of it, the more disgusted did he become—at once with Miss Blank and with her charge. What a cold-hearted wretch the woman must be! How strange that she should not at least 'take an interest' in the girl! To be sure he had made it a special point in her engagement that she should not take an interest. He was right in doing so, he felt sure; but, still, here was an unforeseen crisis, at which it would have been very important to have lighted on some one who would not be bound by a mere bargain. The girl was an unmanageable little fool, determined to have her own way at all risks; and the law would not permit him to shut her up, and keep her in the absolute subjection of a prison. She must have every advantage, forsooth—freedom and society, and Heaven knows what besides; education as much as if she were going to earn her living as a governess; and even that crowning horror, Lovers, when the time came. Yes, there was no law in the realm forbidding an heiress to have lovers. Miss Blank might resign, not wishing to compromise herself: but he, the unhappy guardian, could not resign. It was not illegal for a young man to speak to Kate—any idle fellow, with an introduction, might chatter to her, and drive her protectors frantic, and yet could not be put into prison for it. And there could be little doubt that, simply to spite her guardian, after she had worried him to death in every other way, she would fall in love. She would do it, as sure as fate; and even if she met with opposition she was a girl quite capable of eloping with her lover, giving unbounded trouble, and probably throwing some lasting stigma on herself and her name. It was premature, as Miss Blank said; but Miss Blank was a person of experience, learned in the ways of girls, and doubtless knew what she was saying. She had declined to have anything further to do with Kate; she had declared her own sway and 'lovers' to be quite incompatible. But Mr. Courtenay could not give a month's warning, and what was he to do?

If there was but anybody to be found who would 'take an interest' in the girl! This idea flashed unconsciously through his mind, and he did not even realise that in wishing for this, in perceiving its necessity, he was stultifying all the previous exertions of his guardianship. Theories are all very well, but it is astonishing how ready men are to drop them in an emergency. Mr. Courtenay was in a dreadful emergency at present, and he prayed to his gods for some one to 'take an interest' in this girl. Her Aunt Anderson! The suggestion was so very convenient, it was so delightfully ready a way of escape out of his troubles, that he felt it necessary to pull himself up, and look at it fully. It is not to be supposed that it was a pleasant or grateful suggestion in itself. Had he been in no trouble about Kate, he would have at once, and sternly, declined all invitations (he would have said interference) on the part of her mother's family. The late Mr. Courtenay had made a very foolish marriage, a marriage quite beneath his position; and the sister of the late Mrs. Courtenay had been discouraged in all her many attempts to see anything of the orphan Kate. Fortunately she had not been much in England, and, until the present, these attempts had all been made when Kate was a baby. Had the young lady of Langton-Courtenay been at all manageable, they would have been equally discouraged now. But the very name of Mrs. Anderson, at this crisis, breathed across Mr. Courtenay's tribulations like the sweet south across a bed of violets. It was such a temptation to him as he did not know how to withstand. Her mother's family! They had no right, certainly, to any share of the good things, which were entirely on the Courtenay side; but certainly they had a right to their share of the trouble. This trouble he had borne for fifteen years, and had not murmured. Of course, in the very nature of things, it was their turn now.

Mr. Courtenay reflected very deeply on this subject, looking at it in all its details. Fortunately there were but few remnants of her mother's family. Mrs. Anderson was the widow of a Consul, who had spent almost all his life abroad. She had a pension, a little property, and an only daughter, a little older than Kate. There were but two of them. If they turned out to be of that locust tribe which Mr. Courtenay so feared and hated, they could at least be bought off cheaply, when they had served their purpose. The daughter, no doubt, would marry, and the mother could be bought off. Mr. Courtenay did not enter into any discussion with himself as to the probabilities of carrying out this scheme of buying off. At this moment he did not care to dwell upon any difficulties. In the meantime, he had the one great difficulty, Kate herself, to get settled somehow; and anything which might happen six years hence was so much less pressing. By that time a great many things unforeseen might have happened; and Mr. Courtenay did not choose to make so long an excursion into the unknown. What was he to do with her now? Was he to be compelled to stay in the country, to give up all his pleasures and comforts, and the habits of his life, in order to guard and watch over this girl?—or should she be given over, for the time, to the guardianship of her mother's family? This was the real question he had to decide.

And by degrees he came to think more and more cordially of Mrs. Anderson—more cordially, and, at the same time, contemptuously. What a fool she must be, to offer voluntarily to take all this trouble! No doubt she expected to make her own advantage out of it; but Mr. Courtenay, with a grim smile upon his countenance, felt that he himself was quite capable of taking care of that. He might employ her, but he would take care that her devotion should be disinterested. She would be better than a governess at this crisis of Kate's history! She would be a natural duenna and inspectress of morals, as well as the superintendent of education; and it should, of course, be fully impressed upon her that it was for her interest to discourage lovers, and keep the external world at arm's length. The very place of her residence was favourable. She had settled in the Isle of Wight, a long way from Langton-Courtenay, and happily so far from town that it would not be possible to run up and down and appeal to him at any moment. He thought of this all night, and it was the first subject that returned to his thoughts in the morning. Mrs. Anderson, or unlimited worry, trouble, and annoyance—banishment to the country, severance from all delights. Then let it be Mrs. Anderson! he said to himself, with a sigh. It was hard upon him to have such a decision to make, and yet it was satisfactory to feel that he had decided for the best. He went down to breakfast with a certain solemn composure, as of a man who was doing right and making a sacrifice. It would be the salvation of his personal comfort, and to secure that, at all costs, was fundamentally and eternally right; but it was a sacrifice at once of pride and of principle, and he felt that he had a right to the honours of martyrdom on that score.

After breakfast he called his ward into the library, with a polite little speech of apology to Miss Blank. 'If you will permit me the pleasure of a few words with you at twelve o'clock, I think we may settle that little matter,' he said, with the greatest suavity; leaving upon that lady's mind the impression that Kate was to be bound hand and foot, and delivered over into her hands—which, as Miss Blank had no desire, could she avoid it, to leave the comfort of Langton-Courtenay, was very satisfactory to her; and then he withdrew into the library with the victim.

'Now, Kate,' he said, sitting down, 'I am going to speak to you very seriously.'

'You have been doing nothing but speak to me seriously ever since you came,' said Kate, pouting. 'I wish you would not give yourself so much trouble, Uncle Courtenay. All I want is just yes or no.'

'But a great deal depends on the yes or the no. Look here, Kate, I am willing to let you go—oh! pray don't clap your hands too soon!—I am willing to let you go, on conditions, and the conditions are rather serious. You had better not decide until you hear—'

'I am sure I shall not mind them,' said impetuous Kate, before whose eyes there instantly rose up a prospect of a new world, all full of freshness, and novelty, and interest. Mind!—she would not have minded fire and water to get at an existence which should be altogether new.

'Listen, however,' said Mr. Courtenay. 'My conditions are very grave. If you go to Mrs. Anderson, Kate—'

'Of course I shall go, if you will let me, Uncle Courtenay.'

'If you go,' said Mr. Courtenay, with a wave of his hand deprecating interruption, 'it must not be for a visit only—you must go to stay.'

'To stay!'

Kate's eyes, which grew round with the strain of wonder, interest, and excitement, and which kindled, and brightened, and shone, reflecting like a mirror the shades of feeling that passed through her mind, were a sight to see.

'If you go,' he continued, 'and if Mrs. Anderson is content to receive you, it must be for the remainder of your minority. I have had a great deal of trouble with your education, and now it is just that your mother's family should take their share. Hear me out, Kate. Your aunt, of course, should have an allowance for your maintenance, and you could have as many masters and governesses, and all the rest, as were necessary; but if you go out of my hands, you go not for six weeks, but for six years, Kate.'

Kate had been going to speak half a dozen times, but now, having controlled herself so long, she paused with a certain mixture of feelings. Her delight was certainly toned down. To go and come—to be now Queen of Langton, and now her aunt's amused and petted guest, had been her own dream of felicity. This was a different matter, there could be no doubt. It would be the old story—if not the monotony of Langton, which she knew, the monotony of Shanklin, which she did not know. Various clouds passed over the firmament which had looked so smiling. Perhaps it was possible her Aunt Anderson and Ombra might not turn out desirable companions for six years—perhaps she might regret her native place, her supremacy over the cottagers, whom she sometimes exasperated. The cloud thickened, dropped lower. 'Should I never be allowed to come back?—not even to see Langton, Uncle Courtenay?' she asked in a subdued voice.

'Langton, in that case, ought to be let or shut up.'

'Let!—to other people!—to strangers, Uncle Courtenay!—our house!'

'Well, you foolish child, are we such very superior clay that we cannot let our house? Why, the best people in England do it. The Duke of Brentford does it. You have not quite his pretensions, and he does not mind.'

'But I have quite his pretensions,' cried Kate—'more!—and so have you, uncle. What is he more than a gentleman? and we are gentlemen, I hope. Besides, a Duke has a vulgar sort of grandeur with his title—you know he has—and can do what he pleases; but we must act as gentlefolks. Oh! Uncle Courtenay, not that!'

'Pshaw!' was all that Mr. Courtenay replied. He was not open to sentimental considerations, especially when money was concerned; but, still, he had so much natural prejudice remaining in him for the race and honour of Langton-Courtenay, that he thought no worse of his troublesome ward for what she had said. He would of course pay no manner of attention to it; but still, on the whole, he liked her so to speak.

'Let us waive the question,' he resumed. 'No, not to Langton-Courtenay—I don't choose you should return here, if you quit it. But there might be change of air, once a year or so, to other places.'

'Oh! might we go and travel?—might we go,' cried Kate, looking up to him with shining eyes and eager looks, and lips apart, like an angelic petitioner, 'abroad?'

She said this last word with such a fulness and roundness of sound, as it would be impossible, even in capitals, to convey through the medium of print.

'Well,' he said, with a smile, 'probably that splendour and delight might be permitted to be—if you could afford it off your allowance, being always understood.'

'Oh! of course we could afford it,' said Kate. 'Uncle, I consent at once—I will write to my Aunt Anderson at once. I wish she was not called Anderson—it sounds so common—like the groom in the village. Uncle Courtenay, when can I start? To-morrow? Now, why should you shake your head? I have very few things to pack; and to-morrow is just as good as any other day.'

'Quite as good, I have no doubt; and so is to-morrow week,' said Mr. Courtenay. 'In the first place, you must take till to-morrow to decide.'

'But when I have decided already!' said Kate.

'To-morrow at this time bring me your final answer. There, now run away—not another word.'

Kate went away, somewhat indignant; and for the next twenty-four hours did nothing but plan tours to all the beautiful places she had ever heard or read about. Her deliberations as to the scheme in general were all swallowed up in this. 'I will take them to Switzerland; I will take them to Italy. We shall travel four or five months in every year; and see everything and hear everything, and enjoy everything,' she said to herself, clapping her hands, as it were, under her breath. For she was generous in her way; she was quite clear on the point that it was she who must 'take' her aunt and cousin everywhere, and make everything agreeable for them. Perhaps there was in this a sense of superiority which satisfied that craving for power and influence which belonged to her nature; but still, notwithstanding her defective education, it was never in Kate's mind to keep any enjoyment to herself.

CHAPTER IX

Before four-and-twenty hours had passed, a certain premonition of approaching change had stolen into the air at Langton-Courtenay. Miss Blank, too, had been received by Mr. Courtenay in a private audience, where he treated her with the courtesy due from one crowned head to another; but, nevertheless, gave her fully to understand that her reign was over. This took her all the more by surprise, that she had expected quite the reverse, from his words and looks in the morning; and it was perhaps an exclamation which burst from her as she withdrew, amazed and indignant, to her own room, which betrayed the possibilities of the future to the household. Miss Blank was not prone to exclamations, nor to betraying herself in any way; but to have your resignation blandly accepted, when you expected to be implored, almost with tears, to retain your post, is an experience likely to overcome the composure of any one. The exclamation itself was of the plainest character—it was, 'Oh! I like his politeness—I like that!' These words were heard by a passing housemaid; and not only were the words heard, but the flushed cheek, the indignant step, the air of injury were noted with all that keenness and intelligence which the domestic mind reserves for the study of the secrets of those above them. 'She's got the sack like the rest,' was Jane's remark to herself; and she spread it through the house. The intimation produced a mild interest, but no excitement. But when late in the afternoon Maryanne came rushing downstairs, open-mouthed, to report some unwary words which had dropped from her young mistress, the feelings of the household acquired immediate intensity. It was a suspecting place, and a poor sort of place, where there never were any great doings; but still Langton-Courtenay was a comfortable place, and when Maryanne, with that perverted keenness of apprehension already noticed, which made her so much more clever in divining her mistress's schemes than doing her mistress's work, had put Kate's broken words together, a universal alarm took possession of the house. The housemaid, and the kitchenmaid, and the individual who served in the capacity of man-of-all-work, shook in their shoes. Mrs. Cook, however, who was housekeeper as well, shook out her ample skirts, and declared that she did not mind. 'A house can't take care of itself,' she said, with noble confidence; 'and they ain't that clever to know now to get on without me.' The gardener, also, was easy in his mind, secure in the fact that 'the "place," must be kep' up;' but a thrill of tremulous expectation ran through all those who were liable to be sent away.

These fears were very speedily justified. In as short a time as the post permitted, Mr. Courtenay received an effusive and enthusiastic answer from Mrs. Anderson, to whom he had written very curtly, making his proposal. This proposal was that she should receive Kate, not as a visitor, but permanently, until she attained her majority, giving her what educational advantages were within her reach, getting masters for her, and everything that was needful; and, in short, taking entire charge of her. 'Circumstances prevent me from doing this myself,' he wrote; 'and, of course, a lady is better fitted to take charge of a girl at Kate's troublesome age than I can be.' And then he entered upon the subject of money. Kate would have an allowance of five hundred pounds a year. It was ridiculously large for a child like his niece, he thought to himself; but parsimony was not Mr. Courtenay's weakness. For this she was to have everything a girl could require, with the exception of society, which her guardian forbade. 'It is not my wish that she should be introduced to the world till she is of age, and I prefer to choose the time and the way myself,' he said. With these conditions and instructions, Kate was to go, if her aunt wished it, to the Cottage.

Mrs. Anderson's letter, as we have said, was enthusiastic. She asked, was she really to have her dearest sister's only child under her care? and appealed to heaven and earth to testify that her delight was unspeakable. She said that her desire could only be the welfare, in every point, of 'our darling niece!' That nobody could be more anxious than she was to see her grow up the image of her sweet mother, 'which, in my mind, means an example of every virtue and every grace!' She declared that were she rich enough to give Kate all the advantages she ought to have, she would prove to Mr. Courtenay her perfect disinterestedness by refusing to accept any money with the dear child. But, for Kate's own sake, she must accept it; adding that the provision seemed to be both ample and liberal. Mrs. Anderson went on to say that masters of every kind came to a famous school in her neighbourhood, and that Mr. Courtenay might be quite sure of darling Kate's having every advantage. As for society, there was none, and he need be under no apprehension on that subject. She herself lived the quietest of lives, though of course she understood that, when Mr. Courtenay said society, he did not mean that she was to be interdicted from having a friend now and then to tea. This was the utmost extent of her dissipations, and she understood, as a matter of course, that he did not refer to anything of that description. She would come herself to London, she said, to receive from his hands 'our darling niece,' and he could perhaps then enter into further details as to anything he specially wished in reference to a subject on which their common interest was so great. Mr. Courtenay coughed very much over this letter—it gave him an irritation in his throat. 'The woman is a humbug as well as a fool!' he said to himself. But yet the question was—humbug or no humbug—was she the best person to free him of the charge of Kate? And, however he might resist, his judgment told him that this was the case.

The Rectory people came to return the visit of Mr. and Miss Courtenay while the house was in this confusion and commotion. They made a most decorous call at the proper hour, and in just the proper number—Mr. and Mrs. Hardwick, and one daughter. Kate had fallen from the momentary popularity which she had attained on her first appearance at the Rectory. She was now 'that interfering, disagreeable thing,' to the two girls. Nevertheless, as was right, in consideration of Miss Courtenay's age, Edith, the sensible one, accompanied her mother.

'I am the best one to go,' said Edith to her mother. 'For Minnie, I am sure, would lose her temper, and it is much best not to throw her into temptation.'

'You must be quite sure you can resist the temptation yourself,' said Mrs. Hardwick, who had brought up her children very well indeed, and had early taught them to identify and struggle against their specially besetting sins.

'You know, mamma, though I am sure I am a great deal worse in other things, this kind of temptation is not my danger,' said Edith; and with this satisfactory arrangement, the party took its way to the Hall.

Kate, in the flutter of joyous excitement which attended the new change in her fortunes, was quite a new creature—not the same who had called at the Rectory, and surprised and offended them. She had forgotten all about her own naughtiness. She seized upon Edith, and drew her into a corner, eager for a listener.

'Oh! do you know I am going away?' she said. 'Have you ever been away from home? Have you been abroad? Did you ever go to live among people whom you never saw before? That is what I am going to do.'

'Oh! I am so sorry for you!' said Edith, glad, as she afterwards explained to her mother, to be able to say something which should at once be amiable and true.

'Sorry!' said Kate—'oh! don't be sorry. I am very glad. I am going to my aunt, who is fond of me, though I never saw her. Going to people who are fond of you is different—'

'Are you fond of her?' said Edith.

'I never saw her,' said Kate, opening her eyes.

Here was an opportunity to be instructive such as seldom occurred, even in the schools where Miss Edith's gift was known. The young sage laid her hand upon Kate's, who was considerably surprised by the unlooked-for affectionateness. 'I am older than you,' said Edith—'I am quite grown up. You will not mind my speaking to you? Oh! do you know, dear, what is the best way to make people fond of you?'

'No.'

'To love them,' said Edith, with fervour. Kate looked at her with calm, reflective, fully-opened eyes.

'If you can,' she said—'but then how can you? Besides, it is their business to begin; they are older; they ought to know more about it—to be more in the way; Uncle Courtenay, for instance—I am sure you are very good—a great deal better than I am; but could you be fond of him?'

'If he was my uncle—if it was my duty,' said Edith.

'Oh! I don't know about duty,' said Kate, shaking back her abundant locks. The idea did not all commend itself to her mind. 'It is one's duty to learn lessons,' she went on, 'and keep one's temper, and not to talk too much, and that sort of thing; but to be fond of people—However, never mind; we can talk of that another time. We are going on Monday, and I never was out of Langton-Courtenay for a single night in all my life before.'

'Poor child!—what a trial for you!' said Edith.

At this moment Mrs. Hardwick struck in—'After the first is over, I am sure you will like it very much,' she said. 'It will be such a change. Of course it is always trying to leave home for the first time.'

'Trying!' cried Kate; and she rose up in the very restlessness of delight, with her eyes shining, and her hair streaming behind her. But what was the use of discussing it? Of course they could not understand. It was easier to show them over the house and the grounds than to explain her feelings to them. And both Mrs. Hardwick and Edith were deeply impressed by the splendour of Langton-Courtenay. They gave little glances at Kate of mingled surprise and admiration. After all, they felt, the possessor of such a place—the owner of the lands which stretched out as far as they could see—ought to be excused if she was a little different from other girls. 'What a temptation it must be!' Edith whispered to her mother; and it pleased Mrs. Hardwick to see how tolerant of other people's difficulties her child was. Kate grew quite excited by their admiration. She rushed over all the house, leading them into a hundred quaint corners. 'I shall fill it from top to bottom when I am of age,' she said. 'All those funny bedrooms have been so dreadfully quiet and lonely since ever I was born; but it shall be gay when my time comes.'

'Oh! hush, my dear,' said pious Mrs. Hardwick—'don't make so sure of the future, when we don't know what a day or an hour may bring forth.'

'Well,' said Kate, holding her position stoutly, 'if anything happens, of course there is an end of it; but if nothing happens—if I live, and all that—oh! I just wish I was one-and-twenty, to show you what I should do!'

'Do you think it will make you happy to be so gay?' said Edith, but with a certain wistful inquiry in her eyes, which was not like her old superiority.

'Oh! my dear children, hush!' repeated her mother—'don't talk like this. In the first place, gaiety is nothing—it is good neither for body nor soul; and besides, I cannot let you chatter so about the future. You will forgive me, my dear Miss Courtenay, for I am an old-fashioned person; but when we think how little we know about the future;—and your life will be an important one—a lesson and an example to so many. We ought to try to make ourselves of use to our fellow-creatures—and you must endeavour that the example should be a good one.'

'Fancy me an example!' said Kate, half to herself; and then she was silent, with a philosophy beyond her years. She did not attempt to argue; she had wit enough to see that it would be useless, and to pass on to another subject. But as she ran along the corridor, and into all the rooms, the thought of what she would make of them, when she came back, went like wine through her thrilling veins. She was glad to go away—far more glad than any one could imagine who had never lived the grey, monotonous routine of such an existence, uncheered by companions, unwarmed by love. But she would also be glad to come back—glad to enter splendidly, a young queen among her court. Her head was almost turned by this sublime idea. She would come back with new friends, new principles, new laws; she would be Queen absolute, without partner or help; she would be the lawgiver, redresser of wrongs. Her supremacy would be beneficent as the reign of an ideal sovereign; but she would be supreme!

When her visitors left, she stood on the threshold of her own house, looking with shining eyes into that grand future. The shadows had all faded from her mind. She had almost forgotten, in the excitement of her new plans, all about Miss Blank's sharp words, and the people who hated her. It would have surprised her had any one called that old figment to her recollection. Hate! there was nothing like it in that future. There was power and beneficence, and mirth and brightness. There was everything that was gay, everything that was beautiful; smiles, and bright looks, and wit, and unbounded novelty; and herself the dispenser of everything pleasant, herself always supreme! This was the dream of the future which framed itself in Kate Courtenay's thoughts.

CHAPTER X

While all this agitation was going on over Kate's fate on one side, it is not to be supposed that there was no excitement on the other. Her two relations, the mother and daughter to whom she was about to be confided, were nearly as much disturbed as Kate herself by the prospect of receiving her. It might, indeed, be said to have disturbed them more, for it affected their entire life. They had lately returned to England, and settled down, after a wandering life, in a house of their own. They were not rich, but they had enough. They were not humble, but accustomed to think very well of themselves; and the fact was that, though Mrs. Anderson had, for many reasons, accepted Mr. Courtenay's proposal with enthusiasm, even she felt that the ideal seclusion she had been dreaming of was at once broken up—even she—and still more Ombra, her daughter, who was fanciful, and of a somewhat jealous and contradictory temper, fond of her own way, and of full freedom to carry her fancies out.

Mrs. Anderson, let us say at once, was neither a hypocrite nor a fool, and never, during their whole intercourse, regarded her heiress-niece as a means of drawing advantage to herself, or in a mercenary way. She was a warm-hearted, kind, and just woman; but she had her faults. The chief of these was a very excess of virtue. Her whole soul was set upon not being good only, but appearing so. She could not bear the idea of being deficient in any decorum, in any sentiment which society demanded. No one could have grieved more sincerely than she did for her husband; but a bitterer pang even than that caused her by natural sorrow would have gone through her heart, had she been tempted to smile through her tears a day sooner than public opinion warranted a widow to smile. In every position—even that in which she felt most truly—a sense of what society expected from her was always in her mind. This code of unwritten law went deeper with her even than nature. She had truly longed and yearned over Kate, in her kind heart, from the moment she had reached England; and had she followed her natural instincts, would have rushed at once to Langton-Courtenay, to see the child who was all that remained of a sister whom she had loved. But the world, in that case, would have said that she meant to establish herself at Langton-Courtenay, and that her affection for her niece was feigned or mercenary.

'Let her alone, then,' Ombra said. 'Why should we trouble ourselves? If her friends think we are not good enough for her, let her alone. Why should she think herself better than we?'

'My love, she is very young,' said Mrs. Anderson; 'and, besides, if I took no notice at all of Catherine's only child, what would people suppose? It would be thought either that I had a guilty conscience in respect to the Courtenays, or that I had been repulsed. Nobody would believe that we had simply let her alone, as you say; and, besides, I am longing to see Kate with all my heart.

'What does it matter what people say?' said Ombra. 'I do not see what any one has to do with our private affairs.'

'That is a great delusion,' said Mrs. Anderson, shaking her head; 'every one has to do with every one else's private affairs. If you do not wish to lay yourself open to remark, you will always keep this in mind. And our position is very trying, between your cousin's wealth and our love for her—'

'I don't think I have very much love for her, mamma.'

'My dear child, don't let any one but me hear you say so. She ought to be like a sister to you,' said Mrs. Anderson.

And Ombra let the discussion drop, and permitted her mother, in this respect, to have her own way. But she was not in any respect of her mother's way of thinking. Her temptation was to hate and despise the opinion of society just in proportion to the reverence for it which she had been bred in: a result usual enough with clear-sighted and impetuous young persons, conscious of the defects of their parents. Ombra was a pretty, gentle, soft-mannered girl in outward appearance; but a certain almost fierce independence and determination to guide her own course as she herself pleased, was in her heart. She would not be influenced, as her mother had been, by other people's ideas. She thought, with some recent writers, that the doctrine of self-sacrifice, as taught specially to women, was altogether false, vain, and miserable. She felt that she herself ought to be first in her home and sphere; and she did not feel disposed even to share with, much less to yield to, the rich cousin whom she had never seen. She shrugged her shoulders over Mrs. Anderson's letter to Kate, but she did not interfere further, until Mr. Courtenay's astounding proposal arrived, fluttering the household as a hawk would flutter the dovecots. At the first reading, it drove Ombra frantic. It was impossible, out of the question, not to be thought of for a moment! In this small house, with their two maids, in the quiet of Shanklin, what were they to do with a self-important girl, a creature, no doubt, bred from her cradle to a consciousness of her own greatness, and who wanted all sorts of masters and advantages? Mrs. Anderson knew how to manage her daughter, and for the moment she allowed her to have her way, and pour forth her indignation. The letter came by the early post; and it was only when they were seated at tea in the evening that she brought forward the other side of the question.

'What you say is all very true, Ombra; but we have two spare bedrooms—there would still be one left for a friend, even if we took in poor dear little Kate.'

'Poor Kate! Why is she poor? She could buy us over and over,' said Ombra, in her indignation.

'Buy what?' said her clever mother—'our love?'

'Mamma, please don't speak any nonsense about love!' said Ombra, hastily. 'I can't love people at a moment's notice; because a girl whom I never saw happens to be the child of my aunt, whom I never saw—'

'Then suppose we leave you out,' said her mother. 'She is the child of my sister, whom I knew well, and was very fond of—that alters the question so far as I am concerned.'

'Oh! of course, mamma,' said Ombra, with darkened brows, 'I do not pretend to do more than give my opinion. It is for you to say how it is to be.'

'Do you think I can make a decision without you?' said the mother, pathetically. 'You must try to look at it more reasonably, my dear. Next to you, Kate is the creature most near to me in the world—next to me. Now, listen, Ombra; she is your nearest relation. Think what it will be to have a friend and a sister if anything should happen to me. The house is small, but we cannot truly say that we have not room for a little girl of fifteen in it. And then think of her loneliness—not a soul to care for her, except that old Mr. Courtenay—'

'Oh! that is nonsense; she must have some one to care for her, or else she must be intensely disagreeable,' said Ombra. 'Mamma, remember what I say—if we take her in, we shall repent it all our lives.'

'Nothing of the sort, my dear,' said Mrs. Anderson, eagerly following up this softened opposition. 'Why she is only fifteen—a mere child!—we can mould her as we will. And then, my dearest child, though heaven knows it is not interest I am thinking of, still it will be a great advantage; our income will be doubled. I must say Mr. Courtenay is very liberal, if nothing else. We shall be able to do many things that we could not do otherwise. Why, Ombra, you look as if you thought I meant to rob your cousin—'

'I would not use a penny of her allowance—it should be all spent upon herself!' cried the girl, flushing with indignant passion. 'Our income doubled! Mamma, what can you be thinking of? Do you suppose I could endure to be a morsel the better for that Kate?'

'You are a little fool, and there is no talking to you,' said Mrs. Anderson, with natural impatience; and for half an hour they did not speak to each other. This, however, could not last very long, for providentially, as Mrs. Anderson said, one of the Rectory girls came in at the time when it was usual for the ladies to take their morning walk, and she would not for all the Isle of Wight have permitted Elsie to see that her child and she were not on their usual terms. When Elsie had left them, a slight relapse was threatened, but they were then walking together along the cliff, with one of the loveliest of landscapes before them—the sun setting, the ruddy glory lighting up Sandown Bay, and all the earth and sea watching that last crisis and climax of the day.

'Oh! there is the true daffodil sky!' Ombra exclaimed, in spite of herself, and the breach was healed. It was she herself who resumed the subject some time later, when they turned towards home. 'I do not see,' she said abruptly, 'what we could do about masters for that girl, if she were to come here. To have them down from town would be ruinous, and to be constantly going up to town with her—to you, who so hate the ferry—would be dreadful!'

'My love, you forget Miss Story's school, where they have all the best masters,' said Mrs. Anderson, mildly.

'You could not send her to school.'

'But they would come to us, my dear. Of course they would be very glad to come to us for a little more money, and I should gladly take the opportunity for your music, Ombra. I thought of that. I wish everything could be settled as easily. If you only saw the matter as I do—'

'There is another thing,' said Ombra, hastily, 'which does not matter to me, for I hate society; but if she is to be kept like a nun, and never to see any one—'

Mrs. Anderson smiled serenely. 'My love, who is there to see?—the Rectory children and a few ladies—people whom we ask to tea. Of course, I would not think of taking her to balls or even dinner-parties; but then, I never go to dinner-parties—there is no one to ask us; and as for balls, Ombra, you know what you said about that nice ball at Ryde.'

'I hate them!' said Ombra, vehemently. 'I hope I shall never be forced to go to another in all my life.'

'Then that question is settled very easily,' said Mrs. Anderson, without allowing any signs of triumph to appear in her face. And next day she wrote to Mr. Courtenay, as has been described. When she wrote about 'our darling niece,' the tears were in her eyes. She meant it with all her heart; but, at the same time, it was the right thing to say, and to be anxious and eager to receive the orphan were the right sentiments to entertain. 'It is the most proper arrangement,' she said afterwards to the Rector's wife, who was her nearest neighbour. 'Of course her mother's sister is her most natural guardian. The property is far best in Mr. Courtenay's hands; but the child herself—'

'Poor child!' said Mrs. Eldridge, looking at her own children, who were many, and thinking within herself that to trust them to any one, even an aunt—

'Yes, poor child!' cried Mrs. Anderson, with the tears in her eyes; 'and my Catherine would have made such a mother! But we must do what we can to make it up to her. She will have some one at least to love her here.'

'I am sure you will be—good to her,' said the Rector's wife, looking wistfully, in her pity, into the face of the woman who, to her simple mind, did protest too much. Mrs. Eldridge felt, as many a straightforward person does, that her neighbour's extreme propriety, and regard for what was befitting and 'expected of her,' was the mask of insincerity. She did not understand the existence of true feeling beneath all that careful exterior. But she was puzzled and touched for the moment by the tears in her companion's eyes.

'You can't get up tears, you know, when you will,' she said to her husband, when they discussed poor Kate's prospects of happiness in her aunt's house, that same night.

'I can't,' said the Rector, 'nor you; but one has heard of crocodile tears!'

'Oh! Fred, no—not so bad as that!'

But still both these good people distrusted Mrs. Anderson, through her very anxiety to do right, and show that she was doing it. They were afraid of her excess of virtue. The exaggeration of the true seemed to them false. And they even doubted the amount of Kate's allowance, because of the aunt's frankness in telling them of it. They thought her intention was to raise her own and her niece's importance, and calculated among themselves what the real sum was likely to be. Poor Mrs. Anderson! everybody was unjust to her—even her daughter—on this point.

But it was with no sense of this general distrust, but, on the contrary, with the most genial sense of having done everything that could be required of her, that she left home on a sunny June morning, with her heart beating quicker than usual in her breast, to bring home her charge. Her heart was beating partly out of excitement to see Kate, and partly out of anxiety about the crossing from Ryde, which she hated. The sea looked calm, from Sandown, but Mrs. Anderson knew, by long experience, that the treacherous sea has a way of looking calm until you have trusted yourself to its tender mercies. This thought, along with her eagerness to see her sister's child, made her heart beat.

CHAPTER XI

Mr. Courtenay had stipulated that Kate was to be met by her aunt, not at his house, but at the railway, and to continue her journey at once. His house, he said, was shut up; but his real reason was reluctance to establish any precedent or pretext for other invasions. Kate started in the very highest spirits, scarcely able to contain herself, running over with talk and laughter, making a perpetual comment upon all that passed before her. Even Miss Blank's sinister congratulations, when she took leave of the little travelling party, 'I am sure I wish you joy, sir, and I wish Mrs. Anderson joy!' did not damp Kate's spirits. 'I shall tell my aunt, Miss Blank, and I am sure she will be much obliged to you,' the girl said, as she took her seat in the carriage. And Maryanne, who, red and excited, was seated by her, tittered in sympathy.

When Mr. Courtenay hid himself behind a newspaper, it was on Maryanne that Kate poured forth the tide of her excitement. 'Isn't it delightful!' she said, a hundred times over. 'Oh! yes, miss; but father and mother!' Maryanne answered, with a sob. Kate contemplated her gravely for twenty seconds. Here was a difference, a distinction, which she did not understand. But before the minute was half over her thoughts had gone abroad again in a confusion of expectancy and pleasure. She leant half out of the window, casting eager glances upon the people who were waiting the arrival of the train at the station. The first figure upon which she set her eyes was that of a squat old woman in a red and yellow shawl. 'Oh! can that be my aunt?' Kate said to herself, with dismay. The next was a white-haired, substantial old lady, old enough to be Mrs. Anderson's mother. 'This is she! She is nice! I shall be fond of her!' cried Kate to herself. When the white-haired lady found some one else, Kate's heart sank. Oh! where was the new guardian?

'Miss Kate! oh! please, Miss Kate!' said Maryanne; and turning sharply round, Kate found herself in somebody's arms. She had not time to see who it was; she felt only a warm darkness surround her, the pressure of something which held her close, and a voice murmuring, 'My darling child! my Catherine's child!' murmuring and purring over her. Kate had time to think, 'Oh! how tall she is! Oh! how warm! Oh! how funny!' before she was let loose and kissed—which latter process allowed her to see a tall woman, not in the least like the white-haired grandmother whom she had fixed upon—a woman not old, with hair of Kate's own colour, smiles on her face, and tears in her eyes.

'Let me look at you, my sweet! I should have known you anywhere. You are so like your darling mother!' said the new aunt. And then she wept; and then she said, 'Is it you? Is it really you, my Kate?' And all this took place at the station, with Uncle Courtenay sneering hard by, and strangers looking on.

'Yes, aunt, of course it is me,' said Kate, who scorned grammar; 'who should it be? I came expressly to meet you; and Uncle Courtenay is there, who will tell you it is all right.'

'Dearest! as if I had any need of your Uncle Courtenay,' said Mrs. Anderson; and she kissed her over again, and cried once more, most honest but inappropriate tears.

'Are you sorry?' cried Kate, in surprise; 'because I am glad, very glad to see you. I could not cry for anything—I am as happy as I can be.'

'You darling!' said Mrs. Anderson. 'But you are right, it is too public here. I must take you away to have some luncheon, too, my precious child. There is no time to lose. Oh! Kate, Kate, to think I should have you at last, after so many years!'

'I hope you will be pleased with me now, aunt,' said Kate, a little alarm mingling with her surprise. Was she worth all this fuss? It was fuss; but Kate had no constitutional objection to fuss, and it was pleasant, on the whole. After all the snubbing she had gone through, it was balm to her to be received so warmly; even though the cynicism which she had been trained into was moved by a certain sense of the ludicrous, too.

'Kate says well,' said old Mr. Courtenay. 'I hope you will be pleased with her, now you have her. To some of us she has been a sufficiently troublesome child; but I trust in your hands—your more skilful hands—'

'I am not afraid,' said Mrs. Anderson, with a very suave smile; 'and even if she were troublesome, I should be glad to have her. But we start directly; and the child must have some luncheon. Will you join us, or must we say good-bye? for we shall not be at home till after dinner, and at present Kate must have something to eat?'

'I have an engagement,' said Mr. Courtenay, hastily. What! he lunch at a railway station with a girl of fifteen and this unknown woman, who, by the way, was rather handsome after her fashion! What a fool she must be to think of such a thing! He bowed himself off very politely, with an assurance that now his mind was easy about his ward. She must write to him, he said and let him know in a few days how she liked Shanklin; but in the meantime he was compelled to hurry away.

When Kate felt herself thus stranded as it were upon an utterly lonely and unknown shore, in the hands of a woman she had never seen before, and the last familiar face withdrawn, there ran a little pain, a little thrill, half of excitement, half of dismay, in her heart. She clutched at Maryanne, who stood behind her; she examined once again, with keen eyes, the new guide of her life. This was novelty indeed!—but novelty so sharp and sudden that it took away her breath. Mrs. Anderson's tone had been very different to her uncle from what it was to herself. What did this mean? Kate was bewildered, half frightened, stunned by the change, and she could not make it out.

'My dear, I am sure your uncle has a great many engagements,' said Mrs. Anderson; 'gentlemen who are in society have so many claims upon them, especially at this time of the year; or perhaps he thought it kindest to let us make friends by ourselves. Of course he must be very fond of you, dear; and I must always be grateful for his good opinion: without that he would not have trusted his treasure in my hands.'

'Aunt Anderson,' said Kate, hastily, 'please don't make a mistake. I am sure I am no treasure at all to him, but only a trouble and a nuisance. You must not think so well of me as that. He thought me a great trouble, and he was very glad to get rid of me. I know this is true.'

Mrs. Anderson only smiled. She put her arm through the girl's, and led her away. 'We will not discuss the question, my darling, for you must have something to eat. When did you leave Langton? Our train starts at two—we have not much time to lose. Are you hungry? Oh! Kate, how glad I am to have you! How very glad I am! You have your mother's very eyes.'

'Then don't cry, aunt, if you are glad.'

'It is because I am glad, you silly child. Come in here, and give me one good kiss. And now, dear, we will have a little cold chicken, and get settled in the carriage before the crowd comes.'

And how different was the second part of this journey! Mrs. Anderson got no newspaper—she sat opposite to Kate, and smiled at all she said. She told her the names of the places they were passing; she was alive to every light and shade that passed over her young, changeable face. Then Kate fell silent all at once, and began to think, and cast many a furtive look at her new-found relation; at last she said, in a low voice, and with a certain anxiety—

'Aunt, is it possible that I could remember mamma?'

'Ah! no, Kate; she died just when you were born.'

'Then did I ever see you before?'

'Never since you were a little baby—never that you could know.'

'It is very strange,' the girl said half to herself; 'but I surely know some face like yours. Ah! could it be that?' She stopped, and her face flushed up to her hair.

'Could it be what, dear?'

Then Kate laughed out—the softest, most musical, tender little laugh that ever came from her lips. 'I know,' she said—'it is myself!'

Mrs. Anderson blushed, too, with sudden pleasure. It was a positive happiness to her, penetrating beneath all her little proprieties and pretensions. She took the girl's hands, and bending forward, looked at her in the face; and it was true—they were as like as if they had been mother and daughter—though the elder had toned down, and lost that glory of complexion, that brightness of intelligence; and the younger was brighter, quicker, more intelligent than her predecessor had ever been. This made at once the sweetest, most pleasant link between them; it bound them together by Nature's warm and visible bond. They were both proud of this tie, which could be seen in their faces, which they could not throw off nor cast away.

But after the ferry was crossed—when they were drawing near Shanklin—a silence fell upon both. Kate, with a quite new-born timidity, was shy of inquiring about her cousin; and Mrs. Anderson was too doubtful of Ombra's mood to say more of her than she could help. She longed to be able to say, 'Ombra will be sure to meet us,' but did not dare. And Ombra did not meet them; she was not to be seen, even, as they walked up to the house. It was a pretty cottage, embowered in luxuriant leafage, just under the shelter of the cliff, and looking out over its own lawn, and a thread of quiet road, and the slopes of the Undercliff, upon the distant sea. There was, however, no one at the door, no one at any of the windows, no trace that they were expected, and Mrs. Anderson's heart was wrung by the sight. Naturally she grew at once more prodigal of her welcomes and caresses. 'How glad I am to see you here, my darling Kate! This is your home, dear child. As long as I live, whenever you may want it, my humble house will be yours from this day—always remember that; and welcome, my darling,—welcome home!'

Kate accepted the kisses, but her thoughts were far away. Where was the other who should have given her a welcome too? All the girl's eager soul rushed upon this new track. Did Ombra object to her?—why was not she here? Ombra's mother, though she said nothing, had given many anxious glances round her, which were not lost upon Kate's keen perceptions? Could Ombra object to the intruder? After all her aunt's effusions, this was a new idea to Kate.

The door was thrown open by a little woman in a curious headdress, made out of a coloured handkerchief, whose appearance filled Kate with amazement, and whose burst of greeting she could not for the first moment understand. Kate's eyes went over her shoulder to a commonplace English housemaid behind with a sense of relief. 'Oh! how the young lady is welcome!' cried old Francesca. 'How she is as the light to our eyes!—and how like our padrona—how like! Come in—come in; your chamber is ready, little angel. Oh! how bella, bella our lady must have been at that age!'

'Hush, Francesca; do not put nonsense into the child's head,' said Mrs. Anderson, still looking anxiously round.

'I judge from what I see,' said the old woman; and then she added, in answer to a question from her mistress's eyes, 'Meess Ombra has the bad head again. It was I that made her put herself to bed. I made the room dark, and gave her the tea, as madam herself does it, otherwise she would be here to kiss this new angel, and bid her the welcome. Come in, come in, carissima; come up, I will show you the chamber. Ah! our signorina has not been able to keep still when she heard you, though she has the bad head, the very bad head.'

And then there appeared to Kate, coming downstairs, the slight figure of a girl in a black dress—a girl whom, at the first moment, she thought younger than herself. Ombra was not at all like her mother—she was like her name, a shadowy creature, with no light about her—not even in the doubtful face, pale and fair, which her cousin gazed upon so curiously. She said nothing till she had come up to them, and did not quicken her pace in the least, though they were all gazing at her. To fill up this pause, Mrs. Anderson, who was a great deal more energetic and more impressionable than her daughter, rushed to her across the little hall.

'My darling, are you ill? I know only that could have prevented you from coming to meet your cousin. Here she is, Ombra mia; here we have her at last—my sweet Kate! Now love each other, girls; be as your mothers were; open your hearts to each other. Oh! my dear children, if you but knew how I love you both!'

And Mrs. Anderson cried while the two stood holding each other's hands, looking at each other—on Kate's side with violent curiosity; on Ombra's apparently with indifference. The mother had to do all the emotion that was necessary, with an impulse which was partly love, and partly vexation, and partly a hope to kindle in them the feelings that became the occasion.

'How do you do? I am glad to see you. I hope you will like Shanklin,' said chilly Ombra.

'Thanks,' said Kate; and they dropped each other's hands; while poor Mrs. Anderson wept unavailing tears, and old Francesca, in sympathy, fluttered about the new 'little angel,' taking off her cloak, and uttering aloud her admiration and delight. It was a strange beginning to Kate's new life.

'I wonder, I wonder—' the new-comer said to herself when she was safely housed for the night, and alone. Kate had seated herself at the window, from whence a gleam of moon and sky was visible, half veiled in clouds. She was in her dressing-gown, and with her hair all over her shoulders, was a pretty figure to behold, had there been any one to see. 'I wonder, I wonder!' she said to herself. But she could not have put into words what her wonderings were. There was only in them an indefinite sense that something not quite apparent had run on beneath the surface in this welcome of hers. She could not tell what it was—why her aunt should have wept; why Ombra should have been so different. Was it the ready tears of the one that chilled the other? Kate was not clear enough on the subject to ask herself this question. She only wondered, feeling there was something more than met the eye. But, on the whole, the child was happy—she had been kissed and blessed when she came upstairs; she seemed to be surrounded with an atmosphere of love and care. There was nobody (except Ombra) indifferent—everybody cared; all were interested. She wondered—but at fifteen one does not demand an answer to all the indefinite wonderings which arise in one's heart; and, despite of Ombra, Kate's heart was lighter than it had ever been (she thought) in all her life. Everything was strange, new, unknown to her, yet it was home. And this is a paradox which is always sweet.

CHAPTER XII

There was something that might almost have been called a quarrel downstairs that night over the new arrival. Ombra was cross, and her mother was displeased; but Mrs. Anderson had far too strong a sense of propriety to suffer herself to scold. When she said 'I am disappointed in you, Ombra. I have seldom been more wounded than when I came to the door, and did not find you,' she had done all that occurred to her in the way of reproof.

'But I had a headache, mamma.'

'We must speak to the doctor about your headaches,' said Mrs. Anderson; and Ombra, with something like sullenness, went to bed.

But she was not to escape so easily. Old Francesca had been Ombra's nurse. She was not so very old, but had aged, as peasant women of her nation do. She was a Tuscan born, with the shrill and high-pitched voice natural to her district, and she had followed the fortunes of the Andersons all over the world, from the time of her nursling's birth. She was, in consequence, a most faithful servant and friend, knowing no interests but those of her mistress, but at the same time a most uncompromising monitor. Ombra knew what was in store for her, as soon as she discovered Francesca, with her back turned, folding up the dress she had worn in the morning. The chances are that Ombra would have fled, had she been able to do so noiselessly, but she had already betrayed herself by closing the door.

'Francesca,' she said, affecting an ease which she did not feel, 'are you still here? Are you not in bed? You will tire yourself out. Never mind those things. I will put them away myself.'

'The things might be indifferent to me,' said Francesca, turning round upon her, 'but you are not. My young lady, I have a great deal to say to you.'

This conversation was chiefly in Italian, both the interlocutors changing, as pleased them, from one language to another; but as it is unnecessary to cumber the page with italics, or the reader's mind with two languages, I will take the liberty of putting it in English, though in so doing I may wrong Francesca's phrases. When her old nurse addressed her thus, Ombra trembled—half in reality because she was a chilly being, and half by way of rousing her companion's sympathy. But Francesca was ruthless.

'You have the cold, I perceive,' she said, 'and deserve to have it. Seems to me that if you thought sometimes of putting a little warmth in your heart, instead of covering upon your body, that would answer better. What has the little cousin done, Dio mio, to make you as if you had been for a night on the mountains? I look to see the big ice-drop hanging from your fingers, and the snow-flakes in your hair! You have the cold!—bah! you are the cold!—it is in you!—it freezes! I, whose blood is in your veins, I stretch out my hand to get warm, and I chill, I freeze, I die!'

'I am Ombra.' said the girl, with a smile, 'you know; how can I warm you, Francesca? It is not my nature.'

'Are you not, then, God's making, because they have given you a foolish name?' cried Francesca. 'The Ombra I love, she is the Ombra that is cool, that is sweet, that brings life when one comes out of a blazing sun. You say the sun does not blaze here; but what is here, after all? A piece of the world which God made! When you were little, Santissima Madonna! you were sweet as an olive orchard; but now you are sombre and dark, like a pine-wood on the Apennines. I will call you 'Ghiaccia,'[A] not Ombra any more.'

'It was not my fault. You are unjust. I had a headache. You said so yourself.'

'Ah, disgraziata! I said it to shield you. You have brought upon my conscience a great big—what you call fib. I hope my good priest will not say it was a lie!'

'I did not ask you to do it,' cried Ombra. 'And then there was mamma, crying over that girl as if there never had been anything like her before!'

'The dear lady! she did it as I did, to cover your coldness—your look of ice. Can we bear that the world should see what a snow-maiden we have between us? We did it for your sake, ungrateful one, that no one should see—'

'I wish you would let me alone,' said Ombra; and though she was seventeen—two years older than Kate—and had a high sense of her dignity, she began to cry. 'If you only would be true, I should not mind; but you have so much effusion—you say more than you mean, both mamma and you.'

'Seems to me that it is better to be too kind than too cold,' said Francesca, indignantly. 'And this poor little angel, the orphan, the child of the Madonna—ah! you have not that thought in your icy Protestant; but among us Christians every orphan is Madonna's child. How could I love the holiest mother, if I did not love her child? Bah! you know better, but you will not allow it. Is it best, tell me, to wound the poverina with your too little, or to make her warm and glad with our too mooch?—even if it were the too mooch,' said Francesca, half apologetically; 'though there is nothing that is too mooch, if it is permitted me to say it, for the motherless one—the orphan—the Madonna's child!'

Ombra made no reply; she shrugged her shoulders, and began to let down her hair out of its bands—the worst of the storm was over.

But Francesca had reserved herself for one parting blaze, 'And know you, my young lady, what will come to you, if thus you proceed in your life?' she said. 'When one wanders too mooch on the snowy mountains, one falls into an ice-pit, and one dies. It will so come to you. You will grow colder and colder, colder and colder. When it is for your good to be warm, you will be ice: you will not be able more to help yourself. You will make love freeze up like the water in the torrent; you will lay it in a tomb of snow, you will build the ice-monument over it, and then all you can do will be vain—it will live no more. Signorina Ghiaccia, if thus you go on, this is what will come to you.'

And with this parting address, Francesca darted forth, not disdaining, like a mere mortal and English domestic, to shut the door with some violence. Ombra had her cry out by herself, while Kate sat wondering in the next room. The elder girl asked herself, was it true?—was she really a snow-maiden, or was it some mysterious influence from her name that threw this shade over her, and made her so contradictory and burdensome even to herself?

For Ombra was not aware that she had been christened by a much more sober name. She stood as Jane Catherine in the books of the Leghorn chaplain—a conjunction of respectable appellatives which could not have any sinister influence. I doubt, however, whether she would have taken any comfort from this fact; for it was pleasant to think of herself as born under some wayward star—a shadowy creature, unlike common flesh and blood, half Italian, half spirit. 'How can I help it?' she said to herself. The people about her did not understand her—not even her mother and Francesca. They put the commonplace flesh-and-blood girl on a level with her—this Kate, with half-red hair, with shallow, bright eyes, with all that red and white that people rave about in foolish books. 'Kate will be the heroine wherever we go,' she said, with a smile, which had more pain than pleasure in it. She was a little jealous, a little cross, disturbed in her fanciful soul; and yet she was not heartless and cold, as people thought. The accusation wounded her, and haunted her as if with premonitions of reproaches to come. It was not hard to bear from Francesca, who was her devoted slave; but it occurred dimly to Ombra, as if in prophecy, that the time would come when she should hear the same words from other voices. Not Ombra-Ghiaccia! Was it possible? Could that fear ever come true?

Mrs. Anderson, for her part, was less easy about this change in her household than she would allow. When she was alone, the smiles went off her countenance. Kate, though she had been so glad to see her, though the likeness to herself had made so immediate a bond between them, was evidently enough not the kind of girl who could be easily managed, or who was likely to settle down quietly into domestic peace and order. She had the makings of a great lady in her, an independent, high-spirited princess, to whom it was not necessary to consider the rules which are made for humbler maidens. Already she had told her aunt what she meant to do at Langton when she went back; already she had inquired with lively curiosity all about Shanklin. Mrs. Anderson thought of her two critics at the Rectory, who, she knew by instinct, were ready to pick holes in her, and be hard upon her 'foreign ways,' and trembled for her niece's probable vagaries. It was 'a great responsibility,' a 'trying position,' for herself. Many a 'trying position' she had been in already, the difficulties of which she had surmounted triumphantly. She could only hope that 'proper feeling,' 'proper respect' for the usages of society, would bring her once more safely through. When Francesca darted in upon her, fresh from the lecture she had delivered, Mrs. Anderson's disturbed look at once betrayed her.

'My lady looks as she used to look when the big letters came, saying Go,' said Francesca; 'but, courage, Signora mia, the big letters come no more.'

'No; nor he who received them, Francesca,' said the mistress, sadly. 'But it was not that I was thinking of—it was my new care, my new responsibility.'

'Bah!' cried Francesca; 'my lady will pardon me, I did not mean to be rude. Ah! if my lady was but a Christian like us other Italians! Why there never came an orphan into a kind house, but she brought a blessing. The dear Madonna will never let trouble come to you from her child; and, besides, the little angel is exactly like you. Just so must my lady have looked at her age—beautiful as the day.'

'Ah! Francesca, you are partial,' said Mrs. Anderson, with, however, a returning smile. 'I never was so pretty as Kate.'

'My lady will pardon me,' said Francesca, with quiet gravity; 'in my eyes, senza complimenti, there is no one so beautiful as my lady even now.'

This statement was much too serious and superior to compliment-making, to be answered, especially as Francesca turned at once to the window, to close the shutters, and make all safe for the night.

CHAPTER XIII

Mrs. Anderson's house was situated in one of those nests of warmth and verdure which are characteristic of the Isle of Wight. There was a white cliff behind, partially veiled with turf and bushes, the remains of an ancient landslip. The green slope which formed its base, and which, in Spring, was carpeted with wild-flowers, descended into the sheltered sunny garden, which made a fringe of flowers and greenness round the cottage. On that side there was no need of fence or boundary. A wild little rustic flight of steps led upward to the winding mountain-path which led to the brow of the cliff, and the cliff itself thus became the property of the little house. Both cottage and garden were small, but the one was a mass of flowers, and the airy brightness and lightness of the other made up for its tiny size. The windows of the little drawing-room opened into the rustic verandah, all garlanded with climbing plants; and though the view was not very great, nothing but flowers and verdure, a bit of quiet road, a glimpse of blue sea, yet from the cliff there was a noble prospect—all Sandown Bay, with its white promontory, and the wide stretch of water, sometimes blue as sapphire, though grey enough when the wind brought it in, in huge rollers upon the strand. The sight, and sound, and scent of the sea were all alike new to Kate. The murmur in her ears day and night, now soft, like the hu-ush of a mother to a child, now thundering like artillery, now gay as laughter, delighted the young soul which was athirst for novelty. Here was something which was always new. There was no limit to her enjoyment of the sea. She liked it when wild and when calm, and whatever might be its vagaries, and in all her trials of temper, which occurred now and then, fled to it for soothing. The whole place, indeed, seemed to be made especially for Kate. It suited her to climb steep places, to run down slopes, to be always going up or down, with continual movement of her blood and stir of her spirits. She declared aloud that this was what she had wanted all her life—not flat parks and flowers, but the rising waves to pursue her when she ventured too close to them, the falling tide to open up sweet pools and mysteries, and penetrate her with the wholesome breath of the salt, delightful beach.

'I don't know how I have lived all this time away from it. I must have been born for the seaside!' she cried, as she walked on the sands with her two companions.

Ombra, for her part, shrugged her shoulders, and drew her shawl closer. She had already decided that Kate was one of the race of extravagant talkers, who say more than they feel.

'The sea is very nice,' said Mrs. Anderson, who in this respect was not so enthusiastic as Kate.

'Very nice! Oh! aunt, it is simply delightful! Whenever I am troublesome—as I know I shall be—just send me out here. I may talk all the nonsense I like—it will never tire the sea.'

'Do you talk a great deal of nonsense, Kate?'

'I am afraid I do,' said the girl, with penitence. 'Not that I mean it; but what is one to do? Miss Blank, my last governess, never talked at all, when she could help it, and silence is terrible—anything is better than that; and she said I chattered, and was always interfering. What could I do? One must be occupied about something!'

'But are you fond of interfering, dear?'

'Auntie!' said Kate, throwing back her hair, 'if I tell you the very worst of myself, you will not give me up, or send me away? Thanks! It is enough for me to be sure of that. Well, perhaps I am, a little—I mean I like to be doing something, or talking about something. I like to have something even to think about. You can't think of Mangnall's Questions, now, can you?—or Mrs. Markham? The village people used to be a great deal more interesting. I used to like to hear all that was going on, and give them my advice. Well, I suppose it was not very good advice. But I was not a nobody there to be laughed at, you know, auntie—I was the chief person in the place!'

Here Ombra laughed, and it hurt Kate's feelings.

'When I am old enough, I shall be able to do as I please in Langton-Courtenay,' she said.

'Certainly, my love,' said Mrs. Anderson, interposing; 'and I hope, in the meantime, dear, you will think a great deal of your responsibilities, and all that is necessary to make you fill such a trying position as you ought.'

'Trying!' said Kate, with some surprise; 'do you think it will be trying? I shall like it better than anything. Poor old people, I must try to make it up to them, for perhaps I rather bothered them sometimes, to tell the truth. I am not like you and Ombra, so gentle and nice. And, then, I had never seen people behave as I suppose they ought.'

'I am glad you think we behave as we ought, Kate.'

'Oh! auntie; but then there is something about Ombra that makes me ashamed of myself. She is never noisy, nor dreadful, like me. She touches things so softly, and speaks so gently. Isn't she lovely, aunt?'

'She is lovely to me,' said Mrs. Anderson, with a glow of pleasure. 'And I am so glad you like your cousin, Kate.'

'Like her! I never saw any one half so beautiful. She looks such a lady. She is so dainty, and so soft, and so nice. Could I ever grow like that? Ah! auntie, you shake your head—I don't mean so pretty, only a little more like her, a little less like a—'

'My dear child!' said the gratified mother, giving Kate a hug, though it was out of doors. And at that moment, Ombra, who had been in advance, turned round, and saw the hasty embrace, and shrugged her pretty shoulders, as her habit was.

'Mamma, I wish very much you would keep these bursts of affection till you get home,' said Ombra. 'The Eldridges are coming down the cliff.'

'Oh! who are the Eldridges? I know some people called Eldridge,' said Kate—'at least, I don't know them, but I have heard—'

'Hush! they will hear, too, if you don't mind,' said Ombra. And Kate was silent. She was changing rapidly, even in these few days. Ombra, who snubbed her, who was not gracious to her, who gave her no caresses, had, without knowing it, attained unbounded empire over her cousin. Kate had fallen in love with her, as girls so often do with one older than themselves. The difference in this case was scarcely enough to justify the sudden passion; but Ombra looked older than she was, and was so very different a being from Kate, that her gravity took the effect of years. Already this entirely unconscious influence had done more for Kate than all the educational processes she had gone through. It woke the woman, the gentlewoman, in the child, who had done, in her brief day, so many troublesome things. Ombra suddenly had taken the ideal place in her mind—she had been elevated, all unwitting of the honour, to the shrine in Kate's heart. Everything in her seemed perfection to the girl—even her name, her little semi-reproofs, her gentle coldness. 'If I could but be like Ombra, not blurting things out, not saying more than I mean, not carried away by everything that interests me,' she said, self-reproachfully, with rising compunction and shame for all her past crimes. She had never seen the enormity of them as she did now. She set up Ombra, and worshipped her in every particular, with the enthusiasm of a fanatic. She tried to curb her once bounding steps into some resemblance to the other's languid pace; and drove herself and Maryanne frantic by vain endeavours to smoothe her rich crisp chestnut hair into the similitude of Ombra's shadowy, dusky locks. This sudden worship was independent of all reason. Mrs. Anderson herself was utterly taken by surprise by it, and Ombra had not as yet a suspicion of the fact; but it had already begun to work upon Kate.

It was not in her, however, to make the acquaintance of this group of new people without a little stir in her pulses—all the more as Mrs. Eldridge came up to herself with special cordiality.

'I am sure this is Miss Courtenay,' she said. 'I have heard of you from my nephew and nieces at Langton-Courtenay. They told me you were coming to the Island. I hope you will like it, and think it as pretty as I do. You are most welcome, I am sure, to Shanklin.'

'Are you their aunt at Langton-Courtenay?' said Kate, with eyes which grew round with excitement and pleasure. 'Oh! how very odd! I did not think anybody knew me here.'

'I am aunt to the boys and girls,' said Mrs. Eldridge. 'Mrs. Hardwick is my husband's sister. We must be like old friends, for the Hardwicks' sake.'

'But the Hardwicks are not old friends to me,' said Kate, with a child's unnecessary conscientiousness of explanation. 'Bertie I know, but I have only seen the others twice.'

'Oh! that does not matter,' said the Rector's wife; 'you must come and see me all the same.' And then she turned to Mrs. Anderson, and began to talk of the parish. Kate stood by and listened with wondering eyes as they discussed the poor folk, and their ways and their doings. They did not interfere in her way; but perhaps their way was not much better, on the whole, than Kate's. She had been very interfering, there was no doubt; but then she had interfered with everybody, rich and poor alike, and made no invidious distinction. She stood and listened wondering, while the Rector added his contribution about the mothers' meetings, and the undue expectations entertained by the old women at the almshouses. 'We must guard against any foolish partiality, or making pets of them,' Mr. Eldridge said; and his wife added that Mr. Aston, in the next parish, had quite spoiled his poor people. 'He is a bachelor; he has nobody to keep him straight, and he believes all their stories. They know they have only to send to the Vicarage to get whatever they require. When one of them comes into our parish, we don't know what to do with her,' she said, shaking her head. Kate was too much occupied in listening to all this to perceive that Ombra shrugged her shoulders. Her interest in the new people kept her silent, as they reascended the cliff, and strolled towards the cottage; and it was not till the Rector and his wife had turned homewards, once more cordially shaking hands with her, and renewing their invitation, that she found her voice.

'Oh! auntie, how very strange—how funny!' she said. 'To think I should meet the Eldridges here!'

'Why not the Eldridges?—have you any objection to them?' said Mrs. Anderson.

'Oh, no!—I suppose not.' (Kate put aside with an effort that audacity of Sir Herbert Eldridge, and false assumption about the size of his park.) 'But it is so curious to meet directly, as soon as I arrive, people whom I have heard of—'

'Indeed, my dear Kate, it is not at all wonderful,' said her aunt, didactically. 'The world is not nearly such a big place as you suppose. If you should ever travel as much as we have done (which heaven forbid!), you would find that you were always meeting people you knew, in the most unlikely places. Once, at Smyrna, when Mr. Anderson was there, a gentleman came on business, quite by chance, who was the son of one of my most intimate friends in my youth. Another time I met a companion of my childhood, whom I had lost sight of since we were at school, going up Vesuvius. Our chaplain at Cadiz turned out to be a distant connection of my husband's, though we knew nothing of him before. Such things are always happening. The world looks very big, and you feel as if you must lose yourself in it; but, on the contrary, wherever one goes, one falls upon people one knows.'

'But yet it is so strange about the Hardwicks,' said Kate, persisting; 'they are the only people I ever went to see—whom I was allowed to know.'

'How very pleasant!' said Mrs. Anderson. 'Now I shall be quite easy in my mind. Your uncle must have approved of them, in that case, so I may allow you to associate with the Eldridges freely. How very nice, my love, that it should be so!'

Kate made no reply to this speech. She was not, to tell the truth, quite clear that her uncle approved. He had not cared to hear about Bertie Hardwick; he had frowned at the mention of him. 'And Bertie is the nicest—he is the only one I care for,' said Kate to herself; but she said nothing audibly on the subject. To her, notwithstanding her aunt's philosophy, it seemed very strange indeed that Bertie Hardwick's relatives should be the first to meet her in this new world.

CHAPTER XIV

Kate settled down into her new life with an ease and facility which nobody had expected. She wrote to her uncle that she was perfectly happy; that she never could be sufficiently thankful to him for freeing her from the yoke of Miss Blank, and placing her among people who were fond of her. 'Little fool!' Mr. Courtenay muttered to himself. 'They have flattered her, I suppose.' This was the easiest and most natural explanation to one who knew, or thought he knew, human nature so well.

But Kate was not flattered, except by her aunt's caressing ways and habitual fondness. Nobody in the Cottage recognised her importance as the heiress of Langton-Courtenay. Here she was no longer first, but second—nay third, taking her place after her cousin, as nature ordained. 'Ombra and Kate,' was the new form of her existence—first Ombra, then the new-comer, the youngest of all. She was spoiled as a younger child is spoiled, not in any other way. Mrs. Anderson's theory in education was indulgence. She did not believe in repression. She was always caressing, always yielding. For one thing, it was less troublesome than a continual struggle; but that was not her motive. She took high ground. 'What we have got to do is to ripen their young minds,' she said to the Rector's wife, who objected to her as 'much too good,' a reproach which Mrs. Anderson liked; 'and it is sunshine that ripens, not an east wind!' This was almost the only imaginative speech she had ever made in her life, and consequently she liked to repeat it. 'Depend upon it, it is sunshine that ripens them, and not east wind!'

'The sunshine ripens the wheat and the tares alike, as we are told in Scripture,' said Mrs. Eldridge, with professional seriousness.

'That shows that Providence is of my way of thinking,' said her antagonist. 'Why should one cross one's children, and worry them? They will have enough of that in their lives! Besides, I have practical proof on my side. Look, at Ombra! There is a child that never was crossed since she was born; and if I had scolded till I made myself ill, do you think I could have improved upon that?'

Mrs. Eldridge stood still for a moment, not believing her ears. She had daughters of her own, and to have Ombra set up as a model of excellence! But she recovered herself speedily, and gave vent to her feelings in a more courteous way.

'Ah! it is easy to see you never had any boys,' she said, with that sense of superiority which the mother of both sections of humanity feels over her who has produced but one. 'Ombra, indeed!' Mrs. Eldridge said, within herself. And, indeed, it was a want of 'proper feeling,' on Mrs. Anderson's part, to set up so manifestly her own daughter above other people's. She felt it, and immediately did what she could to atone.

'Boys, of course, are different,' she said; 'but I am sure you will agree with me that a poor child who has never had any one to love her, who has been brought up among servants, a girl who is motherless—'

'Oh! poor child! I can only say you are too good—too good! With such a troublesome disposition, too. I never could be half as good!' cried the Rector's wife.

Thus Mrs. Anderson triumphed in the argument. And as it happened that ripening under the sunshine was just what Kate wanted, the system answered in the most perfect way, especially as a gently chilling breeze, a kind of moral east wind, extremely subdued, but sufficiently keen, came from Ombra, checking Kate's irregularities, without seeming to do so, and keeping her high spirit down. Ombra's influence over her cousin increased as time went on. She was Kate's model of all that was beautiful and sweet. The girl subdued herself with all her might, and clipped and snipped at her own character, to bring it to the same mould as that of her cousin. And as such worship cannot go long unnoted, Ombra gradually grew aware of it, and softened under its influence. The Cottage grew very harmonious and pleasant within doors. When Kate went to bed, the mother and daughter would still linger and have little conversations about her, conversations in which the one still defended and the other attacked—or made a semblance of attacking—the new-comer; but the acrid tone had gone out of Ombra's remarks.

'I don't want to say a word against Kate,' she would say, keeping up her old rôle. 'I think there is a great deal of good about her; but you know we have no longer our house to ourselves.'

'Could we enjoy our house to ourselves, Ombra, knowing that poor child to have no home?' said Mrs. Anderson, with feeling.

'Well, mamma, the poor child has a great many advantages over us,' said Ombra, hesitating. 'I should like to have had her on a visit; but to be always between you and me—'

'No one can be between you and me, my child.'

'That is true, perhaps. But then our little house, our quiet life all to ourselves.'

'That was a dream, my dear—that was a mere dream of your own. People in our position cannot have a life all to ourselves. We have our duties to society; and I have my duty to you, Ombra. Do you think I could be so selfish as to keep you altogether to myself, and never let you see the world, or have your chance of choosing some one who will take care of you better than I can?'

'Please don't,' said Ombra. 'I am quite content with you; and there is not much at Shanklin that can be called society or the world.'

'The world is everywhere,' said Mrs. Anderson, with dignity. 'I am not one of those who confine the term to a certain class. Your papa was but a Consul, but I have seen many an ambassador who was very inferior to him. Shanklin is a very nice place, Ombra; and the society, what there is, is very nice also. I like my neighbours very much—they are not lords and ladies, but they are well-bred, and some of them are well-born.'

'I don't suppose we are among that number,' said Ombra, with a momentary laugh. This was one of her pet perversities, said out of sheer opposition; for though she thrust the fact forward, she did not like it herself.

'I think you are mistaken,' said her mother, with a flush upon her face. 'Your papa had very good connections in Scotland; and my father's family, though it was not equal to the Courtenays, which my sister married into, was one of the most respectable in the county. You are not like Kate—you have not the pedigree which belongs to a house which has landed property; but you need not look down upon your forefathers for all that.'

'I do not look down upon them. I only wish not to stand up upon them, mamma, for they are not strong enough to bear me, I fear,' Ombra said, with a little forced laugh.

'I don't like joking on such subjects,' said Mrs. Anderson. 'But to return to Kate. She admires you very, very much, my darling—I don't wonder at that—'

'Silly child!' said Ombra, in a much softened tone.

'It shows her sense, I think; but it throws all the greater a responsibility on you. Oh! my dear love, could you and I, who are so happy together, dare to shut our hearts against that poor desolate child?'

Once more Ombra slightly, very slightly shrugged her shoulders; but she answered—

'I am sure I have no wish to shut my heart against her, mamma.'

'For my part,' said Mrs. Anderson, 'I feel I cannot pet her too much, or be too indulgent to her, to make up to her for fifteen years spent among strangers, with nobody to love.'

'How odd that she should have found nobody to love!' said Ombra, turning away. She herself was, as she believed, 'not demonstrative,' not 'effusive.' She was one of the many persons who think that people who do not express any feeling at all, must necessarily have more real feeling than those who disclose it—a curious idea, quite frequent in the world; and she rather prided herself upon her own reserve. Yet, reserved as she was, she, Ombra, had always found people to love her, and why not Kate? This was the thought that passed through her mind as she gave up the subject; but still she had grown reconciled to her cousin, had begun to like her, and to be gratified by her eager, girlish homage. Kate's admiration spoke in every look and word, in her abject submission to Ombra's opinion, her concurrence in all that Ombra said, her imitation of everything she did. Ombra was a good musician, and Kate, who had no great faculty that way, got up and practised every morning, waking the early echoes, and getting anything but blessings from her idol, whose bed was exactly above the piano on the next floor. Ombra was a great linguist, by dint of her many travels, and Kate sent unlimited orders for dictionaries and grammars to her uncle, and began to learn verbs with enthusiasm. She had all the masters who came from London to Miss Story's quiet establishment, men whose hours were golden, and whom nobody but an heiress could have entertained in such profusion; and she applied herself with the greatest diligence to such branches of study as were favoured by Ombra, putting her own private tastes aside for them with an enthusiasm only possible to first love. Perhaps Kate's enthusiasm was all the greater because of the slow and rather grudging approbation which her efforts to please elicited. Mrs. Anderson was always pleased, always ready to commend and admire; but Ombra was very difficult. She made little allowance for any weakness, and demanded absolute perfection, as mentors at the age of seventeen generally do; and Kate hung on her very breath. Thus she took instinctively the best way to please the only one in the house who had set up any resistance to her. Over the rest Kate had an easy victory. It was Ombra who, all unawares, and not by any virtue of hers, exercised the best control and influence possible over the head-strong, self-opinioned girl. She was head-strong enough herself, and very imperfect, but that did not affect her all-potent visionary sway.

And nothing could be more regular, nothing more quiet and monotonous, than the routine of life in the Cottage. The coming of the masters was the event in it; and that was a mild kind of event, causing little enthusiasm. They breakfasted, worked, walked, and dined, and then rose next morning to do the same thing over again. Notwithstanding Mrs. Anderson's talk about her duty to society, there were very few claims made upon her. She was not much called upon to fulfil these duties. Sometimes the ladies went out to the Rectory to tea; sometimes, indeed, Mrs. Anderson and Ombra dined there; but on these occasions Kate was left at home, as too young for such an intoxicating pleasure. 'And, besides, my darling, I promised your uncle,' Mrs. Anderson would say. But Kate was always of the party when it was tea. There were other neighbours who gave similar entertainments; and before a year had passed, Kate had tasted the bread and butter of all the houses in the parish which Mrs. Anderson thought worthy of her friendship. But only to tea; 'I made that condition with Mr. Courtenay, and I must hold by it, though my heart is broken to leave you behind. If you knew how trying it was, my dearest child!' she would say with melancholy tones, as she stepped out, with a shawl over her evening toilet; but these were very rare occurrences indeed. And Kate went to the teas, and was happy.

How happy she was! When she was tired of the drawing-room (as happened sometimes), she would rush away to an odd little room under the leads, which was Francesca's work-room and oratory, where the other maids were never permitted to enter, but which had been made free to Mees Katta. Francesca was not like English servants, holding jealously by one special metier. She was cook, and she was housekeeper, but, at the same time, she was Mrs. Anderson's private milliner, making her dresses; and the personal attendant of both mother and daughter. Even Jane, the housemaid, scorned her for this versatility; but Francesca took no notice of the scorn. She was not born to confine herself within such narrow limits as an English kitchen afforded her; and she took compensation for her unusual labours. She lectured Ombra, as we have seen; she interfered in a great many things which were not her business; she gave her advice freely to her mistress; she was one of the household, not less interested than the mistress herself. And when Kate arrived, Francesca added another branch of occupation to the others; or, rather, she revived an art which she had once exercised with great applause, but which had fallen into disuse since Ombra ceased to be a child. She became the minstrel, the improvisatore, the ancient chronicler, the muse of the new-comer. When Kate felt the afternoon growing languid she snatched up a piece of work, and flew up the stairs to Francesca's retreat. 'Tell me something,' she would say; and, sitting at the old woman's feet, would forget her work, and her dulness, and everything in heaven and earth, in the entrancement of a tale. These were not fairy-tales, but bits of those stories, more strange than fairy-tales, which still haunt the old houses of Italy. Francesca's tales were without end. She would begin upon a family pedigree, and work her way up or down through a few generations, without missing a stitch in her work, or dropping a thread in her story. She filled Kate's head with counts and barons, and gloomy castles and great palaces. It was an amusement which combined the delight of gossip and the delight of novel-reading in one.

And thus Kate's life ran on, as noiseless, as simple as the growth of a lily or a rose, with nothing but sunshine all about, warming her, ripening her, as her new guardian said, bringing slowly on, day by day, the moment of blossoming, the time of the perfect flower.

CHAPTER XV

It was summer when Kate arrived at the Cottage, and it was not till the Easter after that any disturbing influences came into the quiet scene. Easter was so late that year that it was almost summer again. The rich slopes of the landslip were covered with starry primroses, and those violets which have their own blue-eyed beauty only to surround them, and want the sweetness of their rarer sisters. The landslip is a kind of fairyland at that enchanted moment. Everything is coming—the hawthorn, the wild roses, all the flowers of early summer, are, as it were, on tiptoe, waiting for the hour of their call; and the primroses have come, and are crowding everywhere, turning the darkest corners into gardens of delight. Then there is the sea, now matchless blue, now veiled with mists, framing in every headland and jutting cliff, without any margin of beach to break its full tone of colour; and above, the new-budded trees, the verdure that grows and opens every day, the specks of white houses everywhere, dotted all over the heights. Spring, which makes everything and every one gay, which brings even to the sorrowful a touch of that reaction of nature that makes pain sorer for the moment, yet marks the new springing of life—fancy what it was to the sixteen-year-old girl, now first emancipated, among people who loved her, never judged her harshly, nor fretted her life with uncalled-for opposition!

Kate felt as if the primroses were a crowd of playmates, suddenly come to her out of the bountiful heart of nature. She gathered baskets full every day, and yet they never decreased. She passed her mornings in delicious idleness making them into enormous bouquets, which gave the Cottage something of the same aspect as the slopes outside. She had a taste for this frivolous but delightful occupation. I am free to confess that to spend hours putting primroses and violets together, in the biggest flat dishes which the Cottage could produce, was an extremely frivolous occupation; most likely she would have been a great deal better employed in improving her mind, in learning verbs, or practising exercises, or doing something useful. But youth has a great deal of leisure, and this bright fresh girl, in the bright little hall of the Cottage, arranging her flowers in the spring sunshine, made a very pretty picture. She put the primroses in, with their natural leaves about them, with sweet bunches of blue violets to heighten the effect, touching them as if she loved them; and, as she did it, she sang as the birds do, running on with unconscious music, and sweetness, and gladness. It was Spring with her as with them. Nothing was as yet required of her but to bloom and grow, and make earth fairer. And she did this unawares and was as happy over her vast, simple bouquet, and took as much sweet thought how to arrange it, as if that had been the great aim of life. She was one with her flowers, and both together they belonged to Spring—the Spring of the year, the Spring of life, the sweet time which comes but once, and never lasts too long.

She was thus employed one morning when steps came through the garden, steps which she did not much heed. For one thing, she but half heard them, being occupied with her 'work,' as she called it, and her song, and having no fear that anything unwelcome would appear at that sunny, open door. No one could come who did not know everybody in the little house, who was not friendly, and smiling, and kind, whose hand would not be held out in pleasant familiarity. Here were no trespassers, no strangers. Therefore Kate heard the steps as though she heard them not, and did not even pause to ask herself who was coming. She was roused, but then only with the mildest expectation, when a shadow fell across her bit of sunshine. She looked up with her song still on her lip, and her hands full of flowers. She stopped singing. 'Oh! Bertie!' she cried, half to herself, and made an eager step forward. But then suddenly she paused—she dropped her flowers. Curiosity, wonder, amazement came over her face. She went on slowly to the door, gazing, and questioning with her eyes.

'Are there two of you?' she said gravely. 'I heard that Bertie Hardwick was coming. Oh! which is you? Stop—don't tell me. I am not going to be mystified. I can find it out for myself.'

There were two young men standing in the hall, who laughed and blushed as they stood submitting to her inspection; but Kate was perfectly serious. She stood and looked at them with an unmoved and somewhat anxious countenance. A certain symbolical gravity and earnestness was in her face; but there was indeed occasion to hesitate. The two who stood before her seemed at the first glance identical. They had the same eyes, the same curling brown hair, the same features, the same figure. Gradually, however, the uncertainty cleared away from Kate's face.

'It must be you,' she said, still very seriously. 'You are not quite so tall, and I think I remember your eyes. You must be Bertie, I am sure.'

'We are both Bertie,' said the young man, laughing.

'Ah! but you must be my Bertie; I am certain of it,' said Kate. Not a gleam of maiden consciousness was in her; she said it with all simplicity and seriousness. She did not understand the colour that came to one Bertie's face or the smile that flashed over the other; and she held out her hand to the one whom she had selected. 'I am so glad to see you. Come in, and tell me all about Langton. Dear old Langton! Though you were so disagreeable about the size of the park—'

'I will never be disagreeable again.'

'Oh, nonsense!' cried Kate, interrupting him. 'As if one could stop being anything that is natural! My aunt is somewhere about, and Ombra is in the drawing-room. Come in. Perhaps, though, you had better tell me who this—other gentleman—Why, Mr. Bertie, I am not quite sure, after all, which is the other and which is you!'

'This is my cousin, Bertie Eldridge,' said her old friend. 'You will soon know the difference. You remember what an exemplary character I am, and he is quite the reverse. I am always getting into trouble on his account.'

'Miss Courtenay will soon know better than to believe you,' said the other; at which Kate started and clapped her hands.

'Oh! I know now that is not your voice. Ombra, please, here are two gentlemen—'

This is how the two cousins were introduced into the Cottage. They had been there before separately; but neither Mrs. Anderson nor her daughter knew how slight was the acquaintance which entitled Kate to qualify one of the new-comers as 'my Bertie.' They were both young, not much over twenty, and their likeness was wonderful; it was, however, a likeness which diminished as they talked, for their expression was as different as their voices. Kate had no hesitation in appropriating the one she knew.

'Tell me about Langton,' she said—'all about it. I have heard nothing for nearly a year. Oh! don't laugh. I know the house stands just where it used to stand, and no one dares to cut down the trees. But itself—Don't you know what Langton means to me?'

'Home?' said Bertie Hardwick, but with a little doubt in his tone.

'Home!' repeated Kate; and then she, too, paused perplexed. 'Not exactly home, for there is no one there I care for—much. Oh! but can't you understand? It is not home; I am much happier here; but, in a kind of a way, it is me!'

Bertie Hardwick was puzzled, and he was dazzled too. His first meeting with her had made no small impression upon him; and now Kate was almost a full-grown woman, and the brightness about her dazzled his eyes.

'It cannot be you now,' he said. 'It is—let.'

Kate gave a fierce little cry, and clenched her hands.

'Oh! Uncle Courtenay, I wish I could just kill you!' she said, half to herself.

'It is let, for four or five years, to the only kind of people who can afford to have great houses now—to Mr. Donkin, who has a large—shop in town.'

Kate moaned again, but then recovered herself.

'I don't see that it matters much about the shop. I think if I were obliged to work, I should not mind keeping a shop. It would be such fun! But, oh! if Uncle Courtenay were only here!'

'It is better not. There might be bloodshed, and you would regret it after,' said Bertie, gravely.

'Don't laugh at me; I mean it. And, if you won't tell me anything about Langton, tell me about yourself. Who is he? What does he mean by being so like you? He is different when he talks; but at the first glance—Why do you allow any one to be so like you, Mr. Bertie? If he is not nice, as you said—'

'I did not mean you to believe me,' said Bertie. 'He is the best fellow going. I wish I were half as good, or half as clever. He is my cousin, and just like my brother. Why, I am proud of being like him. We are taken for each other every day.'

'I should not like it,' said Kate. 'Ombra and I are not like each other, though we are cousins too. Do you know Ombra? I think there never was any one like her; but, on the whole, I think it is best to be two people, not one. Are you still at Oxford?—and is he at Oxford? Mr. Bertie, if I were you, I don't think I should be a clergyman.'

'Why?' said Bertie, who, unfortunately for himself, was much of her mind.

'You might not get a living, you know,' said Kate.

This she said conscientiously, to prepare him for the fact that he was not to have Langton-Courtenay; but his laugh disconcerted her, and immediately brought before her eyes the other idea that his objectionable uncle, who had a park larger than Langton, might have a living too. She coloured high, having begun to find out, by means of her education in the Cottage, when she had committed herself.

'Or,' she went on, with all the calmness she could command, 'when you had a living you might not like it. The Rector here—Oh! of course he must be your uncle too. He is very good, I am sure, and very nice,' said Kate, floundering, and feeling that she was getting deeper and deeper into the mire; 'but it is so strange to hear him talk. The old women in the almshouses, and the poor people, and all that, and mothers' meetings—Of course, it must be very right and very good; but, Mr. Bertie, nothing but mothers' meetings, and old women in almshouses, for all your life—'

'I suppose he has something more than that,' said Bertie, half affronted, half amused.

'I suppose so—or, at least, I hope so,' said Kate. 'Do you know what a mothers' meeting is? But to go to Oxford, you know, for that—! If I were you, I would be something else. There must be a great many other things that you could be. Soldiers are not much good in time of peace, and lawyers have to tell so many lies—or, at least, so people say in books. I will tell you what I should advise, Mr. Bertie. Doctors are of real use in the world—I would be a doctor, if I were you.'

'But I should not at all like to be a doctor,' said Bertie. 'Of all trades in the world, that is the last I should choose. Talk of mothers' meetings! a doctor is at every fool's command, to run here and there; and besides—I think, Miss Courtenay, you have made a mistake.'

'I am only saying what I would do if it was me,' said Kate, softly folding her hands. 'I would rather be a doctor than any of the other things. And you ought to decide, Mr. Bertie; you will not be a boy much longer. You have got something here,' and she put up her hand to her own soft chin, and stroked it gently, 'which you did not have the last time I saw you. You are almost—a man.'

This for Bertie to hear, who was one-and-twenty, and an Oxford man—who had felt himself full grown, both in frame and intellect, for these two years past! He was wroth—his cheek burned, and his eye flashed. But, fortunately, Mrs. Anderson interposed, and drew her chair towards them, putting an end to the tête-à-tête. Mrs. Anderson was somewhat disturbed, for her part. Here were two young men—two birds of prey—intruding upon the stillness which surrounded the nest in which she had hidden an heiress. What was she to do? Was it safe to permit them to come, fluttering, perhaps, the nestling? or did stern duty demand of her to close her doors, and shut out every chance of evil? As soon as she perceived that the conversation between Kate and her Bertie was special and private, she trembled and interposed. She asked the young man all about his family, his sisters, his studies—anything she could think of—and so kept her heiress, as she imagined, safe, and the wild beast at bay.

'You are sure your uncle approved of the Hardwicks as friends for you, Kate?' she said that evening, when the visit had been talked over in full family conclave. Mrs. Anderson might make what pretence she pleased that they were only ordinary visitors, but the two Berties had made a commotion much greater than the Rector and his wife did, or even the schoolboy and schoolgirl Eldridges, noisy and tumultuous as their visits often were.

'He made me go to the Rectory with him,' said Kate, very demurely. 'It was not my doing at all; he wanted me to go.'

And, after that, what could there be to say?

CHAPTER XVI

The two Berties came again next day—they came with their cousins, and they came without them. They joined the party from the Cottage in their walks, with an intuitive knowledge where they were going, which was quite extraordinary. They got up croquet-parties and picnics; they were always in attendance upon the two girls. Mrs. Anderson had many a thought on the subject, and wondered much what her duty was in such a very trying emergency; but there were two things that consoled her—the first that it was Ombra who was the chief object of the two young men's admiration; and the second that they could not possibly stay long. Ombra was their first object. She assured herself of this with a warm and pleasant glow at her heart, though she was not a match-making mother, nor at all desirous of 'marrying off,' and 'getting rid of' her only child. Besides, the young men were too young for anything serious—not very long out of their teens; lads still under strict parental observation and guidance; they were too young to make matrimonial proposals to any one, or to carry such proposals out. But, nevertheless, it was pleasant to Mrs. Anderson to feel that Ombra was their first object, and that her 'bairn' was 'respected like the lave.' 'Thank Heaven, Kate's money has nothing to do with it,' she said to herself; and where was the use of sending away two handsome young men, whom the girls liked, and who were a change to them? Besides, they were going away so soon—in a fortnight—no harm could possibly come.

So Mrs. Anderson tolerated them, invited them, gave them luncheon sometimes, and often tea, till they became as familiar about the house as the young Eldridges were, or any other near neighbours. And the girls did not have their heads at all turned by the new cavaliers, who were so assiduous in their attentions. Ombra gently ridiculed them both, hitting them with dainty little arrows of scorn, smiling at their boyish ways, their impetuosity and self-opinion. Kate, on the contrary, took them up very gravely, with a motherly, not to say grandmotherly interest in their future, giving to him whom she called her old friend the very best of good advice. Mrs. Anderson herself was much amused by this new development of her charge's powers. She said to herself, a dozen times in a day, how ridiculous it was to suppose that boys and girls could not be in each other's company without falling in love. Why, here were two pairs continually in each other's company, and without the faintest shadow of any such folly to disturb them! Perhaps a sense that it was to her own perfect good management that this was owing, increased her satisfaction. She 'kept her eye on them,' never officiously, never demonstratively, but in the most vigilant way; and a certain gentle complacency mingled with her content. Had she left them to roam about as they pleased without her, then indeed trouble might have been looked for; but Mrs. Anderson was heroic, and put aside her own ease, and was their companion everywhere. At the same time (but this was done with the utmost caution) she took a little pains to find out all about Sir Herbert Eldridge, the father of one of the Berties—his county, and the amount of his property, and all the information that was possible. She breathed not a word of this to any one—not even to Ombra; but she put Bertie Eldridge on her daughter's side of the table at tea; and perhaps showed him a little preference, for her own part, a preference, however, so slight, so undiscernible to the vulgar eye, that neither of the young men found it out. She was very good to them, quite irrespective of their family, or the difference in their prospects; and she missed them much when they went away. For go away they did, at the end of their fortnight, leaving the girls rather dull, and somewhat satirical. It was the first invasion of the kind that had been made into their life. The boys at the Rectory were still nothing but boys; and men did not abound in the neighbourhood. Even Ombra was slightly misanthropical when the Berties went away.

'What it is to be a boy!' she said; 'they go where they like, these two, and arrange their lives as they please. What a fuss everybody makes about them; and yet they are commonplace enough. If they were girls like us, how little any one would care—'

'My dear, Mr. Eldridge will be a great landed proprietor, and have a great deal in his power,' said Mrs. Anderson.

'Because he happens to have been born Sir Herbert's son; no thanks to him,' said Ombra, with disdain. 'And most likely, when he is a great landed proprietor he will do nothing worth noticing. The other is more interesting to me; he at least has his own way to make.'

'I wonder what poor Bertie will do?' said Kate, with her grandmother air. 'I should not like to see him a clergyman. What Ombra says is very true, auntie. When one is a great Squire, you know, one can't help one's self; one's life is all settled before one is born. But when one can choose what to be!—For my part,' said Kate, with great gravity, 'I am anxious about Bertie, too. I gave him all the advice I could—but I am not sure that he is the sort of boy to take advice.'

'He is older than you are, my love, and perhaps he may think he knows better,' said Mrs. Anderson with a smile.

'But that would be a mistake,' said Kate. 'Boys have so many things to do, they have no time to think. And then they don't consider things as we do; and besides—' But here Kate paused, doubting the wisdom of further explanations. What she had meant to say was that, having no thinking to do for herself, her own position being settled and established beyond the reach of fate, she had the more time to give to the concerns of her neighbours. But it occurred to her that Ombra had scorned Bertie Eldridge's position, and might scorn hers also, and she held her peace.

'Besides, there is always a fuss made about them, as if they were better than other people. Don't let us talk of them any more; I am sick of the subject,' said Ombra, withdrawing into a book. The others made no objection; they acquiesced with a calmness which perhaps scarcely satisfied Ombra. Mrs. Anderson declared openly that she missed the visitors much; and Kate avowed, without hesitation, that the boys were fun, and she was sorry that they were gone. But the chances are that it was Ombra who missed them most, though she professed to be rather glad than otherwise. 'They were a nuisance, interrupting one whatever one was doing. Boys at that age always are a nuisance,' she said, with an air of severity, and she returned to all her occupations with an immense deal of seriousness.

But this disturbance of their quiet affected her in reality much more than it affected her companions—the very earnestnest of her resumed duties testified to this. She was on the edge of personal life, wondering and already longing to taste its excitements and troubles; and everything that disturbed the peaceful routine felt like that life which was surely coming, and stirred her pulses. It was like the first creeping up of the tide about the boat which is destined to live upon the waves; not enough yet to float the little vessel off from the stays which hold it, but enough to rock and stir it with prophetic sensation of the fuller flood to come.

Ombra was 'viewy,' to use a word which has become well-nigh obsolete. She was full of opinions and speculations, which she called thought; a little temper, a good deal of unconscious egotism, and a reflective disposition, united to make her what is called, a 'thoughtful girl.' She mused upon herself, and upon the few varieties of human life she knew, and upon the world, and all its accidents and misunderstandings, as she had seen them, and upon the subjects which she read about. But partly her youth, and partly her character, made her thoughts like the observations of a traveller newly entered into a strange country, and feeling himself capable, as superficial travellers often are, to lay bare its character, and fathom all its problems at a glance. Other people were, to this young philosopher, as foreigners are to the inexperienced traveller. She was very curious about them, and marked their external peculiarities with sufficient quickness; but she had not imagination enough to feel for them or with them, or to see their life from their own point of view. Her own standing-point was the only one in the world to her. She could judge others only by herself.

Curiously enough, however, with this want of sympathetic imagination there was combined a good deal of fancy. Ombra had written little stories from her earliest youth. She had a literary turn. At this period of her life, when she was nearly eighteen, and the world was full of wonders and delightful mysteries to her, she wrote a great deal, sometimes in verse, sometimes in prose, and now and then asked herself whether it was not genius which inspired her. Some of her poems, as she called them, had been printed in little religious magazines and newspapers—for Ombra's muse was as yet highly religious. She had every reason to believe herself one of the stars that shine unseen—a creature superior to the ordinary run of humanity. She read more than any one she knew, and thought, or believed that she thought, deeply on a great many subjects. And one of these subjects naturally was that of the position of women. She was girl enough, and had enough of nature in her, to enjoy the momentary brightness of the firmament which the two Berties had brought. She liked the movement and commotion as much as the others did—the walks, the little parties, the expeditions, and even the games; and she felt the absence of these little excitements when they came to an end. And thereupon she set herself to reflect upon them. She carried her little portfolio up to a rustic seat which had been made on the cliff, sheltered by some ledges of rock, and covered with flowers and bushes, and set herself to think. And here her thoughts took that turn which is so natural, yet so hackneyed and conventional. No one would, in reality, have been less disposed than Ombra to give up a woman's—a lady's privileges. To go forth into the world unattended, without the shield and guard of honour, which her semi-foreign education made doubly necessary to her, would have seemed to the girl the utmost misery of desolation. She would have resented the need as a wrong done her by fate. But nevertheless she sat up in her rocky bower, and looked over the blue sea, and the white headlands, and said to herself, bitterly, what a different lot had fallen to these two Berties from that which was her own. They could go where they liked, society imposed no restraints upon them; when they were tired of one place, they could pass on to another. Heaven and earth was moved for their education, to make everything known to them, to rifle all the old treasure-houses, to communicate to them every discovery which human wisdom had ever made. And for what slight creatures were all these pains taken; boys upon whom she looked down in the fuller development of her womanhood, feeling them ever so much younger than she was, less serious in their ideas, less able to do anything worth living for! It seemed to Ombra, at that moment, that there was in herself a power such as none of 'these boys' had a conception of—genius, the divinest thing in humanity! But that which would have been fostered and cultivated in them, would be quenched, or at least hampered and kept down in her. 'For I am only a woman!' said Ombra, with a swelling heart.

All this was perfectly natural; and, at the same time, it was quite conventional. It was a little overflow of that depression after a feast, that reaction of excitement, which makes every human creature blaspheme in one way or other. The sound of Kate's voice, singing as she came up the little path to the cliff, made her cousin angry, in this state of her mind and nerves. Here was a girl no better than the boys, a creature without thought, who neither desired a high destiny, nor could understand what it meant.

'How careless you are, Kate!' she cried, in the impulse of the moment. 'Always singing, or some nonsense—and you know you can't sing! If I were as young as you are, I would not lose my time as you do! Do you never think?'

'Yes,' said Kate, with a meekness she never showed but to Ombra, 'a great deal sometimes. But I can't on such a morning. There seems nothing in all the world but sunshine and primroses, and the air is so sweet! Come up to the top of the cliff, and try how far you can see. I think I can make out that big ship that kept firing so the other day. Ombra, if you don't mind, I shall be first at the top!'

'As if I cared who was first at the top! Oh! Kate, Kate, you are as frivolous as—as—the silly creatures in novels—or as these boys themselves!'

'The boys were very good boys!' said Kate. 'If they are silly, they can't help it. Of course they were not as clever as you—no one is; and Bertie, you know—little Bertie, my Bertie—ought to think more of what he is going to do. But they were very nice, as boys go. We can't expect them to be like us. Ombra, do come and try a run for the top.'

'What a foolish child you are!' said Ombra, suffering her portfolio to be taken out of her hands; and then her youth vindicated itself, and she started off like a young fawn up the little path. Kate could have won the race had she tried, but was too loyal to outstrip her princess. And thus the cobwebs were blown away from the young thinker's brain.

CHAPTER XVII

It will be seen, however, that, though Kate's interpretation of the imperfections of 'the boys' was more genial than that of Ombra, yet that still there was a certain condescension in her remarks, and sense that she herself was older, graver, and of much more serious stuff altogether than the late visitors. Her instinct for interference, which had been in abeyance since she came to the Cottage, sprung up into full force the moment these inferior creatures came within her reach. She felt that it was her natural mission, the work for which she was qualified, to set and keep them right. This she had been quite unable to feel herself entitled to do in the Cottage. Mrs. Anderson's indulgence and tenderness, and Ombra's superiority, had silenced even her lively spirit. She could not tender her advice to them, much as she might have desired to do so. But Bertie Hardwick was a bit of Langton, one of her own people, a natural-born subject, for whose advantage all her powers were called forth. She thought a great deal about his future, and did not hesitate to say so. She spoke of it to Mr. Eldridge, electrifying the excellent Rector.

'What a trouble boys must be!' she said, when she ran in with some message from her aunt, and found the whole party gathered at luncheon. There were ten Eldridges, so that the party was a large one; and as the holidays were not yet over, Tom and Herbert, the two eldest, had not returned to school.

'They are a trouble, in the holidays,' said Mrs. Eldridge, with a sigh; and then she looked at Lucy, her eldest girl, who was in disgrace, and added seriously, 'but not more than girls. One expects girls to know better. To see a great creature of fifteen, nearly in long dresses, romping like a Tom-boy, is enough to break one's heart.'

'But I was thinking of the future,' said Kate, and she too gave a little sigh, as meaning that the question was a very serious one indeed.

The Rector smiled, but Mrs. Eldridge did not join him. Somehow Kate's position, which the Rector's wife was fond of talking of, gave her a certain solemnity, which made up for her want of age and experience in that excellent woman's eyes.

'As for us,' Kate continued very gravely, 'either we marry or we don't, and that settles the question; but boys that have to work—Oh! when I think what a trouble they are, it makes me quite sad.'

'Poor Kate!' said the laughing Rector; 'but you have not any boys of your own yet, which must simplify the matter.'

'No,' said Kate gravely, 'not quite of my own; but if you consider the interest I take in Langton, and all that I have to do with it, you will see that it does not make much difference. There is Bertie Hardwick, for instance, Mr. Eldridge—'

The Rector interrupted her with a hearty outburst of laughter.

'Is Bertie Hardwick one of the boys whom you regard as almost your own?' he said.

'Well,' Kate answered stoutly, 'of course I take a great interest in him. I am anxious about what he is to be. I don't think he ought to go into the Church; I have thought a great deal about it, and I don't think that would be the best thing for him. Mr. Eldridge, why do you laugh?'

'Be quiet, dear,' said his wife, knitting her brows at him significantly. Mrs. Eldridge had not a lively sense of humour; and she had pricked up her ears at Bertie Hardwick's name. Already many a time had she regretted bitterly that her own Herbert (she would not have him called Bertie, like the rest) was not old enough to aspire to the heiress. And, as that could not be mended, the mention of Bertie Hardwick's name stirred her into a state of excitement. She was not a mercenary woman, neither had it ever occurred to her to set up as a match-maker; 'but,' as she said, 'when a thing stares you in the face—' And then it would be so much for Kate's good.

'You ought not to laugh,' said Kate, with gentle and mild reproof, 'for I mean what I say. He could not live the kind of life that you live, Mr. Eldridge. I suppose you did not like it yourself when you were young?'

'My dear child, you go too far—you go too fast,' cried the Rector, alarmed. 'Who said I did not like it when I was young? Miss Kate, though I laugh, you must not forget that I think my work the most important work in the world.'

'Oh! yes, to be sure,' said Kate; 'of course one knows—but then when you were young—And Bertie is quite young—he is not much more than a boy; I cannot see how he is to bear it—the almshouses, and the old women, and the mothers' meetings.'

'You must not talk, my child, of things you don't understand,' said the Rector, quite recovered from his laughter. He had ten pairs of eyes turned upon him, ten minds, to which it had never occurred to inquire whether there was anything more important in the world than mothers' meetings. Perhaps had he allowed himself to utter freely his own opinions, he might have agreed with Kate that these details of his profession occupied too prominent a place in it. But he was not at liberty then to enter upon any such question. He had to preserve his own importance, and that of his office, in presence of his family. The wrinkles of laughter all faded from the corners of his mouth. He put up his hand gravely, as if to put her aside from this sacred ark which she was touching with profane hands.

'Kate talks nonsense sometimes, as most young persons do,' said Mrs. Eldridge, interfering. 'But at present it is you who don't understand what she is saying—or, at least, what she means is something quite different. She means that Bertie Hardwick would not like such a laborious life as yours; and, indeed, what she says is quite true; and if you had known all at once what you were coming to, all the toil and fatigues—Ah! I don't like to think of it. Yes, Kate, a clergyman's life is a very trying life, especially when a man is so conscientious as my husband. There are four mothers' meetings in different parts of the parish; and there is the penny club, and the Christmas clothing, and the schools, not to speak of two services every Sunday, and two on Wednesdays and Fridays; and a Curate, who really does not do half so much as he ought. I do not want to say anything against Mr. Sugden, but he does pay very little attention to the almshouses; and as for the infant-school—'

'My dear, the children are present,' said the Rector.

'I am very well aware of that, Fred; but they have ears and eyes as well as the rest of us. After all, the infant-school and the Sunday-schools are not very much to be left to one; and there are only ten old people in the almshouses. And, I must say, my dear, considering that Mr. Sugden is able to walk a hundred miles a day, I do believe, when he has an object—'

'Hush! hush!' said the Rector, 'we must not enter into personal discussions. He is fresh from University life, and has not quite settled down as yet to his work. University life is very different, as I have often told you. It takes a man some time to get accustomed to change his habits and ways of thinking. Sugden is rather lazy, I must say—he does not mean it, but he is a little careless. Did I tell you that he had forgotten to put down Farmer Thompson's name in the Easter list? It was a trifle, you know—it really was not of any consequence; but, still, he forgot all about it. It is the negligent spirit, not the thing itself, that troubles me.'

'A trifle!' said Mrs. Eldridge, indignantly; and they entered so deeply into the history of this offence, that Kate, whose attention had been wandering, had to state her errand, and finish her luncheon without further reference to Bertie. But her curiosity was roused; and when, some time after, she met Mr. Sugden, the Curate, it was not in her to refrain from further inquiries. This time she was walking with her aunt and cousin, and could not have everything her own way; but the curate was only too well pleased to join the little party. He was a young man, tall and strong, looking, as Mrs. Rector said, as if he could walk a hundred miles a day; and his manner was not that of one who would be guilty of indolence. He was glad to join the party from the Cottage, because he was one of those who had been partially enslaved by Ombra—partially, for he was prudent, and knew that falling in love was not a pastime to be indulged in by a curate; but yet sufficiently to be roused by the sight of her into sudden anxiety, to look and show himself at his best.

'Ask him to tea, auntie, please,' said Kate, whispering, as the Curate divided the party, securing himself a place by the side of Ombra. Mrs. Anderson looked at the girl with amazement.

'I have no objection,' she said, wondering. 'But why?'

'Oh! never mind why—to please me,' said the girl. Mrs. Anderson was not in the habit of putting herself into opposition; and besides, the little languor and vacancy caused by the departure of the Berties had not yet quite passed away. She gave the invitation with a smile and a whispered injunction. 'But you must promise not to become one of the young ladies who worship curates, Kate.'

'Me!' said Kate, with indignation, and without grammar; and she gazed at the big figure before her with a certain friendly contempt. Mr. Sugden lived a dull life, and he was glad to meet with the pretty Ombra, to walk by her side, and talk to her, or hear her talk, and even to be invited to tea. His fall from the life of Oxford to the life of this little rural parish had been sudden, and it had been almost more than the poor young fellow's head could bear. One day surrounded by young life and energy, and all the merriment and commotion of a large community, where there was much intellectual stir, to which his mind, fortunately for himself, responded but faintly, and a great deal of external activity, into which he had entered with all his heart; and the next day to be dropped into the grey, immovable atmosphere of rural existence—the almshouses, the infant-schools, and Farmer Thompson! The young man had not recovered it. Life had grown strange to him, as it seems after a sudden and bewildering fall. And it never occurred to anybody what a great change it was, except the Rector, who thought it rather sinful that he could not make up his mind to it at once. Therefore, though he had a chop indifferently cooked waiting for him at home, he abandoned it gladly for Mrs. Anderson's bread and butter. Ombra was very pretty, and it was a variety in the monotonous tenor of his life.

When they had returned to the Cottage, and had seated themselves to the simple and lady-like meal, which did not much content his vigorous young appetite, Mr. Sugden began to be drawn out without quite understanding the process. The scene and circumstances were quite new to him. There was a feminine perfume about the place which subdued and fascinated him. Everything was pleasant to look at—even the mother, who was still a handsome woman; and a certain charm stole over the Curate, though the bread and butter was scarcely a satisfactory meal.

'I hope you like Shanklin?' Mrs. Anderson said, as she poured him out his tea.

'Of course Mr. Sugden must say he does, whether or not,' said Ombra. 'Fancy having the courage to say that one does not like Shanklin before the people who are devoted to it! But speak frankly, please, for I am not devoted to it. I think it is dull; it is too pretty, like a scene at the opera. Whenever you turn a corner, you come upon a picture you have seen at some exhibition. I should like to hang it up on the wall, but not to live in it. Now, Mr. Sugden, you can speak your mind.'

'I never was at an exhibition,' said Kate, 'nor at the opera. I never saw such a lovely place, and you know you don't mean it, Ombra—you, who are never tired of sketching or writing poetry about it.'

'Does Miss Anderson write poetry?' said the Curate, somewhat startled. He was frightened, like most men, by such a discovery. It froze the words on his lips.

'No, no—she only amuses herself,' said the mother, who knew what the effect of such an announcement was likely to be; upon which the poor Curate drew breath.

'Shanklin is a very pretty place,' he said. 'Perhaps I am not so used to pretty places as I ought to be. I come from the Fens myself. It is hilly here, and there is a great deal of sea; but I don't think,' he added, with a little outburst, and a painful consciousness that he had not been eloquent—'I don't think there is very much to do.'

'Except the infant-schools and the almshouses,' said Kate.

'Good Lord!' said the poor young man, driven to his wits' end; and then he grew very red, and coughed violently, to cover, if possible, the ejaculation into which he had been betrayed. Then he did his best to correct himself, and put on a professional tone. 'There is always the work of the parish for me,' he said, trying to look assured and comfortable; 'but I was rather thinking of you ladies; unless you are fond of yachting—but I suppose everybody is who lives in the Isle of Wight?'

'Not me,' said Mrs. Anderson. 'I do not like it, and I would not trust my girls, even if they had a chance, which they have not. Oh! no; we content ourselves with a very quiet life. They have their studies, and we do what we can in the parish. I assure you a school-feast is quite a great event.'

Mr. Sugden shuddered; he could not help it; he had not been brought up to it; he had been trained to a lively life, full of variety, and amusement, and exercise. He tried to say faintly that he was sure a quiet life was the best, but the words nearly choked him. It was now henceforward his rôle to say that sort of thing; and how was he to do it, poor young muscular, untamed man! He gasped and drank a cup of hot tea, which he did not want, and which made him very uncomfortable. Tea and bread and butter, and a school-feast by way of excitement! This was what a man was brought to, when he took upon himself the office of a priest.

'Mr. Sugden, please tell me,' said Kate, 'for I want to know—is it a very great change after Oxford to come to such a place as this?'

'O Lord!' cried the poor Curate again. A groan burst from him in spite of himself. It was as if she had asked him if the change was great from the top of an Alpine peak to the bottom of a crevasse. 'I hope you'll excuse me,' he said, with a burning blush, turning to Mrs. Anderson, and wiping the moisture from his forehead. 'It was such an awfully rapid change for me; I have not had time to get used to it. I come out with words I ought not to use, and feel inclined to do ever so many things I oughtn't to do—I know I oughtn't; but then use, you know, is second nature, and I have not had time to get out of it. If you knew how awfully sorry I was—'

'There is nothing to be awfully sorry about,' said Mrs. Anderson, with a smile. But she changed the conversation, and she was rather severe upon her guest when he went away. 'It is clear that such a young man has no business in the Church,' she said, with a sharpness quite unusual to her. 'How can he ever be a good clergyman, when his heart is so little in it? I do not approve of that sort of thing at all.'

'But, auntie, perhaps he did not want to go into the Church,' said Kate; and she felt more and more certain that it was not the thing for Bertie Hardwick, and that he never would take such a step, except in defiance of her valuable advice.

CHAPTER XVIII

Circumstances after this threw Mr. Sugden a great deal in their way. He lived in a superior sort of cottage in the village, a cottage which had once been the village doctor's, and had been given up by him only when he built that house on the Undercliff, which still shone so white and new among its half-grown trees. It must be understood that it was the Shanklin of the past of which we speak—not the little semi-urban place with lines of new villas, which now bears that name. The mistress of the house was the dressmaker of the district as well, and much became known about her lodger by her means. She was a person who had seen better days, and who had taken up dressmaking at first only for her own amusement, she informed her customers, and consequently she had very high manners, and a great deal of gentility, and frightened her humble neighbours. Her house had two stories, and was very respectable. It could not help having a great tree of jessamine all over one side, and a honeysuckle clinging about the porch, for such decorations are inevitable in the Isle of Wight; but still there were no more flowers than were absolutely necessary, and that of itself was a distinction. The upper floor was Mr. Sugden's. He had two windows in his sitting-room, and one in his bedroom, which commanded the street and all that was going on there; and it was the opinion of the Rector's wife that no man could desire more cheerful rooms. He saw everybody who went or came from the Rectory. He could moralise as much as he pleased upon the sad numbers who frequented the 'Red Lion.' He could see the wheelwright's shop, and the smithy, and I don't know how many more besides. From the same window he could even catch a glimpse of the rare tourists or passing travellers who came to see the Chine. And what more would the young man have?

Miss Richardson, the dressmaker, had many little jobs to do for Kate. Sometimes she took it into her head to have a dress made of more rapidly than Maryanne's leisurely fingers could do it; sometimes she saw a fashion-book in Miss Richardson's window to which she took a sudden fancy; so that there was a great deal of intercourse kept up between the dressmaker's house and the Cottage. This did not mean that Kate was much addicted to dress, or extravagant in that point; but she was fanciful and fond of changes—and Maryanne, having very little to do, became capable of doing less and less every day. Old Francesca made all Mrs. Anderson's gowns and most of Ombra's, besides her other work; but Maryanne, a free-born Briton, was not to be bound to any such slavery. And thus it happened that Miss Richardson went often to the Cottage. She wore what was then called a cottage-bonnet, surrounding, with a border of clean quilted net, her prim but pleasant face, and a black merino dress with white collar and cuffs; she looked, in short, very much as a novice Sister would look now; but England was very Protestant at that moment, and there were no Sisters in Miss Richardson's day.

'My young gentleman is getting a little better used to things, thank you, ma'am,' said Miss Richardson. 'Since he has been a little more taken out of an evening, you and other ladies inviting him to tea, you can't think what a load is lifted off my mind. The way he used to walk about at first, crushing over my head till I thought the house would come down! They all feel it a bit, ma'am, do my gentlemen. The last one was a sensible man, and fond of reading, but they ain't all fond of reading—more's the pity! I've been out in the world myself, and I know how cold it strikes coming right into the country like this.'

'But he has his parish work,' said Mrs. Anderson, with a little severity.

'That is what Mrs. Eldridge says; but, bless you, what's his parish work to a young gentleman like that, fresh from college? He don't know what to say to the folks—he don't know what to do with them. Bless your heart,' said Miss Richardson, warming into excitement, 'what should he know about a poor woman's troubles with her family—or a man's, either, for that part? He just puts his hand in his pocket; that's all he does. "I'm sure I'm very sorry for you, and here's half-a-crown," he says. It's natural. I'd have done it myself when I was as young, before I knew the world, if I'd had the halfcrown; and he won't have it long, if he goes on like this.'

'It is very kind of him, and very nice of him,' said Kate.

'Yes, Miss, it's kind in meaning, but it don't do any good. It's just a way of getting rid of them, the same as sending them off altogether. There ain't one gentleman in a thousand that understands poor folks. Give them a bit of money, and get quit of them; that's what young men think; but poor folks want something different. I've nothing to say against Greek and Latin; they're all very fine, I don't doubt, but they don't tell you how to manage a parish. You can't, you know, unless you've seen life a bit, and understand folk's ways, and how things strike them. Turn round, if you please, Miss, till I fit it under the arm. It's just like as if Miss Ombra there should think she could make a dress, because she can draw a pretty figure. You think you could, Miss?—then just you try, that's all I have got to say. The gentlemen think like you. They read their books, and they think they understand folk's hearts, but they don't, any more than you know how to gore a skirt. Miss Kate, if you don't keep still, I can't get on. The scissors will snip you, and it would be a thousand pities to snip such a nice white neck. Now turn round, please, and show the ladies. There's something that fits, I'm proud to think. I've practised my trade in town and all about; I haven't taken it out of books. Though you can draw beautiful, Miss Ombra, you couldn't make a fit like that.'

Miss Richardson resumed, with pins in her mouth, when she had turned Kate round and round, 'There's nobody I pity in all the world, ma'am, as I pity those young gentlemen. They're very nice, as a rule; they speak civil, and don't give more trouble than they can help. Toss their boots about the room, and smoke their cigars, and make a mess—that's to be looked for; but civil and nice-spoken, and don't give trouble when they think of it. But, bless your heart, if I had plenty to live on, and no work to do but to look out of my window and take walks, and smoke my cigar, I'd kill myself, that's what I'd do! Well, there's the schools and things; but he can't be poking among the babies more than half an hour or so now and then; and I ask you, ladies, as folks with some sense, what is that young gentleman to do in a mothers' meeting? No, ma'am, ask him to tea if you'd be his friend, and give him a little interest in his life. They didn't ought to send young gentlemen like that into small country parishes. And if he falls in love with one of your young ladies, ma'am, none the worse.'

'But suppose my young ladies would have nothing to say to him?' said Mrs. Anderson, smiling upon her child, for whom, surely, she might expect a higher fate. As for Kate, the heiress, the prize, such a thing was not to be thought of. But Kate was only a child; she did not occur to the mother, who even in her heiress-ship saw nothing which could counterbalance the superior attractions of Ombra.

Miss Richardson took the pins out of her mouth, and turned Kate round again, and nodded half a dozen times in succession her knowing head.

'Never mind, ma'am,' she said, 'never mind—none the worse, say I. Them young gentlemen ought to learn that they can't have the first they fancy. Does 'em good. Men are all a deal too confident now-a-days—though I've seen the time! But just you ask him to tea, ma'am, if you'd stand his friend, and leave it to the young ladies to rouse him up. Better folks than him has had their hearts broken, and done 'em good!'

It was not with these bloodthirsty intentions that Mrs. Anderson adopted the dressmaker's advice; but, notwithstanding, it came about that Mr. Sugden was asked a great many times to tea. He began to grow familiar about the house, as the Berties had been; to have his corner, where he always sat; to escort them in their walks. And it cannot be denied that this mild addition to the interests of life roused him much more than the almshouses and the infant schools. He wrote home, to his paternal house in the Fens, that he was beginning, now he knew it better, as his mother had prophesied, to take a great deal more interest in the parish; that there were some nice people in it, and that it was a privilege, after all, to live in such a lovely spot! This was the greatest relief to the mind of his mother, who was afraid, at the first, that the boy was not happy. 'Thank heaven, he has found out now that a life devoted to the service of his Maker is a happy life!' that pious woman said, in the fulness of her heart; not knowing, alas! that it was devotion to Ombra which had brightened his heavy existence.

He fell in love gradually, before the eyes of the older people, who looked on with more amusement than any graver feeling; and, with a natural malice, everybody urged it on—from Kate, who gave up her seat by her cousin's to the Curate, up to Mr. Eldridge himself, who would praise Ombra's beauty, and applaud her cleverness with a twinkle in his eye, till the gratified young man felt ready to go through fire and water for his chief. The only spectators who were serious in the contemplation of this little tragi-comedy were Mrs. Anderson and Mrs. Eldridge, of whom one was alarmed, and the other disapproving. Mrs. Anderson uttered little words of warning from time to time, and did all she could to keep the two apart; but then her anxiety was all for her daughter, who perhaps was the sole person in the parish unaware of the fact of Mr. Sugden's devotion to her. When she had made quite sure of this, I am afraid she was not very solicitous about the Curate's possible heartbreak. He was a natural victim; it was scarcely likely that he could escape that heartbreak sooner or later, and in the meantime he was happy.

'What can I do?' she said to the Rector's wife. 'I cannot forbid him my house; and we have never given him any encouragement—in that way. What can I do?'

'If Ombra does not care for him, I think she is behaving very badly,' said Mrs. Eldridge. 'I should speak to her, if I were in your place. I never would allow my Lucy to treat any man so. Of course, if she means to accept him, it is a different matter; but I should certainly speak to Ombra, if I were in your place.'

'The child has not an idea of anything of the kind,' said Mrs. Anderson, faltering. 'Why should I disturb her unconsciousness?'

'Oh!' said Mrs. Eldridge, ironically, 'I am sure I beg your pardon. I don't, for my part, understand the unconsciousness of a girl of nineteen!'

'Not quite nineteen,' said Ombra's mother, with a certain humility.

'A girl old enough to be married,' said the other, vehemently. 'I was married myself at eighteen and a half. I don't understand it, and I don't approve of it. If she doesn't know, she ought to know; and unless she means to accept him, I shall always say she has treated him very badly. I would speak to her, if it were I, before another day had passed.'

Mrs. Anderson was an impressionable woman, and though she resented her neighbour's interference, she acted upon her advice. She took Ombra into her arms that evening, when they were alone, in the favourite hour of talk which they enjoyed after Kate had gone to bed.

'My darling!' she said, 'I want to speak to you. Mr. Sugden has taken to coming very often—we are never free of him. Perhaps it would be better not to let him come quite so much.'

'I don't see how we can help it,' said Ombra, calmly; 'he is dull, he likes it; and I am sure he is very inoffensive. I do not mind him at all, for my part.'

'Yes, dear,' said Mrs. Anderson, faltering; 'but then, perhaps, he may mind you.'

'In that case he would stop away,' said Ombra, with perfect unconcern.

'You don't understand me, dear. Perhaps he thinks of you too much; perhaps he is coming too often, for his own good.'

'Thinks of me—too much!' said Ombra, with wide-opened eyes; and then a passing blush came over her face, and she laughed. 'He is very careful not to show any signs of it, then,' she said. 'Mamma, this is not your idea. Mrs. Eldridge has put it into your head.'

'Well, my darling, but if it were true—'

'Why, then, send him away,' said Ombra, laughing. 'But how very silly! Should not I have found it out if he cared for me? If he is in love with any one, it is with you.'

And after this what could the mother do?

CHAPTER XIX

Ombra was a young woman, as we have said, full of fancy, but without any sympathetic imagination. She had made a picture to herself—as was inevitable—of what the lover would be like when he first approached her. It was a fancy sketch entirely, not even founded upon observation of others. She had said to herself that love would speak in his eyes, as clearly as any tongue could reveal it; she had pictured to herself the kind of chivalrous devotion which belongs to the age of romance—or, at least, which is taken for granted as having belonged to it. And as she was a girl who did not talk very much, or enter into any exposition of her feelings, she had cherished the ideal very deeply in her mind, and thought over it a great deal. She could not understand any type of love but this one; and consequently poor Mr. Sugden, who did not possess expressive eyes, and could not have talked with them to save his life, was very far from coming up to her ideal. When her mother made this suggestion, Ombra thought over it seriously, and thought over him who was the subject of it, and laughed within herself at the want of perception which associated Mr. Sugden and love together. 'Poor dear mamma,' she said in her heart, 'it is so long since she had anything to do with it, she has forgotten what it looks like.' And all that day she kept laughing to herself over this strange mistake; for Ombra had this other peculiarity of self-contained people, that she did not care much for the opinion of others. What she made out for herself, she believed in, but not much else. Mr. Sugden was very good, she thought—kind to everybody, and kind to herself, always willing to be of service; but to speak of him and love in the same breath! He was at the Cottage that same evening, and she watched him with a little amused curiosity. Kate gave up the seat next to her to the Curate, and Ombra smiled secretly, saying to herself that Kate and her mother were in a conspiracy against her. And the Curate looked at her with dull, light blue eyes, which were dazzled and abashed, not made expressive and eloquent by feeling. He approached awkwardly, with a kind of terror. He directed his conversation chiefly to Mrs. Anderson; and did not address herself directly for a whole half hour at least. The thing seemed simply comical to Ombra. 'Come here, Mr. Sugden,' she said, when she changed her seat after tea, calling him after her, 'and tell me all about yesterday, and what you saw and what you did.' She did this with a little bravado, to show the spectators she did not care; but caught a meaning glance from Mrs. Eldridge, and blushed, in spite of herself. So, then, Mrs. Eldridge thought so too! How foolish people are! 'Here is a seat for you, Mr. Sugden,' said Ombra, in defiance. And the Curate, in a state of perfect bliss, went after her, to tell her of an expedition which she cared nothing in the world about. Heaven knows what more besides the poor young fellow might have told her, for he was deceived by her manner, as the others were, and believed in his soul that, if never before, she had given him actual 'encouragement' to-night. But the Rector's wife came to the rescue, for she was a virtuous woman, who could not see harm done before her very eyes without an attempt to interfere.

'I hope you see what you are doing,' she whispered severely in Ombra's ear before she sat down, and fixed her eyes upon her with all the solemnity of a judge.

'Oh! surely, dear Mrs. Eldridge—I want to hear about this expedition to the fleet,' said Ombra. 'Pray, Mr. Sugden, begin.'

Poor fellow! the Curate was not eloquent, and to feel his Rectoress beside him, noting all his words, took away from him what little faculty he had. He began his stumbling, uncomfortable story, while Ombra sat sweetly in her corner, and smiled and knitted. He could look at her when she was not looking at him; and she, in defiance of all absurd theories, was kind to him, and listened, and encouraged him to go on.

'Yes. I daresay nothing particular occurred,' Mrs. Eldridge said at last, with some impatience. 'You went over the Royal Sovereign, as everybody does. I don't wonder you are at a loss for words to describe it. It is a fine sight, but dreadfully hackneyed. I wonder very much, Ombra, you never were there.'

'But for that reason Mr. Sugden's account is very interesting to me,' said Ombra, giving him a still more encouraging look.

'Dreadful little flirt!' Mrs. Eldridge said to herself, and with virtuous resolution, went on—'The boys, I suppose, will go too, on their way here. They are coming in Bertie's new yacht this time. I am sure I wish yachts had never been invented. I suppose these two will keep me miserable about the children from the moment they reach Sandown pier.'

'Which two?' said Ombra. It was odd that she should have asked the question, for her attention had at once forsaken the Curate, and she knew exactly who was meant.

'Oh! the Berties, of course. Did not you know they were coming?' said Mrs. Eldridge. 'I like the boys very well—but their yacht! Adieu to peace for me from the hour it arrives! I know I shall be put down by everybody, and my anxieties laughed at; and you girls will have your heads turned, and think of nothing else.'

'The Berties!—are they coming?' cried Kate, making a spring towards them. 'I am so glad! When are they coming?—and what was that about a yacht? A yacht!—the very thing one wanted—the thing I have been sighing, dying for! Oh! you dear Mrs. Eldridge, tell me when they are coming. And do you think they will take us out every day?'

'There!' said the Rector's wife, with the composure of despair. 'I told you how it would be. Kate has lost her head already, and Ombra has no longer any interest in your expedition, Mr. Sugden. Are you fond of yachting too? Well, thank Providence you are strong, and must be a good swimmer, and won't let the children be drowned, if anything happens. That is the only comfort I have had since I heard of it. They are coming to-morrow—we had a letter this morning—both together, as usual, and wasting their time in the same way. I disapprove of it very much, for my part. A thing which may do very well for Bertie Eldridge, with the family property, and title, and everything coming to him, is very unsuitable for Bertie Hardwick, who has nothing. But nobody will see it in that light but me.'

'I must talk to him about it,' said Kate, thoughtfully. Ombra did not say anything, but as the Rector's wife remarked, she had no longer any interest in the Curate's narrative. She was not uncivil, she listened to what he said afterwards, but it fell flat upon her, and she asked him if he knew the Berties, and if he did not think yachting would be extremely pleasant? It may be forgiven to him if we record that Mr. Sugden went home that night with a hatred of the Berties, which was anything but Christian-like. He (almost) wished the yacht might founder before it reached Sandown Bay; he wished they might be driven out to sea, and get sick of it, and abandon all thoughts of the Isle of Wight. Of course they were fresh-water sailors, who had never known what a gale was, he said contemptuously in his heart.

But nothing happened to the yacht. It arrived, and everything came true which Mrs. Eldridge had predicted. The young people in the village and neighbourhood lost their heads. There was nothing but voyages talked about, and expeditions here and there. They circumnavigated the island, they visited the Needles, they went to Spithead to see the fleet, they did everything which it was alarming and distressing for a mother to see her children do. And sometimes, which was the greatest wonder of all, she was wheedled into going with them herself. Sometimes it was Mrs. Anderson who was the chaperon of the merry party. The Berties themselves were unchanged. They were as much alike as ever, as inseparable, as friendly and pleasant. They even recommended themselves to the Curate, though he was very reluctant to be made a friend of against his will. As soon as they arrived, the wings of life seemed to be freer, the wheels rolled easier, everything went faster. The very sun seemed to shine more brightly. The whole talk of the little community at Shanklin was about the yacht and its masters. They met perpetually to discuss this subject. The croquet, the long walks, all the inland amusements, were intermitted. 'Where shall we go to-morrow?' they asked each other, and discussed the winds and the tides like ancient mariners. In the presence of this excitement, the gossip about Mr. Sugden died a natural death. The Curate was not less devoted to Ombra. He haunted her, if not night and day, at least by sea and land, which had become the most appropriate phraseology. He kept by her in every company; but as the Berties occupied all the front of the picture, there was no room in any one's mind for the Curate. Even Mrs. Anderson forgot about him—she had something more important on her mind.

For that was Ombra's day of triumph and universal victory. Sometimes such a moment comes even to girls who are not much distinguished either for their beauty or qualities of any kind—girls who sink into the second class immediately after, and carry with them a sore and puzzled consciousness of undeserved downfall. Ombra was at this height of youthful eminence now. The girls round her were all younger than she, not quite beyond the nursery, or, at least, the schoolroom. With Kate and Lucy Eldridge by her, she looked like a half-opened rose, in the perfection of bloom, beside two unclosed buds—or such, at least, was her aspect to the young men, who calmly considered the younger girls as sisters and playmates, but looked up to Ombra as the ideal maiden, the heroine of youthful fancy. Perhaps, had they been older, this fact might have been different; but at the age of the Berties sixteen was naught. As they were never apart, it was difficult to distinguish the sentiments of these young men, the one from the other. But the only conclusion to be drawn by the spectators was that both of them were at Ombra's feet. They consulted her obsequiously about all their movements. They caught at every hint of her wishes with the eagerness of vassals longing to please their mistress. They vied with each other in arranging cloaks and cushions for her.

Their yacht was called the Shadow; no one knew why, except, indeed, its owners themselves, and Mrs. Anderson and Mrs. Eldridge, who made a shrewd guess. But this was a very different matter from the Curate's untold love. The Rector's wife, ready as she was to interfere, could say nothing about this. She would not, for the world, put such an idea into the girl's head, she said. It was, no doubt, but a passing fancy, and could come to nothing; for Bertie Hardwick had nothing to marry on, and Bertie Eldridge would never be permitted to unite himself to Ombra Anderson, a girl without a penny, whose father had been nothing more than a Consul.

'The best thing we can wish for her is that they may soon go away; and I, for one, will never ask them again,' said Mrs. Eldridge, with deep concern in her voice. The Rector thought less of it, as was natural to a man. He laughed at the whole business.

'If you can't tell which is the lover, the love can't be very dangerous,' he said. Thus totally ignoring, as his wife felt, the worst difficulty of all.

'It might be both,' she said solemnly; 'and if it is only one, the other is aiding and abetting. It is true I can't tell which it is; but if I were Maria, or if I were Annie—'

'Thank Heaven you are neither,' said the Rector; 'and with ten children of our own, and your nervousness in respect to them, I think you have plenty on your shoulders, without taking up either Annie's or Maria's share.'

'I am a mother, and I can't help feeling for other mothers,' said Mrs. Eldridge, who gave herself a great deal of trouble unnecessarily in this way. But she did not feel for Ombra's mother in these perplexing circumstances. She was angry with Ombra. It was the girl's fault, she felt, that she was thus dangerous to other women's boys. Why should she, a creature of no account, turn the heads of the young men? 'She is not very pretty, even—not half so pretty as her cousin will be, who is worth thinking of,' she said, in her vexation. Any young man would have been fully justified in falling in love with Kate. But Ombra, who was nobody! It was too bad, she felt; it was a spite of fate!

As for Mrs. Anderson, she, warned by the failure of her former suggestions, said nothing to her child of the possibilities that seemed to be dawning upon her; but she thought the more. She watched the Berties with eyes which, being more deeply interested, were keener and clearer than anybody else's eyes; and she drew her own conclusions with a heart that beat high, and sometimes would flutter, like a girl's, in her breast.

Ombra accepted very graciously all the homage paid to her. She felt the better and the happier for it, whatever her opinion as to its origin might be. She began to talk more, being confident of the applause of the audience. In a hundred little subtle ways she was influenced by it, brightened, and stimulated. Did she know why? Would she choose as she ought? Was it some superficial satisfaction with the admiration she was receiving that moved her, or some dawning of deeper feeling? Mrs. Anderson watched her child with the deepest anxiety, but she could not answer these questions. The merest stranger knew as much as she did what Ombra would do or say.

CHAPTER XX

Things went on in this way for some weeks, while the Shadow lay in Sandown Bay, or cruised about the sunny sea. There was so much to do during this period, that none of the young people, at least, had much time to think. They were constantly together, always engaged with some project of pleasure, chattering and planning new opportunities to chatter and enjoy themselves once more; and the drama that was going on among them was but partially perceived by themselves, the actors in it. Some little share of personal feeling had awakened in Kate during these gay weeks. She had become sensible, with a certain twinge of mortification, that three or four different times when she had talked to Bertie Hardwick, 'my Bertie,' his attention had wandered from her. It was a new sensation, and it would be vain to conceal that she did not like it. He had smiled vacantly at her, and given a vague, murmuring answer, with his eyes turned towards the spot where Ombra was; and he had left her at the first possible opportunity. This filled Kate with consternation and a certain horror. It was very strange. She stood aghast, and looked at him; and so little interest did he take in the matter that he never observed her wondering, bewildered looks. The pang of mortification was sharp, and Kate had to gulp it down, her pride preventing her from showing what she felt. But after awhile her natural buoyancy regained the mastery. Of course it was natural he should like Ombra best—Ombra was beautiful, Ombra was the queen of the moment—Kate's own queen, though she had been momentarily unwilling to let her have everything. 'It is natural,' she said to herself, with philosophy—'quite natural. What a fool I was to think anything else! Of course he must care more for Ombra than for me; but I shall not give him the chance again.' This vengeful threat, however, floated out of her unvindictive mind. She forgot all about it, and did give him the chance; and once more he answered her vaguely, with his face turned towards her cousin. This was too much for Kate's patience. 'Mr. Bertie,' she said, 'go to Ombra if you please—no one wishes to detain you; but she takes no interest in you—to save yourself trouble, you may as well know that; she takes no interest in boys—or in you.'

Upon which Bertie started, and woke up from his abstraction, and made a hundred apologies. Kate turned round in the midst of them and left him; she was angry, and felt herself entitled to be so. To admire Ombra was all very well; but to neglect herself, to neglect civility, to make apologies! She went off affronted, determined never to believe in boys more. There was no jealousy of her cousin in her mind; Kate recognised, with perfect composure and good sense, that it was Ombra's day. Her own was to come. She was not out of short frocks yet, though she was over sixteen, and to expect to have vassals as Ombra had would be ridiculous. She had no fault to find with that, but she had a right, she felt, to expect that her privilege as old friend and feudal suzeraine should be respected; whereas, even her good advice was all thrown back upon her, and she had so much good advice to offer!

Kate reflected very deeply that morning on the nature of the sentiment called love. She had means of judging, having looked on while Mr. Sugden made himself look very ridiculous; and now the Berties were repeating the process. Both of them? She asked herself the question as Mrs. Eldridge had done. It made them look foolish, and it made them selfish; careless of other people, and especially of herself. It was hard; it was an injury that her own old friend should be thus negligent, and thus apologise! Kate felt that if he had taken her into his confidence, if he had said, 'I am in love with Ombra—I can't think of anything else,' she would have understood him, and all would have been well. But boys were such strange creatures, so wanting in perception; and she resolved that, if ever this sort of thing happened to her, she would make a difference. She would not permit this foolish absorption. She would say plainly, 'If you neglect your other friends, if you make yourselves look foolish for me, I will have nothing to do with you. Behave as if you had some sense, and do me credit. Do you think I want fools to be in love with me?' This was what Kate made up her mind she would say, when it came to be her turn.

This gay period, however, came to a strangely abrupt and mysterious end. The party had come home one evening, joyous as usual. They had gone round to Ryde in the morning to a regatta; the day had been perfect, the sea as calm as was compatible with the breeze they wanted, and all had gone well. Mrs. Eldridge herself had accompanied them, and on the whole, though certain tremors had crossed her at one critical moment, when the wind seemed to be rising, these tremors were happily quieted, and she had, 'on the whole,' as she cautiously stated, enjoyed the expedition. It was to be wound up, as most of these evenings had been, by a supper at the Rectory. Mrs. Anderson was in her own room, arranging her dress in order to join the sailors in this concluding feast. She had been watching a young moon rise into the twilight sky, and rejoicing in the beauty of the scene, for her children's sake. Her heart was warm with the thought that Ombra was happy; that she was the queen of the party, deferred to, petted, admired, nay—or the mother's instinct deceived her—worshipped by some. These thoughts diffused a soft glow of happiness over her mind. Ombra was happy, she was thought of as she ought to be, honoured as she deserved, loved; there was the brightest prospect opening up before her, and her mother, though she had spent the long day alone, felt a soft radiance of reflected light about her, which was to her what the moon was in the sky. It was a warm, soft, balmy Summer evening; the world seemed almost to hold its breath in the mere happiness of being, as if a movement, a sigh, would have broken the spell. Mrs. Anderson put up her hair (which was still pretty hair, and worth the trouble), and arranged her ribbons, and was about to draw round her the light shawl which Francesca had dropped on her shoulders, when all at once she saw Ombra coming through the garden alone. Ombra alone! with her head drooped, and a haze of something sad and mysterious about her, which perhaps the mother's eyes, perhaps the mere alarm of fancy, discerned at once. Mrs. Anderson gave a little cry. She dropped the shawl from her, and flew downstairs. The child was ill, or something had happened. A hundred wild ideas ran through her head in half a second. Kate had been drowned—Ombra had escaped from a wreck—the Berties! She was almost surprised to see that her daughter was not drenched with sea-water, when she rushed to her, and took her in her arms.

'What is the matter, Ombra? Something has happened. But you are safe, my darling child!'

'Don't,' said Ombra, withdrawing herself almost pettishly from her mother's arms. 'Nothing has happened. I—only was—tired; and I came home.'

She sat down on one of the rustic seats under the verandah, and turned away her head. The moon shone upon her, on the pretty outline of her arm, on which she leant, and the averted head. She had not escaped from a shipwreck. Had she anything to say which she dared not tell? Was it about Kate?

'Ombra, dear, what is it? I know there is something. Kate?'

'Kate? Kate is well enough. What should Kate have to do with it?' cried the girl, with impatient scorn; and then she suddenly turned and hid her face on her mother's arm. 'Oh! I am so unhappy!—my heart is like to break! I want to see no one—no one but you again!'

'What is it, my darling? Tell me what it is.' Mrs. Anderson knelt down beside her child. She drew her into her arms. She put her soft hand on Ombra's cheek, drawing it close to her own, and concealing it by the fond artifice. 'Tell me,' she whispered.

But Ombra did not say anything. She lay still and sobbed softly, as it were under her breath. And there her mother knelt supporting her, her own eyes full of tears, and her heart of wonder. Ombra, who had been this morning the happiest of all the happy! Dark, impossible shadows crept through Mrs. Anderson's mind. She grew sick with suspense.

'I cannot tell you here,' said Ombra, recovering a little. 'Come in. Take me upstairs, mamma. Nobody has done it; it is my own fault.'

They went up to the little white room opening from her mother's, where Ombra slept. The red shawl was still lying on the floor, where it had fallen from Mrs. Anderson's shoulders. Her little box of trinkets was open, her gloves on the table, and the moonlight, with a soft inquisition, whitening the brown air of the twilight, stole in by the side of the glass in which the two figures were dimly reflected.

'Do I look like a ghost?' said Ombra, taking off her hat. She was very pale; she looked like one of those creatures, half demons, half spirits, which poets see about the streams and woods. Never had she been so shadowy, so like her name; but there was a mist of consternation, of alarm, of trouble, about her. She was scared as well as heartbroken, like one who had seen some vision, and had been robbed of all her happiness thereby. 'Mamma,' she said, leaning upon her mother, but looking in the glass all the time, 'this is the end of everything. I will be as patient as I can, and not vex you more than I can help; but it is all over. I do not care to live any more, and it is my own fault.'

'Ombra, have some pity on me! Tell me, for heaven's sake, what you mean.'

Then Ombra withdrew from her support, and began to take off her little ornaments—the necklace she wore, according to the fashion of the time, the little black velvet bracelets, the brooch at her throat.

'It has all happened since sunset,' she said, as she nervously undid the clasps. 'He was beside me on the deck—he has been beside me all day. Oh! can't you tell without having it put into words?'

'I cannot tell what could make you miserable,' said her mother, with some impatience. 'Ombra, if I could be angry with you—'

'No, no,' she said, deprecating; 'Then you did not see it any more than I? So I am not so much, so very much to blame. Oh! mamma, he told me he—loved me—wanted me to—to—be married to him. Oh! when I think of all he said—'

'But, dear,' said Mrs. Anderson, recovering in a moment, 'there is nothing so very dreadful in this. I knew he would tell you so one day or other. I have seen it coming for a long time—'

'And you never told me—you never so much as tried to help me to see! You would not take the trouble to save your child from—from—Oh! I will never forgive you, mamma!'

'Ombra!' Mrs. Anderson was struck with such absolute consternation that she could not say another word.

'I refused him,' said the girl, suddenly, turning away with a quiver in her voice.

'You refused him?'

'What could I do else? I did not know what he was going to say. I never thought he cared. Can one see into another's heart? I was so—taken by surprise. I was so—frightened—he should see. And then, oh! the look he gave me! Oh! mother! mother! it is all over! Everything has come to an end! I shall never be happy any more!'

'What does it mean?' cried the bewildered mother. 'You—refused him; and yet you—Ombra—this is beyond making a mystery of. Tell me in plain words what you mean.'

'Then it is this, in plain words,' said Ombra, rousing up, with a hot flush on her cheek. 'I was determined he should not see I cared, and I never thought he did; and when he spoke to me, I refused. That is all, in plain words. I did not know what I was doing. Oh! mamma, you might be sorry for me, and not speak to me so! I did not believe him—I did not understand him; not till after—'

'My dear child, this is mere folly,' said her mother. 'If it is only a misunderstanding—and you love each other—'

'It is no misunderstanding. I made it very plain to him—oh! very plain! I said we were just to be the same as usual. That he was to come to see us—and all that! Mother—let me lie down. I am so faint. I think I shall die!'

'But, Ombra, listen to me. I can't let things remain like this. It is a misunderstanding—a mistake even. I will speak to him.'

'Then you shall never see me more!' cried Ombra, rising up, as it seemed, to twice her usual height. 'Mother, you would not shame me! If you do I will go away. I will never speak to you again. I will kill myself rather! Promise you will not say one word.'

'I will say nothing to—to shame you, as you call it.'

'Promise you will not say one word.'

'Ombra, I must act according to my sense of my duty. I will be very careful—'

'If you do not want to drive me mad, you will promise. The day you speak to him of this, I will go away. You shall never, never see me more!'

And the promise had to be made.

CHAPTER XXI

The promise was made, and Ombra lay down in her little white bed, silent, no longer making a complaint. She turned her face to the wall, and begged her mother to leave her.

'Don't say any more. Please take no notice. Oh! mamma, if you love me, don't say any more,' she had said. 'If I could have helped it, I would not have told you. It was because—when I found out—'

'Oh! Ombra, surely it was best to tell me—surely you would not have kept this from your mother?'

'I don't know,' she said. 'If you speak of it again, I shall think it was not for the best. Oh! mother, go away. It makes me angry to be pitied. I can't bear it. Let me alone. It is all over. I wish never to speak of it more!'

'But, Ombra—'

'No more! Oh! mamma, why will you take such a cruel advantage? I cannot bear any more!'

Mrs. Anderson left her child, with a sigh. She went downstairs, and stood in the verandah, leaning on the rustic pillar to which the honeysuckle hung. The daylight had altogether crept away, the moon was mistress of the sky; but she no longer thought of the sky, nor of the lovely, serene night, nor the moonlight. A sudden storm had come into her mind. What was she to do? She was a woman not apt to take any decided step for herself. Since her husband's death, she had taken counsel with her daughter on everything that passed in their life. I do not mean to imply that she had been moved only by Ombra's action, or was without individual energy of her own; but those who have thought, planned, and acted always à deux, find it sadly difficult to put themselves in motion individually, without the mental support which is natural to them. And then Mrs. Anderson had been accustomed all her life to keep within the strict leading-strings of propriety. She had regulated her doings by those rules of decorum, those regulations as to what was 'becoming,' what 'fitting her position,' with which society simplifies but limits the proceedings of her votaries. These rules forbade any interference in such a matter as this. They forbade to her any direct action at all in a complication so difficult. That she might work indirectly no doubt was quite possible, and would be perfectly legitimate—if she could; but how?

She stood leaning upon the mass of honeysuckle which breathed sweetness all about her, with the moonlight shining calm and sweet upon her face. The peacefullest place and moment; the most absolute repose and quietness about her—a scene from which conflict and pain seemed altogether shut out; and yet how much perplexity, how much vexation and distress were there. By-and-by, however, she woke up to the fact that she had no right to be where she was—that she ought at that moment to be at the Rectory, keeping up appearances, and explaining rather than adding to the mystery of her daughter's disappearance. It was a 'trying' thing to do, but Mrs. Anderson all her life had maintained rigidly the principle of keeping up appearances, and had gone through many a trying moment in consequence. She sighed; but she went meekly upstairs, and got the shawl which still lay on the floor, and wrapped it round her, and went away alone, bidding old Francesca watch over Ombra. She went down the still rural road in the moonlight, still working at her tangled skein of thoughts. If he had but had the good sense to speak to her first, in the old-fashioned way—if he would but have the good sense to come and openly speak to her now, and give her a legitimate opening to interfere. She walked slowly, and she started at every sound, wondering if perhaps it might be him hanging about, on the chance of seeing some one. When at last she did see a figure approaching, her heart leaped to her mouth; but it was not the figure she looked for. It was Mr. Sugden, the tall curate, hanging about anxiously on the road.

'Is Miss Anderson ill?' he said, while he held her hand in greeting.

'The sun has given her a headache. She has bad headaches sometimes,' she answered, cheerfully; 'but it is nothing—she will be better to-morrow. She has been so much more out doors lately, since this yachting began.'

'That will not go on any longer,' said the Curate, with a mixture of regret and satisfaction. After a moment the satisfaction predominated, and he drew a long breath, thinking to himself of all that had been, of all that the yacht had made an end of. 'Thank Providence!' he added softly; and then louder, 'our two friends are going, or gone. A letter was waiting them with bad news—or, at least, with news of some description, which called them off. I wonder you did not meet them going back to the pier. As the wind is favourable, they thought the best way was to cross in the yacht. They did not stop even to eat anything. I am surprised you did not meet them.'

Mrs. Anderson's heart gave a leap, and then seemed to stop beating. If she had met them, he would have spoken, and all might have been well. If she had but started five minutes earlier, if she had walked a little faster, if—But now they were out of sight, out of reach, perhaps for ever. Her vexation and disappointment were so keen that tears came to her eyes in the darkness. Yes, in her heart she had felt sure that she could do something, that he would speak to her, that she might be able to speak to him; but now all was over, as Ombra said. She could not make any reply to her companion—she was past talking; and, besides, it did not seem to be necessary to make any effort to keep up appearances with the Curate. Men were all obtuse; and he was not specially clever, but rather the reverse. He never would notice, nor think that this departure was anything to her. She walked on by his side in silence, only saying, after awhile, 'It is very sudden—they will be a great loss to all you young people; and I hope it was not illness, or any trouble in the family—'

But she did not hear what answer was made to her—she took no further notice of him—her head began to buzz, and there was a singing in her ears, because of the multiplicity of her thoughts. She recalled herself, with an effort, when the Rectory doors were pushed open by her companion, and she found herself in the midst of a large party, all seated round the great table, all full of the news of the evening, interspersed with inquiries about the absent.

'Oh! have you heard what has happened? Oh! how is Ombra, Mrs. Anderson? Oh! we are all heart-broken! What shall we do without them?' rose the chorus.

Mrs. Anderson smiled her smile of greeting, and put on a proper look of concern for the loss of the Berties, and was cheerful about her daughter. She behaved herself as a model woman in the circumstances would behave, and she believed, and with some justice, that she had quite succeeded. She succeeded with the greater part of the party, no doubt; but there were two who looked at her with doubtful eyes—the Curate, about whom she had taken no precautions; and Kate, who knew every line of her face.

'I hope it is not illness nor trouble in the family,' Mrs. Anderson repeated, allowing a look of gentle anxiety to come over her face.

'No, I hope not,' said Mrs. Eldridge; 'though I am a little anxious, I allow. But no, really I don't think it. They would never have concealed such a thing from us; though there was actually no time to explain. I had gone upstairs to take off my things, and all at once there was a cry, "The Berties are going!" "My dear boys, what is the matter?" I said; "is there anything wrong at either of your homes? I beg of you to let me know the worst!" And then one of them called to me from the bottom of the stairs, that it was nothing—it was only that they must go to meet some one—one of their young men's engagements, I suppose. He said they would come back; but I tell the children that is nonsense; while they were here they might be persuaded to stay, but once gone, they will never come back this season. Ah! I have only too much reason to know boys' ways.'

'But they looked dreadfully cast down, mamma—as if they had had bad news,' said Lucy Eldridge, who, foreseeing the end of a great deal of unusual liberty, felt very much cast down herself.

'Bertie Hardwick looked as if he had seen a ghost,' said another.

'No, it was Bertie Eldridge,' cried a third.

Kate looked from her end of the table at her aunt's face, and said nothing; and a deep red glow came upon Mr. Sugden's cheeks. These two young people had each formed a theory in haste, from the very few facts they knew, and both were quite wrong; but that fact did not diminish the energy with which they cherished each their special notion. Mrs. Anderson, however, was imperturbable. She sat near Mrs. Eldridge, and talked to her with easy cheerfulness about the day's expedition, and all that had been going on. She lamented the end of the gaiety, but remarked, with a smile, that perhaps the girls had had enough. 'I saw this morning that Ombra was tired out. I wanted her not to go, but of course it was natural she should wish to go; and the consequence is, one of her racking headaches,' she said.

With the gravest of faces, Kate listened. She had heard nothing of Ombra's headache till that moment; still, of course, the conversation which Mrs. Anderson reported might have taken place in her absence; but—Kate was very much disturbed in her soul, and very anxious that the meal should come to an end.

The moon had almost disappeared when the company dispersed. Kate rushed to her aunt, and took her hand, and whispered in her ear; but a sudden perception of a tall figure on Mrs. Anderson's other hand stopped her. 'What do you say, Kate?' cried her aunt; but the question could not be repeated. Mr. Sugden marched by their side all the way—he could not have very well told why—in case he should be wanted, he said to himself; but he did not even attempt to explain to himself how he could be wanted. He felt stern, determined, ready to do anything or everything. Kate's presence hampered him, as his hampered her. He would have liked to say something more distinct than he could now permit himself to do.

'I wish you would believe,' he said, suddenly, bending over Mrs. Anderson in the darkness, 'that I am always at your service, ready to do anything you want.'

'You are very, very kind,' said Mrs. Anderson, with the greatest wonderment. 'Indeed, I am sure I should not have hesitated to ask you, had I been in any trouble,' she added, gently.

But Mr. Sugden was too much in earnest to be embarrassed by the gentle denial she made of any necessity for his help.

'At any time, in any circumstances,' he said, hoarsely. 'Mrs. Anderson, I do not say this is what I would choose—but if your daughter should have need of a—of one who would serve her—like a brother—I do not say it is what I would choose—'

'My dear Mr. Sugden! you are so very good—'

'No, not good,' he said, anxiously—'don't say that—good to myself—if you will but believe me. I would forget everything else.'

'You may be sure, should I feel myself in need, you will be the first I shall go to,' said Mrs. Anderson, graciously. ('What can he mean?—what fancy can he have taken into his head?' she was saying, with much perplexity, all the time to herself.) 'I cannot ask you to come in, Mr. Sugden—we must keep everything quiet for Ombra; but I hope we shall see you soon.'

And she dismissed him, accepting graciously all his indistinct and eager offers of service. 'He is very good; but I don't know what he is thinking of,' she said rather drearily as she turned to go in. Kate was still clinging to her, and Kate, though it was not necessary to keep up appearances with her, had better, Mrs. Anderson thought, be kept in the dark too, as much as was possible. 'I am going to Ombra,' she said. 'Good night, my dear child. Go to bed.'

'Auntie, stop a minute. Oh! auntie, take me into your confidence. I love her, and you too. I will never say a word, or let any one see that I know. Oh! Auntie—Ombra—has she gone with them?—has she—run—away?'

'Ombra—run away!' cried Mrs. Anderson, throwing her niece's arm from her. 'Child, how dare you? Do you mean to insult both her and me?'

Kate stood abashed, drawn back to a little distance, tears coming to her eyes.

'I did not mean any harm,' she said, humbly.

'Not mean any harm! But you thought my child—my Ombra—had run away!'

'Oh! forgive me,' said Kate. 'I know now how absurd it was; but—I thought—she might be—in love. People do it—at least in books. Don't be angry with me, auntie. I thought so because of your face. Then what is the matter? Oh! do tell me; no one shall ever know from me.'

Mrs. Anderson was worn out. She suffered Kate's supporting arm to steal round her. She leant her head upon the girl's shoulder.

'I can't tell you, dear,' she said, with a sob. 'She has mistaken her feelings; she is—very unhappy. You must be very, very kind and good to her, and never let her see you know anything. Oh! Kate, my darling is very unhappy. She thinks she has broken her heart.'

'Then I know!' cried Kate, stamping her foot upon the gravel, and feeling as Mr. Sugden did. 'Oh! I will go after them and bring them back! It is their fault.'

CHAPTER XXII

Mrs. Anderson awaited her daughter's awakening next morning with an anxiety which was indescribable. She wondered even at the deep sleep into which Ombra fell after the agitation of the night—wondered, not because it was new or unexpected, but with that wonder which moves the elder mind at the sight of youth in all its vagaries, capable of such wild emotion at one moment, sinking into profound repose at another. But, after all, Ombra had been for some time awake, ere her watchful mother observed. When Mrs. Anderson looked at her, she was lying with her mouth closely shut and her eyes open, gazing fixedly at the light, pale as the morning itself, which was misty, and rainy, and wan, after the brightness of last night. Her look was so fixed and her lips so firmly shut, that her mother grew alarmed.

'Ombra!' she said softly—'Ombra, my darling, my poor child!'

Ombra turned round sharply, fixing her eyes now on her mother's face as she had fixed them on the light.

'What is it?' she said. 'Why are you up so early? I am not ill, am I!' and looked at her with a kind of menace, forbidding, as it were, any reference to what was past.

'I hope not, dear,' said Mrs. Anderson. 'You have too much courage and good sense, my darling, to be ill.'

'Do courage and good sense keep one from being ill?' said Ombra, with something like a sneer; and then she said, 'Please, mamma, go away. I want to get up.'

'Not yet, dear. Keep still a little longer. You are not able to get up yet,' said poor Mrs. Anderson, trembling for the news which would meet her when she came into the outer world again. What strange change was it that had come upon Ombra? She looked almost derisively, almost threateningly into her mother's face.

'One would think I had had a fever, or that some great misfortune had happened to me,' she said; 'but I am not aware of it. Leave me alone, please. I have a thousand things to do. I want to get up. Mother, for heaven's sake, don't look at me so! You will drive me wild! My nerves cannot stand it; nor—nor my temper,' said Ombra, with a shrill in her voice which had never been heard there before. 'Mamma, if you have any pity, go away.'

'If my lady will permit, I will attend Mees Ombra,' said old Francesca, coming in with a look of ominous significance. And poor Mrs. Anderson was worn out—she had been up half the night, and during the other half she did not sleep, though Ombra slept, who was the chief sufferer. Vanquished now by her daughter's unfilial looks, she stole away, and cried by herself for a few moments in a corner, which did her good, and relieved her heart.

But Francesca advanced to the bedside with intentions far different from any her mistress had divined. She approached Ombra solemnly, holding out two fingers at her.

'I make the horns,' said Francesca; 'I advance not to you again, Mademoiselle, without making the horns. Either you are an ice-maiden, as I said, and make enchantments, or you have the evil eye—'

'Oh! be quiet, please, and leave me alone. I want to get up. I don't want to be talked to. Mamma leaves me when I ask her, and why should not you?'

'Because, Mademoiselle,' said Francesca, with elaborate politeness, 'my lady has fear of grieving her child; but for me I have not fear. Figure to yourself that I have made you like the child of my bosom for eighteen—nineteen year—and shall I stand by now, and see you drive love from you, drive life from you? You think so, perhaps? No, I am bolder than my dear padrona. I do not care sixpence if I break your heart. You are ice, you are stone, you are worse than all the winters and the frosts! Signorina Ghiaccia, you haf done it now!'

'Francesca, go away! You have no right to speak to me so. What have I done?'

'Done!' cried Francesca, 'done!—all the evil things you can do. You have driven all away from you who cared for you. Figure to yourself that a little ship went away from the golf last night, and the two young signorini in it. You will say to me that it is not you who have done it; but I believe you not. Who but you, Mees Ombra, Mees Ice and Snow? And so you will do with all till you are left alone, lone in the world—I know it. You turn to ze wall, you cry, you think you make me cry too, but no, Francesca will speak ze trutt to you, if none else. Last night, as soon as you come home, ze little ship go away—cacciato—what you call dreaven away—dreaven away, like by ze Tramontana, ze wind from ze ice-mountains! That is you. Already I haf said it. You are Ghiaccia—you will leave yourself lone, lone in ze world, wizout one zing to lof!'

Francesca's English grew more and more broken as she rose into fervour. She stood now by Ombra's bedside, with all the eloquence of indignation in her words, and looks, and gestures; her little uncovered head, with its knot of scanty hair twisted tightly up behind, nodding and quivering; her brown little hands gesticulating; her foot patting the floor; her black eyes flashing. Ombra had turned to the wall, as she said. She could discomfit her gentle mother, but she could not put down Francesca. And then this news which Francesca brought her went like a stone to the depths of her heart.

'But I will tell you vat vill komm,' she went on, with sparks of fire, as it seemed, flashing from her eyes—'there vill komm a day when the ice will melt, like ze torrents in ze mountains. There will be a rush, and a flow, and a swirl, and then the avalanche! The ice will become water—it will run down, it will flood ze contree; but it will not do good to nobody, Mademoiselle. They will be gone the persons who would have loved. All will be over. Ze melting and ze flowing will be too late—it will be like the torrents in May, all will go with it, ze home, ze friends, ze comfort that you love, you English. All will go. Mademoiselle will be sorry then,' said Francesca, regaining her composure, and making a vindictive courtesy. She smiled at the tremendous picture she was conscious of having drawn, with a certain complacency. She had beaten down with her fierce storm of words the white figure which lay turned away from her with hidden face. But Francesca's heart did not melt. 'Now I have told you ze trutt,' she said, impressively. 'Ze bath, and all things is ready, if Mademoiselle wishes to get up now.'

'What have you been saying to my child, Francesca?' said Mrs. Anderson, who met her as she left the room, looking very grave, and with red eyes.

'Nozing but ze trutt,' said Francesca, with returning excitement; 'vich nobody will say but me—for I lof her—I lof her! She is my bébé too. Madame will please go downstairs, and have her breakfast,' she added calmly. 'Mees Ombra is getting up—there is nothing more to say. She will come down in quarter of an hour, and all will be as usual. It will be better that Madame says nothing more.'

Mrs. Anderson was not unused to such interference on Francesca's part; the only difference was that no such grave crisis had ever happened before. She was aware that, in milder cases, her own caressing and indulgent ways had been powerfully aided by the decided action of Francesca, and her determination to speak 'ze trutt,' as she called it, without being moved by Ombra's indignation, or even by her tears. Her mistress, though too proud to appeal to her for aid, had been but too glad to accept it ere now. But this was such an emergency as had never happened before, and she stood doubtful, unable to make up her mind what she should do, at the door of Ombra's room, until the sounds within made it apparent that Ombra had really got up, and that there was, for the moment, nothing further to be done. She went away half disconsolate, half relieved, to the bright little dining-room below, where the pretty breakfast-table was spread, with flowers on it, and sunshine straying in through the network of honeysuckles and roses. Kate was at her favourite occupation, arranging flowers in the hall, but singing under her breath, lest she should disturb her cousin.

'How is Ombra?' she whispered, as if the sound of a voice would be injurious to her.

'She is better, dear; I think much better. But oh, Kate, for heaven's sake, take no notice, not a word! Don't look even as if you supposed—'

'Of course not, auntie,' said Kate, with momentary indignation that she should be supposed capable of such unwomanly want of comprehension. They were seated quite cheerfully at breakfast when Ombra appeared. She gave them a suspicious look to discover if they had been talking of her—if Kate knew anything; but Kate (she thanked heaven), knew better than to betray herself. She asked after her cousin's headache, on the contrary, in the most easy and natural way; she talked (very little) of the events of the preceding day. She propounded a plan of her own for that afternoon, which was to drive along the coast to a point which Ombra had wished to make a sketch of. 'It will be the very thing for to-day,' said Kate. 'The rain is over, and the sun is shining; but it is too misty for sea-views, and we must be content with the land.'

'Is it true,' said Ombra, looking her mother in the face, 'that the yacht went away last night?'

'Oh yes,' cried Kate, taking the subject out of Mrs. Anderson's hands, 'quite true. They found letters at the railway calling them off—or, at least, so they said. Some of us thought it was your fault for going away, but my opinion is that they did it abruptly to keep up our interest. One cannot go on yachting for ever and ever; for my part, I was beginning to get tired. Whereas, if they come back again, after a month or so, it will all be as fresh as ever.'

'Are they coming back?'

'Yes,' said, boldly, the undaunted Kate.

Mrs. Anderson spoke not a word; she sat and trembled, pitying her child to the bottom of her heart—longing to take her into her arms, to speak consolation to her, but not daring. The mother, who would have tried if she could to get the moon for Ombra, had to stand aside, and let Francesca 'tell ze trutt,' and Kate give the consolation. Some women would have resented the interference, but she was heroic, and kept silence. The audacious little fib which Kate had told so gayly, had already done its work; the cloud of dull quiet which had been on Ombra's face, brightened. All was perhaps not over yet.

Thus after this interruption of their tranquillity they fell back into the old dull routine. Mr. Sugden was once more master of the field. Ombra kept herself so entirely in subjection, that nobody out of the Cottage guessed what crisis she had passed through, except this one observer, whose eyes were quickened by jealousy and by love. The Curate was not deceived by her smiles, by her expressions of content with the restored quietness, by her eagerness to return to all their old occupations. He watched her with anxious eyes, noting all her little caprices, noting the paleness which would come over her, the wistful gaze over the sea, which sometimes abstracted her from her companions.

'She is not happy as she used to be—she is only making-believe, like the angel she is, to keep us from being wretched,' he said to Kate.

'Mr. Sugden, you talk great nonsense; there is nothing the matter with my cousin,' Kate would reply. On which Mr. Sugden sighed heavily and shook his head, and went off to find Mrs. Anderson, whom he gently beguiled into a corner.

'You remember what I said,' he would whisper to her earnestly—'if you want my services in any way. It is not what I would have wished; but think of me as her—brother; let me act for you, as her brother would, if there is any need for it. Remember, you promised that you would—'

'What does the man want me to bid him do?' Mrs. Anderson would ask in perplexity, talking the matter over with Kate—a relief which she sometimes permitted herself; for Ombra forbade all reference to the subject, and she could not shut up her anxieties entirely in her own heart. But Kate could throw no light on the subject. Kate herself was not at all clear what had happened. She could not make quite sure, from her aunt's vague statement, whether it was Ombra that was in the wrong, or the Berties, or if it was both the Berties, or which it was. There were so many complications in the question, that it was very difficult to come to any conclusion about it. But she held fast by her conviction that they must come back to Shanklin—it was inevitable that they must come back.

CHAPTER XXIII

Kate was so far a true prophet that the Berties did return, but not till Christmas, and then only for a few days. For the first time during the Autumn and early Winter, time hung heavy upon the hands of the little household. Their innocent routine of life, which had supported them so pleasantly hitherto, supplying a course of gentle duties and necessities, broke down now, no one could tell why. Routine is one of the pleasantest stays of monotonous life, so long as no agitating influence has come into it. It makes existence more supportable to millions of people who have ceased to be excited by the vicissitudes of life, or who have not yet left the pleasant creeks and bays of youth for the more agitated and stormy sea; but when that first interruption has come, without bringing either satisfaction or happiness with it, the bond of routine becomes terrible. All the succession of duties and pleasures which had seemed to her as the course of nature a few months before—as unchangeable as the succession of day and night, and as necessary—became now a burden to Ombra, under which her nerves, her temper, her very life gave way. She asked herself, and often asked the others, why they should do the same things every day?—what was the good of it? The studies which she shared with her cousin, the little charities they did—visits to this poor woman or the other, expeditions with the small round basket, which held a bit of chicken, or some jelly, or a pudding for a sick pensioner; the walks they took for exercise, their sketchings and practisings, and all the graceful details of their innocent life—what was the good of them? 'The poor people don't want our puddings and things. I daresay they throw them away when we are gone,' said Ombra. 'They don't want to be interfered with—I should not, if I were in their place; and if we go on sketching till the end of time, we never shall make a tolerable picture—you could buy a better for five shillings; and the poorest pianist in a concert-room would play better than we could, though we spent half the day practising. What is the good of it? Oh! if you only knew how sick I am of it all!'

'But, dear, you could not sit idle all day—you could not read all day. You must do something,' said poor Mrs. Anderson, not knowing how to meet this terrible criticism, 'for your own sake.'

'For my own sake!' said Ombra. 'Ah! that is just what makes it so dreadful, so disgusting! I am to go on with all this mass of nonsense for my own sake. Not that it is, or ever will be, of use to any one; not that there is any need to do it, or any good in doing it; but for my own sake! Oh! mamma, don't you see what a satire it is? No man, nobody who criticises women, ever said worse than you have just said. We are so useless to the world, so little wanted by the world, that we are obliged to furbish up little silly, senseless occupations, simply to keep us from yawning ourselves to death—for our own sakes!'

'Indeed, Ombra, I do not understand what you mean, or what you would have,' Mrs. Anderson would answer, all but crying, the vexation of being unable to answer categorically, increasing her distress at her daughter's contradictoriness; for, to be sure, when you anatomized all these simple habits of life, what Ombra said was true enough. The music and the drawing were done for occupation rather than for results. The visits to the poor did but little practical service, though the whole routine had made up a pleasant life, gently busy, and full of kindly interchanges.

Mrs. Anderson felt that she herself had not been a useless member of society, or one whose withdrawal would have made no difference to the world; but in what words was she to say so? She was partially affronted, vexed, and distressed. Even when she reflected on the subject, she did not know in what words to reply to her argumentative child. She could justify her own existence to herself—for was not she the head and centre of this house, upon whom five other persons depended for comfort and guidance. 'Five persons,' Mrs. Anderson said to herself. 'Even Ombra—what would she do without me? And Kate would have no home, if I were not here to make one for her; and those maids who eat our bread!' All this she repeated to herself, feeling that she was not, even now, without use in the world; but how could she have said it to her daughter? Probably Ombra would have answered that the whole household might be swept off the face of the earth without harm to any one—that there was no use in them;—a proposition which it was impossible either to refute or to accept.

Thus the household had changed its character, no one knew how. When Kate arranged the last winterly bouquets of chrysanthemums and Autumnal leaves in the flat dishes which she had once filled with primroses, her sentiments were almost as different as the season. She was nipped by a subtle cold more penetrating than that which blew about the Cottage in the November winds, and tried to get entrance through the closed windows. She was made uncomfortable in all her habits, unsettled in her youthful opinions. Sometimes a refreshing little breeze of impatience crossed her mind, but generally she was depressed by the change, without well knowing why.

'If we are all as useless as Ombra says, it would be better to be a cook or a housemaid; but then the cook and the housemaid are of use only to help us useless creatures, so they are no good either!' This was the style of reasoning which Ombra's vagaries brought into fashion. But these vagaries probably never would have occurred at all, had not something happened to Ombra which disturbed the whole edifice of her young life. Had she accepted the love which was offered to her, no doubt every circumstance around her would have worn a sweet perfection and appropriateness to her eyes; or had she been utterly fancy-free, and untouched by the new thing which had been so suddenly thrust upon her, the pleasant routine might have continued, and all things gone on as before. But the light of a new life had gleamed upon Ombra, and foolishly, hastily, she had put it away from her. She had put it away—but she could not forget that sudden and rapid gleam which had lighted up the whole landscape. When she looked out over that landscape now, the distances were blurred, the foreground had grown vague and dim with mists, the old sober light which dwelt there had gone for ever, following that sudden, evanescent, momentary gleam. What was the good? Once, for a moment, what seemed to be the better, the best, had shone upon her. It fled, and even the homelier good fled with it. Blankness, futility, an existence which meant nothing, and could come to nothing, was what remained to her now.

So Ombra thought; perhaps a girl of higher mind, or more generous heart, would not have done so—but it is hard to take a wide or generous view of life at nineteen, when one thinks one has thrown away all that makes existence most sweet. The loss; the terrible disappointment; the sense of folly and guilt—for was it not all her own fault?—made such a mixture of bitterness to Ombra as it is difficult to describe. If she had been simply 'crossed in love,' as people say, there would have been some solace possible; there would have been the visionary fidelity, the melancholy delight of resignation, or even self-sacrifice; but here there was nothing to comfort her—it was herself only who was to blame, and that in so ridiculous and childish a way. Therefore, every time she thought of it (and she thought of it for ever), the reflection made her heart sick with self-disgust, and cast her down into despair. The tide had come to her, as it comes always in the affairs of men, but she had not caught it, and now was left ashore, a maiden wreck upon the beach, for ever and ever. So Ombra thought—and this thought in her was to all the household as though a cloud hung over it. Mrs. Anderson was miserable, and Kate depressed, she could not tell why.

'We are getting as dull as the old women in the almshouses,' the latter said, one day, with a sigh. And then, after a pause—'a great deal duller, for they chatter about everything or nothing. They are cheery old souls; they look as if they had expected it all their lives, and liked it now they are there.'

'And so they did, I suppose. Not expected it, but hoped for it, and were anxious about it, and used all the influence they could get to be elected. Of course they looked forward to it as the very best thing that could happen—'

'To live in the almshouses?' said Kate, with looks aghast. 'Look forward to it! Oh, auntie, what a terrible idea!'

'My dear,' Mrs. Anderson said, somewhat subdued, 'their expectations and ours are different.'

'That means,' said Ombra, 'that most of us have not even almshouses to look forward to; nothing but futility, past and present—caring for nothing and desiring nothing.'

'Ombra, I do not know what you will say next,' cried the poor mother, baffled and vexed, and ready to burst into tears. Her child plagued her to the last verge of a mother's patience, setting her on edge in a hundred ways. And Kate looked on with open eyes, and sometimes shared her aunt's impatience; but chiefly, as she still admired and adored Ombra, allowed that young woman's painful mania to oppress her, and was melancholy for company. I do not suppose, however, that Kate's melancholy was of a painful nature, or did her much harm. And, besides her mother, the person who suffered most through Ombra was poor Mr. Sugden, who watched her till his eyes grew large and hollow in his honest countenance; till his very soul glowed with indignation against the Berties. The determination to find out which it was who had ruined her happiness, and to seek him out even at the end of the world, and exact a terrible punishment, grew stronger and stronger in him during those dreary days of Winter. 'As if I were her brother; though, God knows, that is not what I would have wished,' the Curate said to himself. This was his theory of the matter. He gave up with a sad heart the hope of being able to move her now to love himself. He would never vex her even, with his hopeless love, he decided; never weary her with bootless protestations; never injure the confidential position he had gained by asking more than could ever be given to him; but one day he would find out which was the culprit, and then Ombra should be avenged.

Gleams of excitement began to shoot across the tranquil cheeriness of the Winter, when it was known that the two were coming again; and then other changes occurred, which made a diversion which was anything but agreeable in the Cottage. Ombra said nothing to any one about her feelings, but she became irritable, impatient, and unreasonable, as only those whose nerves are kept in a state of painful agitation can be. The Berties stayed but a few days; they made one call at the Cottage, which was formal and constrained, and they were present one evening at the Rectory to meet the old yachting-party, which had been so merry and so friendly in the Summer. But it was merry no longer. The two young men seemed to have lost their gaiety; they had gone in for work, they said, both in a breath, with a forced laugh, by way of apology for themselves. They said little to any one, and next to nothing to Ombra, who sat in a corner all the evening, and furtively watched them, reddening and growing pale as they moved about from one to another. The day after they left she had almost a quarrel with her mother and cousin, to such a pitch had her irritability reached; and then, for the first time, she burst into wild tears, and repented and reproached herself, till Mrs. Anderson and Kate cried their eyes out, in pitiful and wondering sympathy. But poor Ombra never quite recovered herself after this outburst. She gave herself up, and no longer made a stand against the soure irritation and misery that consumed her. It affected her health, after a time, and filled the house with anxiety, and depression, and pain. And thus the Winter went by, and Spring came, and Kate Courtenay, developing unawares, like her favourite primroses, blossomed into the flowery season, and completed her eighteenth year.

CHAPTER XXIV

Kate's eighteenth birthday was in Easter-week; and on the day before that anniversary a letter arrived from her Uncle Courtenay, which filled the Cottage with agitation. During all this time she had written periodically and dutifully to her guardian, Mrs. Anderson being very exact upon that point, and had received occasional notes from him in return; but something had pricked him to think of his duties at this particular moment, though it was not an agreeable subject to contemplate. He had not seen her for three years, and it cannot be affirmed that the old man of the world would have been deeply moved had he never seen his ward again; but something had suggested to him the fact that Kate existed—that she was now eighteen, and that it was his business to look after her. Besides, it was the Easter recess, and a few days' quiet and change of air were recommended by his doctor. For this no place could possibly be more suitable than Shanklin; so he sent a dry little letter to Kate, announcing an approaching visit, though without specifying any time.

The weather was fine, and the first croquet-party of the season was to be held at the Cottage in honour of Kate's birthday, so that the announcement did not perhaps move her so much as it might have done. But Mrs. Anderson was considerably disturbed by the news. Mr. Courtenay was her natural opponent—the representative of the other side of the house—a man who unquestionably thought himself of higher condition, and better blood than herself; he was used to great houses and good living, and would probably scorn the Cottage and Francesca's cooking, and Jane's not very perfect waiting; and then his very name carried with it a suggestion of change. He had left them quiet all this time, but it was certain that their quiet could not last for ever, and the very first warning of a visit from him seemed to convey in it a thousand intimations of other and still less pleasant novelties to come. What if he were coming to intimate that Kate must leave the pleasant little house which had become her home?—what if he were coming to take her away? This was a catastrophe which her aunt shrank from contemplating, not only for Kate's sake, but for other reasons, which were important enough. She had sufficient cause for anxiety in the clouded life and confused mind of her own child—but if such an alteration as this were to come in their peaceable existence!

Mrs. Anderson's eyes ran over the whole range of possibilities, as over a landscape. How it would change the Cottage! Not only the want of Kate's bright face, but the absence of so many comforts and luxuries which her wealth had secured! On the other side, it was possible that Ombra might be happier in her present circumstances without Kate's companionship, which threw her own gloom and irritability into sharper relief. She had always been, not jealous—the mother would not permit herself to use such a word—but sensitive (this was her tender paraphrase of an ugly reality), in respect to Kate's possible interference with the love due to herself. Would she be better alone?—better without the second child, who had taken such a place in the house? It was a miserable thought—miserable not only for the mother who had taken this second child into her heart, but shameful to think of for Ombra's own sake. But still it might be true; and in that case, notwithstanding the pain of separation, notwithstanding the loss of comfort, it might be better that Kate should go. Thus in a moment, by the mere reading of Mr. Courtenay's dry letter, which meant chiefly, 'By-the-way, there is such a person as Kate—I suppose I ought to go and see her,' Mrs. Anderson's mind was driven into such sudden agitation and convulsion as happens to the sea when a whirlwind falls upon it, and lashes it into sudden fury. She was driven this way and that, tossed up to the giddy sky, and down to the salt depths; her very sight seemed to change, and the steady sunshine wavered and flickered before her on the wall.

'Oh! what a nuisance!' Kate had exclaimed on reading the letter; but as she threw it down on the table, after a second reading aloud, her eye caught her aunt's troubled countenance. 'Are you vexed, auntie? Don't you like him to come? Then let me say so—I shall be so glad!' she cried.

'My dearest Kate, how could I be anything but glad to see your guardian?' said Mrs. Anderson, recalling her powers; 'not for his sake, perhaps, for I don't know him, but to show him that, whatever the sentiments of your father's family may have been, there has been no lack of proper feeling on our side. The only thing that troubles me is—The best room is so small; and will Francesca's cooking be good enough? These old bachelors are so particular. To be sure, we might have some things sent in from the hotel.'

'If Uncle Courtenay comes, he must be content with what we have,' said Kate, flushing high. 'Particular indeed! If it is good enough for us, I should just think—I suppose he knows you are not the Duchess of Shanklin, with a palace to put him in. And nobody wants him. He is coming for his own pleasure, not for ours.'

'I would not say that,' said Mrs. Anderson, with dignity. 'I want him. I am glad that he should come, and see with his own eyes how you are being brought up.'

'Being brought up! But I am eighteen. I have stopped growing. I am not a child any longer. I am brought up,' said Kate.

Mrs. Anderson shook her head; but she kissed the girl's bright face, and looked after her, as she went out, with a certain pride. 'He must see how Kate is improved—she looks a different creature,' she said to Ombra, who sat by in her usual languor, without much interest in the matter.

'Do you think he will see it, mamma? She was always blooming and bright,' said neutral-tinted Ombra, with a sigh. And then she added, 'Kate is right, she is grown up—she is a woman, and not a child any longer. I feel the difference every day.'

Mrs. Anderson looked anxiously at her child.

'You are mistaken, dear,' she said. 'Kate is very young in her heart. She is childish even in some things. There is the greatest difference between her and you—what you were at her age.'

'Yes, she is brighter, gayer, more attractive to everybody than ever I was,' said Ombra. 'As if I did not see that—as if I did not feel every hour—'

Mrs. Anderson placed herself behind Ombra's chair, and drew her child's head on to her bosom, and kissed her again and again. She was a woman addicted to caresses; but there was meaning in this excess of fondness. 'My love! my own darling!' she said; and then, very softly, after an interval, 'My only one!'

'Not your only one now,' said Ombra, with tears rushing to her eyes, and a little indignant movement; 'you have Kate—'

'Ombra!'

'Mamma, I am a little tired—a little—out of temper—I don't know—what it is; yes, it is temper—I do know—'

'Ombra, you never had a bad temper. Oh! if you would put a little more confidence in me! Don't you think I have seen how depressed you have been ever since—ever since—'

'Since when?' said Ombra, raising her head, her twilight-face lighting up with a flush and sparkle, half of indignation, half of terror. 'Do you mean that I have been making a show of—what I felt—letting people see—'

You made no show, darling; but surely it would be strange if I did not see deeper than others. Ombra, listen.'—She put her lips to her daughter's cheek, and whispered, 'Since we heard they were coming back. Oh! Ombra, you must try to overcome it, to be as you used to be. You repel him, dear, you thrust him away from you as if you hated him! And they are coming here to-day.'

Ombra's shadowy cheek coloured deeper and deeper, her eyelashes drooped over it; she shrank from her mother's eye.

'Don't say anything more,' she said, with passionate deprecation. 'Don't! Talking can only make things worse. I am a fool! I am ashamed! I hate myself! It is temper—only temper, mamma!'

'My own child—my only child!' said the mother, caressing her; and then she whispered once more, 'Ombra, would it be better for you if Kate were away?'

'Better for me!' The girl flushed up out of her languor and paleness like a sudden storm. 'Oh! do you mean to insult me?' she cried, with passionate indignation. 'Do you think so badly of me? Have I fallen so low as that?'

'My darling, forgive me! I meant that you thought she came between us—that you had need of all my sympathy,' cried the mother, in abject humiliation. But it was some time before Ombra would listen. She was stung by a suggestion which revealed to her the real unacknowledged bitterness in her heart.

'You must despise me,' she said, 'you, my own mother! You must think—oh! how badly of me! That I could be so mean, so miserable, such a poor creature! Oh! mother, how could you say such a dreadful thing to me?'

'My darling!' said the mother, holding her in her arms; and gradually Ombra grew calm, and accepted the apologies which were made with so heavy a heart. For Mrs. Anderson saw by her very vehemence, by the violence of the emotion produced by her words, that they were true. She had been right, but she could not speak again on the subject. Perhaps Ombra had never before quite identified and detected the evil feeling in her heart; but both mother and daughter knew it now. And yet nothing more was to be said. The child was bitterly ashamed for herself, the mother for her child. If she could secretly and silently dismiss the other from her house, Mrs. Anderson felt it had become her duty to do it; but never to say a word on the subject, never to whisper, never to make a suggestion of why it was done.

It may be supposed that after this conversation there was not very much pleasure to either of them in the croquet-party, when it assembled upon the sunny lawn. Such a day as it was!—all blossoms, and brightness, and verdure, and life! the very grass growing so that one could see it, the primroses opening under your eyes, the buds shaking loose the silken foldings of a thousand leaves. The garden of the Cottage was bright with all the spring flowers that could be collected into it, and the cliff above was strewed all over with great patches of primroses, looking like planets new-dropped out of heaven. Under the shelter of that cliff, with the sunshine blazing full upon the Cottage garden, but lightly shaded as yet by the trees which had not got half their Summer garments, the atmosphere was soft and warm as June; and the girls had put on their light dresses, rivalling the flowers, and everything looked like a sudden outburst of Summer, of light, and brightness, and new existence. Though the mother and daughter had heavy hearts enough, the only cloud upon the brightness of the party was in their secret consciousness. It was not visible to the guests. Mrs. Anderson was sufficiently experienced in the world to keep her troubles to herself, and Ombra was understood to be 'not quite well,' which accounted for everything, and earned her a hundred pretty attentions and cares from the others who were joyously well, and in high spirits, feeling that Summer, and all their out-door pleasures, had come back.

Nothing could be prettier than the scene altogether. The Cottage stood open, all its doors and windows wide in the sunshine; and now and then a little group became visible from the pretty verandah, gathering about the piano in the drawing-room, or looking at something they had seen a hundred times before, with the always-ready interest of youth. Outside, upon a bench of state, with bright parasols displayed, sat two or three mothers together, who were neither old nor wrinkled, but such as (notwithstanding the presumption to the contrary) the mothers of girls of eighteen generally are, women still in the full bloom of life, and as pleasant to look upon, in their way, as their own daughters. Mrs. Anderson was there, as in duty bound, with a smile, and a pretty bonnet, smiling graciously upon her guests. Then there was the indispensable game going on on the lawn, and supplying a centre to the picture; and the girls and the boys who were not playing were wandering all about, climbing the cliff, peeping through the telescope at the sea, gathering primroses, putting themselves into pretty attitudes and groups, with an unconsciousness which made the combinations delightful. They all knew each other intimately, called each other by their Christian names, had grown up together, and were as familiar as brothers and sisters. Ombra sat in a corner, with some of the elder girls, 'keeping quiet,' as they said, on the score of being 'not quite well;' but Kate was in a hundred places at once, the very centre of the company, the soul of everything, enjoying herself, and her friends, and the sunshine, and her birthday, to the very height of human enjoyment. She was as proud of the little presents she had received that morning as if they had been of unutterable value, and eager to show them to everybody. She was at home—in Ombra's temporary withdrawal from the eldest daughter's duties, Kate, as the second daughter, took her place. It was the first time this had happened, and her long-suppressed social activity suddenly blossomed out again in full flower. With a frankness and submission which no one could have expected from her, she had accepted the second place; but now that the first had fallen to her, naturally Kate occupied that too, with a thrill of long-forgotten delight. Never in Ombra's day of supremacy had there been such a merry party. Kate inspired and animated everybody. She went about from one group to another with feet that danced and eyes that laughed, an impersonation of pleasure and of youth.

'What a change there is in Kate! Why, she is grown up—she is a child no longer!' the Rector's wife said, looking at her from under her parasol. It was the second time these words had been said that morning. Mrs. Anderson was startled by them, and she, too, looked up, and her first glance of proud satisfaction in the flower which she had mellowed into bloom was driven out of her eyes all at once by the sudden conviction which forced itself upon her. Yes, it was true—she was a child no longer. Ombra's day was over, and Kate's day had begun.

A tear forced itself into her eye with this poignant thought; she was carried away from herself, and the bright groups around her, by the alarmed consideration, what would come of it?—how would Ombra bear it?—when, suddenly looking up, she saw the neat, trim figure of an old man, following Jane, the housemaid, into the garden, with a look of mingled amazement and amusement. Instinctively she rose up, with a mixture of dignity and terror, to encounter the adversary. For of course it must be he! On that day of all days!—at that moment of all moments!—when the house was overflowing with guests, everything in disorder, Francesca's hands fully occupied, high tea in course of preparation, and no possibility of a dinner—it was on that day, we repeat, of all others, with a malice sometimes shown by Providence, that Mr. Courtenay had come!

CHAPTER XXV

With a malice sometimes shown by Providence, we have said; and we feel sure that we are but expressing what many a troubled housewife has felt, and blamed herself for feeling. Is it not on such days—days which seemed to be selected for their utter inconvenience and general wretchedness—that troublesome and 'particular' visitors always do come? When a party is going on, and all the place is in gay disorder, as now it was, is it not then that the sour and cynical guest—the person who ought to be received with grave looks and sober aspect—suddenly falls upon us, as from the unkind skies? The epicure comes when we are sitting down to cold mutton—when the tablecloth is not so fresh as it might be. Everything of this accidental kind, or almost everything, follows the same rule, and therefore it is with a certain sense of malicious intention in the untoward fate which pursues us that so many of us regard such a hazard as this which had befallen Mrs. Anderson. She rose with a feeling of impatient indignation which almost choked her. Yes, it was 'just like' what must happen. Of course it was he, because it was just the moment when he was not wanted—when he was unwelcome—of course it must be he! But Mrs. Anderson was equal to the occasion, notwithstanding the horrible consciousness that there was no room ready for him, no dinner cooked or cookable, no opportunity, even, of murmuring a word of apology. She smoothed her brows bravely, and put on her most cheerful smile.

'I am very glad to see you—I am delighted that you have made up your mind to come to see us at last,' she said, with dauntless courage.

Mr. Courtenay made her his best bow, and looked round upon the scene with raised eyebrows, and a look of criticism which went through and through her. 'I did not expect anything so brilliant,' he said, rubbing his thin hands. 'I was not aware you were so gay in Shanklin.'

Gay! If he could only have seen into her heart!

For at that very moment the two Berties had joined the party, and were standing by Ombra in her corner; and the mother's eye was drawn aside to watch them, even though this other guest stood before her. The two stood about in an embarrassed way, evidently not knowing what to do or say. They paid their respects to Ombra with a curious humility and deprecating eagerness; they looked at her as if to say, 'Don't be angry with us—we did not mean to do anything to offend you;' whereas Ombra, on her side, sat drawn back in her seat, with an air of consciousness and apparent displeasure, which Mrs. Anderson thought everybody must notice. Gay!—this was what she had to make her so; her daughter cold, estranged, pale with passion and disappointment, and an inexpressible incipient jealousy, betraying herself and her sentiments; and the young men so disturbed, so bewildered, not knowing what she meant. They lingered for a few minutes, waiting, it seemed, to see if perhaps a kinder reception might be given them, and then withdrew from Ombra with almost an expression of relief, to find more genial welcome elsewhere; while she sank back languid and silent, in a dull misery, which was lit up by jealous gleams of actual pain, watching them from under her eyelids, noting, as by instinct, everyone they spoke to or looked at. Poor Mrs. Anderson! she turned from this sight, and kept down the ache in her heart, and smiled and said,

'Gay!—oh! no; but the children like a little simple amusement, and this is Kate's birthday.' If he had but known what kind of gaiety it was that filled her!—but had he known, Mr. Courtenay fortunately would not have understood. He had outgrown all such foolish imaginations. It never would have occurred to him to torment himself as to a girl's looks; but there seemed to him much more serious matters concerned, as he looked round the pretty lawn. He had distinguished Kate now, and Kate had just met the two Berties, and was talking to them with a little flush of eagerness. Kate, like the others, did not know which Bertie it was who had thrust himself so perversely into her cousin's life; but it had seemed to her, in her self-communings on the subject, that the thing to do was to be 'very civil' to the Berties, to make the Cottage very pleasant to them, to win them back, so that Ombra might be unhappy no more. Half for this elaborate reason, and half because she was in high spirits and ready to make herself agreeable to everybody, she stood talking gaily to the two young men, with three pair of eyes upon her. When had they come?—how nice it was of them to have arrived in time for her party!—how kind of Bertie Hardwick to bring her those flowers from Langton!—and was it not a lovely day, and delightful to be out in the air, and begin Summer again!

All this Kate went through with smiles and pleasant looks, while they looked at her. Three pairs of eyes, all with desperate meaning in them. To Ombra it seemed that the most natural thing in the world was taking place. The love which she had rejected, which she had thrown away, was being transferred before her very face to her bright young cousin, who was wiser than she, and would not throw it away. It was the most natural thing in the world, but, oh, heaven, how bitter!—so bitter that to see it was death! Mrs. Anderson watched Kate with a sick consciousness of what was passing through her daughter's mind, a sense of the injustice of it and the bitterness of it, yet a poignant sympathy with poor Ombra's self-inflicted suffering.

Mr. Courtenay's ideas were very different, but he was not less impressed by the group before his eyes. And the other people about looked too, feeling that sudden quickening of interest in Kate which her guardian's visit naturally awakened. They all knew by instinct that this was her guardian who had appeared upon the scene, and that something was going to happen. Thus, all at once, the gay party turned into a drama, the secondary personages arranging themselves intuitively in the position of the chorus, looking on and recording the progress of the tale.

'I suppose Kate's guardian must have come to fetch her away. What a loss she will be to the Andersons!' whispered a neighbouring matron, full of interest, in Mrs. Eldridge's ear.

'One never can tell,' said that thoughtful woman. 'Kate is quite grown up now, and with two girls, you never know when one may come in the other's way.'

This was so oracular a sentence, that it was difficult to pick up the conversation after it; but after a while, the other went on—

'Let us take a little walk, and see what the girls are about. I understand Kate is a great heiress—she is eighteen now, is she not? Perhaps she is of age at eighteen.'

'Oh, I don't think so!' said Mrs. Eldridge. 'The Courtenays don't do that sort of thing; they are staunch old Tories, and keep up all the old traditions. But still Mr. Courtenay might think it best; and perhaps, from every point of view, it might be best. She has been very happy here; but still these kind of arrangements seldom last.'

'Ah, yes!' said the other, 'there is no such dreadful responsibility as bringing up other people's children. Sooner or later it is sure to bring dispeace.'

'And a girl is never so well anywhere,' added Mrs. Eldridge, 'as in her father's house.'

Thus far the elder chorus. The young ones said to each other, with a flutter of confused excitement and sympathy, 'Oh, what an old ogre Kate's guardian looks!' 'Has he come to carry her off, I wonder?' 'Will he eat her up if he does?' 'Is she fond of him?' Will she go to live with him when she leaves the Cottage?' 'How she stands talking and laughing to the two Berties, without ever knowing he is here!'

Mrs. Anderson interrupted all this by a word. 'Lucy,' she said, to the eldest of the Rector's girls, 'call Kate to me, dear. Her uncle is here, and wants her; say she must come at once.'

'Oh, it is her uncle!' Lucy whispered to the group that surrounded her.

'It is her uncle,' the chorus went on. 'Well, but he is an old ogre all the same!' 'Oh, look at Kate's face!' 'How surprised she is!' 'She is glad!' 'Oh, no, she doesn't like it!' 'She prefers talking nonsense to the Berties!' 'Don't talk so—Kate never flirts!' 'Oh, doesn't she flirt?' 'But you may be sure the old uncle will not stand that!'

Mr. Courtenay followed the movements of the young messenger with his eyes. He had received Mrs. Anderson's explanations smilingly, and begged her not to think of him.

'Pray, don't suppose I have come to quarter myself upon you,' he said. 'I have rooms at the hotel. Don't let me distract your attention from your guests. I should like only to have two minutes' talk with Kate.' And he stood, urbane and cynical, and looked round him, wondering whether Kate's money was paying for the entertainment, and setting down every young man he saw as a fortune-hunter. They had all clustered together like ravens, to feed upon her, he thought. 'This will never do—this will never do,' he said to himself. How he had supposed his niece to be living, it would be difficult to say; most likely he had never attempted to form any imagination at all on the subject; but to see her thus surrounded by other young people, the centre of admiration and observation, startled him exceedingly.

It was not, however, till Lucy went up to her that he quite identified Kate. There she stood, smiling, glowing, a radiant, tall, well-developed figure, with the two young men standing by. It required but little exercise of fancy to believe that both of them were under Kate's sway. Ombra thought so, looking on darkly from her corner; and it was not surprising that Mr. Courtenay should think so too. He stood petrified, while she turned round, with a flush of genial light on her face. She was glad to see him, though he had not much deserved it. She would have been glad to see any one who had come to her with the charm of novelty. With a little exclamation of pleasant wonder, she turned round, and made a bound towards him—her step, her figure, her whole aspect light as a bird on the wing. She left the young men without a word of explanation, in her old eager, impetuous way, and rushed upon him. Before he had roused himself up from his watch of her, she was by his side, putting out both her hands, holding up her peach-cheek to be kissed. Kate!—was it Kate? She was not only tall, fair, and woman grown—that was inevitable—but some other change had come over her, which Mr. Courtenay could not understand. She was a full-grown human creature, meeting him, as it were, on the same level; but there was another change less natural and more confusing, which Mr. Courtenay could make nothing of. An air of celestial childhood, such as had never been seen in Kate Courtenay, of Langton, breathed about her now. She was younger as well as older; she was what he never could have made her, what no hireling could ever have made her. She was a young creature, with natural relationships, filling a natural place in the earth, obeying, submitting, influencing, giving and receiving, loving and being loved. Mr. Courtenay, poor limited old man, did not know what it meant; but he saw the change, and he was startled. Was it—could it be Kate?

'I am so glad to see you, Uncle Courtenay. So you have really, truly come? I am very glad to see you. It feels so natural—it is like being back again at Langton. Have you spoken to auntie? How surprised she must have been! We only got your letter this morning; and I never supposed you would come so soon. If we had known, we would not have had all those people, and I should have gone to meet you. But never mind, uncle, it can't be helped. To-morrow we shall have you all to ourselves.'

'I am delighted to find you are so glad to see me,' said Mr. Courtenay. 'I scarcely thought you would remember me. But as for the enjoyment of my society, that you can have at once, Kate, notwithstanding your party. Take me round the garden, or somewhere. The others, you know, are nothing to me; but I want to have some talk with you, Kate.'

'I don't know what my aunt will think,' said Kate, somewhat discomfited. 'Ombra is not very well to-day, and I have to take her place among the people.'

'But you must come with me in the meantime. I want to talk to you.'

She lifted upon him for a moment a countenance which reminded him of the unmanageable child of Langton-Courtenay. But after this she turned round, consulted her aunt by a glance, and was back by his side instantly, with all her new youthfulness and grace.

'Come along, then,' she said, gaily. 'There is not much to show you, uncle—everything is so small; but such as it is, you shall have all the benefit. Come along, you shall see everything—kitchen-garden and all.'

And in another minute she had taken his arm, and was walking by his side along the garden path, elastic and buoyant, slim and tall—as tall as he was, which was not saying much, for the great Courtenays were not lofty of stature; and Kate's mother's family had that advantage. The blooming face she turned to him was on a level with his own; he could no longer look down upon it. She was woman grown, a creature no longer capable of being ordered about at any one's pleasure. Could this be the little wilful busybody, the crazy little princess, full of her own grandeur, the meddling little gossip, Kate?

CHAPTER XXVI

Does this sort of thing happen often?' said Mr. Courtenay, leading Kate away round the further side of the garden, much to the annoyance of the croquet players. The little kitchen-garden lay on the other side of the house, out of sight even of the pretty lawn. He was determined to have her entirely to himself.

'What sort of thing, Uncle Courtenay?'

Mr. Courtenay indicated with a jerk of his thumb over his shoulder the company they had just left.

'Oh! the croquet,' said Kate, cheerfully. 'No, not often here—more usually it is at the Rectory, or one of the other neighbours. Our lawn is so small; but sometimes, you know, we must take our turn.'

'Oh! you must take your turn, must you?' he said. 'Are all these people your Rectors, or neighbours, I should like to know?'

'There are more Eldridges than anything else,' said Kate. 'There are so many of them—and then all their cousins.'

'Ah! I thought there must be cousins,' said Mr. Courtenay. 'Do you know you have grown quite a young woman, Kate?'

'Yes, Uncle Courtenay, I know; and I hope I give you satisfaction,' she said, laughing, and making him a little curtsey.

How changed she was! Her eyes, which were always so bright; had warmed and deepened. She was beautiful in her first bloom, with the blush of eighteen coming and going on her cheeks, and the fresh innocence of her look not yet harmed by any knowledge of the world. She was eighteen, and yet she was younger as well as older than she had been at fifteen, fresher as well as more developed. The old man of the world was puzzled, and did not make it out.

'You are altered,' he said, somewhat coldly; and then, 'I understood from your aunt that you lived very quietly, saw nobody—'

'Nobody but our friends,' explained Kate.

'Friends! I suppose you think everybody that looks pleasant is your friend. Good lack! good lack!' said the Mentor. 'Why, this is society—this is dissipation. A season in town would be nothing to it.'

Kate laughed. She thought it a very good joke; and not the faintest idea crossed her mind that her uncle might mean what he said.

'Why, there are four, five, six grown-up young men,' he said, standing still and counting them as they came in sight of the lawn. 'What is that but dissipation? And what are they all doing idle about here? Six young men! And who is that girl who is so unhappy, Kate?'

'The girl who is unhappy, uncle?' Kate changed colour; the instinct of concealment came to her at once, though the stranger could have no way of knowing that there was anything to conceal. 'Oh! I see,' she added. 'You mean my cousin Ombra. She is not quite well; that is why she looks so pale.'

'I am not easily deceived,' he said. 'Look here, Kate, I am a keen observer. She is unhappy, and you are in her way.'

'I, uncle!'

'You need not be indignant. You, and no other. I saw her before you left your agreeable companions yonder. I think, Kate, you had better do your packing and come away with me.'

'With you, uncle?'

'These are not very pleasant answers. Precisely—with me. Am I so much less agreeable than that pompous aunt?'

'Uncle Courtenay, you seem to forget who I am, and all about it!' cried Kate, reddening, her eyes brightening. 'My aunt! Why, she is like my mother. I would not leave her for all the world. I will not hear a word that is not respectful to her. Why, I belong to her! You must forget—I am sure I beg your pardon, Uncle Courtenay,' she added, after a pause, subduing herself. 'Of course you don't mean it; and now that I see you are joking about my aunt, of course you were only making fun of me about Ombra too.'

'I am a likely person to make fun,' said Mr. Courtenay. 'I know nothing about your Ombras; but I am right, nevertheless, though the fact is of no importance. I have one thing to say, however, which is of importance, and that is, I can't have this sort of thing. You understand me, Kate? You are a young woman of property, and will have to move in a very different sphere. I can't allow you to begin your career with the Shanklin tea-parties. We must put a stop to that.'

'I assure you, Uncle Courtenay,' cried Kate, very gravely, and with indignant state, 'that the people here are as good as either you or I. The Eldridges are of very good family. By-the-bye, I forgot to mention, they are cousins of our old friends at the Langton Rectory—the Hardwicks. Don't you remember, uncle? And Bertie and the rest—you remember Bertie?—visit here.'

'Oh! they visit here, do they?' said Mr. Courtenay, with meaning looks.

Something kept Kate from adding, 'He is here now.' She meant to have done so, but could not, somehow. Not that she cared for Bertie, she declared loftily to herself; but it was odious to talk to any one who was always taking things into his head! So she merely nodded, and made no other reply.

'I suppose you are impatient to be back to your Eldridges, and people of good family?' he said. 'The best thing for you would be to consider all this merely a shadow, like your friend with the odd name. But I am very much surprised at Mrs. Anderson. She ought to have known better. What! must I not say as much as that?'

'Not to me, if you please, uncle,' cried Kate, with all the heat of a youthful champion.

He smiled somewhat grimly. Had the girl taken it into her foolish head to have loved him, Mr. Courtenay would have been much embarrassed by the unnecessary sentiment. But yet this foolish enthusiasm for a person on the other side of the house—for one of the mother's people, who was herself an interloper, and had really nothing to do with the Courtenay stock, struck him as a robbery from himself. He felt angry, though he was aware it was absurd.

'I shall take an opportunity, however, of making my opinion very clear,' he said, deliberately, with a pleasurable sense that at least he could make this ungrateful, unappreciative child unhappy. The latter half of this talk was held at the corner of the lawn, where the two stood together, much observed and noted by all the party. The young people all gazed at Kate's guardian with a mixture of wonder and awe. What could he be going to do to her? They felt his disapproval affect them somehow like a cold shade; and Mrs. Anderson felt it also, and was disturbed more than she would show, and once more felt vexed and disgusted indeed with Providence, which had so managed matters as to send him on such a day.

'He looks as if he were displeased,' she said to Ombra, when her daughter came near her, and she could indulge herself in a moment's confidence.

'What does it matter how he looks?' said Ombra, who herself looked miserable enough.

'My darling, it is for poor Kate's sake.'

'Oh! Kate!—always Kate! I am tired of Kate!' said Ombra, sinking down listlessly upon a seat. She had the look of being tired of all the rest of the world. Her mother whispered to her, in a tone of alarm, to bestir herself, to try to exert herself, and entertain their guests.

'People are asking me what is the matter with you already,' said poor Mrs. Anderson, distracted with these conflicting cares.

'Tell them it is temper that is the matter,' said poor Ombra. And then she rose, and made a poor attempt once more to be gay.

This, however, was not long necessary, for Kate came back, flushed, and in wild spirits, announcing that her uncle had gone, and took the whole burden of the entertainment on her own shoulders. Even this, though it was a relief to her, Ombra felt as an injury. She resented Kate's assumption of the first place; she resented the wistful looks which her cousin directed to herself, and all her caressing words and ways.

'Dear Ombra, go and rest, and I will look after these tiresome people,' Kate said, putting her arm round her.

'I don't want to rest—pray take no notice of me—let me alone!' cried Ombra. It was temper—certainly it was temper—nothing more.

'But don't think you have got rid of him, auntie, dear,' whispered Kate, in Mrs. Anderson's ear. 'He says he is coming back to-night, when all these people are gone—or if not to-night, at least to-morrow morning—to have some serious talk. Let us keep everybody as late as possible, and balk him for to-night.'

'Why should I wish to balk him, my dear?' said Mrs. Anderson, with all her natural dignity. 'He and I can have but one meeting-ground, one common interest, and that is your welfare, Kate.'

'Well, auntie, I want to balk him,' cried the girl, 'and I shall do all I can to keep him off. After tea we shall have some music,' she added, with a laugh, 'for the Berties, auntie, who are so fond of music. The Berties must stay as long as possible, and then everything will come right.'

Poor Mrs. Anderson! she shook her head with a kind of mild despair. The Berties were as painful a subject to her as Mr. Courtenay. She was driven to her wits' end. To her the disapproving look of the latter was a serious business; and if she could have done it, instead of tempting them to stay all night, she would fain have sent off the two Berties to the end of the world. All this she had to bear upon her weighted shoulders, and all the time to smile, and chat, and make herself agreeable. Thus the pretty Elysium of the Cottage—its banks of early flowers, its flush of Spring vegetation and blossom, and the gay group on the lawn—was like a rose with canker in it—plenty of canker—and seated deep in the very heart of the bloom.

But Kate managed to carry out her intention, as she generally did. She delayed the high tea which was to wind up the rites of the afternoon. When it was no longer possible to put it off, she lengthened it out to the utmost of her capabilities. She introduced music afterwards, as she had threatened—in short, she did everything an ingenious young woman could do to extend the festivities. When she felt quite sure that Mr. Courtenay must have given up all thought of repeating his visit to the Cottage, she relaxed in her exertions, and let the guests go—not reflecting, poor child, in her innocence, that the lighted windows, the music, the gay chatter of conversation which Mr. Courtenay heard when he turned baffled from the Cottage door at nine o'clock, had confirmed all his doubts, and quickened all his fears.

'Now, auntie, dear, we are safe—at least, for to-night,' she said; 'for I fear Uncle Courtenay means to make himself disagreeable. I could see it in his face—and I am sure you are not able for any more worry to-night.'

'I have no reason to be afraid of your Uncle Courtenay, my dear.'

'Oh! no—of course not; but you are tired. And where is Ombra?—Ombra, where are you? What has become of her?' cried Kate.

'She is more tired than I am—perhaps she has gone to bed. Kate, my darling, don't make her talk to-night.'

Kate did not hear the end of this speech; she had rushed away, calling Ombra through the house. There was no answer, but she saw a shadow in the verandah, and hurried there to see who it was. There, under the green climbing tendrils of the clematis, a dim figure was standing, clinging to the rustic pillar, looking out into the darkness. Kate stole behind her, and put her arm round her cousin's waist. To her amazement, she was thrust away, but not so quickly as to be unaware that Ombra was crying. Kate's consternation was almost beyond the power of speech.

'Oh! Ombra, what is wrong?—are you ill?—have I done anything? Oh! I cannot bear to see you cry!'

'I am not crying,' was the answer, in a voice made steady by pride.

'Don't be angry with me, please. Oh! Ombra, I am so sorry! Tell me what it is!' cried wistful Kate.

'It is temper,' cried Ombra, after a pause, with a sudden outburst of sobs. 'There, that is all; now leave me to myself, after you have made me confess. It is temper, temper, temper—nothing! I thought I had not any, but I have the temper of a fiend, and I am trying to struggle against it. Oh! for heaven's sake, let me alone!'

Kate took away her arm, and withdrew herself humbly, with a grieved and wondering pain in her heart. Ombra with the temper of a fiend! Ombra repulsing her, turning away from her, rejecting her sympathy! She crept to her little white bedroom, all silent, and frightened in her surprise, not knowing what to think. Was it a mere caprice—a cloud that would be over to-morrow?—was it only the result of illness and weariness? or had some sudden curtain been drawn aside, opening to her a new mystery, an unsuspected darkness in this sweet life?

CHAPTER XXVII

Long after Kate's little bedchamber had fallen into darkness, the light still twinkled in the windows of the Cottage drawing-room. The lamp was still alight at midnight, and Ombra and her mother sat together, with the marks of tears on their cheeks, still talking, discussing, going over their difficulties.

'I could bear him to go away,' Ombra had said, in her passion; 'I could bear never to see him again. Sometimes I think I should be glad. Oh! I am ashamed—ashamed to the bottom of my heart to care for one who perhaps cares no longer for me! if he would only go away; or if I could run away, and never more see him again! It is not that, mamma—it is not that. It is my own fault that I am unhappy. After what he said to me, to see him with—her! Yes, though I should die with shame, I will tell you the truth. He comes and looks at me as if I were a naughty child, and then he goes and smiles and talks to her—after all he said. Oh! it is temper, mamma, vile temper and jealousy, and I don't know what! I hate her then, and him; and I detest myself. I could kill myself, so much am I ashamed!'

'Ombra! Ombra! my darling, don't speak so!—it is so unlike you!'

'Yes,' she said, with a certain scorn, 'it is so unlike me that I was appalled at myself when I found it out. But what do you know about me, mother? How can you tell I might not be capable of anything that is bad, if I were only tempted, as well as this?'

'My darling! my darling!' said the mother, in her consternation, not knowing what to say.

'Yes,' the girl went on, 'your darling, whom you have brought up out of the reach of evil, who was always so gentle, and so quiet, and so good. I know—I remember how I have heard people speak of me. I was called Ombra because I was such a shadowy, still creature, too gentle to make a noise. Oh! how often I have heard that I was good; until I was tempted. If I were tempted to murder anybody, perhaps I should be capable of it. I feel half like it sometimes now.'

Mrs. Anderson laid her hand peremptorily on her daughter's arm.

'This is monstrous!' she said. 'Ombra, you have talked yourself into a state of excitement. I will not be sorry for you any longer. It is mere madness, and it must be brought to a close.'

'It is not madness!' she cried—'I wish it were. I sometimes hope it will come to be. It is temper!—temper! and I hate it! And I cannot struggle against it. Every time he goes near her—every time she speaks to him! Oh! it must be some devil, do you think—like the devils in the Bible—that has got possession of me?'

'Ombra, you are ill—you must go to bed,' said her mother. 'Why do you shake your head? You will wear yourself into a fever; and what is to become of me? Think a little of me. I have troubles, too, though they are not like yours. Try to turn your mind, dear, from what vexes you, and sympathise with me. Think what an unpleasant surprise to me to see that disagreeable old man; and that he should have come to-day, of all days; and the interview I shall have to undergo to-morrow—'

'Mamma,' said Ombra, with reproof in her tone, 'how strange it is that you should think of such trifles. What is he to you? A man whom you care nothing for—whom we have nothing to do with.'

'My dear,' said Mrs. Anderson, with eyes steadily fixed upon her daughter, 'I have told you before it is for Kate's sake.'

'Oh! Kate!' Ombra made a gesture of impatience. In her present mood, she could not bear her cousin's name. But her mother had been thinking over many things during this long afternoon, which had been so gay, and dragged so heavily. She had considered the whole situation, and had made up her mind, so far as it was practicable, to a certain course of action. Neither for love's sake, nor for many other considerations, could she spare Kate. Even Ombra's feelings must yield, though she had been so indiscreet even as to contemplate the idea of sacrificing Kate for Ombra's feelings. But now she had thought better of it, and had made up her mind to take it for granted that Ombra too could only feel as a sister to Kate.

'Ombra, you are warped and unhappy just now; you don't do justice either to your cousin or yourself. But even at this moment, surely you cannot have thrown aside everything; you cannot be devoid of all natural feeling for Kate.'

'I have no natural feeling,' she said, hoarsely. 'Have not I told you so? I would not allow myself to say it till you put it into my head. But, mamma, it is true. I want her out of my way. Oh! you need not look so horrified; you thought so yourself this morning. From the first, I felt she was in my way. She deranged all our plans—she came between you and me. Let her go! she is richer than we are, and better off. Why should she stay here, interfering with our life? Let her go! I want her out of my way!'

'Ombra!' said Mrs. Anderson, rising majestically from her chair. She was so near breaking down altogether, and forgetting every other consideration for her child's pleasure, that it was necessary to her to be very majestic. 'Ombra, I should have thought that proper feeling alone—Yes, proper feeling! a sense of what was fit and becoming in our position, and in hers. You turn away—you will not listen. Well, then, it is for me to act. It goes to my heart to feel myself alone like this, having to oppose my own child. But, since it must be so, since you compel me to act by myself, I tell you plainly, Ombra, I will not give up Kate. She is alone in the world; she is my only sister's only child; she is—'

Ombra put her hands to her ears in petulance and anger.

'I know,' she cried; 'spare me the rest. I know all her description, and what she is to me.'

'She is five hundred a year,' said Mrs. Anderson, secretly in her heart, with a heavy sigh, for she was ashamed to acknowledge to herself that this fact would come into the foreground. 'I will not give the poor child up,' she said, with a voice that faltered. Bitter to her in every way was this controversy, almost the first in which she had ever resisted Ombra. Though she looked majestic in conscious virtue, what a pained and faltering heart it was which she concealed under that resolute aspect! She put away the books and work-basket from the table, and lighted the candles, and screwed down the lamp with indescribable inward tremors. If she considered Ombra alone in the matter, and Ombra was habitually, invariably her first object, she would be compelled to abandon Kate, whom she loved—and loved truly!—and five hundred a year would be taken out of their housekeeping at once.

Poor Mrs. Anderson! she was not mercenary, she was fond of her niece, but she knew how much comfort, how much modest importance, how much ease of mind, was in five hundred a year. When she settled in the Cottage at first, she had made up her mind and arranged all her plans on the basis of her own small income, and had anxiously determined to 'make it do,' knowing that the task would be difficult enough. But Kate's advent had changed all that. She had brought relief from many petty cares, as well as many comforts and elegancies with her. They could have done without them before she came, but now what a difference this withdrawal would make! Ombra herself would feel it. 'Ombra would miss her cousin a great deal more than she supposes,' Mrs. Anderson said to herself, as she went upstairs; 'and, as for me, how I should miss her!' She went into Kate's room that night with a sense in her heart that she had something to make up to Kate. She had wronged her in thinking of the five hundred a year; but, for all that, she loved her. She stole into the small white chamber very softly, and kissed the sleeping face with most motherly fondness. Was it her fault that two sets of feelings—two different motives—influenced her? The shadow of Kate's future wealth, of the splendour and power to come, stood by the side of the little white bed in which lay a single individual of that species of God's creation which appeals most forcibly to all tender sympathies—an innocent, unsuspecting girl; and the shadow of worldly disinterestedness came into the room with the kind-hearted woman, who would have been good to any motherless child, and loved this one with all her heart. And it is so difficult to discriminate the shadow from the reality; the false from the true.

Mr. Courtenay came to the Cottage next morning, and had a solemn and long interview with Mrs. Anderson. Kate watched about the door, and hovered in the passages, hoping to be called in. She would have given a great deal to be able to listen at the keyhole, but reluctantly yielded to honour, which forbade such an indulgence. When she saw her uncle go away without asking for her, her heart sank; and still more did her heart sink when she perceived the solemn aspect with which her aunt came into the drawing-room. Mrs. Anderson was very solemn and stately, as majestic as she had been the night before, but there was relief and comfort in her eyes. She looked at the two girls as she came in with a smile of tenderness which looked almost like pleasure. Ombra was writing at the little table in the window—some of her poetry, no doubt. Kate, in a most restless state, had been dancing about from her needlework to her music, and from that to three or four books, which lay open, one here and one there, as she had thrown them down. When her aunt came in she stopped suddenly in the middle of the room, with a yellow magazine in her hand, almost too breathless to ask a question; while Mrs. Anderson seated herself at the table, as if in a pulpit, brimful of something to say.

'What is it, auntie?' cried Kate.

'My dear children, both of you,' said Mrs. Anderson, 'I have something very important to say to you. You may have supposed, Kate, that I did not appreciate your excellent uncle; but now that I know his real goodness of heart, and the admirable feeling he has shown—Ombra, do give up your writing for a moment. Kate, your uncle is anxious to give us all a holiday—he wishes me to take you abroad.'

'Abroad!' cried both the girls together, one in a shrill tone, as of bewilderment and desperation, one joyous as delight could make it. Mrs. Anderson expanded gradually, and nodded her head.

'For many reasons,' she said, significantly, 'your uncle and I, on talking it over, decided that the very best thing for you both would be to make a little tour. He tells me you have long wished for it, Kate. And to Ombra, too, the novelty will be of use—'

'Novelty!' said Ombra, in a tone of scorn. 'Where does he mean us to go, then? To Japan, or Timbuctoo, I suppose.'

'Not quite so far,' said her mother, trying to smile. 'We have been to a great many places, it is true, but not all the places in the world; and to go back to Italy, for instance, will be novelty, even though we have been there before. We shall go with every comfort, taking the pleasantest way. Ombra, my love!'

'Oh! you must settle it as you please,' cried Ombra, rising hastily. She put her papers quickly together; then, with her impetuous movements, swept half of them to the ground, and rushed to the door, not pausing to pick them up. But there she paused, and turned round, her face pale with passion. 'You know you don't mean to consult me,' she said, hurriedly. 'What is the use of making a pretence? You must settle it as you please.'

'What is the matter?' said Kate, after she had disappeared, growing pale with sympathy. 'Oh! auntie dear, what is the matter? She was never like this before.'

'She is ill, poor child,' said the mother, who was distracted, but dared not show it. And then she indulged herself in a few tears, giving an excuse for them which betrayed nothing. 'Oh! Kate, what will become of me if there is anything serious the matter? She is ill, and I don't know what to do!'

'Send for the doctor, aunt,' suggested Kate.

'The doctor can do nothing, dear. It is a—a complaint her father had. She would not say anything to the doctor. She has been vexed and bothered—'

'Then this is the very thing for her,' said Kate. 'This will cure her. They say change is good for every one. We have been so long shut up in this poky little place.'

On other occasions Kate had sworn that the island and the cottage were the spots in all the world most dear to her heart. This was the first effect of novelty upon her. She felt, in a moment, that her aspirations were wide as the globe, and that she had been cooped up all her life.

'Yes,' said Mrs. Anderson, fervently, 'I have felt it. We have not been living, we have been vegetating. With change she will be better. But it is illness that makes her irritable. You must promise me to be very gentle and forbearing with her, Kate.'

'I gentle and forbearing to Ombra!' cried Kate, half laughing, half crying—'I! When I think what a cub of a girl I must have been, and how good—how good you both were! Surely everybody in the world should fail you sooner than I!'

'My dear child,' said Mrs. Anderson, kissing her with true affection; and once more there was a reason and feasible excuse for the tears of pain and trouble that would come to her eyes.

The plan was perfect—everything that could be desired; but if Ombra set her face against it, it must come to nothing. It was with this thought in her mind that she went upstairs to her troublesome and suffering child.

CHAPTER XXVIII

Ombra, however, did not set her face against it. What difficulty the mother might have had with her, no one knew, and she appeared no more that day, having 'a bad headache,' that convenient cause for all spiritual woes. But next morning, when she came down, though her face was pale, there was no other trace in her manner of the struggle her submission had cost her, and the whole business was settled, and even the plan of the journey had begun to be made. Already, in this day of Ombra's retirement, the news had spread far and wide. Kate had put on her hat directly, and had flown across to the Rectory to tell this wonderful piece of news. It was scarcely less interesting there than in the Cottage, though the effect was different. The Eldridges raised a universal wail.

'Oh, what shall we do without you?' cried the girls and the boys—a reflection which almost brought the tears to Kate's own eyes, yet pleased her notwithstanding.

'You will not mind so much when you get used to it. We shall miss you as much as you miss us—oh, I wish you were all coming with us!' she cried; but Mrs. Eldridge poured cold water on the whole by suggesting that probably Mrs. Anderson would let the Cottage for the Summer, and that some one who was nice might take it and fill up the vacant place till they came back; which was an idea not taken in good part by Kate.

On her way home she met Mr. Sugden and told him; she told him in haste, in the lightness of her heart and the excitement of the moment; and then, petrified by the effect she had produced, stood still and stared at him in alarm and dismay.

'Oh, Mr. Sugden! I am sure I did not mean—I did not think—'

'Going away?' he said, in a strange, dull, feelingless way. 'Ah! for six months—I beg your pardon—I am a little confused. I have just heard some—some bad news. Did you say going away?'

'I am so sorry,' said Kate, faltering, 'so very sorry. I hope it is not anything I have said—'

'You have said?' he answered, with a dull smile, 'oh, no! I have had bad news, and I am a little upset. You are going away? It is sudden, is it not?—or perhaps you thought it best not to speak. Shanklin will look odd without you,' he went on, looking at her. He looked at her with a vague defiance, as if daring her to find him out. He tried to smile; his eyes were very lacklustre and dull, as if all the vision had suddenly been taken out of them; and his very attitude, as he stood, was feeble, as if a sudden touch might have made him fall.

'Yes,' said Kate, humbly, 'I am sorry to leave Shanklin and all my friends; but my uncle wishes it for me, and as Ombra is so poorly, we thought it might do her good.'

'Ah!' he said, drawing a long breath; and then he added hurriedly, 'Does she like it? Does she think it will do her good?'

'I don't think she likes it at all,' said Kate, 'she is so fond of home; but we all think it is the best thing. Good-bye, Mr. Sugden. I hope you will come and see us. I must go home now, for I have so much to do.'

'Yes, thanks. I will come and see you,' said the Curate. And then he walked on mechanically—straight on, not knowing where he was going. He was stunned by the blow. Though he knew very well that Ombra was not for him, though he had seen her taken, as it were, out of his very hands, there was a passive strength in his nature which made him capable of bearing this. So long as no active step was taken, he could bear it. It had gone to his heart with a penetrating anguish by times to see her given up to the attentions of another, receiving, as he thought, the love of another, and smiling upon it. But all the while she had smiled also upon himself; she had treated him with a friendly sweetness which kept him subject; she had filled his once unoccupied and languid soul with a host of poignant emotions. Love, pain, misery, consolation—life itself, seemed to have come to him from Ombra. Before he knew her, he had thought pleasantly of cricket and field-sports, conscientiously of his duties, piteously of the mothers' meetings, which were so sadly out of his way, and yet were supposed to be duty too.

But Ombra had opened to him another life—an individual world, which was his, and no other man's. She had made him very unhappy and very glad; she had awakened him to himself. There was that in him which would have held him to her with a pathetic devotion all his life. It was in him to have served the first woman that woke his heart with an ideal constancy, the kind of devotion—forgive the expression, oh, intellectual reader!—which makes a dull man sublime, and which dull men most often exhibit. He was not clever, our poor Curate, but he was true as steel, and had a helpless, obstinate way of clinging to his loves and friendships. Never, whatever happened, though she had married, and even though he had married, and the world had rolled on, and all the events of life had sundered them, could Ombra have been to him like any other woman; and now she was the undisputed queen and mistress of his life. She was never to be his; but still she was his lady and his queen. He was ready to have saved her even by the sacrifice of all idea of personal happiness on his own part. His heart was glowing at the present moment with indignant sorrow over her, with fury towards one of the Berties—he did not know which—who had brought a mysterious shadow over her life; and yet he was capable of making an heroic effort to bring back that Bertie, and to place him by Ombra's side, though every step he took in doing so would be over his own heart.

All this was in him; but it was not in him to brave this altogether unthought-of catastrophe. To have her go away; to find himself left with all life gone out of him; to have the heart torn, as it were, out of his breast; and to feel the great bleeding, aching void which nothing could fill up. He had foreseen all the other pain, and was prepared for it; but for this he was not prepared. He walked straight on, in a dull misery, without the power to think. Going away!—for six months! Which meant simply for ever and ever. Where he would have stopped I cannot tell, for he was young and athletic, and capable of traversing the entire island, if he had not walked straight into the sea over the first headland which came in his way—a conclusion which would not have been disagreeable to him in the present state of his feelings, though he could scarcely have drowned had he tried. But fortunately he met the Berties ere he had gone very far. They were coming from Sandown Pier.

'Have you got the yacht here?' he asked, mechanically; and then, before they could understand, broke into the subject of which his heart and brain were both full. 'Have you heard that the ladies of the Cottage are going away?'

This sudden introduction of the subject which occupied him so much was indeed involuntary. He could not have helped talking about it; but at the same time it was done with a purpose—that he might, if possible, make sure which it was.

'The ladies at the Cottage!' They both made this exclamation in undeniable surprise. And he could not help, even in his misery, feeling a little thrill of satisfaction that he knew better than they.

'Yes,' he said, made bolder by this feeling of superiority, 'they are going to leave Shanklin for six months.'

The two Berties exchanged looks. He caught their mutual consultation with his keen and jealous eyes. What was it they said to each other? He was not clever enough to discover; but Bertie Hardwick drew a long breath, and said, 'It is sudden, surely,' with an appearance of dismay which Mr. Sugden, in his own suffering, was savagely glad to see.

'Very sudden,' he said. 'I only heard it this morning. It will make a dreadful blank to us.'

And then the three stood gazing at each other for nearly a minute, saying nothing; evidently the two cousins did not mean to commit themselves. Bertie Eldridge switched his boot with his cane. 'Indeed!' had been all he said; but he looked down, and did not meet the Curate's eye.

'Have you got the yacht here!' Mr. Sugden repeated, hoping that if he seemed to relax his attention something might be gained.

'Yes, she is lying at the pier, ready for a long cruise,' said Bertie Hardwick. 'We are more ambitious than last year. We are going to—'

'Norway, I think,' said Eldridge, suddenly. 'There is no sport to be had now but in out-of-the-way places. We are bound for Scandinavia, Sugden. Can you help us? I know you have been there.'

'Scandinavia!' the other Bertie echoed, with a half whistle, half exclamation; and an incipient smile came creeping about the corners of the brand-new moustache of which he was so proud.

'I am rather out of sorts to-day,' said the Curate. 'I have had disagreeable news from home; but another time I shall be very glad. Scandinavia! Is the "Shadow" big enough and steady enough for the northern seas?'

And then, as he pronounced the name, it suddenly occurred to him why the yacht was called the 'Shadow.' The thought brought with it a poignant sense of contrast, which went through and through him like an arrow. They could call their yacht after her, paying her just such a subtle, inferred compliment as girls love. And they could go away now, lucky fellows, to new places, to savage seas, where they might fight against the elements, and delude their sick hearts (if they possessed such things) by a struggle with nature. Poor Curate!—he had to stay and superintend the mothers' meetings—which also was a struggle with nature, though after a different kind.

'Oh! she will do very well,' said Bertie Eldridge, hastily. 'Look sharp, Bertie, here is the dogcart. We are going to Ryde for a hundred things she wants. I shall send her round there to-morrow. Will you come!'

'I can't,' said the Curate, almost rudely. And then even his unoffending hand seized upon a dart that lay in his way. 'How does all this yachting suit your studies?' he said.

Bertie Hardwick laughed. 'It does not suit them at all,' he said, jumping into the dogcart. 'Good-bye, old fellow. I think you should change your mind, and come with us to-morrow!'

'I won't,' said the Curate, under his breath. But they did not hear him; they dashed off in very good spirits, apparently nowise affected by his news. As for Mr. Sugden, he ground his teeth in secret. That which he would have given his life, almost his soul for, had been thrown away upon one of these two—and to them it was as nothing. It did not cloud their looks for more than a minute, if indeed it affected them at all; whereas to him it was everything. They were the butterflies of life; they had it in their power to pay pretty compliments, to confer little pleasures, but they were not true to death, as he was. And yet Ombra would never find that out; she would never know that his love—which she did not even take the trouble to be conscious of—was for life and death, and that the other's was an affair of a moment. They had driven off laughing; they had not even pretended to be sorry for the loss which the place was about to suffer. It was no loss to them. What did they care? They were heartless, miserable, without sense or feeling; yet one of them was Ombra's choice.

This incident, however, made Mr. Sugden take his way back to the village. He had walked a great deal further than he had any idea of, and had forgotten all about the poor women who were waiting with their subscriptions for the penny club. And it chafed him, poor fellow, to have to go into the little dull room, and to take the pennies. 'Good heavens! is this all I am good for?' he said to himself. 'Is there no small boy or old woman who could manage it better than I? Was this why the good folks at home spent so much money on me, and so much patience?' Poor young Curate, he was tired and out of heart, and he was six feet high and strong as a young lion; yet there seemed nothing in heaven or earth for him to do but to keep the accounts of the penny club and visit the almshouses. He had done that very placidly for a long time, having the Cottage always to fall back upon, and being a kindly, simple soul at bottom—but now! Were there no forests left to cut down? no East-end lanes within his reach to give him something to fight with and help him to recover his life?

CHAPTER XXIX

The Berties drove away laughing, but when they had got quite out of the Curate's sight, Bertie Eldridge turned to his cousin with indignation.

'How could you be such an ass?' he said. 'You were just going to let out that the yacht was bound for the Mediterranean, and then, of course, their plans would have been instantly changed.'

'You need not snap me up so sharply,' said the other; 'I never said a word about the Mediterranean, and if I had he would have taken no notice. What was it to him, one way or another? I see no good in an unnecessary fib.'

'What was it to him? How blind you are! Why it is as much to him as it is—Did you never find that out?'

'You don't mean to say,' said the other Bertie, with confusion. 'But, by Jove, I might have known, and that's how he found out! He is not such a slow beggar as he looks. Did you hear that about my studies? I dare say he said it with a bad motive, but he has reason, heaven knows! My poor studies!'

'Nonsense! You can't apply adjectives, my dear fellow, to what does not exist.'

'That is all very well for you,' said Bertie Hardwick. 'You have no occasion to trouble yourself. You can't come to much harm. But I am losing my time and forming habits I ought not to form, and disappointing my parents, and all that. You know it, Bertie, and I know it, and even such a dull, good-humoured slug as Sugden sees it. I ought not to go with you on this trip—that is as plain as daylight.'

'Stuff!' said the other Bertie.

'It is not stuff. He was quite right. I ought not to go, and I won't!'

'Look here,' said the other; 'if you don't, you'll be breaking faith with me. You know we have always gone halves in everything all our lives. We are not just like any two other fellows; we are not even like brothers. Sometimes I think we have but one soul between us. You are pledged to me, and I to you, for whatever may happen. If it is harm, we will share it; and if it is good, why there is no telling what advantages to you may be involved as well. You cannot forsake me, Bertie; it would be a treachery not only to me, but to the very nature of things.'

Bertie Hardwick shook his head; a shade of perplexity crossed his face.

'I never was your equal in argument, and never will be,' he said, 'and, besides, you have certain stock principles which floor a fellow. But it is no use struggling; I suppose it is my fate. And a very jolly fate, to tell the truth; though what the people at home will say, and all my godfathers and godmothers, who vowed I was to be honest and industrious, and work for my living—'

'I don't much believe in that noble occupation,' said the other; 'but meantime let us think over what we want at Ryde, which is a great deal more important. Going abroad! I wonder if the old fellow was thinking of you and me when he signed that sentence. It is the best thing, the very best, that could have happened. Everything will be new, and yet there will be the pleasure of bringing back old associations and establishing intercourse afresh. How lucky it is! Cheer up, Bertie. I feel my heart as light as a bird.'

'Mine is like a bird that is fluttering just before its fall,' said Bertie, with gravity which was half mock and half real, shaking his head.

'You envy me my good spirits,' said his companion, 'and I suppose there is not very much ground for them. Thank heaven I don't offend often in that way. It is more your line than mine. But I do feel happier about the chief thing of all than I have done since Easter. Courage, old boy; we'll win the battle yet.'

Bertie Hardwick shook his head again.

'I don't think I shall ever win any battle,' he said, dolorously; 'but, in the meantime, here's the list for fitting out the "Shadow." I suppose you think more of that now than of anything else.'

The other Bertie laughed long and low at his cousin's mournful tone; but they were soon absorbed in the lists, as they bowled along towards Ryde, with a good horse, and a soft breeze blowing in their faces. All the seriousness dispersed from Bertie Hardwick's face as they went on—or rather a far more solemn seriousness came over it as he discussed the necessity of this and that, and all the requirements of the voyage. Very soon he forgot all about the momentary curb that had stopped his imagination in full course. 'My studies!' he said, when the business of the day was over, with a joyous burst of laughter more unhesitating even than his cousin's. He had surmounted that little shock, and his amusement was great at the idea of being reproached with neglect of anything so entirely nominal. He had taken his degree, just saving it, with no honour, nor much blame either; and now for a whole year he had been afloat in the world, running hither and thither, as if that world were but one enormous field of amusement. He ought not to have done so. When he decided to give up the Church, he ought, as everybody said, to have turned his mind to some other profession; and great and many were the lamentations over his thoughtlessness in the Rectory of Langton-Courtenay. But somehow the two Berties had always been as one in the minds of all their kith and kin; and even the Hardwicks regarded with a vague indulgence the pleasant idleness which was thus shared. Sir Herbert Eldridge was rich, and had influence and patronage, and the other Bertie was his only son. It would be no trouble to him to provide 'somehow' for his nephew when the right moment came. And thus, though the father and mother shook their heads, and Mrs. Hardwick would sometimes sigh over the waste of Bertie's abilities and his time, yet they had made no very earnest remonstrances up to this moment; and all had gone on merrily, and all had seemed well.

That evening, however, as it happened, he received an energetic letter on the subject from his father—a letter pointing out to him the folly of thus wasting his best years. Mr. Hardwick reminded his son that he was three-and-twenty, that he had his way to make in the world, and that it was his duty to make up his mind how he was going to do it.

'I don't insist upon the Church,' he said, 'if your mind is not inclined that way—for that is a thing I would never force; but I cannot see you sink into a state of dependence. Your cousin is very kind; but you ought, and you must know it, to be already in the way of supporting yourself.'

Bertie wrote an answer to this letter at once that evening, without waiting to take counsel of the night; perhaps he felt that it was safe to do it at once, while the idea of work still looked and felt like a good joke. This was his reply:—

'MY DEAR FATHER,

'I am very sorry to see that you feel so strongly about my idleness. I know I am an idle wretch, and always was; but it can't last, of course; and after this bout I will do my best to mend. The fact is that for this cruise I am pledged to Bertie. I should be behaving very shabbily to him, after all his kindness, if I threw him over at the last moment. And, besides, we don't go without an object, neither he nor I, of which you will hear anon. I cannot say more now. Give my love to Mamma and the girls; and don't be vexed if I find there is no time to run home before we start. I shall write from the first port we touch at. Home without fail before Christmas. Good-bye.

'Yours affectionately, H. H.'

Bertie was much pleased with this effusion; and even when he read it over in the morning, though it did not appear to strike so perfectly the golden line between seriousness and levity as it had appeared to do at night, it was still a satisfactory production. And it pleased him, in the vanity of his youth, to have made the obscure yet important suggestion that his voyage was 'not without an object.' What would they all think if they ever found out what that object was? He laughed at the thought, though with a tinge of heightened colour. The people at home would suppose that some great idea had come to the two—that they were going on an antiquarian or a scientific expedition; for Bertie Eldridge was a young man full of notions, and had made attempts in both these branches of learning. Bertie laughed at this very comical idea; but though he was thus satisfied with his own cleverness in baffling his natural guardians, there was a single drop of shame, a germ of bitterness, somewhere at the bottom of his heart. He could fence gaily with his father, and forget the good advice which came to him from those who had a right to give it; but that chance dart thrown by the Curate had penetrated a weak point in his armour. Mr. Sugden's suggestion, who was a young man on his own level, a fellow whom he had laughed at, and had no lofty opinion of, clung to him like an obstinate bit of thistledown. It was of no consequence, said with an intention to wound—a mere spiteful expression of envy; but it clung to him, and pricked him vaguely, and made him uncomfortable, in spite of himself.

For Bertie was only thoughtless, not selfish. He was running all the risks involved by positive evil in his levity; but he did not mean it. Had he known what real trouble was beginning to rise in the minds of his 'people' in respect to him, and how even his uncle Sir Herbert growled at the foolish sacrifice he was making, Bertie had manhood enough to have pulled himself up, and abandoned those delights of youth. And indeed a certain uneasiness had begun to appear faintly in his own mind—a sense that his life was not exactly what it might be, which, of itself, might have roused him to better things. But temptation was strong, and life was pleasant; and at twenty-three there still seems so much of it to come, and such plenty of time to make amends for all one's early follies. Then there were a hundred specious excuses for him, which even harder judges than he acknowledged. From their cradles, his cousin Bertie and himself had been as one—they had been born on the same day; they had taken every step of their lives together; they resembled each other as twin brothers sometimes do; and something still more subtle, still more fascinating, than the bond between twin-brothers existed between them. This had been the admiration of their respective families when they were children; and it was with some pride that Lady Eldridge and Mrs. Hardwick had told their friends of the curious sympathy between the boys; how when one was ill, the other was depressed and wretched, though his cousin was at a distance from him, and he had no knowledge, except by instinct, of the malady.

'We know directly when anything is wrong with the other Bertie,' the respective mothers would say, with that pride which mothers feel in any peculiarity of their children.

This strange tie was strengthened by their education; they went to school together on the same day; they kept side by side all through, and though one Bertie might be at the head of the form and another at the bottom, still in the same form they managed to keep, all tutors, masters, and aids to learning promoting, so far as in them lay, the twinship, which everybody found 'interesting.' And they went to the same college, and day for day, and side by side, took every successive step. Bertie Eldridge was the cleverest; it was he who was always at the top; and then he was—a fact which he much plumed himself upon—the eldest by six hours, and accordingly had a right to be the guide and teacher. Thus the very threads of their lives were twisted so close together that it was a difficult thing to pull them asunder; and though all the older people had come by this time to regret the natural weakness which had prompted them to allow this bond to knit itself closer with every year of life, none of them had yet hit upon a plan for breaking it. The reader will easily perceive what a fatal connection this was for the poorer of the two—he who had to make his own way, and had no hereditary wealth to fall back upon. For Bertie Eldridge it was natural and suitable, and as innocent and pleasant as a life without an object can be; but for Bertie Hardwick it was destruction. However, it was difficult, very difficult, for him to realise this. He laughed at his father's remonstrances, even while he assented to them, and allowed that they were perfectly true; yes, everything that was said was quite true—and yet the life itself was so natural, so inevitable. How could he tear himself from it—'break faith with Bertie?' He resolved indefinitely that some time or other it would have to be done, and then plunged, with a light heart, into the victualling and the preparation of the 'Shadow.' But, nevertheless, that arrow of Mr. Sugden's stuck between the joints of his armour. He felt it prick him when he moved; he could not quite forget it, do what he would.

CHAPTER XXX

The next day the whole population of the place surged in and out of the Cottage, full of regrets and wonders. 'Are you really going?' the ladies said, 'so soon? I suppose it was quite a sudden idea? And how delightful for you!—but you can't expect us to be pleased. On the contrary, we are all inconsolable. I don't know what we shall do without you. How long do you intend to stay away?'

'Nothing is settled,' said Mrs. Anderson, blandly. 'We are leaving ourselves quite free. I think it is much better not to be hampered by any fixed time for return.'

'Oh, much better!' said the chorus. 'It is such a bore generally; just when one is beginning to know people, and to enjoy oneself, one has to pack up and go away; but there are few people, of course, who are so free as you are, dear Mrs. Anderson—you have no duty to call you back. And then you know the Continent so well, and how to travel, and all about it. How I envy you! But it will be such a loss for us. I don't know what we shall do all the Summer through without you and dear Ombra and Kate. All our picnics, and our water-parties, and our croquet, and everything—I don't know what we shall do—'

'I suppose you will let the Cottage for the summer?' said Mrs. Eldridge, who was of a practical mind; 'and I hope nice people may come. That will be always some consolation for the rest of us; and we cannot grudge our friends their holiday, can we?' she added, with fine professional feeling, reading a mild lesson to her parishioners, to which everybody replied, with a flutter of protestation, 'Oh, of course not, of course not!'

Mr. Courtenay assisted at the little ceremonial. He sat all the afternoon in an easy-chair by the window, noting everything with a smile. The tea-table was in the opposite corner, and from four till six there was little cessation in the talk, and in the distribution of cups of tea. He sat and looked on, making various sardonic remarks to himself. Partly by chance, and partly by intention, he had drawn his chair close to that of Ombra, who interested him. He was anxious to understand this member of the household, who gave Kate no caresses, who did nothing to conciliate or please her, but rather spoke sharply to her when she spoke at all. He set this down frankly and openly as jealousy, and determined to be at the bottom of it. Ombra was not a 'locust.' She was much more like a secret enemy. He made up his mind that there was some mischief between them, and that Ombra hated the girl whom everybody else, from interested motives, pretended to love; therefore, he tried to talk to her, first, because her gloom amused him, and second, that he might have a chance of finding something out.

'I have been under a strange delusion,' he said. 'I thought there was but a very small population in the Isle of Wight.'

'Indeed, I don't know what the number is,' said Ombra.

'I should say it must be legion. The room has been three times filled, and still the cry is, they come! And yet I understand you live very quietly, and this is an out-of-the-way place. Places which are in the way must have much more of it. It seems to be that Mayfair is less gay.'

'I don't know Mayfair.'

'Then you have lived always in the country,' said Mr. Courtenay, blandly. This roused Ombra. She could have borne a graver imputation better, but to be considered a mere rustic, a girl who knew nothing!—

'On the contrary, I have lived very little in the country,' she said, with a tone of irritation. 'But then the towns I have lived in have belonged to a different kind of society than that which, I suppose, you meet with in Mayfair. I have lived in Madrid, Lisbon, Genoa, and Florence—'

'Ah! in your father's time,' said Mr. Courtenay, gently. And the sound of his voice seemed to say to Ombra, 'In the Consul's time! Yes, to be sure. Just the sort of places he would be sure to live in.' Which exasperated her more than she dared show.

'Yes, that was our happy time!' she cried, hotly. 'The time when we were free of all interference. My father was honoured and loved by everybody.'

'Oh! I don't doubt it, I don't doubt it,' said Mr. Courtenay, hurriedly, for she looked very much as if she might be going to cry. 'Spain is very interesting, and so is Italy. It will be pleasant for you to go back.'

'I don't think it will,' she said, bluntly. 'Things will be so different.' And then, after a pause, she added, with nervous haste, 'Kate may like it, perhaps, but not I.'

Mr. Courtenay thought it best to pause. He had no wish to be made a confidant, or to have Ombra's grievances against Kate poured into his ears. He leaned back in his chair, and watched with grim amusement while the visitors went and came. Mr. Sugden had come in while he had been talking, and was now to be seen standing like a tall shadow by the other side of the window, looking down upon Ombra; and a nervous expectation had become visible in her, which caught Mr. Courtenay's eye. She did not look up when the door opened, but, on the contrary, kept her eyes fixed on the work she held in her hand with a rigidity which betrayed her more than curiosity would have done. She would not look up, but she listened with a hot, hectic flush on the upper part of her cheeks, just under her drooped eyelids, holding her breath, and sitting motionless in the suspense which devoured her. The needle shook in her hand, and all the efforts she made to keep it steady did but reveal the more the excitement of all her nerves. Mr. Courtenay watched her with growing curiosity; he was not sympathetic; but it was something new to him and entertaining, and he watched as if he had been at a theatre. He did not mean to be cruel; it was to him like a child's fit of pouting. It was something about love, no doubt, he said to himself. Poor little fool! Somebody had interfered with her love—her last plaything; perhaps Kate, who looked very capable of doing mischief in such matters; and how unhappy she was making herself about nothing at all!

At last the anxiety came to a sudden stop; the hand gave one jerk more violent than before; the eyes shot out a sudden gleam, and then Ombra was suddenly, significantly still. Mr. Courtenay looked up, and saw that two young men had come into the room, so much like each other that he was startled, and did not know what to make of it. As he looked up, with an incipient smile on his face, he caught the eye of the tall Curate on the other side of the window, who was looking at him threateningly. 'Good heavens! what have I done?' said Mr. Courtenay to himself, much amazed. 'I have not fallen in love with the irresistible Ombra!' He was still more entertained when he discovered that the look which he had thus intercepted was on its way to the new comers, whom Ombra did not look at, but whose coming had affected her so strangely. Here was an entire drama in the smallest possible space. An agitated maiden on the eve of parting with her lover; a second jealous lover looking on. 'Thank heaven it is not Kate!' Mr. Courtenay said from the bottom of his heart. The sight of this little scene made him feel more and more the danger from which he had escaped. He had escaped it, but only by a hair's-breadth; and, thank the kind fates, was looking on with amusement at a story which did not concern him; not with dismay and consternation at a private embarrassment and difficulty of his own. This sense of a hairbreadth escape gave the little spectacle zest. He looked on with genuine amusement, like a true critic, delighted with the show of human emotion which was taking place before his eyes.

'Who are these two young fellows?' he asked Ombra, determined to have the whole advantage of the situation, and draw her out to the utmost of his power.

'What two?' she said, looking up suddenly, with a dull red flush on her cheek and a choked voice. 'Oh! they are Mr. Hardwick and Mr. Eldridge; two—gentlemen—mamma knows.'

They were both talking to Kate, standing one on either side of her in the middle of the room. Ombra gave them a long intent look, with the colour deepening in her face, and the breath coming quick from her lips. She took in the group in every detail, as if it had been drawn in lines of fire. How unconscious Kate looked standing there, talking easily, in all the freedom of her unawakened youth. 'Heaven be praised!' thought Mr. Courtenay once more, pious for the first time in his life.

'What! not brothers? What a strange likeness, then!' he said, tranquilly. 'I suppose one of them is young Hardwick, from Langton-Courtenay, whom Kate knew at home. He is a parson, like his father, I suppose?'

'No,' said Ombra, dropping her eyes once more upon her work.

'Not a parson? That is odd, for the elder son, I know, has gone to the Bar. I suppose he has relations here? Kate and he have met before?'

'Yes.'

It was all that Ombra could say; but in her heart she added, 'Always Kate—Kate knew him—Kate has met him! Is there nobody, then, but Kate in the world to be considered. They think so too.'

The old man, for the first time, had a little pity. He asked no more questions, seeing that she was past all power of answering them; and half in sympathy, half in curiosity, drew his chair back a little, and left the new-comers room to approach. When they did so, after some minutes, Ombra's feverish colour suddenly forsook her cheeks, and she grew very pale. Bertie Eldridge was the first to speak. He came up with a little air of deprecation and humility, which Mr. Courtenay, not knowing the fin mot of the enigma, did not understand.

'I am so sorry to hear you are going away,' he said. 'Is it not very sudden, Miss Anderson? You did not speak of it on Wednesday, I think.'

'Did I see you on Wednesday?' said Ombra. 'Oh! I beg your pardon, I know you were here; but I did not think we had any talk.'

'A little, I believe,' said the young man, colouring. His self-possession seemed to fail him, which was amazing to Mr. Courtenay, for the young men of the period do not often fail in self-possession. He got confused, spoke low, and faltered something about knowing he had no right to be told.

'No,' she replied, with nervous colour and a flash of sudden pride; 'out of our own little cottage I do not know anyone who has a right to be consulted—or cares either,' she added, in an undertone.

'Miss Anderson, you cannot think that!'

'Ah, but I do!' Then there was a little pause; and after some moments, Ombra resumed: 'Kate's movements are important to many people. She will be a great lady, and entitled to have her comings and goings recorded in the newspapers; but we have no such claim upon the public interest. It does not matter to any one, so far as I know, whether we go or stay.'

A silence again. Ombra bent once more over her work, and her needle flew through it, working as if for a wager. The other Bertie, who was behind, had been moving about, in mere idleness, the books on Ombra's writing-table. At him she suddenly looked up with a smile—

'Please, Mr. Hardwick! all my poor papers and books which I have just been putting in order—don't scatter them all over the table again.'

'I beg your pardon,' he said, looking up. He had borne the air of the stage-confidant, till that moment, in Mr. Courtenay's eyes, which were those of a connoisseur in such matters. But now his belief on this subject was shaken. When he glanced up and saw the look which was exchanged by the two, and the gloom with which Mr. Sugden was regarding both, a mist seemed to roll away from the scene. How different the girl's aspect was now!—soft with a dewy brightness in her eyes, and a voice that trembled with some concealed agitation; and there was a glow upon Bertie's face, which made him handsomer. 'My cousins are breaking their hearts over your going,' he said.

'Oh, no fear of their hearts!' said Ombra, lightly; 'they will mend. If the Cottage is let, the new tenants will probably be gayer people than we are, and do more to amuse their neighbours. And if we come back—'

'If?' said the young man.

'Nothing is certain, I suppose, in this world—or, at least, so people say.'

'It is very true,' said Mr. Courtenay. 'It is seldom a young lady is so philosophical—but, as you say, if you come back in a year, the chances are you will find your place filled up, and your friends changed.'

Ombra turned upon him with sparks of fire suddenly flashing from her eyes. Philosopher, indeed!—say termagant, rather.

'It is vile and wretched and horrible to say so!' she cried; 'but I suppose it is true.'

And all this time the tall Curate never took his eyes off the group, but stood still and listened and watched. Mr. Courtenay began to feel very uncomfortable. The scene was deadly real, and not as amusing as he had hoped.

CHAPTER XXXI

In the little bustle of preparation which ensued, there was, of course, a good deal of dressmaking to do, and Miss Richardson, the dressmaker from the village, who was Mr. Sugden's landlady, was almost a resident at the Cottage for the following week. She set out every morning in her close black bonnet and black shawl, with her little parcel of properties—including the last fashion book, done up in a very tight roll. She helped Maryanne, and she helped Francesca, who was more difficult to deal with; and she was helped in her turn by the young ladies themselves, who did not disdain the task. It was very pleasant to Miss Richardson, who was a person of refined tastes, to find herself in such refined society. She was never tired remarking what a pleasure it was to talk to ladies who could understand you, and who were not proud, and took an interest in their fellow creatures; and it was during this busy week that Kate acquired that absolute knowledge of Miss Richardson's private history with which she enlightened her friends at a later period. She sat and sewed and talked in the little parlour which served for Kate's studies, and for many other miscellaneous purposes; and it was there, in the midst of all the litter of dressmaking, that Mrs. Anderson and the girls took their afternoon tea, and that even Mrs. Eldridge and some other intimate friends were occasionally introduced. Mrs. Eldridge knew Miss Richardson intimately, as was natural, and liked to hear from her all that was going on in the village; but the dressmaker's private affairs were not of much interest to the Rector's wife—it required a lively and universal human interest like Kate's to enter into such details.

It was only on the last evening of her labours, however, that Miss Richardson made so bold as to volunteer a little private communication to Mrs. Anderson. The girls had gone out into the garden, after a busy day. All was quiet in the soft April evening; even Mr. Sugden had not come that night. They were all alone, feeling a little excited by the coming departure, a little wearied with their many occupations, a little sad at the thought of leaving the familiar place. At least, such were Mrs. Anderson's feelings, as she stood in the verandah looking out. It was a little more than twilight, and less than night. Ombra was standing in a corner of the low garden wall, looking out upon the sea. Kate was not visible—a certain wistfulness, sadness, farewell feeling, seemed about in the very air. What may have happened before we come back? Mrs. Anderson sighed softly, with this thought in her mind. But she was not unhappy. There was enough excitement in the new step about to be taken to keep all darker shades of feeling in suspense. 'If I might make so bold, ma'am,' said Miss Richardson, suddenly, by her side.

Mrs. Anderson started, but composed herself immediately. 'Surely,' she said, with her habitual deference to other people's wishes. The dressmaker coughed, cleared her throat, and made two or three inarticulate beginnings. At length she burst forth—

'The comfort of speaking to a real lady is, as she don't mistake your meaning, nor bring it up against you after. I'm not one as interferes in a general way. I do think, Mrs. Anderson, ma'am, as I'm well enough known in Shanklin to take upon me to say that. But my heart does bleed for my poor young gentleman; and I must say, even if you should be angry, whatever he is to do, when you and the young ladies go away, is more than I can tell. When I saw his face this morning, though he's a clergyman, and as good as gold, the thing as came into my head—and I give you my word for it, ma'am—was as he'd do himself some harm.'

'You mean Mr. Sugden? I do not understand this at all,' said Mrs. Anderson, who had found time to collect herself. 'Why should he do himself any harm? You mean he will work too much, and make himself ill?'

'No, ma'am,' said Miss Richardson, with dignity. 'I don't apologise for saying it, for you've eyes, ma'am, and can see as well as me what's been a-going on. He's been here, ma'am, spending the evenings, take one week with another, five nights out of the seven—and now you and the young ladies is going away. And Miss Ombra—but I don't speak to one as can't take notice, and see how things is going as well as me.'

'Miss Richardson, I think we all ought to be very careful how we talk of a young man, and a clergyman. I have been very glad to see him here. I have always thought it was good for a young man to have a family circle open to him. But if any gossip has got up about the young ladies, it is perfectly without foundation. I should not have expected from you—'

'Oh! Mrs. Anderson, ma'am!' cried the dressmaker, carried away by her feelings. 'Talk to me of gossip, when I was speaking as a friend! an 'umble friend, I don't say different, but still one that takes a deep interest. Foundation or no foundation, ma'am, that poor young gentleman is a-breaking of his heart. I see it before I heard the news. I said to myself, "Miss Ombra's been and refused him;" and then I heard you and the young ladies were going away. Whether he's spoken, and been refused, or whether he haven't had the courage to speak, it ain't for me to guess; but oh! Mrs. Anderson, ma'am, speak a word of comfort to the poor young gentleman! My heart is in it. I can't stop, even if I make you angry. I'm not one to gossip, and, when I'm trusted, wild horses won't drag a word out of me; but I make bold to speak to you—though you're a lady, and I work for my bread—as one woman to another, ma'am. If you hadn't been a real lady, I wouldn't have dared to a-done it. Oh, if you'd but give him a word of good advice! such as we can't have everything we want; and there's a deal of good left, even though Miss Ombra won't have him; and he oughtn't to be ungrateful to God, and that. He'd take it from you. Oh! ma'am, if you'd give him a word of good advice!'

Miss Richardson wept while she spoke; and at length her emotion affected her companion.

'You are a good soul,' said Mrs. Anderson, holding out her hand; 'you are a kind creature. I will always think better of you for this. But you must not say a word about Miss Ombra. He has never spoken to me; and till a man speaks, you know, a lady has no right to take such a thing for granted. But I will not forget what you have said; and I will speak to him, if I can find an opportunity—if he will give me the least excuse for doing it. He will miss us, I am sure.'

'Oh! miss you, ma'am!' cried Miss Richardson; 'all the parish will miss you, and me among the first, as you've always been so good to; but as for my poor young gentleman, what I'm afraid of is as he'll do himself some harm.'

'Hush! my daughter is coming!' said Mrs. Anderson; and she added, in a louder tone, 'I will see that you have everything you want to-morrow; and you must try to give us two days more. I think two days will be enough, Ombra, with everybody helping a little. Good night. To-morrow, when you come, you must make us all work.'

'Thank you very kindly, ma'am,' said the dressmaker, with a curtsey; 'and good night.'

'What was she talking to you about, mamma?' said Ombra's languid voice, in the soft evening gloom; not that she cared to know—the words came mechanically to her lips.

'About the trimming of your travelling dress, my dear,' said her mother, calmly, with that virtuous composure which accompanies so many gentle fibs. ('And so she was, though not just now,' Mrs. Anderson added to herself, in self-exculpation.)

And then Kate joined them, and they went indoors and lit the lamp. Mr. Sugden had been taking a long walk, that night. Some one was sick at the other end of the parish, to whom the Rector had sent him; and he was glad. The invalid was six miles off, and he had walked there and back. But every piece of work, alas! comes to an end, and so did this; and he found himself in front of the Cottage, he could not tell how, just after this soft domestic light began to shine under the verandah, as under an eyelid. He stood and looked at it, poor fellow! with a sick and sore heart. A few nights more, and that lamp would be lit no longer; and the light of his life would be gone out. He stood and looked at it in a rapture of love and pain. There was no one to see him; but if there had been a hundred, he would not have known nor cared, so lost was he in this absorbing passion and anguish. He had not the heart to go in, though the times were so few that he would see her again. He went away, with his head bent on his breast, saying to himself that if she had been happy he could have borne it; but she was not happy; and he ground his teeth, and cursed the Berties, those two butterflies, those two fools, in his heart!

There was one, however, who saw him, and that was Francesca, who was cutting some salad in the corner of the kitchen-garden, in the faint light which preceded the rising of the moon. The old woman looked over the wall, and saw him, and was sorry. 'The villains!' she said to herself. But though she was sorry, she laughed softly as she went in, as people will, while the world lasts, laugh at such miseries. Francesca was sorry for the young man—so sorry, even, that she forgot that he was a priest, and, therefore, a terrible sinner in thinking such thoughts; but she was not displeased with Ombra this time. This was natural. 'What is the good of being young and beautiful if one has not a few victims?' she said to herself. 'Time passes fast enough and then it is all over, and the man has it his own way. If nostra Ombra did no more harm than that!' And, on the whole, Francesca went in with the salad for her ladies' supper rather exhilarated than otherwise by the sight of the hopeless lover. It was the woman's revenge upon man for a great deal that he makes her suffer; and in the abstract women are seldom sorry for such natural victims.

Next evening, however, Mr. Sugden took heart, and went to the Cottage, and there spent a few hours of very sweet wretchedness, Ombra being unusually good to him—and to the Curate she always was good. After the simple supper had been eaten, and Francesca's salad, Mrs. Anderson contrived that both the girls should be called away to try on their travelling-dresses, at which Miss Richardson and Maryanne were working with passion. The window was open; the night was warm, and the moon had risen over the sea. Mrs. Anderson stepped out upon the verandah with the Curate, and they exchanged a few sentences on the beauty of the night, such as were consistent with the occasion; then she broke off the unreal, and took up the true. 'Mr. Sugden,' she said, 'I wanted to speak to you. It seems vain to take such a thing for granted, but I am afraid you will miss us when we go away.'

'Miss you!' he cried; and then tears came into the poor fellow's eyes, and into his voice, and he took her hand with despairing gratitude. 'Thanks for giving me a chance to speak,' he said—'it is like yourself. Miss you!—I feel as if life would cease altogether after Monday—it won't, I suppose, and most things will go on as usual; but I cannot think it—everything will be over for me.'

'You must not think so,' she said; 'it will be hard upon you at first, but you will find things will arrange themselves better than you expect—other habits will come in instead of this. No, indeed I am not unkind, but I know life better than you do. But for that, you know, we could not go on living, with all the changes that happen to us. We should be killed at the first blow.'

'And so I shall be killed,' he said, turning from her with heavier gloom than before, and angry with the consolation. 'Oh! not bodily, I suppose. One can go on and do one's work all the same; and one good thing is, it will be of importance to nobody but myself.'

'Don't say so,' said kind Mrs. Anderson, with tears in her eyes. 'Oh! my dear boy—if you will let me call you so—think what your visionary loss is in comparison with so many losses that people have to bear every day.'

'It is no visionary loss to me,' he said, bitterly. 'But if she were happy, I should not mind. I could bear it, if all were well with her. I hope I am not such a wretch as to think of myself in comparison. Don't think I am too stupid to see how kind you are to me; but there is one thing—only one thing that could give me real comfort. Promise that, if the circumstances are ever such as to call for a brother's interference, you will send for me. It is not what I would have wished, God knows!—not what I would have wished—but I will be a brother to her, if she needs a brother. Promise. There are some things which a man can do best, and if she is wronged, if her brother could set things right—'

'Dear Mr. Sugden, I don't understand you,' said Mrs. Anderson, faltering.

'But you will, if such a time should come? You will remember that you have promised. I will say good night now. I can't go in again after this and see her without making a fool of myself, and it is best she should keep some confidence in me. Good night.'

Had she fulfilled Miss Richardson's commission?—or had she pledged herself to appeal to him instead, in some incomprehensible contingency? Mrs. Anderson looked after him bewildered, and did not know.

CHAPTER XXXII

Sunday was their last evening at Shanklin, and they were all rather melancholy—even Kate, who had been to church three times, and to the Sunday school, and over the almshouses, and had filled up the interstices between these occupations by a succession of tearful rambles round the Rectory garden with Lucy Eldridge, whose tears flowed at the smallest provocation. 'I will remember everything you have told me,' Lucy protested. 'I will go to the old women every week, and take them their tea and sugar—for oh! Kate, you know papa does not approve of money   and I will see that the little Joliffes are kept at school—and I will go every week to see after your flowers; but oh! what shall I do without you? I shan't care about my studies, or anything; and those duets which we used to play together, and our German, which we always meant to take up—I shall not have any heart for them now. Oh! Kate, I wish you were not going! But that is selfish. Of course I want you to have the pleasure; only—'

'I wish you were going,' said Kate—'I wish everybody was coming; but, as that is impossible, we must just make the best of it; and if anybody should take the Cottage, and you should go and make as great friends with them as you ever did with me—'

'How can you think so?' said Lucy, with fresh tears.

'Well,' said Kate, 'if I were very good, I suppose I ought to hope you would make friends with them; but I am not so frightened of being selfish as you are. One must be a little selfish—but for that, people would have no character at all.'

'Oh! Kate, if mamma were to hear you—'

'I should not mind. Mrs. Eldridge knows as well as I do. Giving in to other people is all very well; but if you have not the heart or the courage to keep something of your very own, which you won't give away, what is the good of you? I don't approve of sacrificing like that.'

'I am sure you would sacrifice yourself, though you speak so,' said Lucy. 'Oh! Kate, you would sacrifice anything—even a—person—you loved—if some one else loved him.'

'I should do nothing of the sort,' said Kate, stoutly. 'In the first place, you mean a man, I suppose, and it is only women who are called persons. I should do nothing of the sort. What right should I have to sacrifice him if he were fond of me, and hand him over to some one else? That is not self-sacrifice—it is the height of impertinence; and if he were not fond of me, of course there would be nothing in my power. Oh, no; I am not that sort of person. I will never give up any one's love or any one's friendship to give it to another. Now, Lucy, remember that. And if you are as great friends with the new people as you are with me—'

'What odd ideas you have!' said Lucy. 'I suppose it is because you are so independent and a great lady; and it seems natural that everybody should yield to you.'

Upon which Kate flushed crimson.

'How mean you must think me! To stand up for my own way because I shall be rich. But never mind, Lucy. I don't suppose you can understand, and I am fond of you all the same. I am fond of you now; but if you go and forget me, and go off after other people, you don't know how different I can be. I shall hate you—I shall—'

'Oh! Kate, don't be so dreadful!' cried Lucy. 'What would mamma say?'

'Then don't provoke me,' said Kate. And then they fell back upon more peaceful details, and the hundred commissions which Lucy undertook so eagerly. I am not sure that Kate was quite certain of the sincerity of her self-sacrificing friend. She made a great many wise reflections on the subject when she had left her, and settled it with a philosophy unusual to her years.

'She does not mean to be insincere,' Kate mused to herself. 'She does not understand. If there is nothing deeper in it, how can she help it? When the new people come, she will be quite sure she will not care for them; and then they will call, and she will change her mind. I suppose I will change my mind too. How queer people are! But, at all events, I don't pretend to be better than I am.' And with a little premonitory smart, feeling that her friend was already, in imagination, unfaithful, Kate walked home, looking tenderly at everything.

'Oh! how lovely the sea is!' she said to herself—'how blue, and grey, and green, and all sorts of colours! I hope it will not be rough when we cross to-morrow. I wonder if the voyage from Southampton will be disagreeable, and how Ombra will stand it. Is Ombra really ill now, or is it only her mind? Of course she cannot turn round to my aunt and say it is her mind, or that the Berties had anything to do with it. I wonder what really happened that night; and I wonder which it is. She cannot be in love with them both at once, and they cannot be both in love with her, or they would not be such friends. I wonder—but, there, I am doing nothing but wondering, and there are so many things that are queer. How beautiful that white headland is with a little light about it, as if the day had forgotten to carry all that belonged to it away! And perhaps I may never see it any more. Perhaps I may never come back to the Cottage, or the cliffs, or the sea. What a long time I have been here—and what a horrid disagreeable girl I was! I think I must be a little better now. I am not so impertinent, at all events, though I do like to meddle. I suppose I shall always like to meddle. Oh! I wonder how I shall feel when I go back again to Langton-Courtenay? I am eighteen past, and in three years I shall be able to do whatever I like. Lucy said a great lady—a great lady! I think, on the whole, I like the idea. It is so different from most other people. I shall not require to marry unless I please, or to do anything that is disagreeable. And if I don't set the parish to rights! The poor folks shall be all as happy as the day is long,' cried Kate to herself, with energy. 'They shall have each a nice garden, and a bit of potato-ground, and grass for a cow. And what if I were to buy a quantity of those nice little Brittany cows when we are abroad? Auntie thinks they are the best. How comfortable everybody will be with a cow and a garden! But, oh dear! what a long time it will be first! and I don't know if I shall ever see this dear Cottage, and the bay, and the headland, and all the cliffs and the landslips, and the ups and the downs again.'

'Mees Katta, you vill catzh ze cold,' said Francesca, coming briskly up to her. 'It is not so beautiful this road, that you should take the long looks, and have the air so dull. Sorry, no, she is not sorry—my young lady is not sorry to go to see Italy, and ze mountains, and ze world—'

'Not quite that, Francesca,' said Kate; 'but I have been so happy at the Cottage, and I was thinking what if I should never see it again!'

'That is what you call non-sense,' said Francesca. 'Why should not Mademoiselle, who is verra young, comm back and zee all she lofs? If it was an old, like me—but I think nothink, nothink of ze kind, for I always comms back, like what you call ze bad penny. This is pretty, but were you once to see Italy, Mees Katta, you never would think no more of this—never no more!'

'Indeed, I should!' cried Kate, indignantly; 'and if this was the ugliest place in England, and your Italy as beautiful as heaven, I should still like this best.'

Francesca laughed, and shook her little brown head.

'Wait till my young lady see,' she said—'wait till she see. The air is never damp like this, but sweet as heaven, as Mees Katta says; and the sea blue, all blue; you never see nozing like it. It makes you well, you English, only to see Italy. What does Mademoiselle say?'

'Oh! do you think the change of air will cure Ombra?' cried Kate.

'No,' said Francesca, turning round upon her, 'not the change of air, but the change of mind, will cure Mees Ombra. What she wants is the change of mind.'

'I do not understand you,' said Kate. 'I suppose you mean the change of scene, the novelty, the—'

'I mean the change of ze mind,' said Francesca; 'when she will understand herself, and the ozer people's; when she knows to do right, and puts away her face of stone, then she will be well—quite well. It is not sickness; it is her mind that makes ill, Mees Katta. When she will put ze ice away and be true, then she shall be well.'

'Oh, Francesca, you talk like an old witch, and I am frightened for you!' cried Kate. 'I don't believe in illness of the mind; you will see Ombra will get better as soon as we begin to move about.'

'As soon as she change her mind she will be better,' said the oracular Francesca. 'There is nobody that tells her the truth but me. She is my child, and I lof her, and I tell her the trutt.'

'I think I see my aunt in the garden,' said Kate, hurrying on; for though she was very curious, she was honourable, and did not wish to discover her cousin's secrets through Francesca's revelations.

'If your aunt kill me, I care not,' said Francesca, 'but my lady is the most good, the most sense—She knows Mees Ombra, and she lets me talk. She is cured when she will change the mind.'

'I don't want to hear any more, please,' said honourable Kate. But Francesca went on nodding her head, and repeating her sentiment: 'When she change the mind, she will be well,' till it got to honest Kate's ears, and mixed with her dreams. The mother and daughter were in the garden, talking not too cheerfully. A certain sadness was in the air. The lamp burned dimly in the drawing-room, throwing a faint, desolate light over the emptiness. 'This is what it will look like to-morrow,' said Kate; and she cried. And the others were very much disposed to follow her example. It was the last night—words which are always melancholy; and presently poor Mr. Sugden stole up in the darkness, and joined them, with a countenance of such despair that poor Kate, excited, and tired, and dismal as she herself felt, had hard ado to keep from laughing. The new-comer added no cheer to the little party. He was dismal as Don Quixote, and, poor fellow, as simple-minded and as true.

And next morning they went away. Mr. Courtenay himself, who had lingered in the neighbourhood, paying a visit to some friends, either from excess of kindness, or determination to see the last of them, met them at Southampton, and put them into the boat for Havre, the nearest French port. Kate had her Maryanne, who, confounded by the idea of foreign travel, was already helpless; and the two other ladies were attended by old Francesca, as brisk and busy as a little brown bee, who was of use to everybody, and knew all about luggage and steamboats. Mr. Sugden, who had begged that privilege from Mrs. Anderson, went with them so far, and pointed out the ships of the fleet as they passed, and took them about the town, indicating all its principal wonders to them, as if he were reading his own or their death-warrants.

'If it goes on much longer, I shall laugh,' whispered Kate, in her aunt's ear.

'It would be very cruel of you,' said that kind woman. But even her composure was tried. And in the evening they sailed, with all the suppressed excitement natural to the circumstances.

'You have the very best time of the year for your start,' said Mr. Courtenay, as he shook hands with them.

'And, thanks to you, every comfort in travelling,' said Mrs. Anderson.

Thus they parted, with mutual compliments. Mr. Sugden wrung her hand, and whispered hoarsely, 'Remember—like her brother!' He stalked like a ghost on shore. His face was the last they saw when the steamboat moved, as he stood in the grey of the evening, grey as the evening, looking after them as long as they were visible. The sight of him made the little party very silent. They made no explanation to each other; but Kate had no longer any inclination to laugh. 'Like a brother!—like her brother!' These words, the Curate, left to himself, said over and over in his heart as he walked back and forward on the pier for hours, watching the way they had gone. The same soft evening breeze which helped them on, blew about him, but refreshed him not. The object of his life was gone.

CHAPTER XXXIII

The little party travelled, as it is in the nature of the British tourist to travel, when he is fairly started, developing suddenly a perfect passion for sight-seeing, and for long and wearisome journeys. Mrs. Anderson, though she was old enough and experienced enough to have known better, took the plunge with the truest national enthusiasm. Even when they paused in Paris, which she knew as well as or better than anything in her own country, she still felt herself a tourist, and went conscientiously over again and saw the sights—for Kate, she said, but also for herself. They rushed across France with the speed of an express train, and made a dash at Switzerland, though it was so early in the year. They had it almost all to themselves, the routes being scarcely open, and the great rush of travellers not yet begun; and who, that does not know it, can fancy how beautiful it is among the mountains in May! Kate was carried entirely out of herself by what she saw. The Spring green brightening and enhancing those rugged heights, and dazzling peaks of snow; the sky of an ethereal blue, all dewy and radiant, and surprised into early splendour, like the blue eyes of a child; the paths sweet with flowers, the streams full with the melting snow, the sense of awakening and resurrection all over the land. Kate had not dreamed of anything so splendid and so beautiful. The weather was much finer than is usual so early in the year, and of course the travellers took it not for an exceptional season, as they ought, but gave the fact that they were abroad credit for every shining day. Abroad! Kate had felt for years (she said all her life) that in that word 'abroad' every delight was included; and now she believed herself. The novelty and movement by themselves would have done a great deal; and the wonderful beauty of this virgin country, which looked as if no crowd of tourists had ever profaned it, as if it had kept its stillness, its stateliness and grandeur, and dazzling light and majestic glooms, all for their enjoyment, elevated her into a paradise of inward delight. Even Maryanne was moved, though chiefly by her mistress's many and oft-repeated efforts to rouse her. When Kate had exhausted everybody else, she rushed upon her handmaid.

'Oh! Maryanne, look! Did you ever see—did you ever dream of anything so beautiful?'

'No, miss,' said Maryanne.

'Look at that stream rushing down the ravine. It is the melted snow. And look at all those peaks above. Pure snow, as dazzling as—as—'

'They looks for all the world like the sugar on a bride-cake, miss,' said Maryanne.

At which Kate laughed, but went on—

'Those cottages are called châlets, up there among the clouds. Look how green the grass is—like velvet. Oh! Maryanne, shouldn't you like to live there—to milk the cows in the evening, and have the mountains all round you—nothing but snow-peaks, wherever you turned your eyes?'

Maryanne gave a shudder.

'Why, miss,' she said, 'you'd catch your death of cold!'

'Wait till Mees Katta see my bella Firenze,' said old Francesca. 'There is the snow quite near enough—quite near enough. You zee him on the tops of ze hills.'

'I never, never shall be able to live in a town. I hate towns,' said Kate.

'Ah!' cried the old woman, 'my young lady will not always think so. This is pleasant now; but there is no balls, no parties, no croquée on ze mountains! Mees Katta shakes her head; but then the Winter will come, and, oh! how beautiful is Firenze, with all the palaces, and ze people, and processions that pass, and all that is gay! There will be the Opera,' said Francesca, counting on her fingers, 'and the Cascine, and the Carnival, and the Veglioni, and the grand Corso with the flowers. Ah! I have seen many young English Mees, I know.'

'I never could have supposed Francesca would be so stupid,' cried Kate, returning to the party on the quarter-deck—for this conversation took place in a steamer on the Lake of Lucerne. 'She does not care for the mountains as much as Maryanne does, even. Maryanne thinks the snow is like sugar on a bride-cake,' she went on, with a laugh; 'but Francesca does nothing but rave about Florence, and balls, and operas. As if I cared for such things—and as if we were going there!'

'But Francesca is quite right, dear,' said Mrs. Anderson, with hesitation. 'When the Summer is over, we shall want to settle down again, and see our fellow-creatures; and really, as Francesca has suggested it, we might do a great deal worse. Florence is a very nice place.'

'In Winter, auntie? Are not we going home?'

'My dear, I know your uncle would wish you to see as much as possible before returning home,' said Mrs. Anderson, faltering, and with considerable confusion. 'I confess I had begun to think that—a few months in Italy—as we are here—'

Kate was taken by surprise. She did not quite know whether she was delighted or disappointed by the idea; but before she could reply, she met the eye of her cousin, whose whole face had kindled into passion. Ombra sprang to her feet, and drew Kate aside with a nervous haste that startled her. She grasped her arm tight, and whispered in her ear, 'We are to be kept till you are of age—I see it all now—we are prisoners till you are of age. Oh! Kate, will you bear it? You can resist, but I can't—they will listen to you.'

It is impossible to describe the shock which was given to Kate's loyalty by this speech. It was the first actual suggestion of rebellion which had been made to her, and it jarred her every nerve. She had not been a submissive child, but she had never plotted—never done anything in secret. She said aloud, in painful wonder—

'Why should we be prisoners?—and what has my coming of age to do with it?' turning round, and looking bewildered into her cousin's face.

Ombra made no reply; she went back to her seat, and retired into herself for the rest of the day. Things had gone smoothly since the journey began up to this moment. She had almost ceased to brood, and had begun to take some natural interest in what was going on about her. But now all at once the gloom returned. She sat with her eyes fixed on the shore of the lake, and with the old flush of feverish red, half wretchedness, half anger, under her eyes. Kate, who had grown happy in the brightening of the domestic atmosphere, was affected by this change in spite of herself. She exchanged mournful looks with her aunt. The beautiful lake and the sunny peaks were immediately clouded over; she was doubly checked in the midst of her frank enjoyment.

'You are wrong, Ombra,' said Mrs. Anderson, after a long pause. 'I don't know what you have said to Kate, but I am sure you have taken up a false idea. There is no compulsion. We are to go only when we please, and to stay only as long as we like.'

'But we are not to return home this year?'

'I did not say so; but I think, perhaps, on the whole, that to go a little further, and see a little more, would be best both for you and Kate.'

'Exactly,' said Ombra, with bitterness, nodding her head in a derisive assent.

Kate looked on with wistful and startled eyes. It was almost the first time that the idea of real dissension between these two had crossed her mind; and still more this infinitely startling doubt whether all that was said to her was true. At least there had been concealment; and was it really, truly the good of Ombra and Kate, or some private arrangement with Uncle Courtenay, that was in her aunt's mind. This suggestion came suddenly into her very heart, wounding her as with an arrow; and from that day, though sometimes lessening and sometimes deepening, the cloud upon Ombra's face came back. But as she grew less amiable, she grew more powerful. Henceforward the party became guided by her wayward fancies. She took a sudden liking for one of the quietest secluded places—a village on the little blue lake of Zug—and there they settled for some time, without rhyme or reason. Green slopes, with grey stone-peaks above, and glimpses of snow beyond, shut in this lake-valley. I agree with Ombra that it is very sweet in its stillness, the lake so blue, the air so clear, and the noble nut-bearing trees so umbrageous, shadowing the pleasant châlets. In the centre was a little white washed village church among its graves, its altar all decked with stately May lilies, the flowers of the Annunciation. The church had no beauty of architecture, no fine pictures—not even great antiquity to recommend it; but Ombra was fond of the sunshiny, still place. She would go there when she was tired, and sit down on one of the rush-bottomed chairs, and sometimes was to be seen kneeling furtively on the white altar steps.

Kate, who roamed up and down everywhere, and had soon all the facility of a young mountaineer, would stop at the open church-door as she came down from the hills, alpenstock in hand, sunburnt and agile as a young Diana.

'You are not going to turn a Roman Catholic, Ombra?' she said. 'I think it would make my aunt very unhappy.'

'I am not going to turn anything,' said Ombra. 'I shall never be different from what I am—never any better. One tries and tries, and it is no good.'

'Then stop trying, and come up on the hills and shake it off,' said Kate.

'Perhaps I might if I were like you; but I am not like you.'

'Or let us go on, and see people and do things again—do all sorts of things. I like this little lake,' said Kate. 'One has a home-feeling. I almost think I should begin to poke about the cottages, and find fault with the people, if we were to stay long. But that is not your temptation, Ombra. Why do you like to stay?'

'I stay because it is so still—because nobody comes here, nothing can happen here; it must always be the same for ever and for ever and ever!' cried Ombra. 'The hills and the deep water, and the lilies in the church—which are artificial, you know, and cannot fade.'

Kate did not understand this little bitter jibe at the end of her cousin's speech; but was overwhelmed with surprise when Ombra next morning suggested that they should resume their journey. They were losing their time where they were, she said; and as, if they were to go to Italy for the Winter, it would be necessary to return by Switzerland next year, she proposed to strike off from the mountains at this spot, to go to Germany, to the strange old historical cities that were within reach. 'Kate should see Nuremberg,' she said; and Kate, to her amazement, found the whole matter settled, and the packing commenced that day. Ombra managed the whole journey, and was a practical person, handy and rational, until they came to that old-world place, where she became reveuse and melancholy once more.

'Do you like this better than Switzerland?' Kate asked, as they looked down from their windows along the three-hundred-years-old street, where it was so strange to see people walking about in ordinary dresses and not in trunkhose and velvet mantles.

'I don't care for any place. I have seen so many, and one is so much like another,' said Ombra. 'But look, Kate, there is one advantage. Anything might happen here; any one might be coming along those streets and you would never feel surprised. If I were to see my father walking quietly this way, I should not think it at all strange.'

'But, Ombra—he is dead!' said Kate, shrinking a little, with natural uneasiness.

'Yes, he is dead, but that does not matter. Look down that hazy street with all the gables. Any one might be coming—people whom we have forgotten—even,' she said, pressing Kate's arm, 'people who have forgotten us.'

'Oh! Ombra, how strangely you speak! People that care for you don't forget you,' cried Kate.

'That does not mend the matter,' said Ombra, and withdrew hurriedly from the window.

Poor Kate tried very hard to make something out of it, but could not; and therefore she shrugged her shoulders and gave her head a little shake, and went to her German, which she was working at fitfully, to make the best of her opportunities. The German, though she thought sometimes it would break her heart, was not so hard as Ombra; and even the study of languages had to her something amusing in it.

One of the young waiters in the hotel kept a dictionary in the staircase window, and studied it as he flew up and down stairs for a new word to experiment with upon the young ladies; and another had, by means of the same dictionary, set up a flirtation with Maryanne; so fun was still possible, notwithstanding all; and whether it was by the mountain paths, or in those hazy strange old streets, Kate walked with her head, as it were, in the clouds, in a soft rapture of delight and pleasantness, taking in all that was sweet and lovely and good, and letting the rest drop off from her like a shower of rain. She even ceased to think of Ombra's odd ways—not out of want of consideration, but with the facility which youth has for taking everything for granted, and consenting to whatever is. It was a great pity, but it could not be helped, and one must make the best of it all the same.

And thus the Summer passed on, full of wonders and delights. Mrs. Anderson and her daughter, and even Francesca, were invaluable to the ignorant girl. They knew how everything had to be done; they were acquainted alike with picture-galleries and railway-tickets, and knew even what to say about every work of art—an accomplishment deeply amazing to Kate, who did not know what to say about anything, and who had several times committed herself by praising vehemently some daub which was beyond the reach of praise. When she made such a mistake as this, her mortification and shame were great; but unfortunately her pride made her hold by her opinion. They saw so many pictures, so many churches, so much that was picturesque and beautiful, that her brain was in a maze, and her intellect had become speechless.

They took their way across the mountains in Autumn, getting entangled in the vast common tide of travellers to Italy; and, after all, Francesca's words came true, and it was a relief to Kate to get back into the stream—it relieved the strain upon her mind. Instead of thinking of more and lovelier pictures still, she was pleased to rest and see nothing; and even—a confession which she was ashamed to make to herself—Kate was as much delighted with the prospect of mundane pleasures as she had been with the scenery. Society had acquired a new charm. She had never been at anything more than 'a little dance,' or a country concert, and balls and operas held out their arms to her. One of the few diplomatic friends whom Mrs. Anderson had made in her consular career was at Florence; and even Mr. Courtenay could not object to his niece's receiving the hospitalities of the Embassy. She was to 'come out' at the Ambassador's ball—not in her full-blown glory, as an heiress and a great lady, but as Mrs. Anderson's niece, a pretty, young, undistinguished English girl. Kate knew nothing about this, nor cared. She threw herself into the new joys as she had done into the old. A new chapter, however it might begin, was always a pleasant thing in her fresh and genial life.

CHAPTER XXXIV

Florence altogether was full of pleasant novelty to the young traveller. To find herself living up two pair of stairs, with windows overlooking the Arno, and at a little distance the quaint buildings of the Ponte Vecchio, was as great a change as the first change had been from Langton-Courtenay to the little Cottage at Shanklin. Mrs. Anderson's apartment on the second floor of the Casa Graziana was not large. There was a drawing-room which looked to the front, and received all the sunshine which Florentine skies could give; and half a mile off, at the other end of the house, there was a grim and spare dining-room, furnished with the indispensable tables and chairs, and with a curious little fireplace in the corner, raised upon a slab of stone, as on a pedestal. It would be difficult to tell how cold it was here as the Winter advanced; but in the salone it was genial as Summer whenever the sun shone. The family went, as it were, from Nice to Inverness when they went from the front to the back, for their meals. Perhaps it might have been inappropriate for Miss Courtenay of Langton-Courtenay to live up two pair of stairs; but it was not at all unsuitable for Mrs. Anderson; and, indeed, when Lady Barker, who was Mrs. Anderson's friend, came to call, she was much surprised by the superior character of the establishment. Lady Barker had been a Consul's daughter, and had risen immensely in life by marrying the foolish young attaché, whom she now kept in the way he ought to go. She was not the Ambassadress, but the

Ambassadress's friend, and a member of the Legation; and, though she was now in a manner a great lady herself, she remembered quite well what were the means of the Andersons, and knew that even the terzo piano of a house on the Lung-Arno was more than they could have ventured on in the ancient days.

'What a pretty apartment,' she said; 'and how nicely situated! I am afraid you will find it rather dear. Florence is so changed since your time. Do you remember how cheap everything used to be in the old days? Well, if you will believe me, you pay just fifteen times as much for every article now.'

'So I perceive,' said Mrs. Anderson. 'We give a thousand francs for these rooms, which ought not to be more than a hundred scudi—and without even the old attraction of a pleasant accessible Court.'

Lady Barker opened her eyes—at once, at the fact of Mrs. Anderson paying a thousand francs a month for her rooms, and at her familiar mention of the pleasant Court.

'Oh, there are some very pleasant people here now!' she said; 'if your young ladies are fond of dancing, I think I can help them to some amusement. Lady Granton will send you cards for her ball. Is Ombra delicate?—do you still call her Ombra? How odd it is that you and I, under such different circumstances, should meet here!'

'Yes—very odd,' said Mrs. Anderson; 'and yet I don't know. People who have been once in Italy always come back. There is a charm about it—a—'

'Ah, we didn't think so once!' said Lady Barker, with a laugh. She could remember the time when the Andersons, like so many other people compelled to live abroad, looked upon everything that was not English with absolute enmity. 'You used to think Italy did not agree with your daughter,' she said; 'have you brought her for her health now?'

'Oh no! Ombra is quite well; she is always pale,' said Mrs. Anderson. 'We have come rather on account of my niece—not for her health, but because she had never seen anything out of her own country. We think it right that she should make good use of her time before she comes of age.'

'Oh! will she come of age?' said Lady Barker, with a glance of laughing curiosity. She decided that the pretty girl at the window, who had two or three times broken into the conversation, was a great deal too pretty to be largely endowed by fortune; and smiled at her old friend's grandiloquence, which she remembered so well. She made a very good story of it at the little cosy dinner-party at the Embassy that evening, and prepared the good people for some amusement. 'A pretty English country girl, with some property, no doubt,' she said. 'A cottage ornée, most likely, and some fields about it; but her aunt talks as if she were heiress to a Grand Duke. She has come abroad to improve her mind before she comes of age.'

'And when she goes back there will be a grand assemblage of the tenantry, no doubt, and triumphal arches, and all the rest of it,' said another of the fine people.

'So Mrs. Vice-Consul allows one to suppose,' said Lady Barker. 'But she is so pretty—prettier than anything I have seen for ages; and Ombra, too, is pretty, the late Vice-Consul's heiress. They will far furore—two such new faces, and both so English; so fresh; so gauche!'

This was Lady Barker's way of backing her friends; but the friends did not know of it, and it procured them their invitation all the same, and Lady Granton's card to put on the top of the few other cards which callers had left. And Mrs. Anderson came to be, without knowing it, the favourite joke of the ambassadorial circle. Mrs. Vice-Consul had more wonderful sayings fastened upon her than she ever dreamt of, and became the type and symbol of the heavy British matron to that lively party. Her friend made her out to be a bland and dignified mixture of Mrs. Malaprop and Mrs. Nickleby. Meanwhile, she had a great many things to do, which occupied her, and drove even her anxieties out of her mind. There was the settling down—the hiring of servants and additional furniture, and all the trifles necessary to make their rooms 'comfortable;' and then the dresses of the girls to be put in order, and especially the dress in which Kate was to make her first appearance.

Mrs. Anderson had accepted Mr. Courtenay's conditions; she had acquiesced in the propriety of keeping silent as to Kate's pretensions, and guarding her from all approach of fortune-hunters. There was even something in this which was not disagreeable to her maternal feelings; for to have Kate made first, and Ombra second, would not have been pleasant. But still, at the same time, she could not restrain a natural inclination to enhance the importance of her party by a hint—an inference. That little intimation about Kate's coming of age, she had meant to tell, as indeed it did, more than she intended; and now her mind was greatly exercised about her niece's ball-dress. 'White tarlatane is, of course, very nice for a young girl,' she said, doubtfully, 'it is all my Ombra has ever had; but, for Kate, with her pretensions—'

This was said rather as one talks to one's self, thinking aloud, than as actually asking advice.

'But I thought Kate in Florence was to be simply your niece,' said Ombra, who was in the room. 'To make her very fine would be bad taste; besides,' she added, with a little sigh, 'Kate would look well in white calico. Nature has decked her so. I suppose I never, at my best, was anything like that.'

Ombra had improved very much since their arrival in Florence. Her fretfulness had much abated, and there was no envy in this sigh.

'At your best, Ombra! My foolish darling, do you think your best is over?' said the mother, with a smile.

'I mean the bloom,' said Ombra. 'I never had any bloom—and Kate's is wonderful. I think she gives a pearly, rosy tint to the very air. I was always a little shadow, you know!'

'You will not do yourself justice,' cried Mrs. Anderson. 'Oh! Ombra, if you only knew how it grieves me! You draw back, and you droop into that dreamy, melancholy way; there is always a mist about you. My darling, this is a new place, you will meet new people, everything is fresh and strange. Could you not make a new beginning, dear, and shake it off!'

'I try,' said Ombra, in a low tone.

'I don't want to be hard upon you, my own child; but, then, dear, you must blame yourself, not any one else. It was not his fault.'

'Please don't speak of it,' cried the girl. 'If you could know how humbled I feel to think that it is that which has upset my whole life! Ill-temper, jealousy, envy, meanness—pleasant things to have in one's heart! I fight with them, but I can't overcome them. If I could only "not care!" How happy people are who can take things easily, and who don't care!'

'Very few people do,' said Mrs. Anderson. 'Those who have command of themselves don't show their feelings, but most people feel more or less. The change, however, will do you good. And you must occupy yourself, my love. How nicely you used to draw, Ombra! and you have given up drawing. As for poetry, my dear, it is very pretty—it is very, very pretty—but I fear it is not much good.'

'It does not sell, you mean, like novels.'

'I don't know much about novels; but it keeps you always dwelling upon your feelings. And then, if they were ever published, people would talk. They would say, "Where has Ombra learned all this? Has she been as unhappy as she says? Has she been disappointed?" My darling, I think it does a girl a great deal of harm. If you would begin your drawing again! Drawing does not tell any tales.'

'There is no tale to tell,' cried Ombra. Her shadowy face flushed with a colour which, for the moment, was as bright as Kate's, and she got up hurriedly, and began to arrange some books at a side-table, an occupation which carried her out of her mother's way; and then Kate came in, carrying a basket of fruit, which she and Francesca had bought in the market. There were scarcely any flowers to be had, she complained, but the grapes, with their picturesque stems, and great green leaves, stained with russet, were almost as ornamental. A white alabaster tazza, which they had bought at Pisa, heaped with them, was almost more effective, more characteristic than flowers.

'I have been trying to talk to the market-women,' she said, 'down in that dark, narrow passage, by the Strozzi Palace. Francesca knows all about it. How pleasant it is going with Francesca—to hear her chatter, and to see her brown little face light up! She tells me such stories of all the people as we go.'

'How fond you are of stories, Kate!'

'Is it wrong? Look, auntie, how lovely this vine-branch looks! England is better for some things, though. There will still be some clematis over our porch—not in flower, perhaps, but in that downy, fluffy stage, after the flower. Francesca promises me everything soon. Spring will begin in December, she says, so far as the flowers go, and then we can make the salone gay. Do you know there are quantities of English people at the hotel at the corner? I almost thought I heard some one say my name as I went by. I looked up, but I could not see anybody I knew.'

'I hope there is nobody we know,' cried Ombra, under her breath.

'My dear children,' said Mrs. Anderson, with solemnity, 'you must recognise this principle in Italy, that there are English people everywhere; and wherever there are English people, there is sure to be some one whom you know, or who knows you. I have seen it happen a hundred times; so never mind looking up at the windows, Kate—you may be sure we shall find out quite soon enough.'

'Well, I like people,' said Kate, carelessly, as she went out of the room. 'It will not be any annoyance to me.'

'She does not care,' said Ombra—'it is not in her nature. She will always be happy, because she will never mind. One is the same as another to her. I wish I had that happy disposition. How strange it is that people should be so different! What would kill me would scarcely move her—would not cost her a tear.'

'Ombra, I am not so sure—'

'Oh! but I am sure, mamma. She does not understand how things can matter so much to me. She wonders—I can see her look at me when she thinks I don't notice. She seems to say, "What can Ombra mean by it?—how silly she is to care!"'

'But you have not taken Kate into your confidence?' said Mrs. Anderson, in alarm.

'I have not taken any one into my confidence—I have no confidence to give,' said Ombra, with the ready irritation which had come to be so common with her. The mother bore it, as mothers have to do, turning away with a suppressed sigh. What a difference the last year had made on Ombra!—oh! what a thing love was to make such a difference in a girl! This is what Mrs. Anderson said to herself with distress and pain; she could scarcely recognise her own child in this changed manifestation, and she could not approve, or even sympathise with her, in the degree, at least, which Ombra craved.

CHAPTER XXXV

The fact was that Ombra, as she said, had not given her confidence to any one; she had betrayed herself to her mother in her first excitement, when she had lost command of herself; but that was all. A real and full confidence she had never given. Ombra's love of sympathy was great, but it was not accompanied, as it generally is, by that open heart which finds comfort in disclosing its troubles. Her heart was not open. She neither revealed herself nor divined others; she was not selfish, nor harsh in temper and disposition; but all that she was certain of was her own feelings. She did not know how to find out what other people were feeling or thinking, consequently she had a very imperfect idea of those about her, and seldom found out for herself what was going on in their minds. This limited her powers of sympathy in a wonderful way, and it was this which was at the root of all her trouble. She had been wooed, but only when it came to a conclusion had she really known what that wooing meant. In her ignorance she had refused the man whom she was already beginning to love, and then had gone on to think about him, after he had revealed himself—to understand all he had been meaning—to love him, with the consciousness that she had rejected him, and with the fear that his affections were being transferred to her cousin. This was what gave the sting to it all, and made poor Ombra complain so mournfully of her temper. She did not divine what her love meant till it was too late; and then she resented the fact that it was too late—resented the reserve which she had herself imposed upon him, the friendly demeanour she had enjoined. She had begged him, when she rejected him, as the greatest of favours, to keep up his intercourse with the family, and be as though this episode had never been. And when the poor fellow obeyed her she was angry with him. I do not know whether the minds of men are ever similarly affected, but this is a weakness not uncommon with women. And then she took his subdued tone, his wistful looks, his seldom approaches to herself, as so many instances that he had got over what she called his folly. Why should he continue to nourish his folly when she had so promptly announced her indifference? And then it was that it became apparent to her that he had transferred his affections to Kate. As it happened, by the fatality which sometimes attends such matters, the unfortunate young man never addressed Kate, never looked at her, but Ombra found him out. When Kate was occupied by others, her cousin took no notice; but when that one step approached, that one voice addressed her, Ombra's eyes and ears were like the lynx. Kate was unconscious of the observation, by means of being absolutely innocent; and the hero himself was unconscious for much the same reason, and because he felt sure that his hopeless devotion to his first love must be so plain to her as to make any other theory on the subject out of the question. But Ombra, who was unable to tell what eyes meant, or to judge from the general scope of action, set up her theory, and made herself miserable. She had been wretched when watching 'them;' she was wretched to go away and be able to watch them no longer. She had left home with a sense of relief, and yet the news that they were not to return home for the winter smote her like a catastrophe. Even the fact that he had loved her once seemed a wrong to her, for then she did not know it; and since then had he not done her the cruel injury of ceasing to love her?

Poor Ombra! this was how she tormented herself; and up to this moment any effort she had made to free herself, to snap her chains, and be once more rational and calm, seemed but to have dug the iron deeper into her soul. Nothing cuts like an imaginary wrong. The sufferer would pardon a real injury a hundred times while nursing and brooding over the supposed one. She hated herself, she was ashamed, disgusted, revolted by the new exhibitions of unsuspected wickedness, as she called it, in her nature. She tried and tried, but got no better. But in the meantime all outward possibilities of keeping the flame alight being withdrawn, her heart had melted towards Kate. It was evident that in Kate's lighter and more sunshiny mind there was no room for such cares as bowed down her own; and with a yearning for love which she herself scarcely understood, she took her young cousin, who was entirely guiltless, into her heart.

Kate and she were sitting together, the morning of the ball to which the younger girl looked forward so joyfully. Ombra was not unmoved by its approach, for she was just one year over twenty, an age at which balls are still great events, and not unapt to influence life. Her heart was a little touched by Kate's anxious desire that her dress and ornaments should be as fresh and pretty and valuable as her own. It was good of her; to be sure, there was no reason why one should wish to outshine the other; but still Kate had been brought up a great lady, and Ombra was but the Consul's daughter. Therefore her heart was touched, and she spoke.

'It does not matter what dress I have, Kate; I shall look like a shadow all the same beside you. You are sunshine—that was what you were born to be, and I was born in the shade.'

'Don't make so much of yourself, Ombra mia,' said Kate. 'Sunshine is all very well in England, but not here. Am I to be given over to the Englishmen and the dogs, who walk in the sun?'

A cloud crossed Ombra's face at this untoward suggestion.

'The Englishmen as much as you please,' she said; and then, recovering herself with an effort, 'I wonder if I shall be jealous of you, Kate? I am a little afraid of myself. You so bright, so fresh, so ready to make friends, and I so dull and heavy as I am, besides all the other advantages on your side. I never was in society with you before.'

'Jealous of me!' Kate thought it was an admirable joke. She laughed till the tears stood in her bright eyes. 'But then there must be love before there is jealousy—or, so they say in books. Suppose some prince appears, and we both fall in love with him? But I promise you, it is I who shall be jealous. I will hate you! I will pursue you to the ends of the world! I will wear a dagger in my girdle, and when I have done everything else that is cruel, I will plunge it into your treacherous heart! Oh! Ombra, what fun!' cried the heroine, drying her dancing eyes.

'That is foolish—that is not what I mean,' said serious Ombra. 'I am very much in earnest. I am fond of you, Kate—'

This was said with a little effort; but Kate, unconscious of the effort, only conscious of the love, threw her caressing arm round her cousin's waist, and kissed her.

'Yes,' she said, softly; 'how strange it is, Ombra! I, who had nobody that cared for me,' and held her close and fast in the tender gratitude that filled her heart.

'Yes, I am fond of you,' Ombra continued; 'but if I were to see you preferred to me—always first, and I only second, more thought of, more noticed, better loved! I feel—frightened, Kate. It makes one's heart so sore. One says to oneself, "It is no matter what I do or say. It is of no use trying to be amiable, trying to be kind—she is sure to be always the first. People love her the moment they see her; and at me they never look." You don't know what it is to feel like that.'

'No,' said Kate, much subdued; and then she paused. 'But, Ombra, I am always so pleased—I have felt it fifty times; and I have always been so proud. Auntie and I go into a corner, and say to each other, "What nice people these are—they understand our Ombra—they admire her as she should be admired!" We give each other little nudges, and nod at each other, and are so happy. You would be the same, of course, if—though it don't seem likely—' And here Kate broke off abruptly, and blushed and laughed.

'You are the youngest,' said Ombra—'that makes it more natural in your case. And mamma, of course, is—mamma—she does not count. I wonder—I wonder how I shall take it—in my way or in yours?'

'Are you so sure it will happen?' said Kate, laughing. Kate herself did not dislike the notion very much. She had not been brought up with that idea of self-sacrifice which is inculcated from their cradles on so many young women. She felt that it would be pleasant to be admired and made much of; and even to throw others into the shade. She did not make any resolutions of self-renunciation. The visionary jealousy which moved Ombra, which arose partly from want of confidence in herself, and partly from ignorance of others, could never have arisen in her cousin. Kate did not think of comparing herself with any one, or dwelling upon the superior attractions of another. If people did not care for her, why, they did not care for her, and there was an end of it; so much the worse for them. To be sure she never yet had been subjected to the temptation which had made Ombra so unhappy. The possibility of anything of the kind had never entered her thoughts. She was eighteen and a half, and had lived for years on terms of sisterly amity with all the Eldridges, Hardwicks, and the 'neighbours' generally; but as yet she had never had a lover, so far as she was aware. 'The boys,' as she called them, were all as yet the same to Kate—she liked some more than others, as she liked some girls more than others; but to be unhappy or even annoyed because one or another devoted himself to Ombra more than to her, such an idea had never crossed the girl's mind. She was fancy free; but it did not occur to her to make any pious resolution on the subject, or to decide beforehand that she would obliterate herself in a corner, in order to give the first place and all the triumph to Ombra. There are young saints capable of doing this; but Kate Courtenay was not one of them. Her eyes shone; her rose-lips parted with just the lightest breath of excitement. She wanted her share of the triumphs too.

Ombra shook her head, but made no reply. 'Oh,' she said, to herself, 'what a hard fate to be always the shadow!' She exerted all the imagination she possessed, and threw herself forward, as it were, into the evening which was coming. Kate was in all the splendour of her first bloom—that radiance of youth and freshness which is often the least elevated kind of beauty, yet almost always the most irresistible. The liquid brightness of her eyes, the wild-rose bloom of her complexion, the exquisite softness, downiness, deliciousness of cheek and throat and forehead, might be all as evanescent as the dew upon the sunny grass, or the down on a peach. It was youth—youth supreme and perfect in its most delicate fulness, the beauté de diable, as our neighbours call it. Ombra, being still so young herself, did not characterise it so; nor, indeed, was she aware of this glory of freshness which, at the present moment, was Kate's crowning charm. But she wondered at her cousin's beauty, and she did not realise her own, which was so different. 'Shall I be jealous—shall I hate her?' she asked herself. At home she had hated her for a moment now and then. Would it be the same again?—was her own mind so mean, her character so low, as that? Thinking well of one's self, or thinking ill of one's self, requires only a beginning; and Ombra's experience had not increased her respect for her own nature. Thus she prepared for the Ambassadress's ball.

It was a strange manner of preparation, the reader will think. Our sympathy has been trained to accompany those who go into battle without a misgiving—who, whatever jesting alarm they may express, are never really afraid of running away; but, after all, the man who marches forward with a terrible dread in his mind that when the moment comes he will fail, ought to be as interesting, and certainly makes a much greater claim upon our compassion, than he who is tolerably sure of his nerves and courage. The battle of the ball was to Ombra as great an event as Alma or Inkermann. She had never undergone quite the same kind of peril before, and she was afraid as to how she should acquit herself. She represented to herself all the meanness, misery, contemptibleness, of what she supposed to be her besetting sin—that did not require much trouble. She summed it all up, feeling humiliated to the very heart by the sense that under other circumstances she had yielded to that temptation before, and she asked herself—shall I fail again? She was afraid of herself. She had strung her nerves, and set her soul firmly for this struggle, but she was not sure of success. At the last moment, when the danger was close to her, she felt as if she must fail.

CHAPTER XXXVI

Kate thought she had never imagined anything so stately, so beautiful, so gay, so like a place for princes and princesses to meet, as the suite of rooms in the Palazzo occupied by the English Embassy, where the ball was held. The vista which stretched before her, one room within another, the lines of light infinitely reflected by the great mirrors—the lofty splendid rooms, rich in gold and velvet; the jewels of the ladies, the glow of uniforms and decorations; the beautiful dresses—all moved her to interest and delight. Delight was the first feeling; and then there came the strangest sensation of insignificance, which was not pleasant to Kate. For three years she had lived in little cottage rooms, in limited space, with very simple surroundings. But the first glance at this new scene brought suddenly before the girl's eyes her native dwelling-place, her own home, which, of course, was but an English country-house, yet was more akin to the size and splendour of the Palazzo than to the apartments on the Lung-Arno, or the little Cottage on the Undercliff. Kate found herself, in spite of herself, making calculations how the rooms at Langton-Courtenay would look in comparison; and from that she went on to consider whether any one here knew of Langton-Courtenay, or was aware that she herself was anything but Mrs. Anderson's niece. She was ashamed of herself for the thought, and yet it went quick as lightning through her excited mind.

Lady Granton smiled graciously upon them, and even shook hands with the lady whom she knew as Mrs. Vice-Consul, with more cordiality than usual, with a gratitude which would have given Mrs. Anderson little satisfaction had she known it, to the woman who had already amused her so much; but then the group passed on like the other groups, a mother and two unusually pretty daughters, as people thought, but strangers, nobodies, looking a little gauche, and out of place, in the fine rooms, where they were known to no one. Ombra knew what the feeling was of old, and was not affronted by it; but Kate had never been deprived of a certain shadow of distinction among her peers. The people at Shanklin had, to their own consciousness, treated her just as they would have done any niece of Mrs. Anderson's; but, unconsciously to themselves, the fact that she was Miss Courtenay, of Langton-Courtenay, had produced a certain effect upon them. No doubt Kate's active and lively character had a great deal to do with it, but the fact of her heiress-ship, her future elevation, had much to do with it also. A certain pre-eminence had been tacitly allowed to her; a certain freedom of opinion, and even of movement, had been permitted, and felt to be natural. She was the natural leader in half the pastimes going, referred to and consulted by her companions. This had been her lot for these three years past. She never had a chance of learning that lesson of personal insignificance which is supposed to be so salutary. All at once, in a moment, she learned it now. Nobody looked up to her, nobody considered her, nobody knew or cared who she was. For the first half-hour Kate was astonished, in spite of all her philosophy, and then she tried to persuade herself that she was amused. But the greatest effort could not persuade her that she liked it. It made her tingle all over with the most curious mixture of pain, and irritation, and nervous excitement. The dancing was going on merrily, and there was a hum of talking and soft laughter all around; people passing and repassing, greeting each other, shaking hands, introducing to each other their common friends. But the three ladies who knew nobody stood by themselves, and felt anything but happy.

'If this is what you call a ball, I should much rather have been at home,' said Kate, with indignation.

'It is not cheerful, is it?' said Ombra. 'But we must put up with it till we see somebody we know. I wish only we could find a seat for mamma.'

'Oh! never mind me, my dear,' said Mrs. Anderson. 'I can stand very well, and it is amusing to watch the people. Lady Barker will come to us as soon as she sees us.'

'Lady Barker! As if any one cared for her!' said Kate; but even Kate, though she could have cried for mortification, kept looking out very sharply for Lady Barker. She was not a great lady, nor of any importance, so far as she herself was concerned, but she held the keys of the dance, of pleasure, and amusement, and success, for that night, at least, for both Ombra and Kate. The two stood and looked on while the pairs of dancers streamed past them, with the strangest feelings—or at least Kate's feelings were very strange. Ombra had been prepared for it, and took it more calmly. She pointed out the pretty faces, the pretty dresses to her cousin, by way of amusing her.

'What do you think of this toilette?' she said. 'Look, Kate, what a splendid dark girl, and how well that maize becomes her! I think she is a Roman princess. Look at her diamonds. Don't you like to see diamonds, Kate?'

'Yes,' said Kate, with a laugh at herself, 'they are very pretty; but I thought we came to dance, not to look at the people. Let us have a dance, you and I together, Ombra—why shouldn't we? If men won't ask us, we can't help that—but I must dance.'

'Oh! hush, my darling,' said Mrs. Anderson, alarmed. 'You must not really think of anything so extraordinary. Two girls together! It was all very well at Shanklin. Try to amuse yourself for a little, looking at the people. There are some of the great Italian nobility here. You can recognise them by their jewels. That is one, for instance, that lady in velvet—'

'It is very interesting, no doubt,' cried Kate, 'and if they were in a picture, or on a stage, I should like to look at them; but it is very queer to come to a ball only to see the people. Why, we might be their maids, standing in a corner to see the ladies pass. Is it right for the lady of the house to ask us, and then leave us like this? Do you call that hospitality? If this was Langton-Courtenay,' said Kate, bringing her own dignity forward unconsciously, for the first time for years, 'and it was I who was giving this ball, I should be ashamed of myself. Am I speaking loud? I am sure I did not mean it; but I should be ashamed—'

'Oh! hush, dear, hush!' cried Mrs. Anderson. 'Lady Barker will be coming presently.'

'But it was Lady Granton who invited us, auntie. It is her business to see—'

'Hush, my dearest child! How could she, with all these people to attend to? When you are mistress of Langton-Courtenay, and give balls yourself, you will find out how difficult it is—'

'Langton-Courtenay?' said some one near. The three ladies instantaneously roused up out of their languor at the sound. Whose voice was it? It came through the throng, as if some one half buried in the crowd had caught up the name, and flung it on to some one else. Mrs. Anderson looked in one direction, Kate, all glowing and smiling, in another, while the dull red flush of old, the sign of surprised excitement and passion, came back suddenly to Ombra's face. Though they had not been aware of it, the little group had already been the object of considerable observation; for the girls were exceptionally pretty, in their different styles, and they were quite new, unknown, and piquant in their obvious strangeness. Even Kate's indignation had been noted by a quick-witted English lady, with an eyeglass, who was surrounded by a little court. This lady was slightly beyond the age for dancing, or, if not really so, had been wise enough to meet her fate half-way, and to retire gracefully from youth, before youth abandoned her. She had taken up her place, resisting all solicitations.

'Don't ask me—my dancing-days are over. Ask that pretty girl yonder, who is longing to begin,' she had said, with a smile, to one of her attendants half an hour before.

'Je ne demande pas mieux, if indeed you are determined,' said he. 'But who is she? I don't know them.'

'Nobody seems to know them,' said Lady Caryisfort; and so the observation began.

Lady Caryisfort was very popular. She was a widow, well off, childless, good-looking, and determined, people said, never to marry again. She was the most independent of women, openly declaring, on all hands, that she wanted no assistance to get through life, but was quite able to take care of herself. And the consequence was that everybody about was most anxious to assist in taking care of her. All sorts of people took all sorts of trouble to help her in doing what she never hesitated to say she could do quite well without them. She was something of a philosopher, and a good deal of a cynic, as such people often are.

'You would not be so good to me if I had any need of you,' she said, habitually; and this was understood to be 'Lady Caryisfort's way.'

'Nobody knows them,' she added, looking at the party through her eyeglass. 'Poor souls, I daresay they thought it was very fine and delightful to come to Lady Granton's ball. And if they had scores of friends already, scores more would turn up on all sides. But because they know nobody, nobody will take the trouble to know them. The younger one is perfectly radiant. That is what I call the perfection of bloom. Look at her—she is a real rosebud! Now, what fainéants you all are!'

'Why are we fainéants?' said one of the court.

'Well,' said Lady Caryisfort, who professed to be a man-hater, within certain limits, 'I am aware that the nicest girl in the world, if she were not pretty, might stand there all the night, and nobody but a woman would ever think of trying to get any amusement for her. But there is what you are capable of admiring—there is beauty, absolute beauty; none of your washy imitations, but real, undeniable loveliness. And there you stand and gape, and among a hundred of you she does not find one partner. Oh! what it is to be a man! Why, my pet retriever, who is fond of pretty people, would have found her out by this, and made friends with her, and here are half a dozen of you fluttering about me!'

There was a general laugh, as at a very good joke; and some one ventured to suggest that the flutterers round Lady Caryisfort could give a very good reason—

'Yes,' said that lady, fanning herself tranquilly, 'because I don't want you. In society that is the best of reasons; and that pretty creature there does want you, therefore she is left to herself. She is getting indignant. Why, she grows prettier and prettier. I wonder those glances don't set fire to something! Delicious! She wants her sister to dance with her. What a charming girl! And the sister is pretty, too, but knows better. And mamma—oh! how horrified mamma is! This is best of all!'

Thus Lady Caryisfort smiled and applauded, and her attendants laughed and listened. But, curiously enough, though she was so interested in Kate, and so indignant at the neglect to which she was subjected, it did not occur to her to take the young stranger under her protection, as she might so easily have done. It was her way to look on—to interfere was quite a different matter.

'Now this is getting quite dramatic,' she cried; 'they have seen some one they know—where is he?—or even where is she?—for any one they know would be a godsend to them. How do you do, Mr. Eldridge? How late you are! But please don't stand between me and my young lady. I am excited about her; they have not found him yet—and how eager she looks! Mr. Eldridge—why, good heavens! where has he gone?'

'Who was it that said Langton-Courtenay?' cried Kate; 'it must be some one who knows the name, and I am sure I know the voice. Did you hear it, auntie? Langton-Courtenay!—I wonder who it could be?'

A whole minute elapsed before anything more followed. Mrs. Anderson looked one way, and Kate another. Ombra did not move. If the lively observer, who had taken so much interest in the strangers, could have seen the downcast face which Kate's bright countenance threw into the shade, her drama would instantly have increased in interest. Ombra stood without moving a hair's-breadth—without raising her eyes—without so much as breathing, one would have said. Under her eyes that line of hot colour had flushed in a moment, giving to her face the look of something suppressed and concealed. The others wondered who it was, but Ombra knew by instinct who had come to disturb their quiet once more. She recognised the voice, though neither of her companions did; and if there had not been any evidence so clear as that voice—had it been a mere shadow, an echo—she would have known. It was she who distinguished in the ever-moving, ever-rustling throng, the one particular movement which indicated that some one was making his way towards them. She knew he—they—were there, without raising her eyes, before Kate's cry of joyful surprise informed her.

'Oh, the Berties!—I beg your pardon—Mr. Hardwick and Mr. Eldridge. Oh, fancy!—that you should be here!'

Ombra neither fell nor fainted, nor did she even speak. The room swam round and round, and then came back to its place; and she looked up, and smiled, and put out her hand.

The two pretty strangers stood in the corner no longer; they stood up in the next dance, Kate in such a glow of delight and radiance that the whole ball-room thrilled with admiration. There had been a little hesitation as to which of the two should be her partner—a pause during which the two young men consulted each other by a look; but she had herself so clearly indicated which Bertie she preferred, that the matter was speedily decided. 'I wanted to have you,' she said frankly to Bertie Hardwick, as he led her off, 'because I want to hear all about home. Tell me about home. I have not thought of Langton for two years at least, and my mind is full of it to-night—I am sure I don't know why. I keep thinking, if I ever give a ball at Langton, how much better I will manage it. Fancy!' cried Kale, flushing with indignation, 'we have been here an hour, and no one has asked us to dance, neither Ombra nor me.'

'That must have been because nobody knew you,' said Bertie Hardwick.

'And whose fault was that? Fancy asking two girls to a dance, and then never taking the trouble to look whether they had partners or not! If I ever give a ball, I shall behave differently, you may be sure.'

'I hope you will give a great many balls, and that I shall be there to see.'

'Of course,' said Kate, calmly; 'but if you ever see me neglecting my duty like Lady Granton, don't forget to remind me of to-night.'

Lady Granton's sister was standing next to her, and, of course, heard what she said.

CHAPTER XXXVII

'It was you who knew them, Mr. Eldridge,' said Lady Caryisfort. 'Tell me about them—you can't think how interested I am. She thinks Lady Granton neglected her duty, and she means to behave very differently when she is in the same position. She is delicious! Tell me who she is.'

'My cousin knows better than I do,' said Bertie Eldridge, drawing back a step. 'She is an old friend and neighbour of his.'

'If your cousin were my son, I should be frightened of so very dangerous a neighbour,' said Lady Caryisfort. It was one of her ways to distinguish as her possible sons men a few years younger than herself.

'Even to think her dangerous would be a presumption in me,' said Bertie Hardwick. 'She is the great lady at home. Perhaps, though you laugh, you may some day see whether she can keep the resolution to behave differently. She is Miss Courtenay, of Langton-Courtenay, Lady Caryisfort. You must know her well enough by name.'

'What!—the Vice-Consul's niece! I must go and tell Lady Granton,' said an attaché, who was among Lady Caryisfort's attendants.

She followed him with her eyes as he went away, with an amused look.

'Now my little friend will have plenty of partners,' she said. 'Oh! you men, who have not even courage enough to ask a pretty girl to dance until you have a certificate of her position. But I don't mean you two. You had the certificate, I suppose, a long time ago?'

'Yes. She has grown very pretty,' said Bertie Eldridge, in a patronising tone.

'How kind of you to think so!—how good of you to make her dance! as the French say. Mr. Hardwick, I suppose she is your father's squire? Are you as condescending as your cousin? Give me your arm, please, and introduce me to the party. I am sure they must be fun. I have heard of Mrs. Vice-Consul—'

'I don't think they are particularly funny,' said Bertie Hardwick, with a tone which the lady's ear was far too quick to lose.

'Ah!' she said to herself, 'a victim!' and was on the alert at once.

'It is the younger one who is Miss Courtenay, I suppose?' she said. 'The other is—her cousin. I see now. And I assure you, Mr. Hardwick, though she is not (I suppose?) an heiress, she is very pretty too.'

Bertie assented with a peculiar smile. It was a great distinction to Bertie Hardwick to be seen with Lady Caryisfort on his arm, and a very great compliment to Mrs. Anderson that so great a personage should leave her seat in order to make her acquaintance. Yet there were drawbacks to this advantage; for Lady Caryisfort had a way of making her own theories on most things that fell under her observation; and she did so at once in respect to the group so suddenly brought under her observation. She paid Mrs. Anderson a great many compliments upon her two girls.

'I hear from Mr. Hardwick that I ought to know your niece "at home," as the schoolboys say,' she said. 'Caryisfort is not more than a dozen miles from Langton-Courtenay. I certainly did not expect to meet my young neighbour here.'

'Her uncle wishes her to travel; she is herself fond of moving about,' murmured Mrs. Anderson.

'Oh! to be sure—it is quite natural,' said Lady Caryisfort; 'but I should have thought Lady Granton would have known who her guest was—and—and all of us. There are so many English people always here, and it is so hard to tell who is who—'

'If you will pardon me,' said Mrs. Anderson, who was not without a sense of her own dignity, 'it is just because of the difficulty in telling who is who that I have brought Kate here. Her guardian does not wish her to be introduced in England till she is of age; and as I am anxious not to attract any special attention, such as her position might warrant—'

'Is her guardian romantic?' said Lady Caryisfort. 'Does he want her to be loved for herself alone, and that sort of thing? For otherwise, do you know, I should think it was dangerous. A pretty girl is never quite safe—'

'Of course,' said Mrs. Anderson, gravely, 'there are some risks, which one is obliged to run—with every girl.'

And she glanced at Bertie Hardwick, who was standing by; and either Bertie blushed, being an ingenuous young man, or Lady Caryisfort fancied he did; for she was very busy making her little version of this story, and every circumstance, as far as she had gone, fitted in.

'But an heiress is so much more dangerous than any other girl. Suppose she should fancy some one beneath—some one not quite sufficiently—some one, in short, whom her guardians would not approve of? Do you know, I think it is a dreadful responsibility for you.'

Mrs. Anderson smiled; but she gave her adviser a sudden look of fright and partial irritation.

'I must take my chance with others,' she said. 'We can only hope nothing will happen.'

'Nothing happen! When it is girls and boys that are in question something always happens!' cried Lady Caryisfort, elevating her eyebrows. 'But here come your two girls, looking very happy. Will you introduce them to me, please? I hope you will not be affronted with me for an inquisitive old woman,' she went on, with her most gracious smile; 'but I have been watching you for ever so long.'

She was watching them now, closely, scientifically, under her drooped eyelids. Bertie had brightened so at their approach, there could be no mistaking that symptom. And the pale girl, the dark girl, the quiet one, who, now that she had time to examine her, proved almost more interesting than the beauty—had changed, too, lighting up like a sky at sunset. The red line had gone from under Ombra's eyes; there was a rose-tint on her cheek which came and went; her eyes were dewy, like the first stars that come out at evening. A pretty, pensive creature, but bright for the moment, as was the other one—the one who was all made of colour and light.

'This is my niece, Lady Caryisfort,' said Mrs. Anderson, with an effort; and she added, in a lower tone, 'This is Ombra, my own child.'

'Do you call her Ombra? What a pretty name! and how appropriate! Then of course the other one is sunshine,' said Lady Caryisfort. 'I hope I shall see something of them while I stay here; and, young ladies, I hope, as I said, that you do not consider me a very impertinent old woman because I have been watching you.'

Kate laughed out the clearest, youthful laugh.

'Are you an old woman?' she said. 'I should not have guessed it.'

Lady Caryisfort turned towards Kate with growing favour. How subtle is the effect of wealth and greatness (she thought). Kate spoke out frankly, in the confidence of her own natural elevation, which placed her on a level with all these princesses and great ladies; while Ombra, though she was older and more experienced, hung shyly back, and said nothing at all. Lady Caryisfort, with her quick eyes, perceived, or thought she perceived, this difference in a moment, and, half-unconsciously, inclined towards the one who was of her own caste.

'Old enough to be your grandmother,' she said; 'and I am your neighbour, besides, at home, so I hope we shall be great friends. I suppose you have heard of the Caryisforts? No! Why, you must be a little changeling not to know the people in your own county. You know Bertie Hardwick, though?'

'Oh! yes—I have known him all my life,' said Kate, calmly, looking up at her.

How different the two girls were! The bright one (Lady Caryisfort remarked to herself) as calm as a Summer day; the shadowy one all changing and fluttering, with various emotions. It was easy to see what that meant.

This conversation, however, had to be broken up abruptly, for already the stream of partners which Lady Caryisfort had prophesied was pouring upon the girls. Lady Barker, indeed, had come to the rescue as soon as the appearance of the two Berties emancipated the cousins. When they did not absolutely require her help, she proffered it, according to Lady Caryisfort's rule; and even Lady Granton herself showed signs of interest. An heiress is not an everyday occurrence even in the highest circles; and this was not a common heiress, a mere representative of money, but the last of an old family, the possessor of fair and solid English acres, old, noble houses, a name any man might be proud of uniting to his own; and a beauty besides. This was filling the cup too high, most people felt—there was no justice in it. Fancy, rich, well-born, and beautiful too! She had no right to have so much.

'I cannot think why you did not tell me,' said Lady Barker, coming to Mrs. Anderson's side. She felt she had made rather a mistake with her Mrs. Vice-Consul; and the recollection of her jokes about Kate's possible inheritance made her redden when she thought of them. She had put herself in the wrong so clearly that even her stupid attaché had found it out.

'I had no desire to tell anybody—I am sorry it is known now,' said Mrs. Anderson.

Long before this a comfortable place had been found for Kate's aunt. Her heiress had raised her out of all that necessity of watching and struggling for a point of vantage which nobodies are compelled to submit to when they venture among the great. But it is doubtful whether Mrs. Anderson was quite happy in her sudden elevation. Her feelings were of a very mixed and uncertain character. So far as Lady Barker was concerned, she could not but feel a certain pride—she liked to show the old friend, who was patronising and kind, that she needed no exercise of condescension on her part; and she was pleased, as that man no doubt was pleased, who, having taken the lower room at the feast, was bidden, 'Friend, go up higher.' That sensation cannot be otherwise than pleasant—the little commotion, the flutter of apologies and regrets with which she was discovered 'to have been standing all this time;' the slight discomfiture of the people round, who had taken no notice, on perceiving after all that she was somebody, and not nobody, as they thought. All this had been pleasant. But it was not so pleasant to feel in so marked and distinct a manner that it was all on Kate's account. Kate was very well; her aunt was fond of her, and good to her, and would have been so independent of her heiress-ship. But to find that her own value, such as it was—and most of us put a certain value on ourselves—and the beauty and sweetness of her child, who, to her eyes, was much more lovely than Kate, should all go for nothing, and that an elevation which was half contemptuous, should be accorded to them solely on Kate's account, was humiliating to the good woman. She took advantage of it, and was even pleased with the practical effect; but it wounded her pride, notwithstanding, in the tenderest point. Kate, whom she had scolded and petted into decorum, whom she had made with her own hands, so to speak, into the semblance she now bore, whose faults and deficiencies she was so sensible of! Poor Mrs. Anderson, the position of dignity 'among all the best people' was pleasant to her; but the thought that she had gained it only as Kate's aunt put prickles in the velvet. And Ombra, her child, her first of things, was nothing but Kate's cousin. 'But that will soon be set to rights,' the mother said to herself, with a smile; and then she added aloud—

'I am very sorry it is known now. We never intended it. A girl in Kate's position has enough to go through at home, without being exposed to—to fortune-hunters and annoyances here. Had I known these boys were in Florence, I should not have come. I am very much annoyed. Nothing could be further from her guardian's wishes—or my own.'

'Oh, well, you can't help it!' said Lady Barker. 'It was not your fault. But you can't hide an heiress. You might as well try to put brown holland covers on a lighthouse. By-the-bye, young Eldridge is very well connected, and very nice—don't you think?'

'He is Sir Herbert Eldridge's son,' said Mrs. Anderson, stiffly.

'Yes. Not at all bad looking, and all that. Nobody could consider him, you know, in the light of a fortune-hunter. But if you take my advice you will keep all those young Italians at arm's length. Some of them are very captivating in their way; and then it sounds romantic, and girls are pleased. There is that young Buoncompagni, that Miss Courtenay is dancing with now. He is one of the handsomest young fellows in Florence, and he has not a sou. Of course he is looking out for some one with money. Positively you must take great care. Ah! I see it is Mr. Eldridge your daughter is dancing with. You are old friends, I suppose?'

'Very old friends,' said Mrs. Anderson; and she was not sorry when her questioner was called away. Perhaps, for the moment, she was not much impressed by Kate's danger in respect to the young Count Buoncompagni. Her eyes were fixed upon Ombra, as was natural. In the abstract, a seat even upon velvet cushions (with prickles in them), against an emblazoned wall, for hours together, with no one whom you know to speak to, and only such crumbs of entertainment as are thrown to you when some one says, 'A pretty scene, is it not? What a pretty dress! Don't you think Lady Caryisfort is charming? And dear Lady Granton, how well she is looking!' Even with such brilliant interludes of conversation as the above, the long vigil of a chaperon is not exhilarating. But when Mrs. Anderson's eye followed Ombra she was happy; she was content to sit against the wall, and gaze, and would not allow to herself that she was sleepy. 'Poor dear Kate, too!' she said to herself, with a compunction, 'she is as happy as possible.' Thus nature gave a compensation to Ombra for being only Miss Courtenay's cousin—a compensation which, for the moment, in the warmth of personal happiness, she did not need.

CHAPTER XXXVIII

'Why should you get up this morning, Signora mia?' said old Francesca. 'The young ladies are fast asleep still. And it was a grand success, a che lo dite. Did not I say so from the beginning? To be sure it was a grand success. The Signorine are divine. If I were a young principe, or a marchesino, I know what I should do. Mees Katta is charming, my dearest lady; but, nostra Ombra—ah! nostra Ombra—'

'Francesca, we must not be prejudiced,' said Mrs. Anderson, who was taking her coffee in bed—a most unusual indulgence—while Francesca stood ready for a gossip at the bedside. The old woman was fond of petting her mistress when she had an opportunity, and of persuading her into little personal indulgences, as old servants so often are. The extra trouble of bringing up the little tray, with the fragrant coffee, the little white roll from the English baker, which the Signora was so prejudiced as to prefer, and one white camelia out of last night's bouquet, in a little Venetian glass, to serve the purpose of decoration, was the same kind of pleasure to her as it is to a mother to serve a sick child who is not ill enough to alarm her. Francesca liked it. She liked the thanks, and the protest against so innocent an indulgence with which it was always accompanied.

'I must not be so lazy again. I am quite ashamed of myself. But I was fatigued last night.'

'Si! si!' cried Francesca. 'To be sure the Signora was tired. What! sit up till four o'clock, she who goes to bed at eleven; and my lady is not twenty now, as she once was! Ah! I remember the day when, after a ball, Madame was fatigued in a very different way.'

'Those days are long past, Francesca,' said Mrs. Anderson, with a smile, shaking her head. She did not dislike being reminded of them. She had known in her time what it was to be admired and sought after; and after sitting for six hours against the wall, it was a little consolation to reflect that she too had had her day.

'As Madame pleases, so be it,' said Francesca; 'though my lady could still shine with the best if she so willed it; but for my own part I think she is right. When one has a child, and such a child as our Ombra—'

'My dear Francesca, we must not be prejudiced,' said Mrs. Anderson. 'Ombra is very sweet to you and me; and I think she is very lovely; but Kate is more beautiful than she is—Kate has such a bloom. I myself admire her very much—not of course so much as—my own child.'

'If the Signora had said it, I should not have believed her,' said Francesca. 'I should be sorry to show any want of education to Madame, but I should not have believed her. Mademoiselle Katta is good child—I love her—I am what you call fond; but she is not like our Ombra. It is not necessary that I should draw the distinction. The Signora knows it is quite a different thing.'

'Yes, yes, Francesca, I know—I know only too well; and I hope I am not unjust,' said Mrs. Anderson. 'I hope I am not unkind—I cannot help it being different. Nothing would make me neglect my duty, I trust; and I have no reason to be anything but fond of Kate—I love her very much; but still, as you say—'

'The Signora knows that I understand,' said Francesca. 'Two gentlemen have called already this morning—already, though it is so early. They are the same young Signorini who came to the Cottage in IsleofWite.' (This Francesca pronounced as one word.) 'Now, if the Signora would tell me, it would make me happy. There is two, and I ask myself—which?'

Mrs. Anderson shook her head.

'And so do I sometimes,' she said; 'and I thought I knew; but last night—My dear Francesca, when I am sure I will tell you. But, indeed, perhaps it is neither of them,' she added, with a sigh.

Francesca shook her head.

'Madame would say that perhaps it is bose.'

I have not thought it necessary always to put down Francesca's broken English, nor the mixture of languages in which she spoke. It might be gratifying to the writer to be able to show a certain acquaintance with those tongues; but it is always doubtful whether the reader will share that gratification. But when she addressed her mistress, Francesca spoke Italian, and consequently used much better language than when she was compelled to toil through all the confusing sibilants and ths of the English tongue.

'I do not know—I cannot tell,' said Mrs. Anderson. 'Take the tray, mia buona amica. You shall know when I know. And now I think I must get up. One can't stay in bed, you know, all day.'

When her mistress thus changed the subject, Francesca saw that it was no longer convenient to continue it. She was not satisfied that Mrs. Anderson did not know, but she understood that she was in the meantime to make her own observations. Keener eyes were never applied to such a purpose, but at the present moment Francesca was too much puzzled to come to any speedy decision on the subject; and notwithstanding her love for Ombra, who was supreme in her eyes, Francesca was moved to a feeling for Kate which had not occurred to the other ladies. 'Santissima Madonna! it is hard—very hard for the little one,' she said to herself, as she mused over the matter. 'Who is to defend her from Fate? She will see them every day—she is young—they are young—what can anyone expect? Ah! Madonna mia, send some good young marchesino, some piccolo principe, to make the Signorina a great lady, and save her from breaking her little heart. It would be good for la patria, too,' Francesca resumed, piously thinking of Kate's wealth.

She was a servant of the old Italian type, to whom it was natural to identify herself with her family. She did not even 'toil for duty, not for meed,' but planned and deliberated over all their affairs with the much more spontaneous and undoubting sentiment that their affairs were her own, and that they mutually belonged to each other. She said 'our Ombra' with as perfect good faith as if her young mistress had been her own child—and so indeed she was. The bond between them was too real to be discussed or even described—and consequently it was with the natural interest of one pondering her own business that Francesca turned it all over in her mind, and considered how she could best serve Kate, and keep her unharmed by Ombra's uncertainty.

When Count Antonio Buoncompagni came with his card and his inquiries, the whole landscape lighted up around her. Francesca was a Florentine of the Florentines. She knew all about the Buoncompagni; her aunt's husband's sister had been cameriera to the old Duchessa, Antonio's grandmother; so that in a manner, she said to herself, she belonged to the family. The Contessina, his mother, had made her first communion along with Francesca's younger sister, Angiola. This made a certain spiritual bond between them. The consequence of all these important facts, taken together, was that Francesca felt herself the natural champion of Count Buoncompagni, who seemed thus to have stepped in at the most suitable moment, and as if in answer to her appeal to the Madonna, to lighten her anxieties, and free her child Ombra from the responsibility of harming another. The Count Antonio was young and very good-looking. He addressed Francesca in those frank and friendly tones which she had so missed in England; he called her amica mia, though he had never seen her before. 'Ah! Santissima Madonna, quella differenza!' she said to herself, as he went down the long stair, and the young Englishmen, who had known her for years, and were very friendly to the old woman, came up, and got themselves admitted without one unnecessary word. They had no caressing friendly phrase for her as they went and came.

Francesca was true as steel to her mistress and all her house; she would have gone through fire and water for them; but it never occurred to her that to take the part of confidante and abettor to the young Count, should he mean to present himself as a suitor to Kate, would be treacherous to them or their trust. Of all things that could happen to the Signorina, the best possible thing—the good fortune most to be desired—would be that she should get a noble young husband, who would be very fond of her, and to whose house she would bring joy and prosperity. The Buoncompagni, unfortunately, though noble as the king himself, were poor; and Francesca knew very well what a difference it would make in the faded grand palazzo if Kate went there with her wealth. Even so much wealth as she had brought to her aunt would, Francesca thought, make a great difference; and what, then, would not the whole fabulous amount of Kate's fortunes do? 'It will be good for la patria, too,' she repeated to herself; and this not guiltily, like a conscious conspirator, but with the truest sense of duty.

She carried in Count Antonio's card to the salone where the ladies were sitting with their visitors. Ombra was seated at one of the windows, looking out; beside her stood Bertie Hardwick, not saying much; while his cousin, scarcely less silent, listened to Kate's chatter. Kate's gay voice was in full career; she was going over all last night's proceedings, giving them a dramatic account of her feelings. She was describing her own anger, mortification, and dismay; then her relief, when she caught sight of the two young men. 'Not because it was you,' she said gaily, 'but because you were men—or boys—things we could dance with; and because you knew us, and could not help asking us.'

'That is not a pleasant way of stating it,' said Bertie Eldridge. 'If you had known our delight and amaze and happiness in finding you, and how transported we were—'

'I suppose you must say that,' said Kate; 'please don't take the trouble. I know you could not help making me a pretty speech; but what I say is quite true. We were glad, not because it was you, but because we felt in a moment, here are some men we know, they cannot leave us standing here all night; we must be able to get a dance at last.'

'I have brought the Signora a card,' said Francesca, interrupting the talk. 'Ah, such a beautiful young Signor! What a consolation to me to be in my own country; to be called amica mia once again. You are very good, you English Signori, and very kind in your way, but you never speak as if you loved us, though we may serve you for years. When one comes like this handsome young Count Antonio, how different! "Cara mia," he says, "put me at the feet of their Excellencies. I hope the beautiful young ladies are not too much fatigued!" Ah, my English gentlemen, you do not talk like that! You say, "Are they quite well—Madame Anderson and the young ladies?" And if it is old Francesca, or a new domestic, whom you never saw before, not one word of difference! You are cold; you are insensible; you are not like our Italian. Signorina Katta, do you know the name on the card?'

'It's Count Antonio Buoncompagni!' said Kate, with a bright blush and smile. 'Why, that was my partner last night! How nice of him to come and call—and what a pretty name! And he dances like an angel, Francesca—I never saw any one dance so well!'

'That is a matter of course, Signorina. He is young; he is a Buoncompagni; his ancestors have all been noble and had education for a thousand years—what should hinder him to dance? If the Signorina will come to me when these gentlemen leave you, I will tell her hundreds of beautiful stories about the Buoncompagni. We are, as it were, connected—the sister-law of my aunt Filomena was once maid to the old Duchessa—besides other ties,' Francesca added, raising her head with a certain careless grandeur. 'Nobody knows better than I do the history of the Buoncompagni; and the Signorina is very fond of stories, as Madame knows.'

'My good Francesca, so long as you don't turn her head with your stories,' said Mrs. Anderson, good-humouredly. And she added, when the old woman had left the room, 'Often and often I have been glad to hear Francesca's stories myself. All these Italian families have such curious histories. She will go on from one to another, as if she never would have done. She knows everybody, and whom they all married, and all about them. And there is some truth, you know, in what she says—we are very kind, but we don't talk to our servants nor show any affection for them. I am very fond of Francesca, and very grateful to her for her faithful service, but even I don't do it. Kate has a frank way with everybody. But our English reserve is dreadful!'

'We don't say everything that comes uppermost,' said one of the young men. 'We do not wear our hearts on our sleeves,' said the other.

'No,' said Ombra; 'perhaps, on the contrary, you keep them so covered up that one never can tell whether you have any hearts at all.'

Ombra's voice had something in it different from the sound of the others; it had a meaning. Her words were not lightly spoken, but fully intended. This consciousness startled all the little party. Mrs. Anderson flung herself, as it were, into the breach, and began to talk fast on all manner of subjects; and Ombra, probably repenting the seriousness of her speech, exerted herself to dissipate the effect of it. But Kate kept the Count's card in her hand, pondering over it. A young Italian noble; the sort of figure which appears in books and in pictures; the kind of person who acts as hero in tale and song. He had come to lay himself at the feet of the beautiful young ladies. Well! perhaps the two Berties meant just as much by the clumsy shy visit which they were paying at that moment—but they never laid themselves at anybody's feet. They were well-dressed Philistines, never allowing any expression of friendship or affectionateness to escape them. Had they no hearts at all, as Ombra insinuated, or would they not be much pleasanter persons if they wore their said hearts on their sleeves, and permitted them to be pecked at? Antonio Buoncompagni! Kate stole out after a while, on pretence of seeking her work, and flew to the other end of the long, straggling suite of rooms to where Francesca sat. 'Tell me all about them,' she said, breathlessly. And Francesca clapped her hands mentally, and felt that her work had begun.

CHAPTER XXXIX

'It is very interesting,' said Kate; 'but it is about this Count's grandfather you are talking, Francesca. Could not we come a little lower down?'

'Signorina mia, when one is a Buoncompagni, one's grandfather is very close and near,' said Francesca. 'There are some families in which a grandfather is a distant ancestor, or perhaps the beginning of the race. But with the Buoncompagni you do not adopt that way of reckoning. Count Antonio's mother is living—she is a thing of to-day, like the rest of us. Then I ask, Signorina Katta, whom can one speak of? That is the way in old families. Doubtless in the Signorina's own house—'

'Oh, my grandpapa is a thousand years off!' said Kate. 'I don't believe in him—he must have been so dreadfully old. Even papa was old. He married when he was about fifty, I suppose, and I never saw him. My poor little mother was different, but I never saw her either. Don't speak of my family, please. I suppose they were very nice, but I don't know much about them.'

'Mademoiselle would not like to be without them,' said Francesca, nodding her little grey head. 'Mademoiselle would feel very strange if all at once it were said to her, "You never had a grandpapa. You are a child of the people, my young lady. You came from no one knows where." Ah, you prefer the old ones to that! Signorina Katta. If you were to go into the Buoncompagni Palazzo, and see all the beautiful pictures of the old Cavalieri in their armour, and the ladies with pearls and rubies upon their beautiful robes! The Contino would be rich if he could make up his mind to sell those magnificent pictures; but the Signorina will perceive in a moment that to sell one's ancestors—that is a thing one could never do.'

'No, I should not like to sell them,' said Kate, thoughtfully. 'But do you mean that? Are the Buoncompagni poor?'

'Signorina mia,' said Francesca, with dignity, 'when were they rich—our grand nobili Italiani! Not since the days when Firenze was a queen in the world, and did what she would. That was ended a long, long time ago. And what, then, was it the duty of the great Signori to do? They had to keep their old palaces, and all the beautiful things the house had got when it was rich, for the good of la patria, when she should wake up again. They had to keep all the old names, and the recollections. Signorina Katta, a common race could not have done this. We poor ones in the streets, we have done what we could; we have kept up our courage and our gaiety of heart for our country. The Buoncompagni, and such like, kept up the race. They would rather live in a corner of the old Palazzo than part with it to a stranger. They would not sell the pictures, and the belle cose, except now and then one small piece, to keep the family alive. And now, look you, Signorina mia, la patria has woke up at last, and ecco! Her old names, and her old palaces, and the belle cose are here waiting for her. Ah! we have had a great deal to suffer, but we are not extinguished. Certainly they are poor, but what then? They exist; and every true Italian will bless them for that.'

This old woman, with her ruddy-brown, dried-up little face, and her scanty hair, tied into a little knot at the top of it—curious little figure, whom Kate had found it hard work to keep from laughing at when she arrived first at Shanklin—was a politician, a visionary, a patriot-enthusiast. Kate now, at eighteen, looked at Francesca with respect, which was just modified by an inclination, far down at the bottom of her heart, to laugh. But for this she took herself very sharply to task. Kate had not quite got over the natural English inclination to be contemptuous of all 'foreigners' who took a different view of their duty from that natural to the British mind. If the Buoncompagni had tried to make money, and improve their position; if they had emigrated, and fought their way in the world; if they had done some active work, instead of vegetating and preserving their old palaces, she asked herself? Which was no doubt an odd idea to have got into the Tory brain of the young representative of an old family, bound to hate revolutionaries; but Kate was a revolutionary by nature, and her natural Toryism was largely tinctured by the natural Radicalism of her age, and that propensity to contradict, and form theories of her own, which were part of her character. It was part of her character still, though it had been smoothed down, and brought under subjection, by her aunt's continual indulgence. She was not so much impressed as she felt she ought to have been by Francesca's speech.

'I am glad they exist,' she said. 'Of course we must all really have had the same number of grandfathers and grandmothers, but still an old family is pleasant. The only thing is, Francesca—don't be angry—suppose they had done something, while the patria, you know, has been asleep; suppose they had tried to get on, to recover their money, to do something more than exist! It is only a suggestion—probably I am quite wrong, but—

'The Signorina perhaps will condescend to inform me,' said Francesca, with lofty satire, 'what, in her opinion, it would have been best for our nobles to do?'

'Oh! I am sure I don't know. I only meant—I don't know anything about it!' cried Kate.

'If the Signorina will permit me to say so, that is very visible,' said Francesca; and then, for full five minutes, she plied her needle, and was silent. This, perhaps, was rather a hard punishment for Kate, who had left the visitors in the drawing-room to seek a more lively amusement in Francesca's company, and who, after the excitement of the ball, was anxious for some other excitement. She revenged herself by pulling the old woman's work about, and asking what was this, and this. Francesca was making a dress for her mistress, and Mrs. Anderson, though she did not despise the fashion, was sufficiently sensible to take her own way, and keep certain peculiarities of her own.

'Why do you make it like this?' said Kate. 'Auntie is not a hundred. She might as well have her dress made like other people. She is very nice-looking, I think, for her age. Don't you think so? She must have been pretty once, Francesca. Why, you ought to know—you knew her when she was young. Don't you think she has been—?'

'Signorina, be so good as to let my work alone,' said Francesca. 'What! do you think there is nothing but youth that is to be admired? I did not expect to find so little education in one of my Signorinas. Know, Mademoiselle Katta, that there are many persons who think Madame handsomer than either of the young ladies. There is an air of distinction and of intelligence. You, for instance, you have the beauté de diable—one admires you because you are so young; but how do you know that it will last? Your features are not remarkable, Signorina Katta. When those roses are gone, probably you will be but an ordinary-looking woman; but my Signora Anderson, she has features, she has the grand air, she has distinction—'

'Oh! you spiteful old woman!' cried Kate, half vexed, half laughing. 'I never said I thought I was pretty. I know I am just like a doll, all red and white; but you need not tell me so, all the same.'

'Mademoiselle is not like a doll,' said Francesca. 'Sometimes, when she has a better inspiration, Mademoiselle has something more than red and white. I did not affirm that it would not last. I said how do you know? But my Signora has lasted. She is noble!—she is distinguished! And as for what she has been—'

'That is exactly what I said,' said Kate.

'We do not last in Italy,' said Francesca, pursuing the subject with the gravity of an abstract philosopher. 'It is, perhaps, our beautiful climate. Your England, which has so much of mist and of rain, keeps the grass green, and it preserves beauty. The Contessa Buoncompagni has lost all her beauty. She was of the Strozzi family, and made her first communion on the same day as my little Angiolina, who is now blessed in heaven. Allow me to say it to you, Signorina mia, they were beautiful as two angels in their white veils. But the Contessina has grown old. She has lost her hair, which does not happen to the English

Signore, and—other things. I am more old than she, and when I see it I grieve. She does not go out, except, of course, which goes without saying, to the Duomo. She is a good woman—a very good woman. If she cannot afford to give the best price for her salad, is it her fault? She is a great lady, as great as anybody in all Firenze—Countess Buoncompagni, born Strozzi. What would you have more? But, dear lady, it is no shame to her that she is not rich. Santissima Madonna, why should one hesitate to say it? It is not her fault.'

'Of course it cannot be her fault; nobody would choose to be poor if they could help it,' said Kate.

'I cannot say, Signorina Katta—I have not any information on the subject. To be rich is not all. It might so happen—though I have no special information—that one would choose to be poor. I am poor myself, but I would not change places with many who are rich. I should esteem more,' said Francesca, raising her head, 'a young galantuomo who was noble and poor, and had never done anything against the patria, nor humbled himself before the Tedeschi, a hundred and a thousand times more than those who hold places and honours. But then I am a silly old woman, most likely the Signorina will say.'

'Is Count Buoncompagni like that?' asked Kate; but she did not look for an answer.

And just then the bell rang from the drawing-room, and Francesca put down her work and bustled away to open the door for the young Englishmen whose company Kate had abandoned. The girl took up Francesca's work, and made half a dozen stitches; and then went to her own room, where Maryanne was also at work. Kate gave a little sketch of the dresses at the ball to the handmaiden, who listened with breathless interest.

'I don't think anyone could have looked nicer than you and Miss Ombra in your fresh tarlatane, Miss,' said Maryanne.

'Nobody took the least notice of us,' said Kate. 'We are not worth noticing among so many handsome, well-dressed people. We were but a couple of girls out of the nursery in our white. I think I will choose a colour that will make some show if I ever go to a ball again.'

'Oh! Miss Kate, you will go to a hundred balls!' cried Maryanne, with fervour.

Kate shrugged her shoulders with sham disdain; but she felt, with a certain gentle complacency, that it was true. A girl who has once been to a ball must go on. She cannot be shut up again in any nursery and school-room; she is emancipated for ever and ever; the glorious world is thrown open to her. The tarlatane which marked her bread-and-butter days would no doubt yield to more splendid garments; but she could not go back—she had made her entry into life.

Lady Caryisfort called next day—an event which filled Mrs. Anderson with satisfaction. No doubt Kate was the chief object of her visit; and as it was the first time that Kate's aunt and cousin had practically felt the great advantage which her position gave her over them, there was, without doubt, some difficulty in the situation. But, fortunately, Ombra's attention was otherwise occupied; and Mrs. Anderson, though she was a high-spirited woman, and did not relish the idea of deriving consequence entirely from the little girl whom she had brought up, had yet that philosophy which more or less is the accompaniment of experience, and knew that it was much better to accept the inevitable graciously, than to fight against it. And if anything could have neutralised the wound to her pride, it would have been the 'pretty manners' of Lady Caryisfort, and the interest which she displayed in Ombra. Indeed,

Ombra secured more of her attention than Kate did—a consoling circumstance. Lady Caryisfort showed every inclination to 'take them up.' It was a thing she was fond of doing; and she was so amiable and entertaining, and so rich, and opened up such perfectly good society to her protégées, that few people at the moment of being taken up realised the fact that they must inevitably be let down again by-and-by—a process not so pleasant.

At this moment nothing could be more delightful than their new friend. She called for them when she went out driving, and took them to Fiesole, to La Pioggia, to the Cascine—wherever fashion went. She lent them her carriage when she was indolent, as often happened, and did not care to go out. She asked them to her little parties when she had 'the best people'—a compliment which Mrs. Anderson felt deeply, and which was very different from the invitation to the big ball at the Embassy, to which everybody was invited. In short, Lady Caryisfort launched the little party into the best society of English at Florence, such as it is. And the pretty English heiress became as well known as if she had gone through a season at home previous to this Italian season. Poor Uncle Courtenay! Had he seen Antonio Buoncompagni, who danced like an angel, leading his ward through the mazes of a cotillon, what would that excellent guardian's feelings have been?

CHAPTER XL

We have said that Ombra's attention was otherwise occupied. Had it not been so, it is probable that she would have resented and struggled against the new and unusual and humiliating consciousness of being but an appendage to her cousin; but fortunately all such ideas had been driven out of her head. A new life, a new world, seemed to have begun for Ombra. All the circumstances of their present existence appeared to lend themselves to the creation of this novel sphere. Old things seemed to have passed away, and all had become new. From the moment of the first call, made in doubt and tribulation, by the two Berties, they had resumed again, in the most natural manner, the habits of their former acquaintance, but with an entirely new aspect. Here there was at once the common bond which unites strangers in a new place—a place full of beauty and wonder, which both must see, and which it is so natural they should see together. The two young men fell into the habit of constant attendance upon the ladies, with a naturalness which defeated all precautions; and an intercourse began to spring up, which combined that charming flavour of old friendship, and almost brotherhood, with any other sentiment that might arise by the way. This conjunction, too, made the party so independent and so complete. With such an escort the ladies could go anywhere; and they went everywhere accordingly—to picture-galleries, to all the sights of the place, and even now and then upon country excursions, in the bright, cold Winter days. 'The boys,' as Kate called them, came and went all day long, bringing news of everything that was to be seen or heard, always with a new plan or suggestion for the morrow.

The little feminine party brightened up, as women do brighten always under the fresh and exhilarating influence of that breath from outside which only 'the boys' can bring. Soon Mrs. Anderson, and even Ombra herself, adopted that affectionate phrase—to throw another delightful, half-delusive veil over all possibilities that might be in the future. It gave a certain 'family feeling,' a mutual right to serve and be served; and at times Mrs. Anderson felt as if she could persuade herself that 'the boys,' who were so full of that kindly and tender gallantry which young men can pay to a woman old enough to be their mother, were in reality her own as much as the girls were—if not sons, nephews at the least. She said this to herself, by way, I fear, of excusing herself, and placing little pleasant shields of pretence between her and the reality. To be sure, she was the soul of propriety, and never left the young people alone together; but, as she said, 'at whatever cost to herself,' bore them company in all their rambles. But yet sometimes a recollection of Mr. Courtenay would cross her mind in an uncomfortable way. And sometimes a still more painful chill would seize her when she thought of Kate, who was thus thrown constantly into the society of the Berties. Kate treated them with the easiest friendliness, and they were sincerely (as Mrs. Anderson believed) brotherly to her. But, still, they were all young; and who could tell what fancies the girl might take into her head? These two thoughts kept her uncomfortable. But yet the life was happy and bright; and Ombra was happy. Her cloud of temper had passed away; her rebellions and philosophies had alike vanished into the air. She was brighter than ever she had been in her life—more loving and more sympathetic. Life ran on like a Summer day, though the Tramontana sometimes blew, and the dining-room was cold as San Lorenzo; but all was warm, harmonious, joyous within.

Kate, for one, never troubled her head to ask why. She accepted the delightful change with unquestioning pleasure. It was perfectly simple to her that her cousin should get well—that the cloud should disperse. In her thoughtlessness she did not even attribute this to any special cause, contenting herself with the happy fact that so it was.

'How delightful it is that Ombra should have got so well!' she said, with genuine pleasure, to her aunt.

'Yes, dear,' said Mrs. Anderson, looking at her wistfully. 'It is the Italian air—it works like a charm.'

'I don't think it is the air,' said Kate—'privately, auntie, I think the Italian air is dreadfully chilly—at least, when one is out of the sun. It is the fun, and the stir, and the occupation. Fun is an excellent thing, and having something to do—Now, don't say no, please, for I am quite sure of it. I feel so much happier, too.'

'What makes you happier, my darling?' said Mrs. Anderson, with a very anxious look.

'Oh! I don't know—everything,' said Kate; and she gave her aunt a kiss, and went off singing, balancing a basket on her head with the pretty action of the girls whom she saw every day carrying water from the fountain.

Mrs. Anderson was alone, and this pretty picture dwelt in her mind, and gave her a great deal of thought. Was it only fun and occupation, as the girl said?—or was there something else unknown to Kate dawning in her heart, and making her life bright, all unconsciously to herself? 'They are both as brothers to her,' Mrs. Anderson said to herself, with pain and fear; and then she repeated to herself how good they were, what true gentlemen, how incapable of any pretence which could deceive even so innocent a girl as Kate. The truth was, Mrs. Anderson's uneasiness increased every day. She was doing by Kate as she would that another should not do by Ombra. She was doubly kind and tender, lavishing affection and caresses upon her, but she was not considering Kate's interest, or carrying out Mr. Courtenay's conditions. And what could she do? The happiness of her own child was involved; she was bound hand and foot by her love for Ombra. 'Then,' she would say to herself, 'Kate is getting no harm. She is eighteen past—quite old enough to be "out"—indeed, it would be wrong of me to deny her what pleasure I can, and it is not as if I took her wherever we were asked. I am sure, so far as I am concerned, I should have liked much better to go to the Morrises—nice, pleasant people, not too grand to make friends of—but I refused, for Kate's sake. She shall go nowhere but in the very best society. Her uncle himself could not do better for her than Lady Granton or Lady Caryisfort—most likely not half so well; and he will be hard to please indeed if he is discontented with that,' Mrs. Anderson said to herself. But notwithstanding all these specious pleadings at that secret bar, where she was at once judge and advocate and culprit, she did not succeed in obtaining a favourable verdict; all she could do was to put the thought away from her by times, and persuade herself that no harm could ensue.

'Look at Ombra now,' Kate said, on the same afternoon to Francesca, whose Florentine lore she held in great estimation. Her conversation with her aunt had brought the subject to her mind, and a little curiosity about it had awakened within her when she thought it over. 'See what change of air has done, as I told you it would—and change of scene.'

'Mees Katta,' said Francesca, 'change of air is very good—I say nothing against that—but, as I have remarked on other occasions, one must not form one's opinion on ze surface. Mademoiselle Ombra has changed ze mind.'

'Oh! yes, I know you said she must do that, and you never go back from what you once said; but, Francesca, I don't understand you in the least. How has she changed her mind?'

'If Mademoiselle would know, it is best to ask Mees Ombra her-self,' said Francesca, 'not one poor servant, as has no way to know.'

'Oh!' cried Kate, flushing scarlet, 'when, you are so humble there is an end of everything—I know that much by this time. There! I will ask Ombra herself; I will not have you make me out to be underhand. Ombra, come here one moment, please. I am so glad you are better; it makes me happy to see you look like your old self; but tell me one thing—my aunt says it is the change of air, and I say it is change of scene and plenty to do. Now, tell me which it is—I want to know.'

Ombra had been passing the open door; she came and stood in the doorway, with one hand upon the lintel. A pretty, flitting, evanescent colour had come upon her pale cheek, and there was now always a dewy look of feeling in her eyes, which made them beautiful. She stood and smiled, in the soft superiority of her elder age, upon the girl who questioned her. Her colour deepened a little, her eyes looked as if there was dew in them, ready to fall. 'I am better,' she said, in a voice which seemed to Kate to be full of combined and harmonious notes—'I am better without knowing why—I suppose because God is so good.'

And then she went away softly, crooning the song which she had been humming to herself, in the lightness of her heart, as her cousin called her. Kate was struck with violent shame and self-disgust. 'Oh, how wicked I am!' she said, rushing to her own room and shutting herself in. And there she had a short but refreshing cry, though she was by no means given to tears. She had been brought up piously, to be sure—going to church, attending to her 'religious duties,' as a well-brought-up young woman ought to do. But it had not occurred to her to give any such visionary reason for anything that had happened to her. Kate preferred secondary causes, to tell the truth. But there was something more than met the ear in what Ombra said. How was it that God had been so good? Kate was very reverential of this new and unanswerable cause for her cousin's restoration. But how was it?—there was still something, which she did not fathom, beyond.

Such pleasant days these were! When 'the boys' came to pay their greetings in the morning, 'Where shall we go to-day?' was the usual question. They went to the pictures two or three days in the week, seeing every scrap of painting that was to be found anywhere—from the great galleries, where all was light and order, to the little out-of-the-way churches, which hid, in the darkness of their heart of hearts, some one precious morsel of an altar-piece, carefully veiled from the common public. And, in the intervals, they would wander through the streets, learning the very houses by heart; gazing into the shop windows, at the mosaics, on the Lung-Arno; at the turquoises and pearls, which then made the Ponte Vecchio a soft blaze of colour, blue and white; at the curiosity shops, and those hung about with copies in which Titian was done into weakness, and Raphael to imbecility. Every bit of Florence was paced over by these English feet, one pair of which were often very tired, but never shrunk from the duty before them. Most frequently 'the boys' returned to luncheon, which even Mrs. Anderson, who knew better, was prejudiced enough to create into a steady-going English meal. In the afternoon, if they drove with Lady Caryisfort to the Cascine, the Berties came to the carriage-windows to tell them all that was going on; to bring them bouquets; to point out every new face. When they went to the theatre or opera in the evening, again the same indefatigable escort accompanied and made everything smooth for them. When they had invitations, the Berties, too, were invariably of the party. When they stayed at home the young men, even when not invited, would always manage to present themselves during the evening, uniting in pleasant little choruses of praise to Mrs. Anderson for staying at home. 'After all, this is the best,' the young hypocrites would say; and one of them would read while the ladies worked; or there would be 'a little music,' in which Ombra was the chief performer. Thus, from the beginning of the day to the end, they were scarcely separated, except for intervals, which gave freshness ever renewed to their meeting. It was like 'a family party;' so Mrs. Anderson said to herself a dozen times in a day.

CHAPTER XLI

'Come and tell me all about yourself, Kate,' said Lady Caryisfort, from her sofa. She had a cold, and was half an invalid. She had kept Kate with her while the others went out, after paying their call. Lady Caryisfort had enveloped her choice of Kate in the prettiest excuses: 'I wish one of you girls would give up the sunshine, and stay and keep me company,' she had said. 'Let me see—no, I will not choose Ombra, for Ombra has need of all the air that is to be had; but Kate is strong—an afternoon's seclusion will not make any difference to her. Spare me Kate, please, Mrs. Anderson. I want some one to talk to—I want something pleasant to look at. Let her stay and dine with me, and in the evening I will send her home.'

So it had been settled; and Kate was in the great, somewhat dim drawing-room, which was Lady Caryisfort's abode. The house was one of the great palazzi in one of the less-known streets of Florence. It was on the sunny side, but long ago the sun had retreated behind the high houses opposite. The great lofty palace itself was like a mountain side, and half way down this mountain side came the tall windows, draped with dark velvet and white muslin, which looked out into the deep ravine, called a street, below. The room was very large and lofty, and had openings on two sides, enveloped in heavy velvet curtains, into two rooms beyond. The two other side walls were covered with large frescoes, almost invisible in this premature twilight; for it was not late, and the top rooms in the palace, which were inhabited by Cesare, the mosaic-worker, still retained the sunshine. All the decorations were of a grandiose character; the velvet hangings were dark, though warm in colour; a cheerful wood fire threw gleams of variable reflection here and there into the tall mirrors; and Lady Caryisfort, wrapped in a huge soft white shawl, which looked like lace, but was Shetland wool, lay on a sofa under one of the frescoes. As the light varied, there would appear now a head, now an uplifted arm, out of the historical composition above. The old world was all about in the old walls, in the waning light, in the grand proportions of the place; but the dainty lady in her shawl, the dainty table with its pretty tea-service, which stood within reach of her hand, and Kate, whose bloom not even the twilight could obliterate, belonged not to the old, but the new. There was a low, round chair, a kind of luxurious shell, covered with the warm, dark velvet, on the other side of the little table.

'Come and sit down beside me here,' said Lady Caryisfort, 'and tell me all about yourself.'

'There is not very much to tell,' said Kate, 'if you mean facts; but if it is me you want to know about, then there is a little more. Which would you like best?'

'I thought you were a fact.'

'I suppose I am,' said Kate, with a laugh. 'I never thought of that. But then, of course, between the facts that have happened to me and this fact, Kate Courtenay, there is a good deal of difference. Which would you like best? Me? But, then, where must I begin?'

'As early as you can remember,' said the inquisitor; 'and, recollect, I should most likely have sought you out, and known all about you long before this, if you had stayed at Langton—so you may be perfectly frank with me.'

To tell the truth, all the little scene had been got up on purpose for this confidential talk; the apparently chance choice of Kate as a companion, and even Lady Caryisfort's cold, were means to an end. Kate was of her own county, she was of her own class, she was thrown into a position which Lady Caryisfort thought was not the one she ought to have filled, and with all the fervour of a lively fancy and benevolent meaning she had thrown herself into this little ambush. The last words were just as near a mistake as it was possible for words to be, for Kate had no notion of being anything but frank; and the little assurance that she might be so safely almost put her on her guard.

'You would not have been allowed to seek me out,' said Kate. 'Uncle Courtenay had made up his mind I was to know nobody—I am sure I don't know why. He used to send me a new governess every year. It was the greatest chance that I was allowed to keep even Maryanne. He thought servants ought to be changed; and I am afraid,' said Kate, with humility, 'that I was not at all nice when I was at home.'

'My poor child! I don't believe you were ever anything but nice.'

'No,' said Kate, taking hold of the caressing hand which was laid on her arm; 'you can't think how disagreeable I was till I was fifteen; then my dear aunt—my good aunt, whom you don't like so much as you might—'

'How do you know that, you little witch?'

'Oh, I know very well! She came home to England, after being years away, and she wrote to my uncle, asking if she might see me, and he was horribly worried with me at the time,' said Kate. 'I had worried him so that he could not eat his dinner even in peace—and Uncle Courtenay likes his dinner—so he wrote and said she might have me altogether if she pleased; and though he gave the very worst account of me, and said all the harm he could, auntie started off directly and took me home.'

'That was kind of her, Kate.'

'Kind of her! Oh, it was a great deal more than kind! Fancy how I felt when she cried and kissed me! I am not sure that anybody had ever kissed me before, and I was such a stupid—such a thing without a soul—that I was quite astonished when she cried. I actually asked her why? Whenever I think of it I feel my cheeks grow crimson.' And here Kate, with a pretty gesture, laid one of Lady Caryisfort's soft rose-tipped fingers upon her burning cheek.

'You poor dear child! Well, I understand why Mrs. Anderson cried, and it was nice of her; but après,' said Kate's confessor.

'Après? I was at home; I was as happy as the day was long. I got to be like other girls; they never paid any attention to me, and they petted me from morning to night.'

'But how could that be?' said Lady Caryisfort, whose understanding was not quite equal to the strain thus put upon it.

'I forgot all about myself after that,' said Kate. 'I was just like other girls. Ombra thought me rather a bore at first; but, fortunately, I never found that out till she had got over it. She had always been auntie's only child, and I think she was a trifle—jealous; I have an idea,' said Kate—'But how wicked I am to go and talk of Ombra's faults to you!'

'Never mind; I shall never repeat anything you tell me,' said the confidante.

'Well, I think, if she has a weakness, it is that perhaps she likes to be first. I don't mean in any vulgar way,' said Kate, suddenly flushing red as she saw a smile on her companion's face, 'but with people she loves. She would not like (naturally) to see her mother love anyone else as much as her! or even she would not like to see me—'

'And how about other people?' cried Lady Caryisfort, amused.

'About other people I do not know what to say; I don't think she has ever been tried,' said Kate, with a grave and puzzled look. 'She has always been first, without any question—or, at least, so I think; but that is puzzling—that is more difficult. I would rather not go into that question, for, by-the-bye, this is all about Ombra—it is not about me.'

'That is true,' said Lady Caryisfort; 'we must change the subject, for I don't want you to tell me your cousin's secrets, Kate.'

'Secrets! She has not any,' said Kate, with a laugh.

'Are you quite sure of that?'

'Sure of Ombra! Of course I must be. If I were not quite sure of Ombra, whom could I believe in? There are no secrets,' said Kate, with a little pride, 'among us.'

'Poor child!' thought Lady Caryisfort to herself; but she said nothing, though, after a while, she asked gently, 'Were you glad to come abroad? I suppose it was your guardian's wish?'

Once more Kate laughed.

'That is the funniest thing of all,' she said. 'He came to pay us a visit; and fancy he, who never could bear me to have a single companion, arrived precisely on my birthday, when we were much gayer than usual, and had a croquet party! It was as good as a play to see his face. But he made my aunt promise to take us abroad. I suppose he thought we could make no friends abroad.'

'But in that he has evidently been mistaken, Kate.'

'I don't know. Except yourself, Lady Caryisfort, what friends have we made? You have been very kind, and as nice as it is possible to be—'

'Thanks, dear. The benefit has been mine,' said Lady Caryisfort, in an undertone.

'But we don't call Lady Granton a friend,' continued Kate, 'nor the people who have left cards and sent us invitations since they met us there. And until we came to Florence we had not met you.'

'But then there are these two young men—Mr. Eldridge and Mr. Hardwick.'

'Oh! the Berties,' said Kate; and she laughed. 'They don't count, surely; they are old friends. We did not require to come to Italy to make acquaintance with them.'

'Perhaps you came to Italy to avoid them?' said Lady Caryisfort, drawing her bow at a venture.

Kate looked her suddenly in the face with a start; but the afternoon had gradually grown darker, and neither could make out what was in the other's face.

'Why should we come to Italy to avoid them?' said Kate, gravely.

Her new seriousness quite changed the tone of her voice. She was thinking of Ombra and all the mysterious things that had happened that Summer day after the yachting. It was more than a year ago, and she had almost forgotten; but somehow, Kate could not tell how, the Berties had been woven in with the family existence ever since.

Lady Caryisfort gave her gravity a totally different meaning, 'So that is how it is,' she said to herself.

'If I were you, Kate,' she said aloud, 'I would write and tell my guardian all about it, and who the people are whom you are acquainted with here. I think he has a right to know. Would he be quite pleased that the Berties, as you call them, should be with you so much? Pardon me if I say more than I ought.'

'The Berties!' said Kate, now fairly puzzled. 'What has Uncle Courtenay to do with the Berties? He is not Ombra's guardian, but only mine: and they have nothing to do with me.'

'Oh! perhaps I am mistaken,' said Lady Caryisfort; and she changed the subject dexterously, leading Kate altogether away from this too decided suggestion. They talked afterwards of everything in earth and heaven; but at the end of that little dinner, which they ate tête-à-tête, Kate returned to the subject which in the meantime had been occupying a great part of her thoughts.

'I have been thinking of what you said about Uncle Courtenay,' she said, quite abruptly, after a pause. 'I do write to him about once every month, and I always tell him whom we are seeing. I don't believe he ever reads my letters. He is always paying visits through the Winter when Parliament is up, and I always direct to him at home. I don't suppose he ever reads them. But that, of course, is not my fault, and whenever we meet anyone new I tell him. We don't conceal anything; my aunt never permits that.'

'And I am sure it is your own feeling too,' cried Lady Caryisfort. 'It is always best.'

And she dismissed the subject, not feeling herself possessed of sufficient information to enter into it more fully. She was a little shaken in her own theory on the subject of the Berties, one of whom at least she felt convinced must have designs on Kate's fortune. That was 'only natural;' but at least Kate was not aware of it. And Lady Caryisfort was half annoyed and half pleased when one of her friends asked admittance in the evening, bringing with her the young Count Buoncompagni, whom Kate had met at the Embassy. It was a Countess Strozzi, an aunt of his, and an intimate of Lady Caryisfort's, who was his introducer. There was nothing to be said against the admission of a good young man who had come to escort his aunt in her visit to her invalid friend, but it was odd that they should have chosen that particular night, and no other. Kate was in her morning dress, as she had gone to make a morning call, and was a little troubled to be so discovered; but girls look well in anything, as Lady Caryisfort said to herself, with a sigh.

CHAPTER XLII

It was about this time, about two months after their arrival in Florence, and when the bright and pleasant 'family life' we have been describing had gone on for about six weeks in unbroken harmony, that there began to breathe about Kate, like a vague, fitful wind, such as sometimes rises in Autumn or Spring, one can't tell how or from whence, a curious sense of isolation, of being somehow left out and put aside in the family party. For some time the sensation was quite indefinite. She felt chilled by it; she could not tell how. Then she would find herself sitting alone in a corner, while the others were grouped together, without being able to explain to herself how it happened. It had happened several times, indeed, before she thought of attempting to explain so strange an occurrence; and then she said to herself that of course it was mere chance, or that she herself must have been sulky, and nobody else was aware.

A day or two, however, after her visit to Lady Caryisfort, there came a little incident which could not be quite chance. In the evening Mrs. Anderson sat down by her, and began to talk about indifferent subjects, with a little air of constraint upon her, the air of one who has something not quite pleasant to say. Kate's faculties had been quickened by the change which she had already perceived, and she saw that something was coming, and was chafed by this preface, as only a very frank and open nature can be. She longed to say, 'Tell me what it is, and be done with it.' But she had no excuse for such an outcry. Mrs. Anderson only introduced her real subject after at least an hour's talk.

'By-the-bye,' she said—and Kate knew in a moment that now it was coming—'we have an invitation for to-morrow, dear, which I wish to accept, for Ombra and myself, but I don't feel warranted in taking you—and, at the same time, I don't like the idea of leaving you.'

'Oh! pray don't think of me, aunt,' said Kate, quickly. A flush of evanescent anger at this mode of making it known suddenly came over her. But, in reality, she was half stunned, and could not believe her ears. It made her vague sense of desertion into something tangible at once. It realised all her vague feelings of being one too many. But, at the same time, it stupefied her. She could not understand it. She did not look up, but listened with eyes cast down, and a pain which she did not understand in her heart.

'But I must think of you, my darling,' said Mrs. Anderson, in a voice which, at this moment, rung false and insincere in the girl's ears, and seemed to do her a positive harm. 'How is it possible that I should not think of you? It is an old friend of mine, a merchant from Leghorn, who has bought a place in the country about ten miles from Florence. He is a man who has risen from nothing, and so has his wife, but they are kind people all the same, and used to be good to me when I was poor. Lady Barker is going—for she, too, you know, is of my old set at Leghorn, and, though she has risen in the world, she does not throw off people who are rich. But I don't think your uncle would like it, if I took you there. You know how very careful I have been never to introduce you to anybody he could find fault with. I have declined a great many pleasant invitations here, for that very reason.'

'Oh! please, aunt, don't think of doing so any more,' cried Kate, stung to the heart. 'Don't deprive yourself of anything that is pleasant, for me. I am very well. I am quite happy. I don't require anything more than I have here. Go, and take Ombra, and never mind me.'

And the poor child had great difficulty in refraining from tears. Indeed, but for the fact that it would have looked like crying for a lost pleasure, which Kate, who was stung by a very different feeling, despised, she would not have been able to restrain herself. As it was, her voice trembled, and her cheeks burned.

'Kate, I don't think you are quite just to me,' said Mrs. Anderson. 'You know very well that neither in love, nor in anything else, have I made a difference between Ombra and you. But in this one thing I must throw myself upon your generosity, dear. When I say your generosity, Kate, I mean that you should put the best interpretation on what I say, not the worst.'

'I did not mean to put any interpretation,' said Kate, drawn two ways, and ashamed now of her anger. 'Why should you explain to me, auntie, or make a business of it? Say you are going somewhere to-morrow, and you think it best I should not go. That is enough. Why should you say a word more?'

'Because I wanted to treat you like a woman, not like a child, and to tell you the reason,' said Mrs. Anderson. 'But we will say no more about it, as those boys are coming. I do hope, however, that you understand me, Kate.'

Kate could make no answer, as 'the boys' appeared at this moment; but she said to herself sadly, 'No, I don't understand—I can't tell what it means,' with a confused pain which was very hard to bear. It was the first time she had been shaken in her perfect faith in the two people who had brought her to life, as she said. She did not rush into the middle of the talk, as had once been her practice, but sat, chilled, in her corner, wondering what had come over her. For it was not only that the others were changed—a change had come upon herself also. She was chilled; she could not tell how. Instead of taking the initiative, as she used to do, in the gay and frank freshness which everybody had believed to be the very essence of her character, she sat still, and waited to be called, to be appealed to. Even when she became herself conscious of this, and tried to shake it off, she could not succeed. She was bound as in chains; she could not get free.

And when the next morning came, and Kate, with a dull amaze which she could not overcome, saw the party go off with the usual escort, the only difference being that Lady Barker occupied her own usual place, her feelings were not to be described. She watched them from the balcony while they got into the carriage, and arranged themselves gaily. She looked down upon them and laughed too, and bade them enjoy themselves. She met the wistful look in Mrs. Anderson's eyes with a smile, and, recovering her courage for the moment, made it understood that she meant to pass an extremely pleasant day by herself. But when they drove away, Kate went in, and covered her eyes with her hands. It was not the pleasure, whatever that might be; but why was she left behind? What had she done that they wanted her no longer?—that they found her in the way? It was the first slight she had ever had to bear, and it went to her very heart.

It was a lovely bright morning in December. Lovely mornings in December are rare in England; but even in England there comes now and then a winter day which is a delight and luxury, when the sky is blue, crisper, profounder than summer, when the sun is resplendent, pouring over everything the most lavish and overwhelming light; when the atmosphere is still as old age is when it is beautiful—stilled, chastened, subdued, with no possibility of uneasy winds or movement of life; but all quietness, and now and then one last leaf fluttering down from the uppermost boughs. Such a morning in Florence is divine. The great old houses stand up, expanding, as it were, erecting their old heads gratefully into the sun and blueness of the sphere; the old towers rise, poising themselves, light as birds, yet strong as giants, in that magical atmosphere. The sun-lovers throng to the bright side of the way, and bask and laugh and grow warm and glad. And in the distance the circling hills stand round about the plain, and smile from all their heights in fellow-feeling with the warm and comforted world below. One little girl, left alone in a sunny room on the Lung-Arno in such a morning, with nothing but her half-abandoned tasks to amuse her, nobody to speak to, nothing to think of but a vague wrong done to herself, which she does not understand, is not in a cheerful position, though everything about her is so cheerful; and Kate's heart sank down—down to her very slippers.

'I don't understand why you shouldn't come,' said some one, bursting in suddenly. 'Oh! I beg your pardon; I did not mean to be so abrupt.'

For Kate had been crying. She dashed away her tears with an indignant hand, and looked at Bertie with defiance. Then the natural reaction came to her assistance. He looked so scared and embarrassed standing there, with his hat in his hand, breathless with haste, and full of compunction. She laughed in spite of herself.

'I am not so ashamed as if it had been anyone else,' she said. 'You have seen me cry before. Oh! it is not for the expedition; it is only because I thought they did not want me, that was all.'

'I wanted you,' said Bertie, still breathless, and under his breath.

Kate looked up wondering, and suddenly met his eye, and they both blushed crimson. Why? She laughed to shake it off, feeling, somehow, a pleasanter feeling about her heart.

'It was very kind of you,' she said; 'but, you know, you don't count; you are only one of the boys. You have come back for something?'

'Yes, Lady Barker's bag, with her fan and her gloves, and her eau-de-Cologne.'

'Oh! Lady Barker's. There it is, I suppose. I hate Lady Barker!' cried Kate.

'And so do I; and to see her in your place—'

'Never mind about that. Go away, please, or you will be late; and I hope you will have a pleasant day all the same.'

'Not without you,' said Bertie; and he took her hand, and for one moment seemed doubtful what to do with it. What was he going to do with it? The thought flashed through Kate's mind with a certain amusement; but he thought better of the matter, and did nothing. He dropped her hand, blushing violently again, and then turned and fled, leaving her consoled and amused, and in a totally changed condition. What did he mean to do with the hand he had taken? Kate held it up and looked at it carefully, and laughed till the tears came to her eyes. He had meant to kiss it, she felt sure, and Kate had never yet had her hand kissed by mortal man; but he had thought better of it. It was 'like Bertie.' She was so much amused that her vexation went altogether out of her mind.

And in the afternoon Lady Caryisfort called and took her out. When she heard the narrative of Kate's loneliness, Lady Caryisfort nodded her head approvingly, and said it was very nice of Mrs. Anderson, and quite what ought to have been. Upon which Kate became ashamed of herself, and was convinced that she was the most ungrateful and guilty of girls.

'A distinction must be made,' said Lady Caryisfort, 'especially as it is now known who you are. For Miss Anderson it is quite different, and her mother, of course, must not neglect her interests.'

'How funny that anyone's interests should be affected by an invitation!' said Kate, with one of those unintentional revelations of her sense of her own greatness which were so amusing to her friends. And Count Buoncompagni came to her side of the carriage when they got to the Cascine. It was entirely under Lady Caryisfort's wing that their acquaintance had been formed, and nobody, accordingly, could have a word to say against it. Though she could not quite get Bertie (as she said) out of her head after the incident of the morning, the young Italian was still a very pleasant companion. He talked well, and told her about the people as none of the English could do. 'There is Roscopanni, who was the first out in '48, he said. 'He was nearly killed at Novara. But perhaps you do not care to hear about our patriots?'

'Oh! but I do,' cried Kate, glowing into enthusiasm; and Count Antonio was nothing loth to be her instructor. He confessed that he himself had been 'out,' as Fergus MacIvor, had he survived it, might have confessed, to the '45. Kate had her little prejudices, like all English girls—her feeling of the inferiority of 'foreigners,' and their insincerity and theatrical emotionalness. But Count Antonio took her imagination by storm. He was handsome; he had the sonorous masculine voice which suits Italian best, and does most justice to its melodious splendour; yet he did not speak much Italian, but only a little now and then, to give her courage to speak it. Even French, however, which was their general medium of communication, was an exercise to Kate, who had little practice in any language but her own. Then he told her about his own family, and that they were poor, with a frankness which went to Kate's heart; and she told him, as best she could, about Francesca, and how she had heard the history of the Buoncompagni—'before ever I saw you,' Kate said, stretching the fact a little.

Thus the young man was emboldened to propose to Lady Caryisfort a visit to his old palace and its faded glories. There were some pictures he thought that ces dames would like to look at. 'Still some pictures, though not much else,' he said, ending off with a bit of English, and a shrug of his shoulders, and a laugh at his own poverty; and an appointment was made before the carriage drove off.

'The Italians are not ashamed of being poor,' said Kate, with animation, as they went home.

'If they were, they might as well give in at once, for they are all poor,' said Lady Caryisfort, with British contempt. But Kate, who was rich, thought all the more of the noble young Florentine, with his old palace and his pictures. And then he had been 'out.'

CHAPTER XLIII

Kate took it upon herself to make unusual preparations for the supper on that particular evening. She decorated the table with her own hands, and coaxed Francesca to the purchase of various dainties beyond the ordinary.

'They will be tired; they will want something when they come back,' she said.

'Mademoiselle is very good; it is angelic to be so kind after what has passed—after the affair of the morning,' said Francesca. 'If I had been in Mademoiselle's place, I do not think I should have been able to show so much education. For my part, it has yet to be explained to me how my lady could go to amuse herself and leave Mees Katta alone here.'

'Francesca, don't talk nonsense,' said Kate. 'I quite approve what my aunt did. She is always right, whatever anyone may think.'

'It is very likely, Mees Katta,' said Francesca; 'but I shall know ze why, or I will not be happy. It is not like my lady. She is no besser than a slave with her Ombra. But I shall know ze why; I shall know ze reason why!'

'Then don't tell me, please, for I don't wish to be cross again,' said Kate, continuing her preparations. 'Only I do hope they won't bring Lady Barker with them,' she added to herself. Lady Barker was the scapegoat upon whom Kate spent her wrath. She forgave the other, but her she had made up her mind not to forgive. It was night when the party came home. Kate rushed to the balcony to see them arrive, and looked on; without, however, making her presence known. There was but lamplight this time, but enough to show how Ombra sprang out of the carriage, and how thoroughly the air of a successful expedition hung about the party. 'Well!' said Kate to herself, 'and I have had a pleasant day too.' She ran to the door to welcome them, but, perhaps, made her appearance inopportunely. Ombra was coming upstairs hand in hand with some one—it was not like her usual gravity—and when the pair saw the door open they separated, and came up the remaining steps each alone. This was odd, and startled Kate. Then, when she asked, 'Have you had a pleasant day?' some one answered, 'The most delightful day that ever was!' with an enthusiasm that wounded her feelings—she could not tell why. Was it indeed Bertie Hardwick who said that? he who had spoken so differently in the morning? Kate stood aghast, and asked no more questions. She would have let the two pass her, but Ombra put an arm round her waist and drew her in.

'Oh Kate, listen, I am so happy!' said Ombra, whispering in her ear. 'Don't be vexed about anything, dear; you shall know it all afterwards. I am so happy!'

This was said in the little dark ante-room, where there were no lights, and Kate could only give her cousin a hasty kiss before she danced away. Bertie, for his part, in the dark, too, said nothing at all. He did not explain the phrase—'The most delightful day that ever was!' 'Well!' said poor Kate to herself, gulping down a little discomfort—'well! I have had a pleasant day too.'

And then what a gay supper it was!—gayer than usual; gayer than she had ever known it! She did not feel as if she were quite in the secret of their merriment. They had been together all day, while she had been alone; they had all the jokes of the morning to carry on, and a hundred allusions which fell flat upon Kate. She had been put on her generosity, it was true, and would not, for the world, have shown how much below the general tone of hilarity she was; but she was not in the secret, and very soon she felt ready to flag. When she put in her experiences of the day, a momentary polite attention was given, but everybody's mind was elsewhere. Mrs. Anderson had a half-frightened, half-puzzled look, and now and then turned affecting glances upon Kate; but Ombra was radiant. Never had she looked so beautiful; her eyes shone like two stars; her faint rose-colour went and came; her face was lit with soft smiles and happiness. All sorts of fancies crossed Kate's mind. She looked at the young men, who were both in joyous spirits—but either her discrimination failed her, or her eyes were dim, or her understanding clouded. Altogether Kate was in a maze, and did not know what to do or think; they stayed till it was very late, and both Ombra and her mother went to close and lock the door after them when they went away, leaving Kate once more alone. She sat still at a corner of the table, and listened to the voices and laughter still at the door. Bertie Hardwick's voice, she thought, was the one she heard most. They were all so happy, and she only listening to it, not knowing what it meant! Then, when the door was finally locked, Mrs. Anderson came back to her alone. 'Ombra has gone to bed,' she said. 'She is tired, though she has enjoyed it so very much. And, my dear child, you must go to bed too. It is too late for you to be up.'

'But you have had a very pleasant day.'

'They have—oh yes!' said Mrs Anderson. 'The young ones have been very happy; but it has not been a pleasant day to me. I have so many anxieties; and then to think of you by yourself at home.'

'I was not by myself,' said Kate. Lady Caryisfort called and took me out.'

'Ah! Lady Caryisfort is very kind,' said Mrs. Anderson, with a tone, however, in which there was neither delight nor gratitude; and then she put her arm round her niece, and leaned upon her. 'Ah!' she said again, 'I can see how it will be! They will wean you away from me. You who have never given me a moment's uneasiness, who have been such a good child to me! I suppose it must be so—and I ought not to complain.'

'But, auntie,' said Kate, bewildered, 'nobody tries to take me from you—nobody wants me, that I know of—even you—'

'Yes,' said Mrs. Anderson, 'even I. I know. And I shall have to put up with that too. Oh! Kate, I know more than one of us will live to regret this day;—but nobody so much as I.'

'I don't understand you. Auntie, you are over-tired. You ought to be asleep.'

'You will understand me some time,' said Mrs. Anderson, 'and then you will recollect what I said. But don't ask me any questions, dear. Good-night.'

Good night! She had been just as happy as any of the party, Kate reflected, half an hour before, and her voice had been audible from the door, full of pleasantness and the melody of content. Was the change a fiction, got up for her own benefit, or was there something mysterious lying under it all? Kate could not tell, but it may be supposed how heart-sick and weary she was when such an idea as that her dearest friend had put on a semblance to deceive her, could have entered her mind. She was very, very much ashamed of it, when she woke in the middle of the night, and it all came back to her. But what was she to think? It was the first mystery Kate had encountered, and she did not know how to deal with it. It made her very uneasy and unhappy, and shook her faith in everything. She lay awake for half an hour pondering it; and that was as much to Kate as a week of sleepless nights would have been to many, for up to this time she had no need to wake o' nights, nor anything to weigh upon her thoughts when she woke.

Next morning, however, dissipated these mists, as morning does so often. Ombra was very gay and bright, and much more affectionate and caressing than usual. Kate and she, indeed, seemed to have changed places—the shadow had turned into sunshine. It was Ombra who led the talk, who rippled over into laughter, who petted her cousin and her mother, and was the soul of everything. All Kate's doubts and difficulties fled before the unaccustomed tenderness of Ombra's looks and words. She had no defence against this unexpected means of subjugation, and for some time she even forgot that no explanation at all was given to her of the events of the previous day. It had been 'a pleasant day,' 'a delightful day,' the walk had been perfect, 'and everything else,' Ombra had said at breakfast, 'except that you were not with us, Kate.'

'And that we could not help,' said Mrs. Anderson, into whose face a shade of anxiety had crept. But she was not as she had been in that mysterious moment on the previous night. There was no distress about her. She had nearly as much happiness in her eyes as that which ran over and overflowed in Ombra's. Had Kate dreamed that last five minutes, and its perplexing appearances? But Mrs. Anderson made no explanations any more than Ombra. They chatted about the day's entertainment, their hosts, and many things which Kate could only half understand, but they did not say, 'We are so happy because of this or that.' Through all this affectionateness and tenderness this one blank remained, and Kate could not forget it. They told her nothing. She was left isolated, separated, outside of some magic circle in which they stood.

The young men joined them very early, earlier even than usual; and then this sense of separation became stronger and stronger in Kate's mind. Would they never have done talking of yesterday? The only thing that refreshed her spirit a little was when she announced the engagement Lady Caryisfort had made—'for us all,' Kate said, feeling a little conscious, and pleasantly so, that she herself was, in this case, certainly to be the principal figure—to visit the Buoncompagni palace. Bertie Hardwick roused up immediately at the mention of this.

'Palace indeed!' he said. 'It is a miserable old house, all mildewed and moth-eaten! What should we do there?'

'I am going, at least,' said Kate, 'with Lady Caryisfort. Count Buoncompagni said there were some nice pictures; and I like old houses, though you may not be of my opinion. Auntie, you will come?'

'Miss Courtenay's taste is peculiar,' said Bertie. 'One knows what an old palace, belonging to an impoverished family, means in Italy. It means mouldy hangings, horrible old frescoes, furniture (and very little of that) crumbling to pieces, and nothing in good condition but the coat of arms. Buoncompagni is quite a type of the class—a young, idle, do-nothing fellow, as noble as you like, and as poor as Job; good for leading a cotillion, and for nothing else in this world; and living in his mouldy old palace, like a snail in its shell.'

'I don't think you need to be so severe,' said Kate, with flashing eyes. 'If he is poor, it is not his fault; and he is not ashamed of it, as some people are. And, indeed, I don't think you young men work so very hard yourselves as to give you a right to speak.'

This was a blow most innocently given, but it went a great deal deeper than Kate had supposed. Bertie's countenance became crimson; he was speechless; he could make no reply; and, like every man whose conscience is guilty, he felt sure that she meant it, and had given him this blow on purpose. It was a strange quarter to be assailed from; but yet, what else could it mean? He sat silent, and bit his nails, and remembered Mr. Sugden, and asked himself how it was that such strange critics had been moved against him. We have said that this episode was refreshing to Kate; but not so were the somewhat anxious arrangements which followed on Mrs. Anderson's part, 'for carrying out Kate's plan, which would be delightful.'

'I always like going over an old palace,' she said, with a certain eagerness; 'and if you gentlemen have not done it already, I am sure it will be worth your while.'

But there was very little response from anyone; and in a few minutes more the interruption seemed to be forgotten, and they had all resumed their discussion of the everlasting history of the previous day. Once more Kate felt her isolation, and after awhile she escaped silently from the room. She did not trust herself to go to her own chamber, but retired to the chilly dining-room, and sat down alone over her Italian, feeling rather desolate. She tried to inspire herself with the idea of putting the Italian into practice, and by the recollection of Count Antonio's pretty compliments to her on the little speeches she ventured to make in answer to his questions. 'I must try not to make any mistakes this time,' she said to herself; but after five minutes she stopped and began thinking. With a conscious effort she tried to direct her mind to the encounter of yesterday—to Lady Caryisfort and Count Buoncompagni; but somehow other figures would always intrude; and a dozen times at least she roused up sharply, as from a dream, and found herself asking again, and yet again, what had happened yesterday? Was it something important enough to justify concealment? Was it possible, whatever it was, that it could be concealed from her? What was it? Alas! poor Count Antonio was but the ghost whom she tried to think of; while these were the real objects that interested her. And all the time the party remained in the drawing-room, not once going out. She could hear their voices now and then when a door was opened. They stayed indoors all the morning—a thing which had never happened before. They stayed to luncheon. In the afternoon they all went out walking together; but even that was not as of old. A change had come over everything—the world itself seemed different; and what was worst of all was that this change was pleasant to all the rest and melancholy only to Kate. She said to herself, wistfully, 'No doubt I would be pleased as well as the rest if only I knew.'

CHAPTER XLIV

For the next few days everything was merry as marriage-bells; and though Kate felt even the fondness and double consideration with which she was treated when she was alone with her aunt and cousin to belong somehow to the mystery, she had no excuse even to herself for finding fault with it. They were very good to her. Ombra, at least, had never been so kind, so tender, so anxious to please her. Why should she be anxious to please her? She had never done so before; it had never been necessary; it was a reversal of everything that was natural; and, like all the rest, it meant something underneath, something which had to be made up for by these superficial caresses. Kate did not go so far as this in her articulate thoughts; but it was what she meant in the confused and painful musings which now so often possessed her. But she could not remonstrate, or say, 'Why are you so unnecessarily, unusually tender? What wrong have you done me that has to be made up for in this way?' She could not say this, however much she might feel it. She had to hide her wonder and dissatisfaction in her own heart.

At last the day came for the visit to the Buoncompagni palace. They were to walk to Lady Caryisfort's, to join her, and all had been arranged on the previous night. The ladies were waiting, cloaked and bonneted, when Bertie Eldridge made his appearance alone.

'I hope I have not kept you waiting,' he said; 'that ridiculous cousin of mine won't come. I don't know what has come over him; he has taken some absurd dislike to poor Buoncompagni, who is the best fellow in the world. I hope you will accept my company alone.'

Ombra had been the first to advance to meet him, and he stood still holding her hand while he made his explanation. She dropped it, however, with an air of disappointment and annoyance.

'Bertie will not come—when he knows that I—that we are waiting for him! What a strange thing to do! Bertie, who is always so good; how very annoying—when he knew we depended on him!'

'I told him so,' said the other,—'I told him what you would say; but nothing had any effect. I don't know what has come to Bertie of late. He is not as he used to be; he has begun to talk of work, and all sorts of nonsense. But to-day he will not come, and there is nothing more to be said. It is humbling to me to see how I suffer without him; but I hope you will try to put up with me by myself for one day.'

'Oh! I cannot think what Bertie means by it. It is too provoking!' said Ombra, with a clouded countenance; and when they got into the street their usual order of march was reversed, and Ombra fell behind with Kate, whose mind was full of a very strange jumble of feeling, such as she could not explain to herself. On ordinary occasions one or other of the Berties was always in attendance on Ombra. To-day she indicated, in the most decided manner, that she did not want the one who remained. He had to walk with Mrs. Anderson, while the two girls followed together. 'I never knew anything so provoking,' Ombra continued, taking Kate's arm. 'It is as if he had done it on purpose—to-day, too, of all days in the world!'

'What is particular about to-day?' said Kate, who, to tell the truth, was at this moment less in sympathy with Ombra than she had ever been before.

'Oh! to-day—why, there is—well,' said Ombra, pausing suddenly, 'of course there is nothing particular about to-day. But he must have known how it would put us out—how it would spoil everything. A little party like ours is quite changed when one is left out. You ought to see that as well as I do. It spoils everybody's pleasure. It changes the feeling altogether.'

'I don't think it does so always,' said Kate. But she was generous even at this moment, when a very great call was made on her generosity. 'I never heard you call Mr. Hardwick Bertie before,' she added, not quite generous enough to pass this over without remark.

'To himself, you mean,' said Ombra with a slight blush. 'We have always called them the Berties among ourselves. But I think it is very ridiculous for people who see so much of each other to go on saying Mr. and Miss.'

'Do they call you Ombra, then?' said Kate, lifting her eyebrows. Poor child! she had been much, if secretly, exasperated, and it was not in flesh and blood to avoid giving a mild momentary prick in return.

'I did not say so,' said Ombra. 'Kate, you, too, are contradictory and uncomfortable to-day; when you see how much I am put out—'

'But I don't see why you should be so much put out,' said Kate, in an undertone, as they reached Lady Caryisfort's door.

What did it mean? This little incident plunged her into a sea of thoughts. Up to this moment she had supposed Bertie Eldridge to be her cousin's favourite, and had acquiesced in that arrangement. Somehow she did not like this so well. Kate had ceased for a long time to call Bertie Hardwick 'my Bertie,' as she had once done so frankly; but still she could not quite divest herself of the idea that he was more her own property than anyone else's—her oldest friend, whom she had known before any of them. And he had been so kind the other morning, when the others had deserted her. It gave her a strange, dull, uncomfortable sensation to find him thus appropriated by her cousin. 'I ought not to mind—it can be nothing to me,' she said to herself; but, nevertheless, she did not like it. She was glad when they came to Lady Caryisfort's door, and her tête-à-tête with Ombra was over; and it was even agreeable to her wounded amour-propre when Count Antonio came to her side, beaming with smiles and self-congratulations at having something to show her. He kept by Lady Caryisfort as they went on to the palazzo, which was close by, with the strictest Italian propriety; but when they had entered his own house the young Count did not hesitate to show that his chief motive was Kate. He shrugged his shoulders as he led them in through the great doorway into the court, which was full of myrtles and greenness. There was a fountain in the centre, which trickled shrilly in the air just touched with frost, and oleanders planted in great vases along a terrace with a low balustrade of marble. The tall house towered above, with all its multitudinous windows twinkling in the sun. There was a handsome loggia, or balcony, over the terrace on the first floor. It was there that the sunshine dwelt the longest, and there it was still warm, notwithstanding the frost. This balcony had been partially roofed in with glass, and there were some chairs placed in it and a small white covered table.

'This is the best of my old house,' said Count Antonio, leading them in, hat in hand, with the sun shining on his black hair. 'Such as it is, it is at the service of ces dames; but its poor master must beg them to be very indulgent—to make great allowances for age and poverty.' And then he turned and caught Kate's eye, and bowed to the ground, and said, 'Sia padrona!' with the pretty extravagance of Italian politeness, with a smile for the others, but with a look for herself which made her heart flutter. 'Sia padrona—consider yourself the mistress of everything,'—words which meant nothing at all, and yet might mean so much! And Kate, poor child, was wounded, and felt herself neglected. She was left out by others—banished from the love and confidence that were her due—her very rights invaded. It soothed her to feel that the young Italian, in himself as romantic a figure as heart could desire, who had been 'out' for his country, whose pedigree ran back to Noah, and perhaps a good deal further, was laying his half-ruined old house and his noble history at her feet. And the signs of poverty, which were not to be concealed, and which Count Antonio made no attempt to conceal, went to Kate's heart, and conciliated her. She began to look at him, smiling over the wreck of greatness with respect as well as interest; and when he pointed to a great empty space in one of the noble rooms, Kate's heart melted altogether.

'There was our Raphael—the picture he painted for us. That went off in '48, when my father fitted out the few men who were cut to pieces with him at Novara. I remember crying my eyes out, half for our Madonna, half because I was too small to go with him. Nevare mind' (he said this in English—it was one of his little accomplishments of which he was proud). 'The country is all the better; but no other picture shall ever hang in that place—that we have sworn, my mother and I.'

Kate stood and gazed up at the vacant place with an enthusiasm which perhaps the picture itself would scarcely have called from her. Her eyes grew big and luminous, 'each about to have a tear.' Something came into her throat which prevented her from speaking; she heard a little flutter of comments, but she could not betray the emotion she felt by trying to add to them. 'Oh!' she said to herself with that consciousness of her wealth which was at times a pleasure to her—'oh! if I could find that Madonna, and buy it and send it back!' And then other thoughts involuntarily rushed after that one—fancies, gleams of imagination, enough to cover her face with blushes. Antonio turned back when the party went on, and found her still looking up at the vacant place.

'It is a sad blank, is it not?' he said.

'It is the most beautiful thing in all the house,' said Kate; and one of the tears fell as she looked at him, a big blob of dew upon her glove. She looked at it in consternation, blushing crimson, ashamed of herself.

Antonio did what any young Italian would have done under the circumstances. Undismayed by the presence of an audience, he put one knee to the ground, and touched the spot upon Kate's little gloved thumb with his lips; while she stood in agonies of shame, not knowing what to do.

'The Signorina's tear was for Italy,' he said, as he rose; 'and there is not an Italian living who would not thank her for it on his knees.'

He was perfectly serious, without the least sense that there could be anything ridiculous or embarrassing in the situation; but it may be imagined what was the effect upon the English party, all with a natural horror of a scene.

Lady Caryisfort, I am sorry to say, showed herself the most ill-bred upon this occasion—she pressed her handkerchief to her lips, but could not altogether restrain the very slightest of giggles. Ombra opened her eyes, and looked at her mother; while poor Kate, trembling, horrified, and overwhelmed with shame, shrank behind Mrs. Anderson.

'It was not my fault,' she gasped.

'Don't think anything of it, my love,' whispered Mrs. Anderson, in consolation. 'They mean nothing by it—it is the commonest thing in the world.' A piece of consolation which was not, however, quite so consolatory as it was intended to be.

But she kept her niece by herself after this incident as long as it was practicable; and so it came about that the party divided into three. Lady Caryisfort and Antonio went first, Mrs. Anderson and Kate next, and Ombra and Bertie Eldridge last of all. As Kate moved gradually on, she heard that a very close and low-toned conversation was going on behind her; and Ombra did not now seem so much annoyed by Bertie Hardwick's absence as she had been a little while ago. Was she—an awful revelation seemed to burst upon Kate—was Ombra a coquette? She dismissed the thought from her mind as fast as possible; but after feeling so uncomfortable about her cousin's sudden interest in Bertie, she could not help feeling now a certain pity for him, as if he too, like herself, were slighted now. Not so would Kate herself have treated anyone. It was not in her, she said to herself, to take up and cast down, to play with any sentiment, whether friendship or anything else; and in her heart she condemned Ombra, though secretly she was not sorry. She was a coquette—that was the explanation. She liked to have both the young men at her feet, without apparently caring much for either. This was a sad accusation to bring against Ombra, but somehow Kate felt more kindly disposed towards her after she had struck this idea out.

When they reached the loggia, the table was found to be covered with an elegant little breakfast, which reminded Kate of the pretty meals to be seen in a theatre, which form part of so many pretty comedies. It was warm in the sunshine, and there was a scaldina, placed Italian fashion, under the table, for the benefit of the chilly; and an old man, in a faded livery, served the repast, which he had not cooked, solely because it had been ordered from an hotel, to poor old Girolamo's tribulation. But his master had told him the reason why, and the old servant had allowed that the expenditure might be a wise one. Kate found, to her surprise, that she was the special object of the old man's attention. He ran off with a whole string of 'Che! che's,' when he had identified her, which he did by consultation of his master's eye. 'Bella Signorina, this is from the old Buoncompagni vineyards,' he said, as he served to her some old wine; and, with another confidential movement, touched her arm when he handed her the fruit, 'From the gardens, Signorina mia,' he whispered; and the honey 'from Count Antonio's own bees up on the mountains;' and, 'Cara Signorina mia, this the Contessa's own hands prepared for those beautiful lips,' he said, with the preserves. He hung about her; he had eyes for no one else.

'What is the old man saying to you, Kate?' said her aunt.

'Nothing,' answered Kate, half amused and half distressed; and she met Count Antonio's eye, and they both blushed, to the admiration of the beholders.

This was how the visit terminated. Old Girolamo followed them obsequiously down the great staircase, bowing, with his hand upon his breast, and his eyes upon the young English lady, who was as rich as the Queen of Sheba, and as beautiful as the Holy Mother herself. And Kate's heart beat with all the little magic flutter of possibilities that seemed to gather round her. If her heart had been really touched, she would not have divined what it all meant so readily; but it was only her imagination that was touched, and she saw all that was meant. It was the first time that she had seen a man pose himself before her in the attitude of love, and (though no doubt it is wrong to admit it) the thing pleased her. She was not anxious, as she ought to have been, to preserve Antonio's peace of mind. She was flattered, amused, somewhat touched. That was what he meant. And for herself, she was not unwilling to breathe this delicate incense, and be, as other women, wooed and worshipped. Her ideas went no further. Up to this moment it was somewhat consolatory, and gave her something pleasant to think of. Poor old Girolamo! Poor old palace! She liked their master all the better for their sake.

CHAPTER XLV

In the few weeks that followed it happened that Kate was thrown very much into the society of Lady Caryisfort. It would have been difficult to tell why; and not one of the party could have explained how it was that Ombra and her mother were always engaged, or tired, or had headaches, when Lady Caryisfort called on her way to the Cascine. But so it happened; and gradually Kate passed into the hands of her new friend. Often she remained with her after the drive, and went with her to the theatre, or spent the evening with her at home. And though Mrs. Anderson sometimes made a melancholy little speech on the subject, and half upbraided Kate for this transference of her society, she never made any real effort to withstand it, but really encouraged—as her niece felt somewhat bitterly—a friendship which removed Kate out of the way, as she had resolved not to take her into her confidence. Kate was but half happy in this strange severance, but it was better to be away, better to be smiled upon and caressed by Lady Caryisfort, than to feel herself one too many, to be left out of the innermost circle at home.

And the more she went to the Via Maggio the more she saw of Count Buoncompagni. Had it been in any other house than her own that Kate had encountered this young, agreeable, attractive, honest fortune-hunter, Lady Caryisfort would have been excited and indignant. But he was an habitué of her own house, an old friend of her own, as well as the relation of her dearest and most intimate Italian friend; and she was too indolent to disturb her own mind and habits by the effort of sending him away.

'Besides, why should I? Kate cannot have some one to go before her to sweep all the young men out of her path,' she said, with some amusement at her own idea. 'She must take her chance, like everybody else; and he must take his chance. 'By way of setting her conscience at rest, however, she warned them both. She said to Count Antonio seriously,

'Now, don't flirt with my young lady. You know I dislike it. And I am responsible for her safety when she is with me; and you must not put any nonsense into her head.'

'Milady's commands are my law,' said Antonio, meaning to take his own way. And Lady Caryisfort said lightly to Kate,

'Don't you forget, dear, that all Italians are fortune-hunters. Never believe a word these young men say. They don't even pretend to think it disgraceful, as we do. And, unfortunately, it is known that you are an heiress.'

All this did not make Kate happier. It undermined gradually her confidence in the world, which had seemed all so smiling and so kind. She had thought herself loved, where now she found herself thrust aside. She had thought herself an important member of a party which it was evident could go on without her; and the girl was humbled and downcast. And now to be warned not to believe what was said to her, to consider all those pleasant faces as smiling, not upon herself, but upon her fortune. It would be difficult to describe in words how depressed she was. And Antonio Buoncompagni, though she had been thus warned against him, had an honest face. He looked like the hero in an opera, and sang like the same; but there was an honest simplicity about his face, which made it very hard to doubt him. He was a child still in his innocent ways, though he was a man of the world, and doubtless knew a great deal of both good and evil which was unknown to Kate. But she saw the simplicity, and she was pleased, in spite of herself, with the constant devotion he showed to her. How could she but like it? She was wounded by other people's neglect, and he was so kind, so amiable, so good to her. She was pleased to see him by her side, glad to feel that he preferred to come; not like those who had known her all her life, and yet did not care.

So everything went on merrily, and already old Countess Buoncompagni had heard of it at the villa, and meditated a visit to Florence, to see the English girl who was going to build up the old house once more. And even, which was most wonderful of all, a sense that she might have to do it—that it was her fate, not to be struggled against—an idea half pleasant, half terrible, sometimes stole across the mind even of Kate herself.

Lady Caryisfort received more or less every evening, but most on the Thursdays; and one of these evenings the subject was brought before her too distinctly to be avoided. That great, warm-coloured, dark drawing-room, with the frescoes, looked better when it was full of people than when its mistress was alone in it. There were quantities of wax lights everywhere, enough to neutralise the ruby gloom of the velvet curtains, and light up the brown depths of the old frescoes, with the faces looking out of them. All the mirrors, as well as the room itself, were full of people in pretty dresses, seated in groups or standing about, and there were flowers and lights everywhere. Lady Caryisfort herself inhabited her favourite sofa near the fire, underneath that great fresco; she had a little group round her as she always had; but something rather unusual had occurred. Among all the young men who worshipped and served this pretty woman, who treated them as boys and professed not to want them—and the gay young women who were her companions—there had penetrated one British matron, with that devotion to her duties, that absolute virtuousness and inclination to point out their duty to others, which sometimes distinguishes that excellent member of society. She had been putting Lady Caryisfort through a catechism of all her doings and intentions, and then, as ill-luck would have it, her eye lighted upon pretty Kate, with the young man who was the very Count of romance—the primo tenore, the jeune premier, whom anyone could identify at a glance.

'Ah! I suppose I shall soon have to congratulate you on that,' she said, nodding her head with airy grace in the direction where Kate was, 'for you are a relation of Miss Courtenay's, are you not? I hope the match will be as satisfactory for the lady as for the gentleman—as it must be indeed, when it is of your making, dear Lady Caryisfort. What a handsome couple they will make!'

'Of my making!' said Lady Caryisfort. And the crisis was so terrible that there was a pause all round her—a pause such as might occur in Olympus before Jove threw one of his thunderbolts. All who knew her, knew what a horrible accusation this was. 'A match—of my making!' she repeated. 'Don't you know that I discourage marriages among my friends? I—to make a match!—who hate them, and the very name of them!'

'Oh, dear Lady Caryisfort, you are so amusing! To hear you say that, with such a serious look! What an actress you would have made!'

'Actress,' said Lady Caryisfort, 'and match-maker! You do not compliment me; but I am not acting just now. I never made a match in my life—I hate to see matches made! I discourage them; I throw cold water upon them. Matches!—if there is a thing in the world I hate—'

'But I mean a nice match, of course; a thing most desirable; a marriage such as those, you know,' cried the British matron, with enthusiasm, 'which are made in heaven.'

'I don't believe in anything of the kind,' said the mistress of the house, who liked to shock her audience now and then.

'Oh, dear Lady Caryisfort!'

'I do not believe in anything of the kind. Marriages are the greatest nuisance possible; they have to be, I suppose, but I hate them; they break up society; they disturb family peace; they spoil friendship; they make four people wretched for every two whom they pretend to make happy!'

'Lady Caryisfort—Lady Caryisfort! with all these young people about!'

'I don't think what I say will harm the young people; and, besides, everybody knows my feelings on this subject. I a match-maker! Why, it is my horror! I begin to vituperate in spite of myself. I—throw away my friends in such a foolish way! The moment you marry you are lost—I mean to me. Do you hear, young people? Such of you as were married before I knew you I can put up with. I have accepted you in the lump, as it were. But, good heavens! fancy me depriving myself of that child who comes and puts her pretty arms round my neck and tells me all her secrets! If she were married to-morrow she would be prim and dignified, and probably would tell me that her John did not quite approve of me. No, no; I will have none of that.'

'Lady Caryisfort is always sublime on this subject,' said one of her court.'

'Am I sublime? I say what I feel,' said Lady Caryisfort, languidly leaning back upon her cushions. 'When I give my benediction to a marriage, I say, at the same time, bon jour. I don't want to be surrounded by my equals. I like inferiors—beings who look up to me; so please let nobody call me a match-maker. It is the only opprobrious epithet which I will not put up with. Call me anything else—I can bear it—but not that.'

'Ah! dear Lady Caryisfort, are not you doing wrong to a woman's best instincts?' said her inquisitor, shaking her head with a sigh.

Lady Caryisfort shrugged her shoulders.

'Will some one please to give me my shawl?' she said; and half-a-dozen pair of hands immediately snatched at it. 'Thanks; don't marry—I like you best as you are,' she said, with a careless little nod at her subjects before she turned round to plunge into a conversation with Countess Strozzi, who did not understand English. The British matron was deeply scandalised; she poured out her indignant feelings to two or three people in the room before she withdrew, and next day she wrote a letter to a friend in England, asking if it was known that the great heiress, Miss Courtenay, was on the eve of being married to an Italian nobleman—'or, at least, he calls himself Count Somebody; though of course, one never believes what these foreigners tell one,' she wrote. 'If you should happen to meet Mr. Courtenay, you might just mention this, in case he should not know how far things had gone.'

Thus, all unawares, the cloud arose in the sky, and the storm prepared itself. Christmas had passed, and Count Antonio felt that it was almost time to speak. He was very grateful to Providence and the saints for the success which had attended him. Perhaps, after all, his mother's prayers in the little church at the villa, and those perpetual novenas with which she had somewhat vexed his young soul when she was with him in Florence, had been instrumental in bringing about this result. The Madonna, who, good to everyone, is always specially good to an only son, had no doubt led into his very arms this wealth, which would save the house. So Antonio thought quite devoutly, without an idea in his good-natured soul that there was anything ignoble in his pursuit or in his gratitude. Without money he dared not have dreamed of marrying, and Kate was not one whom he could have ventured to fall in love with apart from the necessity of marriage. But he admired her immensely, and was grateful to her for all the advantages she was going to bring him. He even felt himself in love with her, when she looked up at him with her English radiance of bloom, singling him out in the midst of so many who would have been proud of her favour. There was not a thought in the young Italian's heart which was not good, and tender, and pleasant towards his heiress. He would have been most kind and affectionate to her had she married him, and would have loved her honestly had she chosen to love him; but he was not impassioned—and at the present moment it was to Antonio a most satisfactory, delightful, successful enterprise, which could bring nothing but good, rather than a love-suit, in which his heart and happiness were engaged.

However, things were settling steadily this way when Christmas came. Already Count Antonio had made up his mind to begin operations by speaking to Lady Caryisfort on the subject, and Kate had felt vaguely that she would have to choose between the position of a great lady in England on her own land and that of a great lady in beautiful Florence. The last was not without its attractions, and Antonio was so kind, while other people were so indifferent. Poor Kate was not as happy as she looked. More and more it became apparent to her that something was going on at home which was carefully concealed from her. They even made new friends, whom she did not know—one of whom, in particular, a young clergyman, a friend of the Berties, stared at her now and then from a corner of the drawing-room in the Lung-Arno, with a curiosity which she fully shared. 'Oh! he is a friend of Mr. Hardwick's; he is here only for a week or two; he is going on to Rome for the Carnival,' Mrs. Anderson said, without apparently perceiving what an evidence Kate's ignorance was of the way in which their lives had fallen apart. And the Berties now were continually in the house. They seemed to have no other engagements, except when, now and then, they went to the opera with the ladies. Sometimes Kate thought one or the other of them showed signs of uneasiness, but Ombra was bright as the day, and Mrs. Anderson made no explanation. And how could she, the youngest of the household, the one who was not wanted—how could she interfere or say anything? The wound worked deeper and deeper, and a certain weariness and distrust crept over Kate. Oh, for some change!—even Antonio's proposal, which was coming. For as it was only her imagination and her vanity, not her heart, which were interested, Kate saw with perfect clear-sightedness that the proposal was on its way.

But before it arrived—before any change had come to the state of affairs in the Lung-Arno—one evening, when Kate was at home, and, as usual, abstracted over a book in a corner; when the Berties were in full possession, one bending over Ombra at the piano, one talking earnestly to her mother, Francesca suddenly threw the door open, with a vehemence quite unusual to her, and without a word of warning—without even the announcement of his name to put them on their guard—Mr. Courtenay walked into the room.

CHAPTER XLVI

The scene which Mr. Courtenay saw when he walked in suddenly to Mrs. Anderson's drawing-room, was one so different in every way from what he had expected, that he was for the first moment as much taken aback as any of the company. Francesca, who remembered him well, and whose mind was moved by immediate anxiety at the sight of him, had not been able to restrain a start and exclamation, and had ushered him in suspiciously, with so evident a feeling of alarm and confusion that the suspicious old man of the world felt doubly convinced that there was something to conceal. But she had neither time nor opportunity to warn the party; and yet this was how Mr. Courtenay found them. The drawing-room, which looked out on the Lung-Arno, was not small, but it was rather low—not much more than an entresol. There was a bright wood fire on the hearth, and near it, with a couple of candles on a small table by her side, sat Kate, distinctly isolated from the rest, and working diligently, scarcely raising her eyes from her needlework. The centre table was drawn a little aside, for Ombra had found it too warm in front of the fire; and about this the other four were grouped—Mrs. Anderson, working, too, was talking to one of the young men; the other was holding silk, which Ombra was winding; a thorough English domestic party—such a family group as should have gladdened virtuous eyes to see. Mr. Courtenay looked at it with indescribable surprise. There was nothing visible here which in the least resembled a foreign Count; and Kate was, wonderful to tell, left out—clearly left out. She was sitting apart at her little table near the fire, looking just a little weary and forlorn—a very little—not enough to catch Mrs. Anderson's eye, who had got used to this aspect of Kate. But it struck Mr. Courtenay, who was not used to it, and who had suspected something very different. He was so completely amazed, that he could not think it real. That little old woman must have given some signal; they must have been warned of his coming; otherwise it was altogether impossible to account for this extraordinary scene. They all jumped to their feet at his appearance. There was first a glance of confusion and embarrassment exchanged, as he saw; and then everyone rose in their wonder.

'Mr. Courtenay! What a great, what a very unexpected—,' said Mrs. Anderson. She had meant to say pleasure; but even she was so much startled and confounded that she could not carry her intention out.

'Is it Uncle Courtenay?' said Kate, rising, too. She was not alarmed—on the contrary, she looked half glad, as if the sight of him was rather a relief than otherwise. 'Is it you, Uncle Courtenay? Have you come to see us? I am very glad. But I wonder you did not write.'

'Thanks for your welcome, Kate. Thanks, Mrs. Anderson. Don't let me disturb you. I made up my mind quite suddenly. I had not thought of it a week ago. Ah! some more acquaintances whom I did not expect to see.'

Mr. Courtenay was very gracious—he shook hands all round. The Berties shrank, no one could have quite told how—they looked at each other, exchanging a glance full of dismay and mutual consultation. Mr. Courtenay's faculties were all on the alert; but he had been thinking only of his niece, and the young men puzzled him. They were not near Kate, they were not 'paying her attention;' but, then, what were they doing here? He was not so imaginative nor so quick in his perceptions as to be able to shift from the difficulty he had mastered to this new one. What he had expected was a foreign adventurer making love to his niece; and instead of that here were two young Englishmen, not even looking at his niece. He was posed; but ever suspicious. For the moment they had baffled him; but he would find it out, whatever they meant, whatever they might be concealing from him; and with that view he accepted the great arm-chair blandly, and sat down to make his observations with the most smiling and ingratiating face.

'We are taking care of Kate—she is a kind of invalid, as you will see,' said Mrs. Anderson. 'It is not bad, I am glad to say, but she has a cold, and I have kept her indoors, and even condemned her to the fireside corner, which she thinks very hard.'

'It looks very comfortable,' said Mr. Courtenay. 'So you have a cold, Kate? I hear you have been enjoying yourself very much, making troops of friends. But pray don't let me disturb anyone. Don't let me break up the party—'

'It is time for us to keep our engagement,' said Bertie Hardwick, who had taken out his watch. 'It is a bore to have to go, just as there is a chance of hearing news of home; but I hope we shall see Mr. Courtenay again. We must go now. It is actually nine o'clock.'

'Yes. I did not think it was nearly so late,' said his cousin, echoing him. And they hurried away, leaving Mr. Courtenay more puzzled than ever. He had put them to flight, it was evident—but why? For personally he had no dread of them, nor objection to them, and they had not been taking any notice of Kate.

'I have disturbed your evening, I fear,' he said to Mrs. Anderson. She was annoyed and uncomfortable, though he could not tell the reason why.

'Oh! no, not the least. These boys have been in Florence for some little time, and they often come in to enliven us a little in the evenings. But they have a great many engagements. They can never stay very long,' she said, faltering and stammering, as if she did not quite know what she was saying. But for this Kate would have broken out into aroused remonstrance. Can never stay very long! Why, they stayed generally till midnight, or near it. These words were on Kate's lips, but she held them back, partly for her aunt's sake, partly—she could not tell why. Ombra, overcast in a moment from all her brightness, sat behind, drawing her chair back, and began to arrange and put away the silk she had been winding. It shone in the lamplight, vivid and warm in its rich colour. What a curious little picture this made altogether! Kate, startled and curious, in her seat by the fire; Mrs. Anderson, watchful, not knowing what was going to happen, keeping all her wits about her, occupied the central place; and Ombra sat half hidden behind Mr. Courtenay's chair, a shadowy figure, with the lamplight just catching her white hands, and the long crimson thread of the silk. In a moment everything had changed. It might have been Shanklin again, from the aspect of the party. A little chill seemed to seize them all, though the room was so light and warm. Why was it? Was it a mere reminiscence of his former visit which had brought such change to their lives? He was uncomfortable, and even embarrassed, himself, though he could not have told why.

'So Kate has a cold!' he repeated. 'From what I heard, I supposed you were living a very gay life, with troops of friends. I did not expect to find such a charming domestic party. But you are quite at home here, I suppose, and know the customs of the place—all about it? How sorry I am that your young friends should have gone away because of me!'

'Oh! pray don't think of it. It was not because of you. They had an engagement,' said Mrs. Anderson. Yes, I have lived in Florence before; but that was in very different days, when we were not left such domestic quiet in the evenings,' she added, elevating her head a little, yet sighing. She did not choose Mr. Courtenay, at least, to think that it was only her position as Kate's chaperon which gave her importance here. And it was quite true that the Consul's house had been a lively one in its day. Two young wandering Englishmen would not have represented society then; but perhaps all the habitués of the house were not exactly on a level with the Berties. 'I have kept quiet, not without some trouble,' she continued, 'as you wished it so much for Kate.'

'That was very kind of you,' he said; 'but see, now, what odd reports get about. I heard that Kate had plunged into all sorts of gaiety—and was surrounded by Italians—and I don't know what besides.'

'And you came to take care of her?' said Ombra, quietly, at his elbow.

Mr. Courtenay started. He did not expect an assault on that side also.

'I came to see you all, my dear young lady,' he said; 'and I congratulate you on your changed looks, Miss Ombra. Italy has made you look twice as strong and bright as you were in Shanklin. I don't know if it has done as much for Kate.'

'Kate has a cold,' said Mrs. Anderson, 'but otherwise she is in very good looks. As for Ombra, this might almost be called her native air.'

This civil fencing went on for about half an hour. There was attack and defence, but both stealthy, vague, and general; for the assailant did not quite know what he had to find fault with, and the defenders were unaware what would be the point of assault. Kate, who felt herself the subject of contention, and who did not feel brave enough or happy enough to take up her rôle as she had done at Shanklin, kept in her corner, and said very little. She coughed more than was at all necessary, to keep up her part of invalid; but she did not throw her shield over her aunt as she had once done. With a certain mischievous satisfaction she left them to fight it out: they did not deserve Mr. Courtenay's wrath, but yet they deserved something. For that one night Kate, who was somewhat sick and sore, felt in no mood to interfere. She could not even keep back one little arrow of her own, when her uncle had withdrawn, promising an early visit on the morrow.

'As you think I am such an invalid, auntie,' she said, with playfulness, which was somewhat forced, when the door closed upon that untoward visitor, 'I think I had better go to bed.'

'Perhaps it will be best,' said Mrs. Anderson, offended. And Kate rose, feeling angry and wicked, and ready to wound, she could not tell why.

'It is intolerable that that old man should come here with his suspicious looks—as if we meant to take advantage of him or harm her,' cried Ombra, in indignation.

'If it is me whom you call her, Ombra—'

'Oh! don't be ridiculous!' cried Ombra, impatiently. 'I am sure poor mamma has not deserved to be treated like a governess or a servant, and watched and suspected, on account of you.'

By this time, however, Mrs. Anderson had recovered herself.

'Hush,' she said, 'Ombra; hush, Kate—don't say things you will be sorry for. Mr. Courtenay has nothing to be suspicious about, that I know of, and it is only manner, I dare say. It is a pity that he should have that manner; but it is worse for him than it is for me.'

Now Kate did not love her Uncle Courtenay, but for once in her life she was moved to defend him. And she did love her aunt; but she was wounded and sore, and felt herself neglected, and yet had no legitimate ground for complaint. It was a relief to her to have this feasible reason for saying something disagreeable. The colour heightened in her face.

'My Uncle Courtenay has always been good to me,' she said, 'and if anxiety about me has brought him here, I ought to be grateful to him at least. He does not mean to be rude to anyone, I am sure; and if I am the first person he thinks of, you need not grudge it, Ombra. There is certainly no one else in the world so foolish as to do that.'

The tears were in Kate's eyes; she went away hastily, that they might not fall. She had never known until this moment, because she had never permitted herself to think, how hurt and sore she was. She hurried to her own room, and closed her door, and cried till her head ached. And then the dreadful thought came—how ungrateful she had been!—how wicked, how selfish! which was worse than all.

The two ladies were so taken by surprise that they stood looking after her with a certain consternation. Ombra was the first to recover herself, and she was very angry, very vehement, against her cousin.

'Because she is rich, she thinks she should always be our tyrant!' she cried.

'Oh! hush, Ombra, hush!—you don't think what you are saying,' said her mother.

'You see now, at least, what a mistake it would have been to take her into our confidence, mamma. It would have been fatal. I am so thankful I stood out. If she had us in her power now what should we have done?' Ombra added, more calmly, after the first irritation was over.

But Mrs. Anderson shook her head.

'It is never wise to deceive anyone; harm always comes of it,' she said, sadly.

'To deceive! Is it deceiving to keep one's own secrets?'

'Harm always comes of it,' answered Mrs. Anderson, emphatically.

And after all was still in the house, and everybody asleep, she stole through the dark passage in her dressing-room, and opened Kate's door softly, and went in and kissed the girl in her bed. Kate was not asleep, and the tears were wet on her cheeks. She caught the dark figure in her arms.

'Oh! forgive me. I am so ashamed of myself!' she cried.

Mrs. Anderson kissed her again, and stole away without a word. 'Forgive her! It is she who must forgive me. Poor child! poor child!' she said, in her heart.

CHAPTER XLVII

Next morning, when Mr. Courtenay took his way from the hotel to the Lung-Arno, his eye was caught by the appearance of a young man who was walking exactly in front of him with a great bouquet of violets in his hand. He was young, handsome, and well-dressed, and the continual salutes he received as he moved along testified that he was well known in Florence. The old man's eye (knowing nothing about him) dwelt on him with a certain pleasure. That he was a genial, friendly young soul there could be no doubt; so pleasant were his salutations to great and small, made with hat and hand and voice, as continually as a prince's salutations to his subjects. Probably he was a young prince, or duke, or marchesino; at all events, a noble of the old blue blood, which, in Italy, is at once so uncontaminated and so popular.

Mr. Courtenay had no premonition of any special interest in the stranger, and consequently he looked with pleasure on this impersonation of youth and good looks and good manners. Yes, no doubt he was a nobleman of the faithful Italian blood, one of those families which had kept in the good graces of the country, by what these benighted nations considered patriotism. A fine young fellow—perhaps with something like a career before him, now that Italy was holding up her head again among the nations—altogether an excellent specimen of a patrician; one of those well-born and well-conditioned beings whom every man with good blood in his own veins feels more or less proud of. Such were the thoughts of the old English man of the world, as he took his way in the Winter sunshine to keep his appointment with his niece.

It was a bright cold morning—a white rim of snow on the Apennines gave a brilliant edge to the landscape, and on the smaller heights on the other side of Arno there was green enough to keep Winter in subjection. The sunshine was as warm as Summer; very different from the dreary dirty weather which Mr. Courtenay had left in Bond Street and Piccadilly, though Piccadilly sometimes is as bright as the Lung-Arno. Though he was as old as Methuselah in Kate's eyes, this ogre of a guardian was not so old in his own. And he had once been young, and when young had been in Florence; and he had a flower in his button-hole and no overcoat, which made him happy. And though he was perplexed, he could not but feel that the worst that he been threatened with had not come true, and that perhaps the story was false altogether, and he was to escape without trouble. All this made Mr. Courtenay walk very lightly along the sunny pavement, pleased with himself, and disposed to be pleased with other people; and the same amiable feelings directed his eyes towards the young Italian, and gave him a friendly feeling to the stranger. A fine young fellow; straight and swift he marched along, and would have distanced the old man, but for those continual greetings, which retarded him. Mr. Courtenay was just a little surprised when he saw the youth whom he had been admiring enter the doorway to which he was himself bound; and his surprise may be imagined when, as he climbed the stairs towards the second floor where his niece lived, he overheard a lively conversation at Mrs. Anderson's very door.

'Amica mia, I hope your beautiful young lady is better,' said the young man. 'Contrive to tell her, my Francesca, how miserable I have been these evil nights, while she has been shut up by this hard-hearted lady-aunt. You will say, cara mia, that it is the Lady Caryisfort who sends the flowers, and that I am desolated—desolated!—and all that comes into your good heart to say. For you understand—I am sure you understand.'

'Oh, yes, I understand, Signor Cont' Antonio,' said Francesca. 'Trust to me, I know what to say. She is not very happy herself, the dear little Signorina. It is dreary for her seeing the other young lady with her lovers; but, perhaps, my beautiful young gentleman, it is not bad for you. When one sees another loved, one wishes to be loved one's self; but it is hard for Mees Katta. She will be glad to have the Signor Conte's flowers and his message.'

'But take care, Francesca mia, you must say they are from my Lady Caryisfort,' said Count Antonio, 'and lay me at the feet of my little lady. I hunger—I thirst—I die to see her again! Will she not see my Lady

Caryisfort to-day? Is she too ill to go out to-night? The new prima donna has come, and has made a furore. Tell her so, cara mia. Francesca make her to come out, that I may see her. You will stand my friend—you were always my friend.'

'The Signor Conte forgets what I have told him; that I am as a connection of the family. I will do my very best for him. Hist! hush! oh, miserecordia! Ecco il vecchio!' cried Francesca, under her breath.

Mr. Courtenay had heard it all, but as his Italian was imperfect he had not altogether made it out, and he missed this warning about il vecchio altogether. The young man turned and faced him as he reached the landing. He was a handsome young fellow, with dark eyes, which were eloquent enough to get to any girl's heart. Mr. Courtenay felt towards him as an old lady in the best society might feel, did she see her son in the fatal clutches of a penniless beauty. The fact that Kate was an heiress made, as it were, a man of her, and transferred all the female epithets of 'wilful' and 'designing' to the other side. Antonio, with the politeness of his country, took off his hat and stood aside to let the older man pass. 'Thinks he can come over me too, with his confounded politeness,' Mr. Courtenay said to himself—indeed, he used a stronger word than confounded, which it would be unladylike to repeat. He made no response to the young Italian's politeness, but pushed on, hat on head, after the vigorous manner of the Britons. 'Who are these for?' he asked, gruffly, indicating with his stick the bunch of violets which made the air sweet.

'For ze young ladies, zare,' said Francesca, demurely, as she ushered him out of the dark passage into the bright drawing-room.

Mr. Courtenay went in with suppressed fury. Kate was alone in the room waiting for him, and what with the agitation of the night, and the little flutter caused by his arrival, she was pale, and seemed to receive him with some nervousness. He noticed, too, that Francesca carried away the bouquet, though he felt convinced it was not intended for Ombra. She was in the pay of that young adventurer!—that Italian rogue and schemer!—that fortune-hunting young blackguard! These were the intemperate epithets which Mr. Courtenay applied to his handsome young Italian, as soon as he had found him out!

'Well, Kate,' he said, sitting down beside her, 'I am sorry you are not well. It must be dull for you to be kept indoors, after you have had so much going about, and have been enjoying yourself so much.'

'Did you not wish me to enjoy myself?' said Kate, whom her aunt's kiss the night before had once more enlisted vehemently on the other side.

'Oh! surely,' said her guardian. 'What do persons like myself exist for, but to help young people to enjoy themselves. It is the only object of our lives!'

'You mean to be satirical, I see,' said Kate, with a sigh, 'but I don't understand it. I wish you would speak plainly out. You taunted me last night with having made many friends, and having enjoyed myself—was it wrong? If you will tell me how few friends you wish me to have, or exactly how little enjoyment you think proper for me, I will endeavour to carry out your wishes—as long as I am obliged.'

This was said in an undertone, with a grind and setting of Kate's white teeth which, though very slight, spoke volumes. She had quite taken up again the colours which she had almost let fall last night. Mr. Courtenay was prepared for remonstrance, but not for such a vigorous onslaught.

'You are civil, my dear, he said, 'and sweet and submissive, and, indeed, everything I could have expected from your character and early habits; but I thought Mrs. Anderson had brought you under. I thought you knew better by this time than to attempt to bully me.'

'I don't want to bully you,' cried Kate, with burning cheeks; 'but why do you come like this, with your suspicious looks, as if you came prepared to catch us in something?—whereas, all the world may know all about us—whom we know, and what we do.'

'This nonsense is your aunt's, I suppose, and I don't blame you for it,' said Mr. Courtenay. 'Let us change the subject. You are responsible to me, as it happens, but I am not responsible to you. Don't make yourself disagreeable, Kate. Tragedy is not your line, though it is your cousin's. By the way, that girl is looking a great deal better than she did; she is a different creature. She has grown quite handsome. Is it because Florence is her native air, as her mother said?'

'I don't know,' said Kate. Though she had taken up her aunt's colours again vehemently, she did not feel so warmly towards Ombra. A certain irritation had been going on in her mind for some time. It had burst forth on the previous night, and Ombra had offered no kiss, said no word of reconciliation. So she was not disposed to enter upon any admiring discussion of her cousin. She would have resented anything that had been said unkindly, but it was no longer in her mind to plunge into applause of Ombra. A change had thus come over them both.

Mr. Courtenay looked at her very keenly—he saw there was something wrong, but he could not tell what it was—Some girlish quarrel, no doubt, he said to himself. Girls were always quarrelling—about their lovers, or about their dresses, or something. Therefore he went over this ground lightly, and returned to his original attack.

'You like Florence?' he said. 'Tell me what you have been doing, and whom you have met. There must be a great many English here, I suppose?'

However, he had roused Kate's suspicions, and she was not inclined to answer.

'We have been doing what everybody else does,' she said—'going to see the pictures and all the sights; and we have met Lady Caryisfort. That is about all, I think. She has rather taken a fancy to me, because she belongs to our own country. She takes me to drive sometimes; and I have seen a great deal of her—especially of late.'

'Why especially of late?'

'Oh! I don't know—that is, my aunt and Ombra found some old friends who were not fine enough, they said, to please you, so they left me behind; and I did not like it, I suppose being silly; so I have gone to Lady Caryisfort's more than usual since.'

'Oh-h!' said Mr. Courtenay, feeling that enlightenment was near. 'It was very honourable of your aunt, I am sure. And this Lady Caryisfort?—is she a match-maker, Kate?'

'A match-maker! I don't understand what you mean, uncle.'

'You have met a certain young Italian, a Count Buoncompagni, whom I have heard of, there?'

Kate reddened, in spite of herself—being on the eve of getting into trouble about him, she began to feel a melting of her heart to Antonio.

'Do you know anything about Count Buoncompagni?' she asked, with elaborate calm. This, then, was what her uncle meant—this was what he had come from England about. Was it really so important as that?

'I have heard of him,' said Mr. Courtenay, drily. 'Indeed, five minutes ago, I followed him up the stairs, without knowing who he was, and heard him giving a string of messages and a bunch of flowers to that wretched old woman.'

'Was it me he was asking for?' said Kate, quite touched. 'How nice and how kind he is! He has asked for me every day since I have had this cold. The Italians are so nice, Uncle Courtenay. They are so sympathetic, and take such an interest in you.'

'I have not the least doubt of it,' he said, grimly. 'And how long has this young Buoncompagni taken an interest in you? It may be very nice, as you say, but I doubt if I, as your guardian, can take so much pleasure in it as you do. I want to hear all about it, and where and how often you have met.'

Kate wavered a moment—whether to be angry and refuse to tell, or to keep her temper and disarm her opponent. She chose the latter alternative, chiefly because she was beginning to be amused, and felt that some 'fun' might be got out of the matter. And it was so long now (about two weeks and a half) since she had had any 'fun.' She did so want a little amusement. Whereupon she answered very demurely, and with much conscious skill,

'I met him first at the Embassy—at Lady Granton's ball.

'At Lady Granton's ball?'

'Yes. There were none but the very best people there—the crême de la crême, as auntie says. Lady Granton's sister introduced him to me. He is a very good dancer—just the sort of man that is nice to waltz with; and very pleasant to talk to, uncle.'

'Oh! he is very pleasant to talk to, is he?' said Uncle Courtenay, still more grimly.

'Very much so indeed. He talks excellent French, and beautiful Italian. It does one all the good in the world talking to such a man. It is better than a dozen lessons. And then he is so kind, and never laughs at one's mistakes. And he has such a lovely old palace, and is so well known in Florence. He may not be very rich, perhaps—'

'Rich!—a beggarly adventurer!—a confounded fortune-hunter!—an Italian rogue and reprobate! How this precious aunt of yours could have shut her eyes to such a piece of folly; or your Lady Caryisfort, forsooth—'

'Why forsooth, uncle? Do you mean that she is not Lady Caryisfort, or that she is unworthy of the name? She is very clever and very agreeable. But I was going to say that though Count Buoncompagni is not rich, he gave us the most beautiful little luncheon the day we went to see his pictures. Lady Caryisfort said it was perfection. And talking of that—if he brought some flowers, as you say, I should like to have them. May I go and speak to Francesca about them?—or perhaps you would rather ring the bell?'

It was thus that Kate evaded the further discussion of the question. She went off gaily bounding along the long passage. 'Francesca, Francesca, where are my flowers?' she cried. Her heart had grown light all at once. A little mischief, and a little opposition, and the freshness, yet naturalness, of having Uncle Courtenay to fight with, exhilarated her spirits. Yes, it felt natural. To be out of humour with her aunt was a totally different matter. That was all pain, with no compensating excitement; but the other was 'fun.' It filled her with wholesome energy and contradictoriness. 'If Uncle Courtenay supposes I am going to give up poor Antonio for him—'—she said in her heart, and danced along the passage, singing snatches of tunes, and calling to Francesca. 'Where are my flowers?—I know there are some flowers for me. Some one cares to know whether I am dead or alive,' she said.

Francesca came out of the dining-room, holding up her hands to implore silence. Oh! my dear young lady,' said Francesca, 'you must not be imprudent. When we receive flowers from a beautiful young gentleman, we take them to our chamber, or we put them in our bosoms—we don't dance and sing over them—or, at least, young ladies who have education, who know what the world expects of them, must not so behave. In my room, Mees Katta, you will find your flowers. They are sent from the English milady—Milady Caryisfort,' Francesca added, demurely folding her arms upon her breast.

'Oh! are they from Lady Caryisfort?' said Kate, with a little disappointment. After all, it was not so romantic as she thought.

'My young lady understands that it must be so,' said Francesca, 'for young ladies must not be compromised; but the hand that carried them was that of the young Contino, and as handsome a young fellow as any in Florence. I am very glad I am old—I might be his grandmother; for otherwise, look you, Mademoiselle, his voice is so mellow, and he looks so with his eyes, and says Francesca mia, cara amica, and such like, that I should be foolish, even an old woman like me. They have a way with them, these Buoncompagni. His father, I recollect, who was very like Count Antonio, very nearly succeeded in turning the head of my Angelina, my little sister that died. No harm came of it, Mees Katta, or I would not have told. We took her away to the convent at Rocca, where we had a cousin, a very pious woman, well known throughout the country, Sister Agnese, of the Reparazione; and there she got quite serious, and as good as a little saint before she died.'

'Was it his fault that she died?' cried Kate, always ready for a story. 'I should have thought, Francesca, that you would have hated him for ever and ever.'

'I had the honour of saying to the Signorina that no harm was done,' said Francesca, with gravity. 'Why should I hate the good Count for being handsome and civil? It is a way they have, these Buoncompagni. But, for my part, I think more of Count Antonio than I ever did of his father. Milady Caryisfort would speak for him, Mees Katta. She is a lady that knows the Italians, and understands how to speak. She has always supported the Contino's suit, has not she? and she will speak for him. He is desolated, desolated—he has just told me—to be so many days without seeing Mademoiselle; and, indeed, he looked very sad. We other Italians don't hide our feelings as you do in your country. He looked sad to break one's heart; and, Mees Katta, figure to yourself my feelings when I saw the Signora's uncle come puff-puff, with his difficulty of breathing, up the stair.

'What did it matter?' said Kate, putting the best face upon it. 'Of course I will not conceal anything from my uncle—though there is nothing to conceal.'

'Milady Caryisfort will speak. If I might be allowed to repeat it to the Signorina, she is the best person to speak. She knows him well through his aunt, who is dei Strozzi, and a very great lady. You will take the Signor Uncle there, Mees Katta, if you think well of my advice.'

'I do not want any advice—there is nothing to be advised about,' cried Kate, colouring deeply, and suddenly recognising the character which Francesca had taken upon herself. She rushed into Francesca's room, and brought out the violets, all wet and fragrant. They were such a secret as could not be hid. They perfumed all the passages as she hurried to her own little room, and separated a little knot of the dark blue blossoms to put in her bodice. How sweet they were! How 'nice' of Antonio to bring them! How strange that he should say they were from Lady Caryisfort! Why should he say they were from Lady Caryisfort? And was he really sad because he did not see her? How good, how kind he was! Other people were not sad. Other people did not care, she supposed, if they never saw her again. And here Kate gave a little sigh, and blushed a great indignant blush, and put her face down into the abundant fragrant bouquet. It was so sweet, and love was sweet, and the thought that one was cared for, and thought of, and missed! This thought was very grateful and pleasant, as sweet as the flowers, and it went to Kate's heart. She could have done a great deal at that moment for the sake of the tender-hearted young Italian, who comforted her wounded feelings, and helped to restore the balance of her being by the attentions which were so doubly consoling in the midst—she said to herself—of coldness and neglect.

Lady Caryisfort called soon afterwards, and was delighted to make Mr. Courtenay's acquaintance; and, as Kate was better, she took them both to the Cascine. That was the first morning—Kate remembered afterwards, with many wondering thoughts—that the Berties had not called before luncheon, and Ombra did not appear until that meal, and was less agreeable than she had been since they left Shanklin. But these thoughts soon fled from her mind, and so did a curious, momentary feeling, that her aunt and cousin looked relieved when she went away with Lady Caryisfort. They did not go. Mrs. Anderson, too, had a cold, she said, and would not go out that day, and Ombra was busy.

'Ombra is very often busy now,' said Lady Caryisfort, as they drove off. 'What is it, Kate? She and Mrs. Anderson used to find time for a drive now and then at first.'

'I don't know what it is,' Kate said, with some pain; and then a little ebullition of her higher spirits prompted her to add an explanation, which was partly malicious, and partly kind, to save her cousin from remark. 'She writes poetry,' said Kate, demurely. 'Perhaps it is that.'

'Oh! good heavens, if I had known she was literary!' cried Lady Caryisfort, with gentle horror. But here were the Cascine, and the flower-girls, and the notabilities who had to be pointed out to the new-comer; and the Count, who had appeared quite naturally by Kate's side of the carriage. Mr. Courtenay said little, but he kept his eyes open, and noted everything. He looked at the lady opposite to him, and listened to her dauntless talk, and heard all the compliments addressed to her, and the smiling contempt with which she received them. This sort of woman could not be aiding and abetting in a vulgar matrimonial scheme, he said to himself. And he was puzzled what to make of the business, and how to put a stop to it. For the Italian kept his place at Kate's side, without any attempt at concealment, and was not a person who could be sneered down by the lordly British stare, or treated quite as a nobody. Mr. Courtenay knew the world, and he knew that an Englishman who should be rude to Count Buoncompagni on his own soil, on the Cascine at Florence, must belong to a different class of men from the class which, being at the top of the social ladder, is more cosmopolitan than any other, except the working people, who are at its lower level. An indignant British uncle from Bloomsbury or Highgate might have done this, but not one whose blood was as blue as that of the Buoncompagni. It was impossible. And yet it was hard upon him to see all this going on under his very eyes. Lady Caryisfort had insisted that he and Kate should dine with her, and it was with the farewell of a very temporary parting glance that Count Antonio went away. This was terrible, but it must be fully observed before being put a stop to. He tried to persuade himself that to be patient was his only wisdom.

'But will not your aunt be vexed, be affronted, feel herself neglected, if we go to dine with Lady Caryisfort? Ladies, I know, are rather prompt to take offence in such matters,' he said.

'Oh! my aunt!—she will not be offended. I don't think she will be offended,' said Kate, in the puzzled tone which he had already noticed. And the two young men of last night were again in the drawing-room when he went upstairs. Was there some other scheme, some independent intrigue, in this? But he shrugged his shoulders and said, what did it matter? It was nothing to him. Miss Ombra had her mother to manage her affairs. Whatever their plans might be they were not his business, so long as they had the good sense not to interfere with Kate.

The dinner at Lady Caryisfort's was small, but pleasant. The only Italian present was a Countess Strozzi, a well-bred woman, who had been Ambassadress from Tuscany once at St. James's, and whom Mr. Courtenay had met before—but no objectionable Counts. He really enjoyed himself at that admirable table. After all, he thought, there is no Sybarite like your rich, accomplished, independent woman—no one who combines the beautiful and dainty with the excellent in such a high degree; so long as she understands cookery; for the choice of guests and the external arrangements are sure to be complete. And Lady Caryisfort did understand cookery. It was the pleasantest possible conclusion to his hurried journey and his perplexity. It was London, and Paris, and Florence all in one; the comfort, the exquisite fare, the society, all helped each other into perfection; and there was a certain flavour of distance and novelty in the old Italian palace which enhanced everything—the flavour of the past. This was not a thing to be had every day, like a Paris dinner. But in the evening Mr. Courtenay was less satisfied. When the great salon, with its warm velvet hangings and its dim frescoes, began to fill, Buoncompagni turned up from some corner or other, and appeared as if by magic at Kate's side. The guardian did the only thing which could be done in the circumstances. He approached the sofa under the picture, which was the favourite throne of the lady of the house, and waited patiently till there was a gap in the circle surrounding her, and he could find an entrance. She made room for him at last, with the most charming grace.

'Mr. Courtenay, you are not like the rest of my friends. I have not heard all your good things, nor all your news, as I have theirs. You are a real comfort to talk to, and I did not have the good of you at dinner. Sit by me, please, and tell me something new. Nobody does,' she added, with a little flutter of her fan,—'nobody ever seems to think that fresh fare is needful sometimes. Let us talk of Kate.'

'If I am bound to confine myself to that subject,' said the old man of society, 'I reserve the question whether it is kind to remind me thus broadly that I am a Methuselah.'

'Oh! I am a Methusela myself, without the h,' said Lady Caryisfort. 'The young people interest me in a gentle, grandmotherly way. I like to see them enjoy themselves, and all that.'

'Precisely,' said Mr. Courtenay. 'I quite understand and perceive the appropriateness of the situation. You are interested in that, for example?' he said, suddenly changing his tone, and indicating a group at the other side of the room. Kate, with some flowers in her hand, which had dropped from the bouquet still in her bosom, with her head drooping over them, and a vivid blush on her cheek—while Count Antonio, bending over her, seemed asking for the flowers, with a hand half extended, and stooping so low that his handsome head was close to hers. This attitude was so prettily suggestive of something asked and granted, that a bewildered blush flushed up upon Lady Caryisfort's delicate face at the sight. She turned to her old companion with a startled look, in which there was something almost like pain.

'Well?' she said, with mingled excitement, surprise, and defiance, which he did not understand.

'I don't think it is well,' he said. 'Will you tell me—and pardon an old disagreeable guardian for asking—how far this has gone?'

'You see as well as I do,' she said, with a little laugh; and then, changing her tone—'But, however far it is gone, I have nothing to do with it. It seems extremely careless on my part; but I give you my word, Mr. Courtenay, I never really noticed it till to-night.'

This was true enough, notwithstanding that she had perceived the dangers of the situation, and warned both parties against it at the outset. For up to this moment she had not seen the least trace of emotion on the part of Kate.

'Nothing could make me doubt a lady's word,' said the old man; 'but one knows that in such matters the code of honour is held lightly.'

'I am not holding it lightly,' she said, with sudden fire; and then, pausing with an effort—'It is true I had not noticed it before. Kate is so frank and so young; such ideas never seem to occur to one in connection with her. But, Mr. Courtenay, Count Buoncompagni is no adventurer. He may be poor, but he is—honourable—good—'

'The woman is agitated,' Mr. Courtenay said to himself. 'What fools these women are! My stars!' But he added, with grim politeness, 'It is utterly out of the question, Lady Caryisfort. You are the girl's countrywoman—even her countywoman. You are not one to incur the fatal reputation of match-making. Help me to break off this folly completely, and I will be grateful to you for ever. It must be done, whether you will help me or not.'

As he spoke, somehow or other she recovered her calm.

'Are you so hard-hearted,' she said,—'so implacable a model of guardians? And I, innocent soul, who had supposed you romantic and Arcadian, wishing Kate to be loved for herself alone, and all the sentimental et ceteras. So it must be put a stop to, must it? Well, if there is nothing to be said for poor Antonio, I suppose, as it is my fault, I must help.'

'There can be no doubt of it,' said Mr. Courtenay.

Lady Caryisfort kept her eyes upon the two, and her lively brain began to work. The question interested her, there could be no doubt. She was shocked at herself, she said, that she had allowed things to go so far without finding it out. And then the two people of the world laid their heads together, and schemed the destruction of Kate's fanciful little dream, and of poor Antonio's hopes. Mr. Courtenay had no compunction; and though Lady Caryisfort smiled and made little appeals to him not to look so implacable, there was a certain gleam of excitement quite unusual to her about her demeanour also.

They had settled their plan before Kate had decided that, on the whole, it was best to thrust the dropped violets back into her belt, and not to give them to Antonio. It was nice to receive the flowers from him; but to give one back, to accept the look with which it was asked, to commit herself in his favour—that was a totally different question. Kate shrank into herself at the suit which was thus pressed a hair's-breadth further than she was prepared for. It was just the balance of a straw whether she should have yielded or taken fright. And, happily for her, with those two pair of eyes upon her, it was the fright that won the day, and not the impulse to yield.

CHAPTER XLIX

Kate had a good deal to think of when she went home that evening, and shut herself up in the room which was full of the sweetness of Antonio's violets. Francesca, with an Italian's natural terror of flower-scents, had carried them away; but Kate had paused on her way to her room to rescue the banished flowers.

'They are enough to kill Mademoiselle in her bed, and leave us all miserable,' said Francesca.

'I am not a bit afraid of violets,' said Kate.

On the contrary, she wanted them to help her. For she did not go into the drawing room, though it was still early. The two young men, she heard, were there; and Kate felt a little sick at heart, and did not care to go where she was not wanted—'Where her absence,' as she said to herself, 'was never remarked.' Oh! how different it was from what it had been! Only a few weeks ago she had been unable to form an idea of herself detached from her aunt and cousin, who went everywhere with her, and shared everything. Even Lady Caryisfort had shown no favouritism towards Kate at first. She had been quite as kind to Ombra, quite as friendly to Mrs. Anderson. It was their own doing altogether. They had snatched, as it were, at Lady Caryisfort, as one who would disembarrass them of the inconvenient cousin—'the third, who was always de trop,' poor Kate said to herself, with a sob in her throat, and a dull pang in her heart. They still went through all the formulas of affection, but they got rid of her, they did not want her. When she had closed the door of her room even upon Maryanne, and sat down over the fire in her dressing-gown, she reflected upon her position, as she had never reflected on it before. She was nobody's child. People were kind to her, but she was not necessary to anyone's happiness; she belonged to no home of her own, where her presence was essential. Her aunt loved her in a way, but, so long as she had Ombra, could do without Kate. And her uncle did not love her at all, only interfered with her life, and turned it into new channels, as suited him. She was of no importance to anyone, except in relation to Langton-Courtenay, and her money, and estates.

This is a painful and dangerous discovery to be made by a girl of nineteen, with a great vase full of violets at her elbow, the offering of such a fortune-hunter as Antonio Buoncompagni, one who was mercenary only because it was his duty to his family, and in reality meant no harm. He was a young man who was quite capable of having fallen in love with her, had she not been so rich and so desirable a match; and as it was he liked her, and was ready to swear that he loved her, so as to deceive not only her, but himself. But perhaps, after all, it was he, and not she, who was most easily deceived. Kate, though she did not know it, had an instinctive inkling of the real state of the case, which was the only thing which saved her from falling at once and altogether into Antonio's net. Had she been sure that he loved her, nothing could have saved her; for love in the midst of neglect, love which comes spontaneous when other people are indifferent, is the sweetest and most consolatory of all things. Sometimes she had almost persuaded herself that this was the case, and had been ready to rush into Antonio's arms; but then there would come that cold shudder of hesitation which precedes a final plunge—that doubt—that consciousness that the Buoncompagni were poor, and wanted English money to build them up again. As for the poverty itself, she cared nothing; but she felt that, had her lover been even moderately well off, it would have saved her from that shrinking chill and suspicion. And then she turned, and rent herself, so to speak, remembering the sublime emptiness of that space on the wall where the Madonna dei Buoncompagni used to be.

'If I can ever find it out anywhere, whatever it may cost, I will buy it, and send it back to him,' Kate said, with a flush on her cheek. And next moment she cried with real distress, feeling for his disappointment, and asking herself why should not she do it?—why not? To make a man happy, and raise up an old house, is worth a woman's while, surely, even though she might not be very much in love. Was it quite certain that people were always very much in love when they married? A great many things, more important, were involved in any alliance made by a little princess in her own right; and such was Kate's character to her own consciousness, and in the eyes of other people. The violets breathed all round her, and the soft silence and loneliness of the night enveloped her; and then she heard the stir in the drawing-room, the movement of the visitors going away, and whispering voices which passed her door, and Ombra's laugh, soft and sweet, like the very sound of happiness—

Ombra was happy; and what cared anyone for Kate? She was the one alone in this little loving household—and that it should be so little made the desolation all the greater. She was one of three, and yet the others did not care what she was thinking, how she was feeling. Kate crept to bed silently, and put out her light, that her aunt might not come to pity her, after she had said good night to her own happy child, whom everybody thought of. 'And yet I might have as good,' Kate said to herself. 'I am not alone any more than Ombra. I have my violets too—my beau chevalier—if I like.' Ah! the beau chevalier! Some one had sung that wistful song at Lady Caryisfort's that night. It came back upon Kate's mind now in the dark, mingled with the whispering of the voices, and the little breath of chilly night air that came when the door opened.

'Ne voyez vous pas que la nuit est profonde,
Et que le monde
N'est que souci.'

Strange, at nineteen, in all the sweetness of her youth, the heiress of Langton had come to understand how that might be!

Lady Caryisfort took more urgent measures on her side than Mr. Courtenay had thought it wise to do. She detained her friend, the Countess Strozzi, and her friend's nephew, when all the other guests were gone. This flattered Antonio, who thought it possible some proposition might be about to be made to him, and made the Countess uncomfortable, who knew the English better than he. Lady Caryisfort made a very bold assault upon the two. She took high ground, and assured them that, without her consent and countenance, to mature a scheme of this kind under her wing, as it were, was a wrong thing to do. She was so very virtuous, in short, that Countess Strozzi woke up to a sudden and lively hope that Lady Caryisfort had more reasons than those which concerned Kate for disliking the match; but this she kept to herself; and the party sat late and long into the night discussing the matter. Antonio was reluctant, very reluctant, to give up the little English maiden, whom he declared he loved.

'Would you love her if she were penniless—if she had no lands and castles, but was as her cousin?' said Lady Caryisfort; and the young man paused. He said at last that, though probably he would love her still better in these circumstances, he should not dare to ask her to marry him. But was that possible? And then it was truly that Lady Caryisfort distinguished herself. She told him all that was possible to a ferocious English guardian—how, though he could not take the money away, he could bind it up so that it would advantage no one; how he could make the poor husband no better than a pensioner of the rich wife, or even settle it so that even the rich wife should become poor, and have nothing in her power except the income, which, of course, could not be taken from her. 'Even that she will not have till she is of age, two long years hence,' Lady Caryisfort explained; and then gave such a lucid sketch of trustees and settlements that the young Italian's soul shrank into his boots. His face grew longer and longer as he listened.

'But I am committed—my honour is involved,' he said.

'Ah! pazzo, allora hai parlato?' cried his kinswoman.

'No, I have not spoken, not in so many words; but I have been understood,' said Antonio, with that imbecile smile and blush of vanity which women know so well.

'I think you may make yourself easy in that respect,' said Lady Caryisfort. 'Kate is not in love with you,' a speech which almost undid what she had been labouring to do; for Antonio's pride was up, and could scarcely be pacified. He had committed himself; he had given Kate to understand that he was her lover, and how was he now to withdraw? 'If he proposes, she is a romantic child—no more than a child—and she is capable of accepting him,' Lady Caryisfort said to his aunt in their last moment of consultation.

'Leave him to me, cara mia,' said the Countess—'leave him to me.' And that noble lady went away with her head full of new combinations. 'The girl will not be of age for two years, and in that time anything may happen. It would be hard for you to wait two years, Antonio mio; let us think a little. I know another, young still, very handsome, and with everything in her own power—'

Antonio was indignant, and resented the suggestion; but Countess Strozzi was not impatient. She knew very well that to such arguments, in the long run, all Antonios yield.

Mr. Courtenay entered the drawing room in the Lung-Arno next day at noon, and found all the ladies there. Again the Berties were absent, but there was no cloud that morning upon Ombra's face. Kate had made her appearance, looking pale and ill, and the hearts of her companions had been touched. They were compunctious and ashamed, and eager to make up for the neglect of which she had never complained. Even Ombra had kissed her a second time after the formal morning salutation, and had said 'Forgive me!' as she did so.

'For what?' said Kate, with the intention of being proud and unconscious. But when she had looked up, and met her aunt's anxious look, and Ombra's eyes with tears in them, her own overflowed. 'Oh! I am so ill-tempered,' she said, 'and ungrateful. Don't speak to me.'

'You are just as I was a little while ago,' said Ombra. 'But, Kate, with you it is all delusion, and soon, very soon, you will know better. Don't be as I was.'

As Ombra was! Kate dried her eyes, yet she did not know whether to be gratified or to be angry. Why should she be as Ombra had been? But yet even these few words brought about a better understanding. And the three were seated together, in the old way, when Mr. Courtenay entered. He had the air of a man full of business. In his hand he carried a packet of letters, some of which he had not yet opened.

'I have just had letters from Langton,' he said. 'I don't know if you take any interest in Langton—or these ladies, who have never even seen it—'

'Of course I do, uncle,' cried Kate. 'Take interest in my own house, my dear old home!'

'It does not follow that young ladies who are fond of Italy should care about a dull old place in the heart of England,' said this wily old man. 'Grieve tells me it is going to rack and ruin, which is not pleasant news. He says it is wicked and shameful to leave it so long without inhabitants; that the village is discontented, and dirty, and wretched, with no one to look after it. In short, ladies, if I look miserable, you must forgive me, for I have not got over Grieve's letter.'

'Who is Grieve, uncle?'

'The new estate-agent, Kate. Didn't you know? Ah! you must begin to take an interest in the estate. My time is drawing to a close, and I shall be glad, very glad, to be rid of it. If I could go down and live there, I might do something; but as that is impossible, I suppose things must continue going to the bad till you come of age.'

Kate sat upright in her chair; her cheeks began to glow, and her eyes to shine.

'Why should things go to the bad?' she said. 'I would rather they did not, for my part.'

'How can they do otherwise,' said Mr. Courtenay, 'while the house is shut up, and there is no one to see to anything? Grieve is a good fellow, but I can't give him Langton to live in, or make him into a Courtenay.'

'I should hope not,' said Kate, setting her small white teeth. By this time her whole countenance began to gleam with excitement and resolution, and that charm to which she always responded with such delight and readiness, the charm of novelty. Then she made a pause, and drew in her breath. 'Uncle,' she said, 'I am not a child any longer. Why shouldn't I go home, and open the house, and live as I ought? I want something to do. I want duty, such as other people have. It is my business to look after Langton. Let me go home.'

'You foolish child!' he said; which was a proof, though Kate did not see it, that everything was working as he wished. 'You foolish child! How could you, at nineteen, go and live in that house alone?'

She looked up. Her crimson cheek grew white, her eyes went in one wistful, imploring look from her aunt to Ombra, from Ombra back again to Mrs. Anderson. Her lips parted in her eagerness, her eyes shone out like lights. She was as if about to speak—but stopped short, and referred to them, as it were, for the answer. Mr. Courtenay looked at them too, not without a little anxiety; but the interest in his face was of a very different kind from that shown by Kate.

'If you mean,' said Mrs. Anderson, faltering, and, for her part, consulting Ombra with her eyes, 'that you would like me to go with you—Kate, my darling, thank you for wishing it—oh! thank you, I have not deserved—But most likely your uncle would not like it, Kate.'

'On the contrary,' said Mr. Courtenay, with his best bow, 'if you would entertain the idea—if it suits with your other plans to go to Langton till Kate comes of age, it would be everything that I could desire.'

The three looked at each other for a full moment in uncertainty and wonder. And then Kate suddenly jumped up, overturned the little table by her side, on which stood the remains of her violets, and danced round the room with wild delight.

'Oh! let us go at once!—let us leave this horrid old picture-gallery! Let us go home, home!' she cried, in an outburst of joy. The vase was broken, and the dead violets strewed over the carpet. Francesca came in and swept them away, and no one took any notice. That was over. And now for home—for home!

CHAPTER L

The success of this move had gone far beyond Mr. Courtenay's highest hopes. He was unprepared for the suddenness of its acceptance. He went off and told Lady Caryisfort, with a surprise and satisfaction that was almost rueful. 'Since that woman came into my niece's affairs,' he said, 'I have had to sacrifice something for every step I have gained; and I find that I have made the sacrifice exactly when it suited her—to buy a concession she was dying to make. I never meant her to set foot in Langton, and now she is going there as mistress; and just, I am certain, at the time it suits her to go. This is what happens to a simple-minded man when he ventures to enter the lists with women. I have a great mind to put everything in her hands and retire from the field.'

'I don't think she is so clever as you give her credit for,' said Lady Caryisfort, who was somewhat languid after the night's exertions. 'I suspect it was you who found out the moment that suited you rather than she.'

But she gave him, in her turn, an account of what she had done, and they formed an alliance offensive and defensive—a public treaty of friendship for the world's inspection, and a secret alliance known only to themselves, by the conditions of which Lady Caryisfort bound herself to repair to London and take Kate under her charge when it should be thought necessary and expedient by the allied powers. She pledged herself to present the heiress and watch over her and guard her from all match-makers, that the humble chaperon might be dismissed, and allowed to go in peace. When he had concluded this bargain Mr. Courtenay went away with a lighter heart, to make preparations for his niece's return. He had been most successful in his pretence to get her away from Florence; and now this second arrangement to get rid of the relations who would be no longer necessary, seemed to him a miracle of diplomacy. He chuckled to himself over it, and rubbed his hands.

'Kate must not be treated as a child any longer—she is grown up, she has a judgment of her own,' he said, with a delicious sense of humour; and then he listened very gravely to all her enthusiastic descriptions of what she was to do when she got to Langton. Kate, however, after the first glow of her resolution, did not feel the matter so easy as it appeared. She had no thought of the violets, which Francesca swept up, at the moment; but afterwards the recollection of them came back to her. She had allowed them to be swept away without a thought. What a cold heart—what an ungrateful nature—she must have! And poor Antonio! In the light of Langton, Antonio looked to her all at once impossible—as impossible as it would be to transplant his old palace to English soil. No way could the two ideas be harmonised. She puckered her brows over it till she made her head ache. Count Buoncompagni and Langton-Courtenay! They would not come together—could not—it was impossible! Indeed the one idea chased the other from her mind. And how was she to intimate this strange and cruel fact to him? How was she to show that all his graceful attentions must be brought to an end?—that she was going home, and all must be over! And the worst was that it could not be done gradually; but one way or another must be managed at once.

The next day Lady Caryisfort came, as usual, on her way to the Cascine; but, to Kate's surprise and relief, and, it must be owned, also to her disappointment, Antonio was not there. She declined the next invitation to Lady Caryisfort's, inventing a headache for the occasion, and growing more and more perplexed the longer she thought over that difficult matter. It was while she was musing thus that Bertie Hardwick one day managed to get beside her for a moment, while Ombra was talking to his cousin. Bertie Eldridge had raised a discussion about some literary matter, and the two had gone to consult a book in the little ante-room, which served as a kind of library; the other Bertie was left alone with Kate, a thing which had not happened before for weeks. He went up to her the moment they were gone, and stood hesitating and embarrassed before her.

'Miss Courtenay,' he said, and waited till she looked up.

Something moved in Kate's heart at the sound of his voice—some chord of early recollection—remembrances which seemed to her to stretch so far back—before the world began.

'Well, Mr. Hardwick?' she said, looking up with a smile. Why there should be something pathetic in that smile, and a little tightness across her eyelids, as if she could have cried, Kate could not have told, and neither can I.

'Are you pleased to go home?—is it with your own will? or did your uncle's coming distress you?' he said, in a voice which was—yes, very kind, almost more than friendly; brotherly, Kate said to herself.

'Distress me?' she said.

'Yes; I have thought you looked a little troubled sometimes. I can't help noticing. Don't think me impertinent, but I can't bear to see trouble in your face.'

Kate made no reply, but she looked up at him—looked him straight in the eyes. Once more she did not know why she did it, and she did not think of half the meanings which he saw written in her face. He faltered; he turned away; he grew red and grew pale; and then came back to her with an answering look which did not falter; but for the re-entrance of the others he must have said something. But they came back, and he did not speak. If he had spoken, what would he have said?

This gave a new direction to Kate's thoughts, but still it was with a heavy heart that she entered Lady Caryisfort's drawing-room, not more than a week after that evening when Antonio had asked for the violets, and she had hesitated whether she would give them. She had hesitated! It was this thought which made her so much ashamed. She had been lonely, and she had been willing to accept his heart as a plaything; and how could she say to him now, 'I am no longer lonely. I am going home; and I could not take you, a stranger, back, to be master of Langton?' She could not say this, and what was she to say? Antonio Buoncompagni was not much more comfortable; he had been thoroughly schooled, and he had begun to accept his part. He even saw, and that clearly, that a pretty, independent bird in the hand, able to pipe as he wished, was better than a fluttering, uncertain fledgling in the bush; but he had a lively sense of honour, and he had committed himself. The young lady, he thought, ought at least to have the privilege of refusing him. 'Go, then, and be refused—pazzo!' said his aunt. 'Most people avoid a refusal, but thou wishest it. It is a pity that thou shouldst not be satisfied.' But, having obtained this permission, the young Count was not, perhaps, so ready to avail himself of it. He did not care to be rejected any more than other men, but he was anxious to reconcile his conscience to his desertion; and he had a tender sense that he himself—Antonio—was not one to be easily forgotten. He watched Kate from the moment of her entry, and persuaded himself that she was pale. 'Poverina!' he said, beneath his moustache. Alas! the sacrifice must be made; but then it might be done in a gentle way.

The evening, however, was half over before he had found his way to her side—a circumstance which filled Kate with wonder, and kept her in a curious suspense; for she could not talk freely to anyone else while he was within sight, to whom she had so much (she thought) to say. He came, and Kate was confused and troubled. Somehow she felt he was changed. Was he less handsome, less tall, less graceful? What had happened to him? Surely there was something. He was no longer the young hero who had dropped on his knee, and kissed her hand for Italy. She was confused, and could not tell how it was.

'You are going to leave Florence?' he said. 'It is sudden—it is too sad to think of. Miss Courtenay, I hope it is not you who wish to leave our beautiful Italy—you, who have understood her so well?'

'No, it is not I,' said Kate. 'I should not have gone of my own free will; but yet I am very willing—I am ready to go—it is home,' she added, hastily, and with meaning. 'It is the place I love best in the world.'

'Ah!' he said, 'I had thought—I had hoped you loved Italy too.'

'Oh! so I do, Count Buoncompagni—and I thought I did still more,' cried the girl, eager to make her hidden and shy, yet brave apology. 'I thought I could have lived and died here, where people were so good to me. But, you know, whenever I heard the name of home, it made my blood all dance in my veins. I felt I had been making a mistake, and that there was nothing in the world I loved like Langton-Courtenay. I made a great mistake, but I did not mean it. I hope nobody will think it is unkind of me, or that I am fond of change.'

Count Antonio stood and listened to this speech with a grim smile on his face, and a look in his eyes which was new to Kate. He, too, was making a disagreeable discovery, and he did not like it. He made her a bow, but he did not make any answer. He stood by her side a few moments, and then he asked her suddenly, 'May I get you some tea?—can I bring you anything?' with a forced quietness; and when Kate said 'No,' he went away, and devoted himself for all the rest of the evening to Lady Caryisfort. There was pique in his manner, but there was something more, which she could not make out; and she sat rather alone for the rest of the evening. She was left to feel her mistake, to wonder, to be somewhat offended and affronted; and went back to the Lung-Arno impatient to hurry over all the packing, and get home at once. But she never found out that in thus taking the weight of the breaking off on her own shoulders, she had saved Count Antonio a great deal of trouble.

When Lady Caryisfort found out what had passed, her amusement was very great. 'She will go now and think all her life that she has done him an injury, and broken his heart, and all kinds of nonsense,' she said to herself. 'Poor Antonio! what a horrible thing money is! But he has escaped very cheaply, thanks to Kate, and she will make a melancholy hero of him, poor dear child, for the rest of her life.'

In this, however, Lady Caryisfort, not knowing all the circumstances, was wrong; for Kate felt vaguely that there was something more than the honourable despair of a young Paladin in her Count's acceptance of her explanation. He accepted it too readily, with too little attempt to resist or remonstrate. She was more angry than pitiful, ignorant as she was. A man who takes a woman so entirely at her first word almost insults her, even though the separation is her own doing. Kate felt this vaguely, and a hot blush rose to her cheek for two or three days after, at the very mention of Antonio's name.

The person, however, who felt this breaking off most was old Francesca, who had gone to an extra mass for weeks back, to promote the suit she had so much at heart. She cried herself sick when she saw it was all over, and said to herself, she knew something evil would happen as soon as il vecchio came. Il vecchio's appearance was always the signal for mischief. He had come, and now once more the party was on the wing, and she herself was to be torn from her native place, the Florence she adored, for this old man's caprice. Francesca thought with a little fierce satisfaction that, when his soul went to purgatory, there would be nobody to pray him out, and that his penance would be long enough. The idea gave her a great deal of satisfaction. She would not help him out, she was certain—not so much as by a single prayer.

But all the time she got on with her packing, and the ladies began to frequent the shops to buy little souvenirs of Florence. It was a busy time, and there was a great deal of movement, and so much occupation that the members of the little party lost sight of each other, as it were, and pursued their different preparations in their own way. 'She is packing,' or, 'she is shopping,' was said, first of one, and then of another; and no further questions were asked. And thus the days crept on, and the time approached when they were to set out once more on the journey home.

CHAPTER LI

Yes, packing, without doubt, takes up a great deal of time, and that must have been the reason why Mrs. Anderson and Ombra were so much occupied. They had so many things to do. Francesca, of course, was occupied with the household; she did the greater part of the cooking, and superintended everything, and consequently had not time for the manifold arrangements—the selection of things they did not immediately want, which were to be sent off direct from Leghorn, and of those which they would require to carry with them. And in this work the ladies toiled sometimes for days together.

Kate had no occasion to make a slave of herself. She had Maryanne to attend to all her immediate requirements, and, in her own person, had nothing better to do than to sit alone, and read, or gaze out of the window upon the passengers below, and the brown Arno running his course in the sunshine, and the high roofs blazing into the mellow light on the other side, while the houses below were in deepest shadow. Kate was too young, and had too many requirements, and hungers of the heart, to enjoy this scene for itself so much, perhaps, as she ought to have done. Had there been somebody by to whom she could have pointed out, or who would have pointed out to her, the beautiful gleams of colour and sunshine, I have no doubt her appreciation of it all would have been much greater. As it was, she felt very solitary; and often after, when life was running low with her, her imagination would bring up that picture of the brown river, and the housetops shining in the sun, and all the people streaming across the Ponte della Trinità, to the other side of the Arno—stranger people, whom she did not know, who were always coming and going, coming and going. Morning made no difference to them, nor night, nor the cold days, nor the rain. They were always crossing that bridge. Oh! what a curious, tedious thing life was, Kate thought—always the same thing over again, year after year, day after day. It was so still that she almost heard her own breathing within the warm, low room, where the sunshine entered so freely, but where nothing else entered all the morning, except herself.

To be sure, this was only for a few days; but, after all, what a strange end it was to the life in Florence, which had begun so differently! In the afternoon, to be sure, it was not lonely. Her uncle would come, and Lady Caryisfort, and the Berties, but not so often as usual. They never came when Mr. Courtenay was expected; but Kate felt, by instinct, that when she and her uncle were at Lady Caryisfort's, the two young men reappeared, and the evenings were spent very pleasantly. What had she done to be thus shut out? It was a question she could not answer. Now and then the young clergyman would appear, who was the friend of Bertie Eldridge, a timid young man, with light hair and troubled eyes. And sometimes she caught Bertie Hardwick looking at herself with a melancholy, anxious gaze, which she still less understood. Why should he so regard her? she was making no complaint, no show of her own depression; and why should her aunt look at her so wistfully, and beg her pardon in every tone or gesture? Kate could not tell; but the last week was hard upon her, and still more hard was a strange accident which occurred at the end.

This happened two or three days before they left Florence. She was roused early, she did not know how, by a sound which she could not identify. Whether it was distant thunder, which seemed unlikely, or the shutting of a door close at hand, she could not tell. It was still dark of the winter morning, and Kate, rousing up, heard some early street cries outside, only to be heard in that morning darkness before the dawn, and felt something in the air, she could not tell what, which excited her. She got up, and cautiously peered into the ante-room out of which her own room opened. To her wonder she saw a bright fire burning. Was it late, she thought? and hastened to dress, thinking she had overslept herself. But when she had finished her morning toilette, and came forth to warm her cold fingers at that fire, there was still no appearance of anyone stirring. What did it mean? The shutters were still closed, and everything was dark, except this brisk fire, which must have been made up quite recently. Kate had taken down a book, and was about to make herself comfortable by the fireside, when the sound of some one coming startled her. It was Francesca, who looked in, with her warm shawl on.

'I thought I heard some one,' said Francesca. 'Mees Katta, you haf give me a bad fright. Why do you get up so early, without warning anyone? I hear the sound, and I say to myself my lady is ill—and behold it is only Mees Katta. It does not show education, waking poor peoples in ze cold out of their good warm bet.'

'But, Francesca, I heard noises too; and what can be the matter?' said Kate, becoming a little alarmed.

'Ah! but there is nosing the matter. Madame sleep—she would not answer even when I knocked. And since you have made me get up so early, it shall be for ze good of my soul, Mees Katta. I am going to mass.'

'Oh! let me go too,' said Kate. 'I have never been at church so early. Don't say a word, Francesca, because I know my aunt will not mind. I will get my hat in a minute. See, I am ready.'

'The Signorina will always have her way,' said Francesca; and Kate found herself, before she knew, in the street.

It was still dark, but day was breaking; and it was by no means the particularly early hour that Kate supposed. There were no fine people certainly about the streets, but the poorer population was all awake and afoot. It was very cold—the beginning of January—the very heart of winter. The lamps were being extinguished along the streets; but the cold glimmer of the day neither warmed nor cleared the air to speak of; and through that pale dimness the great houses rose like ghosts. Kate glanced round her with a shiver, taking in a strange wild vision, all in tints of grey and black, of the houses along the side of the Arno, the arched line of the bridge, the great dim mass of the other part of the town beyond, faint in the darkness, and veiled, indistinct figures still coming and going. And then she followed Francesca, with scarcely a word, to the little out-of-the-way church, with nothing in it to make a show, which Francesca loved, partly because it was humble. For poor people have a liking for those homely, mean little places, where no grandeur of ornament nor pomp of service can ever be. This is a fact, explain it as they can, who think the attractions of ritualistic art and splendid ceremonial are the chief charms of the worship of Rome.

Francesca found out this squalid little church by instinct, as a poor woman of her class in England would find a Bethesda chapel. But at this moment the little church looked cheery, with its lighted altar blazing into the chilly darkness. Kate followed into one of the corners, and knelt down reverently by her companion. Her head was confused by the strangeness of the scene. She listened, and tried to join in what was going on, with that obstinate English prejudice which makes common prayer a necessity in a church. But it was not common prayer that was to be found here. The priest was making his sacrifice at the altar; the solitary kneeling worshippers were having their private intercourse with God, as it were, under the shadow of the greater rite. While Francesca crossed herself and muttered her prayer under her breath, Kate, scarcely capable of that, covered her eyes with her hand, and pondered and wondered. Poor little church, visited by no admiring stranger; poor unknown people, snatching a moment from their work, market-people, sellers of chestnuts from the streets, servants, the lowliest of the low; but morning after morning their feeble candles twinkled into the dark, and they knelt upon the damp stones in the unseen corners. How strange it was! Not like English ideas—not like the virtuous ladies who patronised the daily service at Shanklin. Kate's heart felt a great yearning towards those badly-dressed poor folks, some of whom smelled of garlic. She cried a little silently, the tears dropping one by one, like the last of a summer shower, from behind the shelter of her hand. And when Francesca had ended her prayers, and Kate, startled from her thinking, took her hand from her eyes, the little grey church was all full of the splendour of the morning, the candles put to flight, the priest's muttering over.

'If my young lady will come this way,' whispered Francesca, 'she will be able to kiss the shrine of the famous Madonna—she who stopped the cholera in the village, where my blessed aunt Agnese, of the Reparazione, was so much beloved.'

'I would rather kiss you, Francesca,' cried Kate, in a little transport, audible, so that some praying people raised their heads to look at her, 'for you are a good woman.'

She spoke in English; and the people at their prayers looked down again, and took no more notice. It was nothing wonderful for an English visitor to talk loud in a church.

It was bright daylight when they came out, and everything was gay. The sun already shone dazzling on all the towers and heights, for it was no longer early; it was half-past eight o'clock, and already the forenoon had begun in that early Italian world. As they returned to the Lung-Arno the river was sparkling in the light, and the passengers moving quickly, half because of the cold, and half because the sun was so warm and exhilarating.

'My aunt and Ombra will only be getting up,' said Kate, with a little laugh of superiority; when suddenly she felt herself clutched by Francesca, and, looking round, suddenly stopped short also in the uttermost amaze. In front of her, walking along the bright street, were the two whom she had just named—her aunt and Ombra—and not alone. The two young men were walking with them—one with each lady. Ombra was clinging to the arm of the one by her side; and they all kept close together, with a half-guilty, half clandestine air. The sight of them filled Kate with so much consternation, as well as wonder, that these particulars recurred to her afterwards, as do the details of an accident to those who have been too painfully excited to observe them at the moment of their occurrence.

Francesca clutched her close and held her back as the group went on. They passed, almost brushing by the two spectators, yet in their haste perceiving nothing. But Kate had no inclination to rush forward and join herself to the party, as the old woman feared. After a moment's interval the two resumed their walk, slowly, in speechless wonder. What did it mean? Perhaps Francesca guessed more truly than Kate did; but even she was not in the secret. Before, however, they reached the door, Kate had recovered herself. She quickened her steps, though Francesca held her back.

'They must know that we have seen them,' she said over and over to herself, with a parched throat.

And when the door was reached, the two parties met. It was Ombra who made the discovery first. She had turned round upon her companion to say some word of parting; her face was pale, but full of emotion; she was like one of the attendant saints at a martyrdom, so pale was she, and with a strange look of trance and rapture. But when her eye caught Kate behind, Ombra was strangely moved. She gave a little cry, and without another word ran into the house and up the stairs. Mrs. Anderson turned suddenly round when Ombra disappeared. She stood before the door of the house, and faced the new comers.

'What, Kate!' she said, half frightened, half relieved, 'is it you? What has brought you out so early—and with Francesca, too?'

'You too are out early, aunt.'

'That is true; but it is not an answer,' said Mrs. Anderson with a flush that rose over all her face.

And the two young men stood irresolute, as if they did not know whether to go or stay. Bertie Eldridge, it seemed to Kate, wore his usual indifferent look. He was always blasé and languid, and did not give himself much trouble about anything; but Bertie Hardwick was much agitated. He turned white, and he turned red, and he gave Kate looks which she could not understand. It seemed to her as if he were always trying to apologise and explain with his eyes; and what right had Bertie Hardwick to think that she wanted anything explained or cared what he did? She was angry, she did not quite know why—angry and wounded—hurt as if some one had struck her, and she did not care to stop and ask or answer questions. She followed Mrs. Anderson upstairs, listening doubtfully to Francesca's voluble explanation—how Mademoiselle had been disturbed by some sounds in the house, 'possibly my lady herself, though I was far from thinking so when I left,' said Francesca, pointedly; and how Mees Katta had insisted upon going to mass with her?

Mrs. Anderson shook her head, but turned round to Kate at the door with a softened look, which had something in it akin to Bertie's. She kissed Kate, though the girl half averted her face.

'I do not blame you, my dear, but your uncle might not like it. You must not go again,' she said, thus gently placing the inferior matter in the first place.

And they went in, to find the fire in the ante-room burning all alone, as when Kate had left, and the calm little house looking in its best order, as if nothing had ever happened there.

CHAPTER LII

That was a curious day—a day full of strange excitement and suppressed feeling—suppressed on all sides, yet betraying itself in some unexplainable way. Mrs. Anderson made no explanation whatever of her early expedition—at least to Kate; she did not even refer to it. She gave her a little lecture at breakfast, while they sat alone together—for Ombra did not appear—about the inexpediency of going with Francesca to church. 'I know that you did not mean anything, my darling,' she said, tenderly; 'but it is very touching to see the poor people at their prayers, and I have known a girl to be led away so, and to desert her own church. Such an idea must never be entertained for you; you are not a private individual, Kate—you are a woman with a great stake in the country, an example to many—'

'Oh, I am so tired of hearing that I have a stake in the country!' cried Kate, who at that moment, to tell the truth, was sick of everything, and loathed her life heartily, and everything she heard and saw.

'But that is wrong,' said Mrs. Anderson. 'You must not be tired of such an honour and privilege. You must be aware, Kate, that an ordinary girl of your years would not be considered and studied as you have been. Had you been only my dear sister's child, and not the mistress of Langton-Courtenay, even I should have treated you differently; though, for your own good,' Mrs. Anderson added, 'I have tried as much as possible to forget your position, and look upon you as my younger child.'

Kate's heart was full—full of a yearning for the old undoubting love, and yet a sense that it had been withdrawn from her by no fault of hers, which made it impossible for her to make overtures of tenderness, or even to accept them. She said, 'I like that best;' but she said it low, with her eyes fixed upon her plate, and her voice choking. And perhaps her aunt did not hear. Mrs. Anderson had deliberately mounted upon her high horse. She had invoked, as it were, the assistance of her chief weakness, and was making use of it freely. She said a good deal more about Kate's position—about the necessity of being faithful to one's church, not only as a religious, but a public duty; and thus kept up the discussion till breakfast was fairly over. Then, as usual, Kate was left alone. Francesca had a private interview after in her mistress's room, but what was said to her was never known to anyone. She left it looking as if tears still lay very near her eyes, but not a word did she repeat of any explanation given to her—and, indeed, avoided Kate, so that the girl was left utterly alone in the very heart of that small, and once so tender, household.

And thus life went on strangely, in a mist of suppressed excitement, for some days. How her aunt and cousin spent that time Kate could not tell. She saw little of them, and scarcely cared to note what visits they received, or what happened. In the seclusion of her own room she heard footsteps coming and going, and unusual sounds, but took no notice; and from that strange morning encounter, saw no more of the Berties until they made their appearance suddenly one day in the forenoon, when Mr. Courtenay was there; when they announced their immediate departure, and took their leave at one and the same moment. The parting was a strange one; they all shook hands stiffly with each other, as if they had been mere acquaintances. They said not a word of meeting again; and the young men were both agitated, looking pale and strange. When they left at last, Mr. Courtenay, in his airy way, remarked that he did not think Florence had agreed with them. 'They look as if they were both going to have the fever,' he said; 'though, by-the-bye, it is in Rome people have the fever, not in Florence.'

'I suppose they are sorry to leave,' said Mrs. Anderson, steadily; and then the subject dropped.

It seemed to Kate as if the world went round and round, and then suddenly settled back into its place. And by this time all was over—everything had stopped short. There was no more shopping, nor even packing. Francesca was equal to everything that remained to be done; and the moment of their own departure drew very near.

Ombra drew down her veil as they were carried away out of sight of Florence on the gentle bit of railway which then existed, going to the north. And Mrs. Anderson looked back upon the town with her hands clasped tight together in her lap, and tears in her eyes. Kate noted both details, but even in her own mind drew no deductions from them. She herself was confused in her head as well as in her heart, bewildered, uncertain, walking like some one in a dream. The last person she saw in the railway-station was Antonio Buoncompagni, with a bunch of violets in his coat. He walked as far as he could go when the slow little train got itself into motion, and took off his hat, with a little gesture which went to Kate's heart. Poor Antonio!—had she perhaps been unkind to him after all? There was something sad, and yet not painful—something almost comforting in the thought.

And so they were really on their way again, and Florence was over like yesterday when it is past, and like a tale that is told! How strange to think so! A place never perhaps to be entered again—never, certainly, with the same feelings as now. Ombra's veil was down, and it was thick, and concealed her, and tears stood in Mrs. Anderson's eyes. They had their own thoughts, too, though Kate had no clue to them. No clue! Probably these thoughts dwelt upon things absolutely unknown to her—probably they too were saying to themselves, 'How strange to leave Florence in the past—to be done with it!' But had they left it in the past?

As for Mr. Courtenay, he read his paper, which he had just received from England. There was a debate in it about some object which interested him, and the Times was full of abuse of some of his friends. The old man chuckled a little over this, as he sat on the comfortable side, with his back towards the engine, and his rug tucked over his knees. He did not so much as give Florence a glance as they glided away. What was Hecuba to him, or he to Hecuba? Nothing had happened to him there. Nothing happened to him anywhere—though his ward gave him a good deal of trouble. As for this journey of his, it was a bore, but still it had been successful, which was something, and he made himself extremely comfortable, and read over, as they rolled leisurely along, every word of the Times.

And thus they travelled home.

CHAPTER LIII

It is a curious sensation to return, after a long interval, to the home of one's youth, especially if one has had very great ideas of that home, and thought it magnificent. Even a short absence changes most curiously this first conception of grandeur. When Kate ran into Langton-Courtenay on her return, rushing through the row of new servants, who bowed and curtseyed in the hall, her sense of mortification and disappointment was intense. Everything had shrunken somehow; the rooms were smaller, the ceilings lower, the whole place diminished. Were these the rooms which she had compared in her mind with the suite in which the English ambassadress gave her ball? Kate stood aghast, blushing up to the roots of her hair, and felt so mortified that she did not remember to do the honours to her aunt and cousin. When she recollected, she went back to where they had placed themselves in the great old hall, round the great fireplace. There was a comfortable old-fashioned settle by it, and on this Mrs. Anderson had seated herself, to warm her frozen fingers, and give Kate time to recover herself.

'I have not the least doubt we shall find everything very comfortable,' she said to the new housekeeper, who stood before her, curtseying in her rustling silk gown, and wondering already whether she was to have three mistresses, or which was to be the 'lady of the house.' Mrs. Spigot felt instinctively that the place was not likely to suit her, when Kate ran against the new housemaid, and made the new butler (Mr. Spigot) fall back out of her way. This was not a dignified beginning for a young lady coming home; and if the aunt was to be mistress, it was evident that the situation would not be what the housekeeper thought.

'My niece is a little excited by coming home,' said Mrs. Anderson. 'To-morrow Miss Courtenay will be rested, and able to notice you all.' And she nodded to the servants, and waved her hand, dismissing them. If a feeling passed through Mrs. Anderson's mind, as she did so, that this was truly the position that she ought to have filled, and that Kate, a chit of nineteen, was not half so well endowed for it by nature as she herself would have been, who can blame her? She gave a sigh at this thought, and then smiled graciously as the servants went away, and felt that to have such a house, and so many servants under her control, even provisionally, would be pleasant. The housemaids thought her a very affable lady; but the upper servants were not so enthusiastic. Mrs. Anderson had mounted upon her very highest horse. She had put away all the vagaries of Italian life, and settled down into the very blandest of British matrons. She talked again about proper feeling, and a regard for the opinions of society. She had resumed all the caressing and instructive ways which, at the very beginning of their intercourse, she had adopted with Kate. And all these sentiments and habits came back so readily that there were moments in which she asked herself, 'Had she ever been in Italy at all?' But yes, alas, yes! Never, if she lived a thousand years, could she forget the three months just past.

Kate came back with some confusion to the hall, to find Ombra kneeling on the great white sheepskin mat before the fire; while Mrs. Anderson sat benignly on the settle, throwing off her shawls, and loosing her bonnet. Ombra's veil was thrown quite back; the ruddy glow threw a pink reflection on her face, and her eyes seemed to have thawed in the cheery, warm radiance. They were bright, and there seemed to be a little moisture in them. She held out her hand to her cousin, and drew her down beside her.

'This is the warmest place,' said Ombra; 'and your hands are like ice, Kate. But how warm it feels to be at home in England! and I like your house—it looks as if it had never been anything but a home.'

'It is delightful!—it is much larger and handsomer than I supposed,' said Mrs. Anderson, from the settle. 'With such a place to come home to, dear, I think you may be pardoned a little sensation of pride.'

'Oh! do you think so?' said Kate, gratified. 'I am so very glad you like it. It seems to me so insignificant, after all we have seen. I used to think it was the biggest, the finest, the most delightful house in the world; but if you only knew how the roofs have come down, and the rooms have shrunk!—I feel as if I could both laugh and cry.'

'That is quite natural—quite natural. Kate, I have sent the servants away. I thought you would be better able to see them to-morrow,' said Mrs. Anderson. 'But when you have warmed yourself, I think we may ask for Mrs. Spigot again, and go over the rooms, and see which we are to live in. It will not be necessary to open the whole house for us three, especially in Winter. Besides our bed-rooms and the dining-room, I think a snug little room that we can make ourselves comfortable in—that will be warm, and not too large—'

It pleased Mrs. Anderson to sit there in the warmth and stillness, and make all these suggestions. The big house gave her a sensible pleasure. It was delicious to think that a small room might be chosen for comfort, while there were miles of larger ones all at her orders. She smiled and beamed upon the two girls on the hearth. And indeed it was a pretty picture—Kate began to glow and brighten, with her hat off, and her bright hair shining in the firelight. Her travelling-dress was trimmed round the throat with white fur, like a bird's plumage, which caught a pink tinge too from the firelight, and seemed to caress her, nestling against her pretty cheek. The journey, and the arrival, and all the excitement had driven away, for the moment at least, all mists and clouds, and there was a pretty conflict in her face—half pleasure to be at home, half whimsical discontent with home. Ombra with her veil quite back, and her face cleared also of some other mystical veil, had her hand on Kate's shoulder, and was looking at her kindly, almost tenderly; and one of Ombra's cheeks was getting more than pink—it was crimson in the genial glow; she held up her hand to shield it, which looked transparent against the firelight. Mrs. Anderson looked very complacently, very fondly at both. Now that everything was over, she said to herself, and they had got home, surely at least a little interval of calm might come. She shut her eyes and her ears, and refused to look forward, refused to think of the seeds sown, and the results that must come from them. She had been carried away to permit and even sanction many things that her conscience disapproved; but perhaps the Fates would exact no vengeance this time—perhaps all would go well. She looked at Ombra, and it seemed to her that her child, after so many agitations, looked happy—yes, really happy—not with feverish joy or excitement, but with a genial quiet that belonged to home. Oh! if it might be so?—and why might it not be so?—at least for a time.

Mr. Courtenay had stayed in town, and the three ladies were alone in the house. They settled down in a few days into ease and comfort which, after their travelling, was very sweet. Things were different altogether from what they had been in the Shanklin cottage; and though Mrs. Anderson was in the place of Kate's guardian, yet Kate was no longer a child, to be managed for and ruled in an arbitrary way. It was now that the elder lady showed her wisdom. It was a sensible pleasure to her to govern the great house; here at last she seemed to have scope for her powers; but yet, though she ruled, she did so from the background; with heroic self-denial she kept Kate in the position she was so soon to occupy by right, trained her for it, guided her first steps, and taught her what to do.

'When you are of age, this is how you must manage,' she would say.

'But when I am of age, why should not you manage for me?' Kate replied; and her aunt made no answer.

They had come together again, and the old love had asserted itself once more. The mysteries unexplained had been buried by common consent. Kate lulled her own curiosity to rest, and when various questions came to the very tip of her tongue, she bit and stilled that unruly member, and made a not unsuccessful effort to restrain herself. But it was a hard discipline, and strained her strength. Sometimes, when she saw the continual letters which her aunt and cousin were always receiving, curiosity would give her a renewed pinch. But generally she kept herself down, and pretended not to see the correspondence, which was so much larger than it ever used to be. She was so virtuous even as not to look at the addresses of the letters. What good would it do her to know who wrote them? Of course some must be from the Berties, one, or both—what did it matter? The Berties were nothing to Kate; and, whatever the connection might be, Kate had evidently nothing to do with it, for it had never been told her. With this reasoning she kept herself down, though she was always sore and disposed to be cross about the hour of breakfast. Mrs. Anderson, for her part, would never see the crossness. She petted Kate, and smoothed her down, and read out, with anxious conciliation, scraps from Lady Barker's letters, and others of a similarly indifferent character; while, in the meantime, the other letters, ones which were not indifferent nor apt for quotation, were read by Ombra. The moment was always a disagreeable one for Kate—but she bore it, and made no sign.

But to live side by side with a secret has a very curious effect upon the mind; it sharpens some faculties and deadens others in the strangest way. Kate had now a great many things to think of, and much to do; people came to call, hearing she had come home; and she made more acquaintances in a fortnight than she had done before in a year. And yet, notwithstanding this, I think it was only a fortnight that the reign of peace and domestic happiness lasted. During that time, she made the most strenuous effort a girl could make to put out of her mind the recollection that there was something in the lives of her companions that had been concealed from her. Sometimes, indeed, when she sat by her cousin's side, there would suddenly rise up before her a glimpse of that group at the doorway on the Lung-Arno, and the scared look with which Ombra had rushed away; or some one of the many evening scenes when she was left out, and the other four, clustered about the table, would glide across her eyes like a ghost. Why was she left out? What difference would it have made to them, if they had made her one of themselves—was she likely to have betrayed their secret? And then Bertie Hardwick's troubled face would come before her, and his looks, half-apologetic, half-explanatory; looks, which, now she thought of them, seemed to have been so very frequent. Why was he always looking at her, as if he wanted to explain; as if he were disturbed and ill at ease; as if he felt her to be wronged? Though, of course, she was not in the least wronged, Kate said to herself, proudly; for what was it to her if all the Berties in the world had been at Ombra's feet?—Kate did not want them! Of that, at least, she was perfectly sure.

Mrs. Anderson's room was a large one; opening into that of Ombra on the one side, and into an ante-room, which they could sit in, or dress in, or read and write in, for it was furnished for all uses. It was a petit appartement, charmingly shut in and cosy, one of the best set of rooms in the house, which Kate had specially chosen for her aunt. Here the mother and daughter met one night after a very tranquil day, over the fire in the central room. It was a bright fire, and the cosy chairs that stood before it were luxurious, and the warm firelight flickered through the large room, upon the ruddy damask of the curtains, and the long mirror, and all the pretty furnishings. Ombra came in from her own room in her dressing-gown, with her dusky hair over her shoulders. Dusky were her looks altogether, like evening in a Winter's twilight. Her dressing-gown was of a faint grey-blue—not a pretty colour in itself, but it suited Ombra; and her long hair fell over it almost to her waist. She came in noiselessly to her mother's room, and it was her voice which first betrayed her presence there. Mrs. Anderson had been sitting thinking, with a very serious face; she started at her child's voice.

'I have been trying my very best to bear it—I think I have done my very best; I have smiled, and kept my temper, and tried to look as if I were not ready to die of misery. Oh! mamma, mamma, can this go on for ever? What am I to do?'

'Oh! Ombra, for God's sake have patience!' cried her mother—'nothing new has happened to-day?'

'Nothing new!—is it nothing new to have those girls here from the Rectory, jabbering about their brother? and to know that he is coming—next week, they say? We shall be obliged to meet—and how are we to meet? when I think how I took leave of him last! My life is odious to me!' cried the girl, sinking down in a chair, and covering her face with her hands. 'I don't know how to hold up my head and look those people in the face; and it is worse when no one comes. To live for a whole long, endless day without seeing a strange face, with Kate's eyes going through and through me—'

'Don't make things worse than they are,' said her mother, 'Oh! Ombra, have a little patience! Kate suspects nothing.'

'Suspects!' cried Ombra—'she knows there is something—not what it is, but that there is something. Do you think I don't see her looks in the morning, when the letters come? Poor Kate! she will not look at them; she is full of honour—but to say she does not suspect!'

'I don't know what to say to satisfy you, Ombra,' said her mother. 'Did not I beg you on my knees to take her into your confidence? It would have made everything so much easier, and her so much happier.'

'Oh! mamma, my life is hard enough of itself—don't make it harder and harder!' cried Ombra; and then she laid down her head upon her mother's shoulder, and wept. Poor Mrs. Anderson bore it all heroically; she kissed and soothed her child, and persuaded her that it could not last long—that Bertie would bring good news—that everything would be explained and atoned for in the end. 'There can be no permanent harm, dear—no permanent harm,' she repeated, 'and everybody will be sorry and forgive.' And so, by degrees, Ombra was pacified, and put to bed, and forgot her troubles.

This was the kind of scene which took place night after night in the tranquil house, where all the three ladies seemed so quietly happy. Kate heard no echo of it through the thick walls and curtains, yet not without troubles of her own was the heiress. The intimation of Bertie's coming disturbed her too. She thought she had got quite composed about the whole matter, willing to wait until the secret should be disclosed, and the connection between him and her cousin, whatever it was, made known. But to have him here again, with his wistful looks, and the whole mystery to be resumed, as if there had been no interruption of it—this was more than Kate felt she could bear.

CHAPTER LIV

The news which had made so much commotion in the Hall came from the Rectory in a very simple way. Edith and Minnie had come up to call. Their mother rather wished them to do so frequently. She urged upon them that it might demand a little sacrifice of personal feeling, yet that personal feeling was always a thing that ought to be sacrificed—it was a good moral exercise, irrespective of everything else; and Miss Courtenay was older, and, no doubt, more sensible than when she went away—not likely to shock them as she did then—and that it would be good for her to see a good deal of them, and pleasant for people to know that they went a good deal to the Hall. All this mass of reasoning was scarcely required, yet Edith and Minnie, on the whole, were glad to know that it was their duty to visit Kate. They both felt deeply that a thing which you do as a duty takes a higher rank than a thing you do as a pleasure; and their visits might have taken that profane character had not all this been impressed upon them in time.

'Oh! Miss Courtenay, we have such news,' said Edith; and Minnie added, in a parenthesis ('We are so happy!') 'Dear Bertie is coming home for a few days. He wrote that he was so busy, he could not possibly come; but papa insisted' ('I am so glad papa insisted,' from Minnie, who was the accompaniment), 'and so he is coming—just for two days. He is going to bring us the things he bought for us at Florence.' ('Oh! I do so want to see them!') 'You saw a great deal of him at Florence, did you not?'

'Yes, we saw him—a great many times,' said Kate, noticing, under her eyelids, how Ombra suddenly caught her breath.

'He used to mention you in his letters at first—only at first. I suppose you made too many friends to see much of each other.' ('Bertie is such a fellow for society.') 'He is reading up now for the bar. Perhaps you don't know that he has given up the church?'

'I think I heard him say so,' answered Kate.

And then there was a little pause. The Hardwick girls thought their great news was received very coldly, and were indignant at the want of interest shown in 'our Bertie!' After awhile Edith explained, with some dignity:

'Of course my brother is very important to us' ('He is just the very nicest boy that ever was!' from Minnie), 'though we can't expect others to take the same interest—'

Kate had looked up by instinct, and she caught Ombra's eyes, which were opened in a curious little stare, with an elevation of the eyebrows which spoke volumes. Not the same interest! Kate's heart grew a little sick—she could not tell why—and she turned away, making some conventional answer, she did not know what. A pause again, and then Mrs. Anderson asked, without looking up from her work:

'Is Mr. Hardwick coming to the Rectory alone?'

'Oh, yes! At least we think so,' said the two girls in one.

'I ask because he and his cousin were so inseparable,' said Mrs. Anderson, smiling. 'We used to say that when one was visible the other could not be far off.'

'Oh! you mean Bertie Eldridge,' said Edith. 'No, I am sure he is not coming. Papa does not like our Bertie to be so much with him as he has been. We do not think Bertie Eldridge a nice companion for him,' said the serious young woman, who rather looked down upon the boys, and echoed her parents' sentiments, without any sense of inappropriateness. 'No, we don't at all like them to be so much together,' said Minnie. Again Kate turned round instinctively. This time Ombra was smiling, almost laughing, with quite a gay light in her eyes.

'Of course that is a subject beyond me,' said Mrs. Anderson. 'They seemed much attached to each other.' And then the matter dropped, and the girls entered upon parish news, which left them full scope for prattle. Edith was engaged to be married to a neighbouring clergyman, and, accordingly, she was more than ever clerical and parochial in all her ways of thinking; while Minnie looked forward with a flutter, half of fear and half of excitement, to becoming the eldest Miss Hardwick, and having to manage the Sunday School and decorate the church by herself.

'What shall I do when Edith is married?' was the burden of all the talk she ventured upon alone. 'Mamma is so much occupied, she can't give very much assistance,' she said. 'Oh! dear Miss Courtenay, if you would come and help me sometimes when Edith goes away!'

'I will do anything I can,' said Kate, shortly. And the two girls withdrew at last, somewhat chilled by the want of sympathy. Had they but known what excitement, what commotion, their simple news carried into that still volcano of a house!

He was to come in a week. Kate schooled herself to be very strong, and think nothing of it, but her heart grew sick when she thought of the Florence scenes all over again—perhaps worse, for at Florence at least there were two. And to Ombra the day passed with feverish haste, and all her pretences at tranquillity and good humour began to fail in the rising tide of excitement.

'I shall be better again when he has gone away,' she said to her mother. 'But, oh! how can I—how can I take it quietly? Could you, if you were in my position? Think of all the misery and uncertainty. And he must be coming for a purpose. He would not come unless he had something to say.'

'Oh! Ombra, if there was anything, why should it not be said in a letter?' cried her mother. 'You have letters often enough. I wish you would just put them in your pocket, and not read them at the breakfast table. You keep me in terror lest Kate should see the handwriting or something. After all our precautions—'

'Can you really suppose that Kate is so ignorant?' said Ombra. 'Do you think she does not know well enough whom my letters are from?'

'Then, for God's sake, if you think so, let me tell her, and be done with this horrible secret,' cried her mother. 'It kills me to keep up this concealment; and if you think she knows, why, why should it go on?'

'You are so impetuous, mamma!' said Ombra, with a smile. 'There is a great difference between her guessing and direct information procured from ourselves. And how can we tell what she might do? She would interfere; it is her nature. You could not trust anything so serious to such a child.'

'Kate is not a child now,' said Mrs. Anderson. 'And oh! Ombra, if you will consider how ungrateful, how untrue, how unkind it is—'

'Stop, mamma!' cried Ombra, with a flush of angry colour. 'That is enough—that is a great deal too much—ungrateful! Are we expected to be grateful to Kate? You will tell me next to look up to her, to reverence her—'

'Ombra, you have always been hard upon Kate.'

'It is not my fault,' cried Ombra, suddenly giving way to a little burst of weeping. 'If you consider how different her position is—All this wretched complication—everything that has happened lately—would have been unnecessary if I had had the same prospects as Kate. Everything would have gone on easily then. There would have been no need for concealment—no occasion for deceit.'

'That is not Kate's fault,' said Mrs. Anderson, who was at her wit's end.

'Oh! mother, mother, don't worry me out of my senses. Did I say it was Kate's fault? It is no one's fault. But all we poor miserables must suffer as if it were. And there is no help for it; and it is so hard, so hard to bear!'

'Ombra, I told you to count the cost,' said Mrs. Anderson. 'I told you it would be no easy business. You thought you had strength of mind for the struggle then.'

'And it turns out that I have no strength of mind,' cried Ombra, almost wildly. And then she started up and went to her own room again, where her mother could hear her sighing and moaning till she fell asleep.

These night scenes took away from Mrs. Anderson's enjoyment of the great mansion and the many servants, and that luxurious room which Kate's affection had selected for her aunt. She sat over the fire when she was left alone, and would wonder and ask herself what would come of it, what could ever come of it, and whether it was possible that she should ever be happy again. She looked back with a longing which she could not subdue upon the humble days at Shanklin, when they were all so happy. The little tiny cottage, the small rooms, all rose up before her. The drawing-room itself was not half so large as Mrs. Anderson's bed-room at Langton-Courtenay. But what happy days these had been! She was not an old woman, though she was Ombra's mother. It was not as if life was nearly over for her, as if she could look forward to a speedy end of all her troubles. And she knew better than Ombra that somehow or other the world always exacts punishment, whether immediately or at an after period, from those who transgress its regulations. She said to herself mournfully that things do not come right in life as they do in story-books. Her daughter had taken a weak and foolish step, and she too had shared in the folly by consenting to it. She had done so, she could not explain to herself why, in a moment of excitement. And though Ombra was capable of hoping that some wonderful chain of accidents might occur to solve every difficulty, Mrs. Anderson was not young enough, or inexperienced enough, to think anything of the kind possible. Accidents happen, she was aware, when you do not want them, not when you do. When a catastrophe is foreseen and calculated upon, it never happens. In such a case, the most rotten vessel that ever sunk in a storm will weather a cyclone. Fate would not interfere to help; and when Mrs. Anderson considered how slowly and steadily the ordinary course of nature works, and how little it is likely to suit itself to any pressure of human necessity, her heart grew sick within her. She had a higher opinion of her niece than Ombra had, and she knew that Kate would have been a tower of strength and protection to them, besides all the embarrassment that would have been avoided, and all the pain and shame of deceit. But what could she do? The young people were stronger than she, and had overridden all her remonstrances; and now all that could be done was to carry on as steadily as possible—to conceal the secret—to hope that something might happen, unlikely though she knew that was.

Thus was this gentle household distracted and torn asunder; for there is no such painful thing in the world to carry about with one as a secret;—it will thrust itself to the surface, notwithstanding the most elaborate attempts to heap trifles and the common routine of life over it. It is like a living thing, and moves, or breathes, or cries out at the wrong moment, disclosing itself under the most elaborate covers; and finally, howsoever people may deceive themselves, it is never really hidden. While we are throwing the embroidered veil over it, and flattering ourselves that it is buried in concealment dark as night, our friends all the time are watching it throb under the veil, and wondering with a smile or a sigh, according to their dispositions, how we can be so foolish as to believe that it is hidden from them. The best we can do for our secret is to confuse the reality of it, most often making it look a great deal worse than it is. And this was what Ombra and her mother were doing, while poor Kate looked on wistful, seeing all their transparent manœuvres; and a choking, painful sense of concealment was in the air—a feeling that any moment some volcano might burst forth.

CHAPTER LV

It was a week later before Bertie came. He was brought to call by his mother and sisters in great delight and pomp; and then there ensued the strangest scene, of which only half the company had the least comprehension. The room which Kate had chosen as their sitting-room was an oblong room, with another smaller one opening from it. This small room was almost opposite the fireplace in the larger one, and made a draught which some people—indeed, most people—objected to; but as the broad open doorway was amply curtained, and a great deal of sun came in along with the imaginary draught, the brightness of the place won the day against all objections. The little room was thus preserved from the air of secrecy and retirement common to such rooms. No one could retire to flirt there; no one could listen unseen to conversations not intended for them. The piano was placed in it, and the writing-table, under the broad recessed window, which filled the whole end of it. It was light as a lantern, swept by the daylight from side to side, and the two fires kept it as warm as it was bright. When Mrs. Hardwick sailed in, bearing under her convoy her two blooming girls close behind her, and the tall brother towering over their heads, a more proud or happy woman could not be.

'I have brought my Bertie to see you,' she said, all the seriousness of that 'sense of duty' which weighed upon her ordinary demeanour melting for the moment in her motherly delight and pride. 'He was so modest, we could scarcely persuade him to come. He thought you might think he was presuming on your acquaintance abroad, and taking as much liberty as if he had been an intimate—'

'I think Mr. Hardwick might very well take as much liberty as that,' cried Kate, moved, in spite of herself, to resentment with this obstinate make-believe. Her aunt looked up at her with such pain in her eyes as is sometimes seen in the eyes of animals, who can make us no other protest.

'We are very glad to see Mr. Bertie again,' said Mrs. Anderson, holding out her hand to him with a smile. 'He is a Shanklin acquaintance, too. We are old friends.'

And he shook hands with all of them solemnly, his face turning all manner of colours, and his eyes fixed on the ground. Ombra was the last to approach, and as she gave him her hand, she did not say a word; neither did she lift her eyes to look at him. They stood by each other for a second, hand in hand, with eyes cast down, and a flush of misery upon both their faces. Was it merely misery? It could not but be painful, meeting thus, they who had parted so differently; but Kate, who could not remove her eyes from them, wondered, out of the midst of the sombre cloud which seemed to have come in with Bertie, and to have wrapped her round—wondered what other feeling might be in their minds. Was it not a happiness to stand together even now, and here?—to be in the same room?—to touch each other's hands? Even amid all this pain of suppression and concealment was not there something more in it? She felt as if fascinated, unable to withdraw her eyes from them; but they remained together only for a moment; and Bertie's sisters, who did not think Miss Anderson of much importance, did not even notice the meeting. Bertie himself withdrew to Mrs. Anderson's side, and began to talk to her and to his mother. The girls, disappointed (for naturally they would have preferred that he should make himself agreeable to the heiress), sat down by Kate. Ombra dropped noiselessly on a chair close to the doorway between the two rooms; and after a few minutes she said to her cousin, 'Will you pardon me if I finish my letter for the post?' and went into the inner room, and sat down at the writing-table.

'She writes a great deal, doesn't she?' said Edith Hardwick. 'Is she literary, Miss Courtenay? I asked Bertie, but he could not tell me. I thought she would not mind doing something perhaps for the "Parish Magazine."'

'Edith does most of it herself,' said Minnie. ('Oh! Minnie, for shame!') 'And do you know, Miss Courtenay, she had something in the last "Monthly Packet."' ('Please don't, Minnie, please! What do you suppose Miss Courtenay cares?') 'I shall bring it up to show you next time I come.'

'Indeed, you shall do nothing of the kind!' said Edith, blushing. And Kate made a pretty little civil speech, which would have been quite real and genuine, had not her mind been so occupied with other things; but with the drama actually before her eyes, how could she think of stories in the 'Monthly Packet?' Her eyes went from one to another as they sat with the whole breadth of the room between them; and this absorption made her look much more superior and lofty than she was in reality, or had any thought of being. Yes, she said to herself, it was best so—they could not possibly talk to each other as strangers. It was best that they should thus get out of sight of each other almost—avoid any intercourse. But how strange it was!

'Don't you think it is odd that Bertie, knowing the world as he does, should be so shy?' said Edith. ('Oh! he is so shy!' cried Minnie.) 'He made as many excuses as a frightened little girl. "They won't want to see me," he said. "Miss Courtenay will know it is not rudeness on my part if I don't call. Why should I go and bother them?" We dragged him here!'

'We dragged him by the hair of his head,' said Minnie, who was the wit of the family.

And Kate did her best to laugh.

'I did not think he had been so shy,' she said. 'He wanted, I suppose, to have you all to himself, and not to lose his time making visits. How long is he to stay?'

Edith and Minnie looked at each other. The question had already been discussed between their mother and themselves whether Bertie would be asked to dinner, or whether, indeed, they might not all be asked, with the addition of Edith's betrothed, who was visiting also at the Rectory. They all thought it would be a right thing for Kate to do; and, of course, as Mrs. Anderson was there, it would be so easy, and in every way so nice. They looked at each other, accordingly, with a little consciousness.

'He is to stay till Monday, I think,' said Edith; 'or perhaps we might coax him to give us another day, if—' She was going to say if there was any reason, but that seemed a hint too plain.

'That is not a very long visit,' said Kate. And then, without a hint of a dinner-party, she plunged into the parish, that admirable ground of escape in all difficulties.

They had got into the very depths of charities, and coals, and saving-clubs, when Mrs. Hardwick rose.

'We are such a large party, we must not inflict ourselves upon you too long,' said Mrs. Hardwick. She, too, was a little disappointed that there was not a word about a dinner. She thought Mrs. Anderson should have known what her duty was in the circumstances, and should have given her niece a hint; 'but I hope we shall all meet again before my son goes away.'

And then there was a second shaking of hands. When all was over, and the party were moving off, Kate turned to Bertie, who was last.

'You have not taken leave of Ombra,' she said, looking full at him.

He coloured to his hair; he made her a confused bow, and hurried into the room where Ombra was. Kate, with a sternness which was very strange to her, watched the two figures against the light. Ombra did not move. She spoke to him apparently without even looking up from her letter. A dozen words or so—no more. Then there came a sudden cry from the other door, by which the mother and daughters were going 'Oh! we have forgotten Miss Anderson!' and the whole stream flowed back.

'Indeed, it is Ombra's fault; but she was writing for the post,' exclaimed her mother, calling to her.

Ombra came forward to the doorway, very pale, even to her lips, but smiling, and shook hands three times, and repeated that it was her fault. And then the procession streamed away.

'That girl looks very unhealthy,' Mrs. Hardwick said, when they were walking down the avenue. 'I shall try and find out from her mother if there is consumption in the family, and advise them to try the new remedy. Did you notice what a colour her lips were? She is very retiring, poor thing; and, I must say, never puts herself the least in the way.'

'Do you think she is pretty, Bertie?' said the sisters, together.

'Pretty? Oh! I can't tell. I am no judge,' said Bertie. 'Look here, mamma, I am going to see old Stokes, the keeper. He used to be a great friend of mine. If I don't make up to you before you reach home, I'll be back at least before it is dark.'

'Before it is dark!' said Mrs. Hardwick, in dismay. But Bertie was gone. 'I suppose young men must have their way,' she said, looking after him. 'But you must not think, girls, that people are any the happier for having their way. On the contrary, you who have been educated to submit have a much better preparation for life. I hope dear Bertie will never meet with any serious disappointment,' she added, with a sigh.

'Oh! mamma, serious disappointment! when he has always succeeded in everything!' cried the girls, in their duet.

'For he could not bear it,' said Mrs. Hardwick, shaking her head. 'It would be doubly, doubly hard upon him; for he has never been trained to bear it—never, I may say, since he left the nursery, and got out of my hands.'

At this time it was nearly three o'clock, a dull Winter afternoon, not severe, but dim and mournful. It was the greyness of frost, however, not of damp, which was in the air; and Kate, who was restless, announced her intention of taking a long walk. She was glad to escape from this heavy atmosphere of home; she said, somewhat bitterly, that it was best to leave them together to unbosom themselves, to tell each other all those secrets which were not to be confided to her; and to compare notes, no doubt, as to how he was looking, and how they were to find favourable opportunities of meeting again, Kate's heart was sore—she was irritated by the mystery which, after all, was so plain to her. She saw the secret thing moving underneath the cover—the only difficulty she had was to decide what kind of secret it was. What was the relationship between Bertie and Ombra? Were they only lovers?—were they something more?—and what had Bertie Eldridge to do with it? Kate, indignant, would not permit herself to think; but the questions came surging up in her mind against her will. She had a little basket in her hand. She was carrying some grapes and wine to old Stokes, the disabled keeper, who was dying, and whom everybody made much of. On her way to his cottage she had to pass that little nook where the brook was, and where she had first seen Bertie Hardwick. It was the first time she had seen it since her return, and she paused, half in anger and bitterness, half with a softening swell of recollection. How rich, and sweet, and warm, and delicious it had been that Summer evening, with the blossom still on the hawthorns, and the grass like velvet, and the soft little waterfall tinkling! How everything was changed!—the bushes all black with frost, the trees bare of their foliage, with here and there a ragged red leaf at the end of a bough, the brook tinkling with a sharp metallic sound. Everything else was frozen and still—all the insect life of Summer, all the movements and rustlings of grass and leaves and flowers. The flowers and the leaves were gone; the grass bound fast in an icy coat. 'But not more different,' Kate thought, 'than were other matters—more important than the grass and flowers.'

She was roused from her momentary reverie by the sound of a footstep ringing clear and sharp along the frosty road; and before she could get out of the shelter of the little coppice which encircled that haunt of her childhood, Bertie Hardwick came suddenly up to her. The sight of her startled the young man—but in what way? A flush of delight rushed over his face—he brightened all over, as it seemed, eyes and mouth and every feature. He came forward to her with impetuous steps, and took her hand before she was aware.

'I was thinking of you,' he cried; 'longing to meet you just here, not believing it possible—oh, Kate!—Miss Courtenay, I beg your pardon. I—I forget what I was going to say.'

He did not give up her hand, though; he stood and gazed at her with such pleasure in his eyes as could not be misconstrued. And then the most curious phenomenon came into being—a thing most wonderful, not to be explained. All the anger and the suspicion and the bitterness, suddenly, in a moment, fled out of Kate's heart—they fled like evil spirits exorcised and put to flight by something better than they. Kate was too honest to conceal what was in her mind. She did not draw away her hand; she looked at him full with her candid eyes.

'Mr. Bertie, I am very glad to have met you here. I can't help remembering; and I should be glad—very glad to meet you anywhere; but—'

He dropped her hand; he put up both his own to his face, as if to cover its shame; and then, with a totally changed tone, and a voice from which all the gladness had gone, he said slowly:

'I know; but I am not allowed to explain—I cannot explain. Oh! Kate, you know no harm of me, do you? You have never known or heard that I was without sense of honour? trust me, if you can! Nothing in it, not any one thing, is my fault.'

Kate started as if she had been struck, and everything that had wounded her came back in sevenfold strength. She could not keep even a tone of contempt out of her voice.

'I have heard,' she said, 'that there was honour among thieves: do you throw the blame upon Ombra—all the blame? I suppose it is the way men do. Good-bye, Mr. Hardwick!' And, before he could say a word, she was gone—flying past him, indignant, contemptuous, wounded to the core.

As she came back from the keeper's cottage, when the afternoon was duller than ever, and the sky seemed to be dropping over the tree-tops, Kate thought she saw, in one of the roads which crossed the avenue, the flutter of a lady's shawl. The girl was curious in her excitement, and she paused behind a tree to watch. After a short time the fluttering shawl drew nearer. It was Ombra, clinging close to Bertie Hardwick's arm—turning to him a pale face full of care and anxiety. They were discussing their dark concerns—their secrets. Kate rushed home without once stopping or drawing breath.

CHAPTER LVI

This incident passed as all incidents do, and the blank of common life returned. How short those moments of action are in existence, and how long are the dull intervals—those intervals which count for nothing, and yet are life itself! Bertie Hardwick went away only after sundry unsuccessful efforts on the part of his family to unite the party from the Hall with that at the Rectory. Mrs. Hardwick would willingly, very willingly, have asked them to dinner, even after the disappointment of discovering that they did not mean to ask Bertie. She was stopped, however, by a very commonplace hindrance—where was she to find gentlemen enough on short notice to balance all those three ladies? Mr. Hardwick, Bertie, and Edith's betrothed made the tale correct to begin with—but three more gentlemen in a country parish on two days' notice! It was impossible. All that Mrs. Hardwick could do was to ask, deprecatingly, that the ladies would come to a family dinner, 'very quiet,' she said; 'you must not suppose I mean a party.' Mrs. Anderson, with her best and most smiling looks, accepted readily. 'But Ombra is not very well,' she said; 'I fear I must ask you to excuse her. And dear Kate has such a bad cold—she caught it walking across the park the other evening to old Stokes the keeper's cottage.'

'To old Stokes!' cried Mrs. Hardwick. 'Why, my Bertie was there too.' And she added, looking grave, after that burst of radiance, 'The old man was a great favourite with everybody. We all go to see him.'

'So I hear,' said Mrs. Anderson, smiling; and next day she put on her best gown, poor soul! and went patiently down to the Rectory to dinner, and made a great many apologies for her girls. She did not enjoy it much, and she had to explain that the first chill of England after Italy had been too much for Kate and Ombra. 'We had lived in the Isle of Wight for some years before,' she added, 'so that this is almost their first experience of the severity of Winter. But a few days indoors I hope will make them all right.'

Edith Hardwick could not believe her eyes when, next day, the day before Bertie left, she saw Miss Anderson walking in the park. 'Do you think it possible it was not true?' she and her sister asked each other in consternation; but neither they, nor wiser persons than they, could have determined that question. Ombra was not well, nor was Kate. They were both disturbed in their youthful being almost beyond the limits of self-control. Mrs. Anderson had, in some respects, to bear both their burdens; but she said to herself, with a sigh, that her shoulders were used to it. She had borne the yoke in her youth, she had been trained to bear a great deal, and say very little about it. And so the emotion of the incident gradually died away, growing fainter and larger in the stillness, and the monotony came back as of old!

But, oh! how pleasant the monotony of old would have been, how delightful, had there been nothing but the daily walks, the daily talks, the afternoon drives, the cheerful discussions, and cheerful visits, which had made their simple life at Shanklin so sweet! All that was over, another cycle of existence had come in.

I think another fortnight had elapsed since Bertie's visit, and everything had been very quiet—and the quiet had been very intolerable. Sometimes almost a semblance of confidential intercourse would be set up among them, and Ombra would lean upon Kate, and Kate's heart melt towards Ombra. This took place generally in the evening, when they sat together in the firelight before the lamp was brought, and talked the kind of shadowy talk which belongs to that hour.

'Look at my aunt upon the wall!' Kate cried, one evening, in momentary amusement. 'How gigantic she is, and how she nods and beckons at us!' Mrs. Anderson was chilly, and had placed her chair in front of the fire.

'She is no more a shadow than we all are,' said Ombra. 'When the light comes, that vast apparition will disappear, and she will be herself. Kate, don't you see the parable? We are all stolen out of ourselves, made into ghosts, till the light comes.'

'I don't understand parables,' said Kate.

'I wish you did this one,' said Ombra, with a sigh, 'for it is true.' And then there was silence for a time, a silence which Kate broke by saying,

'There is the new moon. I must go and look at her.'

Not through the glass, dear—it is unlucky,' said Mrs. Anderson; but Kate took no notice. She went into the inner room, and watched the new moon through the great window. A cold, belated, baby moon, looking as if it had lost its way somehow in that blue waste of sky. And the earth looked cold, chilled to the heart, as much as could be seen of it, the tree-tops cowering together, the park frozen. She stood there in a reverie, and forgot about the time, and where she was. The bustle behind her of the lamp being brought in did not disturb Kate, and seeing her at the window, the servant who came with the lights discreetly forbore to disturb her, and left the curtains undrawn. But, from what followed, it was evident that nobody else observed Kate, and she was still deep in her musings, when she was startled, and brought to instant life, by a voice which seemed to ring through the room to her like a trumpet-note of defiance.

'Mother, this cannot go on!' Ombra cried out all at once. 'If it lasts much longer I shall hate her. I shall want to kill her!'

'Ombra!'

'It is true, I shall want to kill her! Oh! not actually with my hands! One never knows what one could do till one is tempted. Still I think I would not touch her. But, God help us, mother, God help us! I hate her now!'

'God help you, indeed, my unhappy child!' cried her mother. 'Oh! Ombra, do you know you are breaking my heart?'

'My own was broken first,' cried Ombra; and there was a ferocious and wild force in what she said, which thrilled through and through the listener, now just beginning to feel that she should not be here, but unable to stir in her great horror and astonishment. 'My own was broken first. What does it matter? I thought I could brave everything; but to have him sent here for her sake—because she would be the most fit match for him! to have her come again between him and me—'

'She never came between him and you—poor Kate!—she never thought of him. Has it not been proved that it was only a fancy? Oh! Ombra, how ungrateful, how unkind you are to her!'

'What must I be grateful for?' cried Ombra. 'She has always been in my way, always! She came between you and me. She took half away from me of what was all mine. Would you hesitate, and doubt, and trouble, as you do, if it were not for Kate? She has always been in my way! She has been my enemy, not my friend. If she did not really come between him and me, then I thought so, and I had all the anguish and sorrow as if it had been true. And now he is to be sent here to meet her—and I am to put up with it, he says, as it will give us means of meeting. But I will not put up with it!' cried Ombra, her voice rising shrill with passion—'I cannot; it is asking too much. I would rather not meet him than meet him to be watched by Kate's eyes. He has no right to come here on such a pretence. I would rather kill her—I would rather never see him again!'

'Oh! Ombra, how can you tell who may hear you?' cried her mother, putting up her hand as if to stop her mouth.

'I don't care who hears me!' said Ombra, pale and sullen.

And then there was a rustle and movement, and both started, looking up with one impulse. In the twilight right beyond the circle of the lamplight, white as death, with a piteous gaze that neither could ever forget, stood Kate. Mrs. Anderson sprang to her feet with a cry; Ombra said not a word—she sat back in her chair, and kept her startled eyes upon her cousin—great dilated eyes, awakened all in a minute to what she had done.

'Kate, you have heard what she has said?'

'Yes, I have heard it,' she said, faintly. 'I did not mean to; but I was there, and I thought you knew. I have heard everything. Oh! it does not matter. It hurts at present, but it will go off after a while.'

She tried to smile, and then she broke down and cried. Mrs. Anderson went to her and threw her arms around her; but Kate put her aunt gently away. She looked up through her tears, and shook her head with the best smile she could muster.

'No, it is not worth while,' she said,—'not any more. I have been wrong all the time. I suppose God did not mean it so. I had no natural mother or sister, and you can't get such things except by nature. Don't let us say any more about it,' she added, hastily brushing the tears from her eyes. 'I am very sorry you have suffered so much on my account, Ombra. If I had only known—And I never came between you and anyone—never dreamt of doing it—never will, never—you may be sure of that. I wanted my aunt to love me—that was natural—but no one else.'

'Kate, I did not mean it,' faltered Ombra, her white face suddenly burning with a blush of passionate shame. She had never realised the meanness of her jealousies and suspicions till this moment. Her mother's remonstrances had never opened her eyes; but in a moment, in this anguish of being found out, she found out herself, and saw through her cousin's eyes, as it were, how contemptible it all was.

'I think you meant it. I don't think you could have spoken so had you not meant it,' said Kate, with composure. And then she sat down, and they all looked at each other, Mrs. Anderson standing before the two girls, wringing her hands. I think they realised what had happened better than she did. Her alarm and misery were great. This was a quarrel between her two children—a quarrel which it was very dreadful to contemplate. They had never quarrelled before; little misunderstandings might have arisen between them, but these it was always possible to smooth down; but this was a quarrel. The best thing to do, she felt, was that they should have it out. Thus for once her perception failed her. She stood frightened between them, looking from one to another, not certain on which side the volcano would burst forth. But no volcano burst forth; things had gone too far for that.

As for Kate, she did not know what had come over her. She had become calm without knowing how. All her agitation passed away, and a dead stillness succeeded—a stillness which made her afraid. Two minutes ago her heart and body had been tingling with darts of pain. She had felt the blow everywhere—on her head, which ached and rung as if she had been struck—on her heart, which seemed all over dull pain—even in her limbs, which did not feel able to support her. But now all had altered; a mysterious numbness crept from her feet up to her heart and her head. She did not feel anything; she saw Ombra's big, startled eyes straining at her, and Mrs. Anderson, standing by, wringing her hands; but neither the one nor the other brought any gleam of feeling to her mind.

'It is a pity we came here,' she said, slowly—'a great pity, for people will discuss everything—I suppose they always do. And I don't know, indeed, what is best; I am not prepared to propose anything; all seems dark to me. I cannot go on standing in Ombra's way—that is all I know. I will not do it. And perhaps, if we were all to think it over to-night, and tell what we think to-morrow morning—' she said, with a smile, which was very faint, and a strong indication to burst forth instead into tears.

'Oh! my darling!' said Mrs. Anderson, bewildered by this extraordinary calm.

Kate made a little strange gesture. It was the same with which she had put her aunt away. 'Don't!' she said, under her breath. She could bear what Ombra had said after the first astonishing outburst, but she could not bear that caressing—those sweet names which belong only to those who are loved. Don't! A touch would have made her recoil—a kiss would have driven her wild and raving, she thought. This was the horror of it all—not that they had quarrelled, but that they had pretended to love her, and all the time had been hating her—or, at the best, had been keeping each other up to the mark by thought of the gratitude and kindness they owed her. Kindness and gratitude!—and yet they had pretended to love.

'Perhaps it is better I should not say anything,' said Ombra, with another flush, which this time was that of rising anger. 'I ought not to have spoken as I did, but I make no apologies—it would be foolish to do so. You must form your own opinion, and nothing that I could say would change it. Of course it is no excuse to say that I would not have spoken as I did had I known you were there.'

'I did not mean to listen,' said Kate, colouring a little. 'You might have seen me all the time; but it is best to say nothing at all now—none of us had better speak. We have to get through dinner, which is a pity. But after that, let us think it over quietly—quite quietly—and in the morning we shall see better. There is no reason,' she said, very softly, 'why, because you do not feel for me as I thought you did, we should quarrel; for really there is nothing to quarrel about. One's love is not in one's own gift, to be bestowed as one pleases. You have been very kind to me—very kind.'

'Oh! Kate—oh! my dear child, do you think I don't love you? Oh! Kate, do not break my heart!'

'Don't, aunt, please,' she said, with a shiver. 'I don't feel quite well, and it hurts me. Don't—any more—now!'

CHAPTER LVII

That was the horrible sting of it—they had made believe to love her, and it had not been true. Now love, Kate reflected (as she went slowly to her room, feeling, somehow, as if every step was a mile), was not like anything else. To counterfeit any other emotion might be pardoned, but to counterfeit love was the last injury anyone could do you. Perhaps it was the wound to her pride which helped the wound to her affections, and made it so bitter. As she thought it all over, she reflected that she had, no doubt, accepted this love much too easily when she went first to her aunt's charge. She had leapt into their arms, as it were. She had left them no room to understand what their real feelings were; she had taken it for granted that they loved her. She writhed under the humiliation which this recollection brought her. After all it was not, perhaps, they who were in the wrong, but she who had insisted on believing what they had never taken much pains to persuade her of. After all, when she came to think of it, Ombra had made no pretence whatever. The very first time they met, Ombra had repulsed her—she was honest, at least!

To be sure, Mrs. Anderson had been very caressing, but that was her nature. She said dear and darling to every child that came in her way—she petted everybody. Why, then, should Kate have accepted her petting as any sign of special love? It was herself that had been a vain fool, all along. She had taken it for granted: she had assumed it as necessary and certain that they loved her; and they, embarrassed by this faith, had been reluctant to hurt her feelings by undeceiving her; this was how it was. What stings, what tortures of pride and pain, did she give herself as she thought these things over! Gradually she pulled down all the pleasant house that had sheltered her these four—nearly five long years. She plucked it down with her hands. She laid her weary head on her little sofa beside the fire in her room, and watched the flickering shadows, and said to herself that here she was, back in the only home that belonged to her, alone as she had been when she left it. Four cold walls, with so much furniture, new unknown servants, who could not love her—who did not even know her; a cold, cold miserable world outside, and no one in it to whom it would make the difference of a meal or a night's rest, whether she lived or died. Oh, cold, terrible remorseless fate! back again in Langton-Courtenay, which, perhaps, she ought never to have left, exactly in the same position as when she left it. Kate could not find any solace in tears; they would not come. All her youth of heart, her easy emotions, her childish laughing and crying, were gone. The sunshine of happiness that had lighted up all the world with dazzling lights had been suddenly quenched. She saw everything as it was, natural and true. It was like the sudden enlightenment which came to the dreamer in fairy-land; shrivelled up all the beautiful faces, turning the gold into dross, and the sweetness into corruption.

How far these feelings were exaggerated and overdone, the reader can judge. The spectator, indeed, always sees how much too far the bent bow rebounds when the string is cut, and how far the sufferer goes astray in disappointment and grief, as well as in the extravagances of hope. But, unfortunately, the one who has to go through it never gets the benefit of that tranquilising knowledge. And to Kate all that she saw now seemed too real—more real than anything she had known before—and her desertion complete. She lay on her sofa, and gazed into the fire, and felt her temples beating and her eyes blazing, but could not cry to relieve herself. When Maryanne came upstairs to light her mistress's candles, and prepare her dress for dinner, she shrieked out to see the flushed face on the sofa-pillow.

'I have a headache—that is all. Don't make a fuss,' cried poor Kate.

'Miss Kate, you must be going to have a fever. Let me call Mrs. Anderson—let me send for the doctor,' cried the girl, in dismay. But Kate exerted her authority, and silenced her. She sent her downstairs with messages that she had a headache, and could not come down again, but was going to bed, and would rather not be disturbed.'

Late in the evening, when Mrs. Anderson came to the door, Maryanne repeated the message. 'I think, ma'am, Miss Kate's asleep. She said she was not to be disturbed.'

But Maryanne did not know how to keep this visitor out. She dared not oppose her, as she stole in on noiseless foot, and went to the bedside. Kate was lying with all her pretty hair in a mass on the pillow, with her eyes closed, and the flush which had frightened Maryanne still on her face. Was she asleep? Mrs. Anderson would have thought so, but for seeing two big teardrops just stealing from her closed eyelashes. She stooped over and kissed her softly on the forehead. 'God bless you, my dear child, my dear child!' she whispered, almost wishing she might not be heard; and then stole away to her own room, to the other child, much more tumultuous and exciting, who awaited her. Poor Mrs. Anderson! of all the three she was the one who had the most to bear.

Ombra was pacing up and down the large bed-room, so luxurious and wealthy, her breath coming quick with excitement, her whole frame full of pulses and tinglings of a hundred pains. She, too, had gone through a sharp pang of humiliation; but it had passed over. She was not lonely, like Kate. She had her mother to fall back upon in the meantime; and even failing her mother, she had some one else, another who would support her, upon whom she could lean, and who would give her moral sacking and sympathy. All this makes a wonderful difference in the way people receive a downfall. Ombra had been thunderstruck at first at her own recklessness, and the wounds she had given; but now a certain irritation possessed her, inflaming all the sore places in her mind, and they were not few. She was walking up and down, thinking what she would do, what she would say, how she would no longer be held in subjection, and forced to consider Kate's ways and Kate's feelings, Kate this and that. She was sorry she had said what she did—that she could avow without hesitation. She had not meant to hurt her cousin, and of course she had not meant really that she hated her, but only that she was irritated and unhappy, and not in a position to choose her words. Kate was rich, and could have whatever she pleased; but Ombra had nothing but the people who loved her, and she could not bear any interference with them. It was the parable of the ewe-lamb over again, she said to herself; and thus was exciting herself, and swelling her excitement to a higher and higher pitch, when her mother went in—her mother, for whom all this tempest was preparing and upon whom it was about to fall.

'You have been to see her, mamma! You never think of your own dignity! You have been petting her, and apologising to her!'

'She is asleep,' said Mrs. Anderson, sitting down, and leaning her head on her hand. She did not feel able for any more contention. Kate, she felt sure, was not really asleep, but she accepted the semblance, that no more might be said.

Ombra laughed, and, though the laugh sounded mocking, there was a great deal of secret relief in it.

'Oh! she is asleep! Did not I say she was no more than a child? She has got over it already. When she wakes up she will have forgotten all about it. How excellent those easy-going natures are! I knew it was only for the moment. I knew she had no feelings to speak of. For once, mama, you must acknowledge yourself in the wrong!'

And Ombra sat down too, with an immense weight lifted from her mind. She had not owned it even to herself, but the relief was so great that she felt now what her anxiety had been. 'Little foolish thing,' she said, 'to be so heroical, and make such a noise—' Ombra laughed almost hysterically—'and then to go to bed and fall asleep, like a baby! She is little more than a baby—I always told you so, mamma.'

'You have always been wrong, Ombra, in your estimation of Kate, and you are wrong now. Whether she was asleep or not, I can't say; she looked like it. But this is a very serious matter all the same. It will not be so easily got over as you think.'

'I don't wish it to be got over!' cried Ombra. 'It is a kind of life I cannot endure, and it ought not to be asked of me—it is too much to ask of me. You saw the letter. He is to be sent here, with the object of paying his addresses to her, because she is an heiress, and it is thought he ought to marry money. To marry—her! Oh! mamma! he ought not to have said it to me. It was wicked and cruel to make such an explanation.'

'I think so too,' said Mrs. Anderson, under her breath.

'And he does not seem to be horrified by the thought. He says we shall be able to meet—Oh! mother, before this happens let us go away somewhere, and hide ourselves at the end of the earth!'

'Ombra, my poor child, you must not hide yourself. There are your rights to be considered. It is not that I don't see how hard it is; but you must not be the one to judge him harshly. We must make allowances. He was alone—he was not under good influence, when he wrote.'

'Oh! mother, and am I to believe of him that bad influences affect him so? This is making it worse—a thousand times worse! I thought I had foreseen everything that there could be to bear; but I never thought of this.'

'Alas! poor child, how little did you foresee!' said Mrs. Anderson, in a low voice—'not half nor quarter part. Ombra, let us take Kate's advice. La nuit porte conseil—let us decide nothing to-night.'

'You can go and sleep, like her,' said Ombra, somewhat bitterly. 'I think she is more like you than I am. You will say your prayers, and compose yourself, and go to sleep.'

Mrs. Anderson smiled faintly. 'Yes, I could have done that when I was as young as you,' she said, and made no other answer. She was sick at heart, and weary of the discussion. She had gone over the same ground so often, and how often soever she might go over it, the effect was still the same. For what could anyone make of such a hopeless, dreary business?

After all, it was Ombra, with all her passion, who was asleep the first. Her sighs seemed to steal through the room like ghosts, and sometimes a deeper one than usual would cause her mother to steal through the open doorway to see if her child was ill. But after a time the sighs died away, and Mrs. Anderson lay in the darkness of the long Winter night, watching the expiring fire, which burned lower and lower, and listening to the wind outside, and asking herself what was to be the next chapter—where she was to go and what to do. She blamed herself bitterly for all that had happened, and went over it step by step and asked herself how it could have been helped. Of itself, had it been done in the light of day, and with consent of all parties, there had been no harm. She had her child's happiness to consider chiefly, and not the prejudices of a family with whom she had no acquaintance. How easy it is to justify anything that is done and cannot be undone! and how easy and natural the steps seem by which it was brought about! while all the time something keeps pricking the casuist, whispering, 'I told you so.' Yes, she had not been without her warnings; she had known that she ought not to have given that consent which had been wrung from her, as it were, at the sword's point. She had known that it was weak of her to let principle and honour go, lest Ombra's cheek should be pale, and her face averted from her mother.

'It was not Ombra's fault,' she said to herself. 'It was natural that Ombra should do anything she did; but I who am older, who know the world, I should have known better—I should have had the courage to bear even her unhappiness, for her good. Oh, my poor child! and she does not know yet, bad as she thinks it, half of what she may have to bear.'

Thus the mother lay and accused herself, taking first one, and then the other, upon her shoulders, shedding salt tears under the veil of that darkness, wondering where she should next wander to, and what would become of them, and whether light could ever come out of this darkness. How her heart ached!—what fears and heaviness overwhelmed her! while Ombra slept and dreamed, and was happy in the midst of the wretchedness which she had brought upon herself!

CHAPTER LVIII

They were all very subdued when they met next day. It was now, perhaps, more than at any former time that Kate's position told. Instinctively, without a word of it to each other, Mrs. Anderson and her daughter felt that on her aspect everything depended. They would not have said it to each other, or even to themselves; but, nevertheless, there could not be any doubt on the subject. There were two of them, and they were perfectly free to go and come as they pleased; but the little one—the younger child—the second daughter, who had been quietly subject to them so long, was the mistress of the situation; she was the lady of the house, and they were but her guests. In a moment their positions were changed, and everything reversed. And Kate felt it too. They were both in the breakfast-room when she came in. She was very quiet and pale, unlike her usual self; but when she made her usual greetings, a momentary glow of red came over her face. It burned as she touched Ombra's cheek with her own. After all that had passed, these habitual kisses were the most terrible thing to go through. It was so hard to break the bond of custom, and so hard to bestow what means love solely for custom's sake. The two girls reddened as if they had been lovers as they thus approached each other, though for a very different cause; but no stranger, unless he had been very quick-sighted, would have seen the subtle, unexpressed change which each of them felt dropping into their very soul. Kate left the others as soon as breakfast was over, and was absent the whole morning. At lunch she was again visible, and once more they sat and talked, with walls of glass or ice between them. This time, however, Kate gave more distinct indication of her policy.

'Would you like to have the carriage this afternoon?' she said.

'I don't know,' said Mrs. Anderson, doubtfully, trying to read her niece's pleasure in her eyes. 'If there is anywhere you want to go to, dear—'

'Oh! if you don't think of going out, I shall drive to Westerton, to get some books,' said Kate. 'I want some German books. It is a long time since I have done any German; but if you want the carriage, never mind—I can go some other day.'

'I do not want it,' said Mrs. Anderson, with a chill of dismay; and she turned to Ombra, and made some anxious suggestion about walking somewhere. 'It will be a nice opportunity while Kate is occupied,' said the poor soul, scheming to keep things smooth; 'you said you wanted to see that part of the park.'

'Yes,' said Ombra, depressed too, though she would have been too proud to confess it; and thus it was arranged.

Kate drove away alone, and had a hearty cry in the carriage, and was very unhappy; and the mother and daughter went and walked against time in the frost-bound park. It was a bright Winter afternoon, with a pleasant sharpness in the air, and a gorgeous sunset of red and gold. They stopped and pointed it out to each other, and dwelt on all the different gradations of colour, with an artificial delight. The change had come in a way which they had not expected, and they did not know how to face it. It was the only situation which Mrs. Anderson, in her long musings, had not foreseen, and she did not know how to meet it. There was nothing but dismay in her mind—dismay and wonder. All her sagacity was at fault.

This went on for some time. Kate was very kind to her guests; but more and more every day they came to feel themselves guests in the house. She was scarcely ever with them, except at meals; and they would sit together all the long morning, and sometimes all the long afternoon, silent, saying nothing to each other, and hear Kate's voice far off, perhaps singing as she went through one of the long passages, perhaps talking to Maryanne, or to a dog whom she had brought in from the stable. They sat as if under a spell, for even Ombra was hushed. Her feelings had somehow changed. Instead of the horror with which she had regarded the probable arrival of her lover, she seemed now possessed with a feverish desire to receive him, to see him when he came, to watch him, perhaps to make sure that he was true to her.

'How can I go away, and know that he is here, and endure it?' she said to her mother. 'I must stay!—I must stay! It is wretched; but it would be more wretched to go.'

This was her mood one day; and the next she would be impatient to leave Langton-Courtenay at once, and found the yoke which was upon her intolerable. These were terrible days, as smiling and smooth as of old to all beholders, but with complete change within. Kate was as brave as a lion in carrying out the rôle she had marked out for herself. Even when her heart failed her, she hid it, and went on stoutly in the almost impossible way.

'I will not interfere with them—I will not ask anything; but otherwise there shall be no change,' she said to herself, with something of the arrogance of youth, ready to give all, and to believe that it could be accepted without the return of anything. But sometimes it was very hard for her to keep it up; sometimes the peculiar aspect of the scene would fill her with sudden compunctions, sudden longings. Everything looked so like the old, happy days, and yet it was all so different! Sometimes a tone of her aunt's voice, a movement or a look of Ombra, would bring some old tender recollection back to her mind, and she would feel driven to the last extremity to prevent herself from bursting into tears, or making a wild appeal to them to let things be as they were again. But she resisted all these impulses, saying to herself, with forlorn pride, that the old love had never existed, that it had been but a delirium of her own, and that consequently there was nothing to appeal to. She resumed her German, and worked at it with tremendous zeal in the library by herself. German is an admirable thing when one has been crossed in love, or mortified in friendship. How often has it been resorted to in such circumstances—and has always afforded a certain consolation! And Kate plunged into parish business, to the great delight and relief of Minnie Hardwick, and showed all her old love of the 'human interest' of the village, the poor folk's stories and their difficulties. She tired herself out, and went back and put off her grey frock, and arrayed herself, and sat down at the table with Ombra, languid and heavy-eyed, and Mrs. Anderson, who greeted her with faint smiles. There was little conversation at the table; and it grew less and less as the days went on. These dinners were not amusing; and yet they had some interest too, for each watched the other, wondering what she would next do or say.

I cannot tell exactly how long this lasted. It seemed to all three an eternity. But one afternoon, when Kate came in from a long walk to the other side of the parish, she found a letter conspicuously placed on the hall-table, where she could not fail to see it. She trembled a little when she saw her aunt's handwriting. And there were fresh carriage-wheels marking the way down the avenue; she had noticed this as she came up. She sat down on the settle in the hall, where Mrs. Anderson had placed herself on the day of their return, and read the following letter with surprise, and yet without surprise. It gave her a shock as of suddenness and strangeness; and yet she had known that it must happen all along.

'MY DEAREST KATE,

'If you can think, when you read this, that I do not mean what I say, you will be very, very wrong. All these years I have loved you as if you were my own child. I could not have done otherwise—it is not in nature. But this is not what I want to say. We are going away. It is not with my will, and yet it is not against my will; for even to leave you alone in the house is better than forcing you to live this unnatural life. Good-bye, my dear, dear child! I cannot tell you—more's the pity!—the circumstances that have made my poor Ombra bitter with everything, including her best friends; but she is very, very sorry, always, after she has said those dreadful words which she does not mean, but which seem to give a little relief to her suffering and bitterness. This is all I can tell you now. Some time or other you will know everything; and then, though you may blame us, you will pity us too. I want to tell you that it never was my wish to keep the secret from you—nor even Ombra's. At least, she would have yielded, but the other party to the secret would not. Dearest child, forgive me! I go away from you, however, with a very sore heart, and I don't know where we shall go, or what we shall do. Ever your most affectionate

'A. ANDERSON.

'P.S.—I have written to your uncle, that unavoidable circumstances, over which I have no control, compelled my leaving. I should prefer that you did not say anything to him about what these circumstances were.'

Kate sat still for some time after she had read her letter. She had expected it—it was inevitable; but, oh! with what loneliness the house began to fill behind her! She sat and gazed into the fire, dumb, bearing the blow as she best could. She had expected it, and yet she never believed it possible. She had felt sure that something would turn up to reconcile them—that one day or another, sooner or later, they would all fall upon each other's necks, and be at one again. She was seized suddenly by that fatal doubt of herself which always comes too late. Had she done right, after all? People must be very confident of doing right who have such important matters in hand. Had she sufficient reason? Was it not mean and paltry of her, in her own house, to have resented a few unconsidered words so bitterly? In her own house! And then she had been the means of turning these two, whom she loved, whether they loved her or not, out upon the world. Kate sat without stirring while the early darkness fell. It crept about her imperceptibly, dimness, and silence, and solitude. The whole great house was a vast desert of silence—not a sound, not a voice, nothing audible but the fall of the ashes on the hearth. The servants' rooms were far away, shut off by double doors, that no noises might disturb their mistress. Oh! what would not Kate have given for the cheerful sound of the kitchen, that used to be too audible at Shanklin, which her aunt always complained of. Her aunt! who had been like her mother! And where was she now? She began to gasp and sob hysterically, but could not cry. And there was nobody to take any notice. She heard her own voice, but nobody else heard it. They were gone! Servants, new servants, filled the house, noiseless creatures, decorous and well-bred, shut in with double doors, that nobody might hear any sound of them. And she alone!—a girl not twenty!—alone in a house which could put up fifty people!—in a house where there was no sound, no light, no warmth, no fire, no love!

She sat there till it was dark, and never moved. Why should she move? There was no fireside to go to, no one whose presence made home. She was as well on the settle in the hall as anywhere else. The darkness closed over her. What did she care? She sat stupefied, with the letter in her hand.

And there she was found when Mr. Spigot, the butler, came to light the lamp. He gave a jump when he saw something in the corner of the settle. And that something started too, and drew itself together, and said, 'Is it so late? I did not know!' and put her hands across her dazzled eyes.

'I beg you a thousand pardons, miss,' said Spigot, confused, for he had been whistling under his breath. 'I didn't know as no one wasn't there.'

'Never mind,' said Kate. 'Give me a candle, please. I suppose I must have dropped asleep.'

Had she dropped asleep really 'for sorrow?'—had she fainted and come to again, nobody being the wiser? Kate could not tell—but there had been a moment of unconsciousness one way or the other; and when she crept upstairs with her candle, a solitary twinkle like a glow-worm in the big staircase, she felt chilled to the bone, aching and miserable. She crept upstairs into the warmth of her room, and, looking in the glass, saw that her face was as the face of a ghost. Her hair had dropped down on one side, and the dampness of the evening had taken all the curl out of it. It fell straight and limp upon her colourless cheek. She went and kneeled down before the fire and warmed herself, which seemed the first necessity of all. 'How cold one gets when one is unhappy!' she said, half aloud; and the murmur of her own voice sounded strange in her ear. Was it the only voice that she was now to hear?

When Maryanne came with the candles, it was a comfort to Kate. She started up from the fire. She had to keep up appearances—to look as if nothing had happened. Maryanne, for her part, was running over with the news.

'Have you heard, miss, as Mrs. Anderson and Miss Ombra is gone?' she asked, as soon as decency would permit. The whole house had been moved by this extraordinary departure, and the entire servants' hall hung upon Maryanne for news.

'Yes,' said Kate, calmly. 'I thought I should be back in time, but I was too late. I hope my aunt had everything comfortable. Maryanne, as I am all alone, you can bring me up some tea here—I can't take the trouble to dine—alone.'

'Very well, miss,' said Maryanne; 'it will be a deal comfortabler. If Mrs. Spigot had known as the ladies was going, she would have changed the dinner—but it was so sudden-like.'

'Yes, it was very sudden,' said Kate. And thus Maryanne carried no news downstairs.

CHAPTER LIX

Kate's life seemed to stop at this point. For a few days she did not know what she did. She would have liked to give in, and be ill, but dared not, lest her aunt (who did not love her) should be compromised. Therefore she kept up, and walked and went to the parish and chattered with Minnie Hardwick, and even tried her German, though this latter attempt was not very successful.

'My aunt was called away suddenly on business,' she explained to Mrs. Hardwick.

'What! and left you alone—quite alone in that great house?' cried Mrs. Hardwick. 'It is not possible! How lonely for you! But I suppose she will only be gone for a few days?'

'I scarcely know. It is business that has taken her away, and nobody can answer for business,' said Kate, with an attempt at a laugh. 'But the servants are very good, and I shall do very well. I am not afraid of being alone.'

'Not afraid, I daresay, but dreadfully solitary. It ought not to be,' said Mrs. Hardwick, in a tone of reproof. And the thought passed through her mind that she had never quite approved of Mrs. Anderson, who seemed to know much more of Bertie than was at all desirable, and, no doubt, had attempted to secure him for that pale girl of hers. 'Though what any gentleman could see in her, or how anyone could so much as look at her while Kate Courtenay was by, I don't understand,' she said, after discussing the question in private.

'Oh, mamma! I think she is so sweet and pretty,' said Edith. 'But I am sure Bertie does not like her. Bertie avoided her—he was scarcely civil. I am sure if there is anyone that Bertie admires it is Kate.'

Mrs. Hardwick shook her head.

'Bertie knows very well,' she said, 'that Miss Courtenay is out of his reach—delightful as she is, and everything we could desire—except that she is rather too rich; but that is no reason why he should go and throw himself away on some girl without a penny. I don't put any faith in his avoiding Miss Anderson. When a young man avoids a young woman it is much the same as when he seeks her society. But, Minnie, run away and look after your club books; you are too young yet to hear such matters discussed.'

'Edith is only a year older than I am,' said Minnie, within herself, 'but then she is almost a married lady.' And with this she comforted her heart, which was not without its private flutters too.

And Kate kept on her way, very bravely holding up her little flag of resolution. She sat in the room which they had all occupied together, and had coals heaped upon the two fires, and could not get warm. The silence of the place made her sick and faint. She got up and walked about, in the hope of hearing at least her own step, and could not on the soft carpet. When she coughed, it seemed to ring all through the house. She got frightened when she caught a glimpse of herself in the great mirror, and thought it was a ghost. She sent to Westerton for all the novels that were to be had, and these were a help to her; but still, to sit in a quiet room, with yourself now and then seen passing through the glass like a thief, and nothing audible but the ashes falling from the grate, is a terrible experience for a girl. She heard herself breathing; she heard her cough echo down all the long galleries. She had her stable dog washed and brushed, and made fit for good society, in the hope that he would take to the drawing-room, and live with her, and give her some one to speak to. But, after all, he preferred the stables, being only a mongrel, without birth or breeding. This rather overcame Kate's bravery; but only once did she thoroughly break down. It was the day after her aunt left, and, with a sudden recollection of companionship and solace still remaining, she had said to Maryanne, 'Go and call old Francesca.' 'Francesca, miss!—oh! bless you, she's gone with her lady,' said Maryanne; and Kate, who had not expected this, broke down all at once, and had a fit of crying.

'Never mind—it is nothing. I thought they meant to leave Francesca,' she said, incoherently. Thus it became evident to her that they were gone, and gone for ever. And Kate went back to her melancholy solitude, and took up her novel; but when she had read the first page, she stopped, and began to think. She had done no wrong to anyone. If there was wrong, it had been done to her. She had tried even to resist all feelings of resentment, and to look as if she had forgotten the wrong done her. Yet it was she who was being punished, as if she were the criminal. Nobody anywhere, whatever harm they might have done, had been punished so sorely. Solitary confinement!—was not that the worst of all—the thing that drives people mad?

Then Mr. Courtenay wrote in a state of great fret and annoyance. What did Mrs. Anderson mean by leaving him in the lurch just then, she and her daughter? She had not even given him an address, that he might write to her and remonstrate (he had intended to supersede her in Spring, to be sure, but he did not think it necessary to mention that); and here he was in town, shut up with a threatening of bronchitis, and it was as much as his life was worth to travel now. Couldn't she get some one to stay with her, or get along somehow until Lady Caryisfort came home?

Kate wrote him a brave little letter, saying that of course she could get on—that he need not be at all troubled about her—that she was quite happy, and should prefer being left as she was. When she had written it, she lay down on the rug before the fire, and had a cry, and then came to herself, and sent to ask if Minnie Hardwick might spend the evening with her. Minnie's report brought her mother up next morning, who found that Kate had a bad cold, and sent for the doctor, and kept her in bed; and all the fuss of this little illness—though Kate believed she hated fuss—did her good. Her own room was pleasanter than the drawing-room. It was natural to be alone there; and as she lay on the sofa, and was read to by Minnie, there seemed at times a possibility that life might mend. And next day and the next, though she recovered, this companionship went on. Minnie was not very wise, but she chattered about everything in heaven and earth. She talked of her brother—a subject in which Kate could not help taking an interest, which was half anger, half something else. She asked a hundred questions about Florence—

'Did you really see a great deal of Bertie? How funny that he should not have told us! Men are so odd!' cried Minnie. 'If it had been I, I should have raved about you for ever and ever!'

'Because you are silly and—warm-hearted,' said Kate, with a sigh. 'Yes, I think we saw them pretty often.'

'Why do you say them?'

'Why?—because the two were always together! We never expected to see one without the other.'

'Like your cousin and you,' said innocent Minnie. And then she laughed.

'Why do you laugh?' said Kate.

'Oh! nothing—an idea that came into my head. I have heard of two sisters marrying two brothers, but never of two pair of cousins—it would be funny.'

'But altogether out of the question, as it happens,' said Kate, growing stately all at once.

'Oh! don't be angry. I did not mean anything. Was Bertie very attentive to Miss Anderson in Florence? We wonder sometimes. For I am sure he avoided her here; and mamma says she puts no faith in a gentleman avoiding a lady. It is as bad as—what do you think?—unless you would rather not say,' added Minnie, shyly; 'or if you think I oughtn't to ask—'

'I don't know anything about Mr. Bertie Hardwick's feelings,' said Kate. And then she added, with a little sadness which she could not quite conceal, 'Nor about anybody, Minnie. Don't ask me, please. I am not clever enough to find things out; and nobody ever confides in me.'

'I am sure I should confide in you first of all!' cried Minnie, with enthusiasm. 'Oh! when I recollect how much we used to be frightened for you, and what a funny girl we thought you; and then to think I should know you so well now, and have got so—fond of you—may I say so?' said the little girl, who was proud of her post.

Kate made no answer for a full minute, and then she said,

'Minnie, you are younger than I am, a great deal younger—'

'I am eighteen,' said Minnie, mortified.

'But I am nineteen and a half, and very, very old for my age. At your age one does not know which is the real thing and which is the shadow—there are so many shadows in this world; and sometimes you take them for truth, and when you find it out it is hard.'

Minnie followed this dark saying with a puzzled little face.

'Yes,' she said, perplexed, 'like Narcissus, you mean, and the dog that dropped the bone. No, I don't mean that—that is too—too—common-place. Oh! did you ever see Bertie Eldridge's yacht? I think I heard he had it at the Isle of Wight. It was called the Shadow. Oh! I would give anything to have a sail in a yacht!'

Ah! that was called the Shadow too. Kate felt for a moment as if she had found something out; but it was a delusion, an idea which she could not identify—a Will-o'-the-Wisp, which looked like something, and was nothing. 'I have a shadow too,' she murmured, half to herself. But before Minnie's wondering eyes and tongue could ask what it meant, Spigot came solemnly to the door. He had to peer into the darkness to see his young mistress on the sofa.

'If you please, Miss Courtenay,' he said, 'there is a gentleman downstairs wishes to see you; and he won't take no answer as I can offer. He says if you hear his name—'

'What is his name?' cried Kate. She did not know what she expected, but it made her heart beat. She sat up, on her sofa, throwing off her wraps, notwithstanding Minnie's remonstrances. Who could it be?—or rather, what?

'The Reverend Mr. Sugden, Miss,' said Mr. Spigot.

'Mr. Sugden!' She said the name two or three times over before she could remember. Then she rose, and directed Spigot to light the candles. She did not know how it was, but new vigour somehow seemed to come into her veins.

'Minnie,' she said, 'this is a gentleman who knows my aunt. He has come, I suppose, about her business. I want you to stay just now; but if I put up my hand so, will you run upstairs and wait for me in my room? Take the book. You will be a true little friend if you will do this.'

'Leave you alone!—with a gentleman!' said Minnie. 'But then of course he must be an old gentleman, as he has come about business,' she said to herself; and added hastily, 'Of course I will. And if you don't put up your hand—so—must I stay?'

'I am sure to put it up,' said Kate.

The room by this time was light and bright, and Spigot's solemn step was heard once more approaching. Kate placed herself in a large chair. She looked as imposing and dignified as she could, poor child!—the solitary mistress of her own house. But how strange it was to see the tall figure come in—the watchful, wistful face she remembered so well! He held out his large hand, in which her little one was drowned, just as he used to do. He glanced round him in the same way, as if Ombra might be somewhere about in the corners. His Shadow too! Kate could not doubt that. But when she gave Minnie her instructions, she had taken it for granted that there would have been certain preliminaries to the conversation—inquiries about herself, or information about what she was doing. But Mr. Sugden was full of excitement and anxiety. He took her small hand into his big one, which swallowed it up, as we have said, and he held it, as some men hold a button.

'I hear they have left you,' he said. 'Tell me, is it true?'

'Yes,' said Kate, too much startled to give her signal, 'they have left me.'

'And you don't know where they have gone?'

She remembered now, and Minnie disappeared, curious beyond all description. Then Kate withdrew her hand from that mighty grasp.

'I don't know where they have gone. Have you heard anything of them, Mr. Sugden? Have you brought me, perhaps, a message?'

He shook his head.

'I heard it all vaguely, only vaguely; but you know how I used to feel, Miss Kate. I feel the same still. Though it is not what I should have wished—I am ready to be a brother to her. Will you tell me all that has passed since you went away?'

'All that has passed?'

'If you will, Miss Kate—as you would be kind to one who does not care very much what happens to him! You are kind, I know—and you love her!'

The tears came to Kate's eyes. She grew warm and red all over, throwing off, as it were, in a moment, the palsy of cold and misery that had come over her.

'Yes,' she said suddenly, 'I love her,' and cried. Mr. Sugden looked on, not knowing why.

Kate felt herself changed as in a moment; she felt—nay, she was herself again. What did it matter whether they loved her?—she loved them. That was, after all, what she had most to do with. She dried her tears, and she told her story, straight off, like a tale she had been taught, missing nothing. And he drank it all in to the end, not missing a word. When she had finished he sat silent, with a sombre countenance, and not a syllable was spoken between them for ten minutes at least. Then he said aloud, as if not talking, but thinking,

'The question is which?' Then he raised his eyes and looked at her. 'Which?' he repeated.

Kate grew pale again, and felt a choking in her throat. She bowed her head, as if she were accepting her fate.

'Mr. Bertie Hardwick!' she said.

CHAPTER LX

This strange little incident, which at the moment it was occurring seemed to be perfectly natural, but as soon as that moment was over became inexplicable, dropped into Kate's life as a stone drops into water. It made a curious commotion and a bustle for the moment, and stirred faintly for a little while afterwards, and then disappeared, and was thought of no more.

Mr. Sugden would not stay, he would not even eat in the house. He had come down from town to the station six miles off, the nearest station for Langton-Courtenay, and there he meant to return again as soon as he had his information. Kate had been much troubled as to how she, in her unprotected condition, was to ask him to stay; but when she found out he would not stay, an uncomfortable sensation as of want of hospitality came over her. But when he was actually gone, and Minnie Hardwick called back, somehow the entire incident appeared like a dream, and it seemed impossible that anything important had happened. Minnie was not curious; business was to her a sacred word, which covered all difficulties. The Curate was not old, as she had supposed; but otherwise being a friend of Mrs. Anderson's, and involved in her affairs, his sudden visit seemed perfectly natural. Just so men would come down from town, and be shut up with her father for an hour or two, and then disappear; and Kate as a great lady, as an heiress and independent person, no doubt must have the same kind of visitors.

Kate, however, thought a great deal of it that night—could not sleep, indeed, for thinking of it; but less the next morning, and still less the day after, till at length the tranquillity settled back into its old stillness. Mr. Sugden had done her good, so far that he had roused her to consciousness of a hearty sentiment in herself, independent of anything from without—the natural affection which was her own independent possession, and not a reflection of other people's love. What though they did not love her even? she loved them; and as soon as she became conscious of this, she was saved from the mental harm that might have happened to her. It gave Kate pain when day after day passed on, and no word came from those who had departed from her so suddenly. But then she was young, and had been brought up in the persuasion that everything was likely to turn out right at the end, and that permanent unhappiness was a very rare thing. She was not alarmed about the safety of those who had deserted her; they were two, nay, three people together; they were used to taking care of themselves; so far as she knew, they had money enough and all that was required. And then her own life was so strange; it occupied her almost like a fairy-life. She thought she had never heard of any one so forlorn and solitary. The singularity of her position did her good. She was half proud, half amused by it; she smiled when her visitors would remark upon her singular loneliness—'Yes, it seems strange to you, I suppose,' she said; but I don't mind it.' It was a small compensation, but still it was a kind of compensation, indemnifying her for some at least of her trouble. The Andersons had disappeared into the great darkness of the world; but some day they would turn up again and come back to her and make explanations. And although she had been impressed by Mr. Sugden's visit, she was not actually anxious about the future of her aunt and cousin; some time or other things naturally would put themselves right.

This, however, did not prevent the feeling of her loneliness from being terrible to her—insupportable; but it removed all complications from her feelings, and made them simple. And thus she lived on for months together, as if in a dream, always assuring Mr. Courtenay that she did very well, that she wanted nothing, getting a little society in the Rectory with the Hardwicks, and with some of her county neighbours who had called upon her. Minnie got used to the carriage, and to making expeditions into Westerton, the nearest town, and liked it. And strangely and stilly as ever Châtelaine lived in an old castle, in such a strange maiden seclusion lived Kate.

Where had the others gone? She ascertained before long that they were not at Shanklin—the Cottage was still let to 'very nice people,' about whom Lucy Eldridge wrote very enthusiastic letters to her cousin—letters which Kate would sometimes draw her innocent moral from, not without a little faint pain, which surprised her in the midst of all graver troubles. She pointed out to Minnie how Lucy Eldridge had rejected the very idea of being friendly with the new comers, much less admitting them to a share in the place Kate held in her heart. 'Whereas now you see I am forgotten altogether,' Kate said, with a conscious melancholy that was not disagreeable to her. Minnie protested that with her such a thing could never happen—it was impossible; and Kate smiled sadly, and shook her head in her superior knowledge. She took Minnie into her intimacy with a sense of condescension. But the friendship did her good. And Mrs. Hardwick was very kind to her. They were all anxious to 'be of use' to the heiress, to help her through her melancholy hours.

When Bertie came down for his next flying visit, she manœuvred so that she succeeded in avoiding him, though he showed no desire this time to avoid her. But, Kate said to herself, this was something that she could not bear. She could not see him as if he were an indifferent stranger, when she knew well that he could reveal to her everything she wanted to know, and set the tangle right at last. He knew where they were without doubt—he knew everything. She could not meet him calmly, and shake hands with him, and pretend she did not remember the past. She was offended with him, both for their sake and her own—for Ombra's sake, because of the secret; and for her own, because of certain little words and looks which were an insult to her from Ombra's lover. No, she could not see him. She had a bad headache when he came with his mother to call; she was not able to go out when she was asked to the Rectory. She saw him only at church, and did nothing but bow when he hurried to speak to her in the churchyard. No, that she would not put up with. There was even a certain contempt mingled with her soreness. Mrs. Anderson had put all the blame upon him—the 'other party to the secret;' while he, poor creature, would not even take the responsibility upon his own shoulders bravely, but blamed Ombra. Well! well! Kate resolved that she would keep her solitude unbroken, that she would allow no intrusion upon her of all the old agitations that once had made her unhappy. She would not consent to allow herself to be made unhappy any longer, or even to think of those who had given her so much pain.

Unfortunately, however, after she had made this good resolution, she thought of nothing else, and puzzled herself over the whole business, and especially Bertie's share in it, night and day. He would suddenly start up into her mind when she was thinking of something else, with a glow over his face, and anxious gleam in his eyes, as she had seen him at the church door. Perhaps, then, though so late, he had meant to explain. Perhaps he intended to lay before her what excuses there might be—to tell her how one thing followed another, how they had been led into clandestine ways.

Kate would make out an entire narrative to herself and then would stop short suddenly, and ask herself what she meant by it? It was not for her to explain for them, but for them to explain to her. But she did not want to think badly of them. Even when her wounds had been deepest, she did not wish to think unkindly; and it would have given her a kind of forlorn pleasure to be able to find out their excuses beforehand. This occupied her many an hour when she sat alone in the stillness, to which she gradually became accustomed. After awhile her own reflection in the glass no longer struck her as looking like a ghost or a thief; she grew used to it. And then the way in which she threw herself into the parish did one good to see. Minnie Hardwick felt that Kate's activity and Kate's beneficence took away her breath. She filled the cottages with what Mrs. Hardwick felt to be luxuries, and disapproved of. She rushed into Westerton continually, to buy things for the old women. One had an easy-chair, another a carpet, another curtains to keep out the wind from the draughty cottage room.

'My dear, you will spoil the people; these luxuries are quite out of their reach. We ought not to demoralize them,' said the clergywoman, thinking of the awful consequences, and of the expectations and discontents that would follow.

'If old Widow Morgan belonged to me—if she was my grandmother, for instance,' said revolutionary Kate, 'would there be anything in the world too good for her? We should hunt the draughts out of every corner, and pad everything with velvet. And I suppose an old woman of eighty in a cottage feels it just as much.'

Mrs. Hardwick was silenced, but not convinced; she was, indeed, shocked beyond measure at the idea of Widow Morgan requiring as many comforts as Kate's grandmother. 'The girl has no discrimination whatever; she does not see the difference; it is of no use trying to explain to her,' she said, with a troubled countenance. But, except these little encounters, there was no real disagreement between them. Bertie Hardwick's family, indeed, took an anxious interest in Kate. They were not worldly-minded people, but they could not forget that their son had been thrown a great deal into the society of a great heiress, both in the Isle of Wight and in Italy. The knowledge that he was in Kate's vicinity had indeed made them much more tolerant, though nobody said so, of his wanderings. They had not the heart, they said, to separate him from his cousin, to whom he was so much attached; but behind this there was perhaps lurking another reason. Not that they would ever have forced their son's affections, or advised, under any circumstances, a mercenary marriage; but only, all other things being so suitable—Mrs. Hardwick, who liked to manage everybody, and did it very well, on the whole, took Kate into her hands with a glow of satisfaction. She would have liked to form her and mould her, and make her all that a woman in her important position ought to be; and, of course, no one could tell what might happen in the future. It was well to be prepared for all.

Mr. Courtenay, for his part, though not quite so happy about his niece, and troubled by disagreeable pricks of conscience in respect to her, made all right by promises. He would come in a week or two—as soon as his cold was better—when he had got rid of the threatening of the gout, which rather frightened his doctor. Finally, he promised without doubt that he would come in the Easter recess, and make everything comfortable. But in the Easter recess it became absolutely necessary for him, for important private affairs, to go down to the Duke of Dorchester's marine palace, where there were some people going whom it was absolutely essential that he should meet. And thus it came to pass that Kate spent her twentieth birthday all alone at Langton-Courtenay. Nobody knew or remembered that it was her birthday. There was not so much as an old servant about the place to think of it. Maryanne, to be sure, might have remembered, but did not until next morning, when she broke forth with, 'La, Miss Kate!' into good wishes and regrets, which Kate, with a flushed face and sore heart, put a stop to at once. No, no one knew. It is a hard thing, even when one is old, to feel that such domestic anniversaries have fallen into oblivion, and no one cares any longer for the milestones of our life; but when one is young—!

Kate went about all day long with this secret bursting in her heart. She would not tell it for pride, though; if she had, all the Hardwick family, at least, would have been ready enough with kisses and congratulations. She carried it about with her like a pain that she was hiding. 'It is my birthday,' she said to herself, when she paused before the big glass, and looked at her own solitary figure, and tried to make a little forlorn fun of herself; 'good morning, Kate, I will give you a present. It will be the only one you will get to-day,' she said, laughing, and nodding at her representative in the glass, whose eyes were rather red; 'but I will not wish you many returns, for I am sure you don't want them. Oh! you poor, poor girl!' she cried, after a moment—'I am so sorry for you! I don't think there is anyone so solitary in all the world.' And then Kate and her image both sat down upon the floor and cried.

But in the afternoon she went to Westerton, with Minnie Hardwick all unconscious beside her in the carriage, and bought herself the present she had promised. It was a tiny little cross, with the date upon it, which Minnie marvelled at much, wondering if it was to herself that this memento was to be presented. Kate had a strong inclination to place the words 'Infelicissimo giorno' over the date, but stopped, feeling that it might look romantic; but it was the unhappiest day to her—the worst, she thought, she had ever yet had to bear.

When she came home, however, a letter was put into her hands. It was from Mrs. Anderson at last.

CHAPTER LXI

Kate's existence, however, was too monotonous to be dwelt upon for ever, and though all that can be afforded to the reader is a glimpse of other scenes, yet there are one or two such glimpses which may help him to understand how other people were affected by this complication of affairs. Bertie Hardwick went up to London after that second brief visit at the Rectory, when Miss Courtenay had so successfully eluded seeing him, with anything but comfortable feelings. He had never quite known how she looked upon himself, but now it became apparent to him that whatever might be the amount of knowledge which she had acquired, it had been anything but favourable to him. How far he had a right to Kate's esteem, or whether, indeed, it was a right thing for him to be anxious about it, is quite a different question. He was anxious about it. He wanted to stand well in the girl's eyes. He had known her all his life, he said to himself. Of course they could only be acquaintances, not even friends, in all probability, so different must their lines of life be; but still it was hard to feel that Kate disliked him, that she thought badly of him. He had no right to care, but he did care. He stopped in his work many and many a day to think of it. And then he would lay down his book or his pen, and gnaw his nails (a bad habit, which his mother vainly hoped she had cured him of), and think—till all the law went out of his head which he was studying.

This was very wrong, and he did not do it any more than he could help; but sometimes the tide of rising thought was too much for him. Bertie was settling to work, as he had great occasion to do. He had lost much time, and there was not a moment to be lost in making up for it. Within the last three months, indeed, his careless life had sustained a change which filled all his friends with satisfaction. It was but a short time to judge by, but yet, if ever man had seen the evil of his ways, and set himself, with true energy, to mend them, it was Bertie, everybody allowed. He had left his fashionable and expensive cousin the moment they had arrived in London. Instead of Bertie Eldridge's fashionable quarters, in one of the streets off Piccadilly, which hitherto he had shared, he had established himself in chambers in the Temple, up two pair of stairs, where he was working, it was reported, night and day. Bertie Eldridge, indeed, had so frightened all his people by his laughing accounts of the wet towels which bound the other Bertie's head of nights, while he laboured at his law books, that the student received three several letters on the subject—one from each of his aunts, and one from his mother.

'My dear, it goes to my heart to hear how you are working,' the latter said. 'I thank God that my own boy is beginning to see what is necessary to hold his place in life. But not too much, dearest Bertie, not too much. What would it avail me if my son came to be Lord Chancellor, and lost his health, or even his life, on the way?'

This confusing sentence did not make Bertie ridicule the writer, for he was, strange to say, very fond of his mother, but he wrote her a merry explanation, and set her fears at rest. However, though he did not indulge in wet towels, he had begun to work with an energy no one expected of him. He had a motive. He had seen the necessity, as his mother said. To wander all over the world with Bertie Eldridge, whose purse was carelessly free, but whose way it was, unconsciously, while intending to save his friends from expense, to draw them into greater and ever greater outlay, was not a thing which could be done, or which it would be at all satisfactory to do for life. And many very grave thoughts had come to Bertie on the journey home. Perhaps he had grown just a little disgusted with his cousin, who saw everything from his own point of view, and could not enter into the feelings and anxieties of a poorer man.

'Oh! bother! All will come right in the end,' he would say, when his cousin pointed out to him the impossibility for himself of the situation, so far as he himself was concerned.

'How can it come right for me?' Hardwick had asked.

'How you do worry!' said Bertie Eldridge. 'Haven't we always shared everything? And why shouldn't we go on doing so? I may be kept out of it, of course, for years and years, but not for ever. Hang it, Bertie, you know all must come right in the end; and haven't we shared everything all our lives?'

This is a sort of speech which it is very difficult to answer. It is so much easier for the richer man to feel benevolent and liberal than for the poorer man to understand his ground of gratitude in such a partnership. Bertie Eldridge, had, no doubt, shared many of his luxuries with his cousin. He had shared his yacht for instance—a delight which Bertie Hardwick could by no means have procured himself—but, while doing this, he had drawn the other into such waste of time and money as he never could have been tempted to otherwise. Bertie Hardwick knew that had he not 'shared everything' with his cousin he would have been a wealthier man: and how then could he be grateful for that community of goods which the other Bertie was so lavishly conscious of?

'He can have spent nothing while we were together,' the latter was always saying. 'He must have saved, in short, out of the allowance my uncle gives him.'

Bertie Hardwick knew that the case was very different, but he could not be so ungenerous as to insist upon this in face of his cousin's delightful sense of liberality. He held his tongue, and this silence did not make him more amiable. In short, the partnership had been broken, as partnerships of the kind are generally broken, with a little discomfort on both sides.

Bertie Eldridge continued his pleasant, idle life—did what he liked, and went where he liked, though, perhaps, with less freedom than of old; while Bertie Hardwick retired to Pump Court and worked—as the other said—night and day. He was hard at work one of those Spring afternoons which Kate spent down at Langton. His impulse towards labour was new, and, as yet, it had many things to struggle against. He had not been brought up to work; he had been an out-of-door lad, fond of any pursuit that implied open air and exercise. Most young men are so brought up now-a-days, whether it is the best training for them or not; and since he took his degree, which had not been accompanied by any distinction, he had been yachting, travelling, amusing himself—none of which things are favourable to work in Pump Court, upon a bright April afternoon. His window was open, and the very air coming in tantalized and tempted him. It plucked at his hair; it disordered his papers; it even blew the book close which he was bending over. 'Confound the wind!' said Bertie. But, somehow, he could not shut the window. How fresh it blew! even off the questionable Thames, reminding the solitary student of walks and rides through the budding woods; of the first days of the boating season; of all the delights of the opening year; confound the wind! He opened his book, and went at it again with a valorous and manful heart, a heart full of anxieties, yet with hope in it too, and, what is almost better than hope—determination. The book was very dry, but Bertie applied to it that rule which is so good in war—so good in play—capital for cricket and football, in the hunting-field, and wherever daring and patience are alike necessary—he would not be beat! It is, perhaps, rather a novel doctrine to apply to a book about conveyancing—or, at least, such a use of it was novel to Bertie. But it answered all the same.

And it was just as he was getting the mastery of his own mind, and forgetting, for the moment, the fascinations of the sunshine and the errant breeze, that some one came upstairs with a resounding hasty footstep and knocked at his door. 'It's Bertie,' he said to himself, with a sigh, and opened to the new-comer. Now he was beat, but not by the book—by fate, and the evil angels—not by any fault of his own.

Bertie Eldridge came in, bringing a gust of fresh air with him. He seated himself on his cousin's table, scorning the chairs. His brow was a little clouded, though he was like one of the butterflies who toil not, neither do they spin.

'By Jove! to see you there grinding night and day, makes a man open his eyes—you that were no better than other people. What do you think you'll ever make of it, old fellow? Not the Woolsack, mind you—I give in to you a great deal, but you're not clever enough for that.'

'I never thought I was,' said the other, laughing, but not with pleasure; and then there was a pause, and I leave it to the reader to judge which were the different interlocutors in the dialogue which follows, for to continue writing 'Bertie,' and 'the other Bertie,' is more than human patience can bear.

'You said you had something to say to me—out with it! I have a hundred things to do. You never were so busy in your life as I am. Indeed, I don't suppose you know what being occupied means.'

'Of course it is the old subject I want to talk of. What could it be else! What is to be done? You know everything that has happened as well as I do. Busy! If you knew what my reflections are early and late, waking and sleeping—'

'I think I can form an idea. Has something new occurred—or is it the old question, the eternal old business, which you never thought of, unfortunately, till it was too late?'

'It is no business of yours to taunt me, nor is it a friend's office. I am driven to my wit's ends. For anything I can see, things may go on as they are for a dozen years.'

'Everybody must have felt so from the beginning. How you could be so mad, both she and you; you most, in one way, for you knew the world better; she most, in another, for it is of more importance to a woman.'

'Shut up, Bertie. I won't have any re-discussion of that question. The thing is, what is to be done now? I was such a fool as to write to her about going down to Langton, at my father's desire; and now I dare not go, or she will go frantic. Besides, she says it must be acknowledged before long: she must do it, if I can't.'

'Good God!'

'What is there to be horrified about? It was all natural. The thing is, what is to be done? If she would keep quiet, all would be right. I am sure her mother could manage everything. One place is as good as another to live in. Don't look at me like that. I am distracted—going mad—and you won't give me any help.'

'The question is, what help can I give?'

'It is easy enough—as easy as daylight. If I were to go, it would only make us both miserable, and lead to imprudences. I know it would. But if you will do it for me—'

'Do you love her, Bertie?'

'Love her! Good heavens! after all the sacrifices I have made! Look at me, as I am, and ask me if I love her! But what can I do? If I speak now we are all ruined; but if she could only be persuaded to wait—only to wait, perhaps for a few days, or a few months—'

'Or a few years! And to wait for what? How can you expect any good to come to you, when you build everything upon your—'

'Shut up, I tell you! Is it my fault? He ought to treat me differently. I never would have entertained such a thought, but for—Bertie, listen to me. Will you go? They will hear reason from you.'

'They ought not to hear reason. It is a cowardly shame! Yes, I don't mind your angry looks—it is a shame! You and I have been too long together to mince matters between ourselves. I tell you I never knew anything more cowardly and wretched. It is a shame—a—'

'The question is, not what you think of it,' said the other sullenly, 'but will you go?'

'I suppose I must,' was the reply.

When the visitor left, half an hour later, after more conversation of this same strain, can it be wondered at if Bertie Hardwick's studies were no longer so steady as they had been? He shut up his books at last, and went out and walked towards the river. It was black and glistening, and very full with the Spring rains. The tide was coming up—the river was crowded with vessels of all kinds. Bertie walked to Chelsea, and got a boat there, and went up to Richmond with the tide. But he did not go to the 'Star and Garter,' where his cousin was dining with a brilliant party. He walked back again to his chambers, turning over in his tired brain a hundred anxieties. And that night he did sit up at work, and for half an hour had recourse to the wet towel. Not because he was working day and night, but because these anxieties had eaten the very heart out of his working day.

CHAPTER LXII

From Pump Court, in the Temple, it is a long way to the banks of a little loch in Scotland, surrounded by hills, covered with heather, and populous with grouse—that is, of course, in the season. The grouse in this early Summer were but babies, chirping among the big roots of the ling, like barndoor chickens; the heather was not purple but only greening over through the grey husks of last year's bloom. The gorse blossoms were forming; the birch-trees shaking out their folded leaves a little more and more day by day against the sky, which was sometimes so blue, and sometimes so leaden. At that time of the year, or at any other, it is lovely at Loch Arroch. Seated on the high bank behind the little inn, on the soft grass, which is as green as emeralds, but soft as velvet, you can count ten different slopes of hills surrounding the gleaming water, which receives them all impartially; ten distinct ridges, all as various as so many sportsmen, distinct in stature and character—from the kindly birch-crowned heads in front here, away to the solemn distant altitudes, folded in snow-plaids or cloud-mantles, and sometimes in glorious sheen of sunset robes, that dazzle you—which fill up the circle far away. The distant giants are cleft into three peaks, and stand still to have their crowns and garments changed, with a benign patience, greeting you across the loch. There are no tourists, and few strangers, except the fishermen, who spend their days not thinking of you or of the beauties of nature, tossed in heavy cobbles upon the stormy loch, or wading up to their waist in ice-cold pools of the river. The river dashes along its wild channel through the glen, working through rocks, and leaping precipitous corners, shrouding itself, like a coy girl, with the birchen tresses which stream over it, till it comes to another loch—a big silvery clasp upon its foaming chain. Among these woods and waters man is still enough; but Nature is full of commotion. She sings about all the hillsides in a hundred burns, with delicatest treble; she makes her own bass under the riven rocks, among the foam of the greater streams; she mutters over your head with deep, sonorous melancholy utterance in the great pine-trees, and twitters in the leaflets of the birch. Lovely birks!—sweetest of all the trees of the mountains! Never were such haunts for fairies, or for mountain girls as agile and as fair as those sweet birchen woods. 'Stern and wild,' do you say? And surely we say it, for so Sir Walter said before us. But what an exquisite idea was that of Nature—what a sweet, fantastic conceit, just like her wayward wealth of resource, to clothe the slopes of those rude hills with the Lady of the Woods! She must have laughed with pleasure, like a child, but with tears of exquisite poet satisfaction in her eyes, when she first saw the wonderful result. And as for you poor people who have never seen Highland loch or river shine through the airy foliage, the white-stemmed grace and lightness of a birch-wood, we are sorry for you, but we will not insult your ignorance; for, soft in your ear, the celebrated Mr. Cook, and all his satellites who make up tours in the holiday season, have never, Heaven be praised! heard of Loch Arroch; and long may it be before the British tourist finds out that tranquil spot.

I cannot tell how Mrs. Anderson and her daughter found it out. The last Consul, it is true, had been from Perthshire, but that of itself gave them little information. They had gone to Edinburgh first, and then, feeling that scarcely sufficiently out of the way, had gone further north, until at last Kinloch-Arroch received them; and they stayed there, they could not tell why, partly because the people looked so kind.

The note which Kate received on her birthday had no date, and the post-mark on it was of a distant place, that no distinct clue might be given to their retreat; but Ombra always believed, though without the slightest ground for it, that this note of her mother's, like all her other injudicious kindnesses to Kate, had done harm, and been the means of betraying them. For it was true that they were now in a kind of hiding, these two women, fearing to be recognised, not wishing to see any one, for reasons which need not be dwelt upon here. They had left Langton-Courtenay with a miserable sense of friendlessness and loneliness, and yet it had been in some respects a relief to them to get away; and the stillness of Loch Arroch, its absolute seclusion, and the kind faces of the people they found there, all concurred in making them decide upon this as their resting-place. They were to stay all the summer, and already they were known to everybody round. Old Francesca had already achieved a great succès in the Perthshire village. The people declared that they understood her much better than if she had been 'ane o' thae mincing English.' She was supposed to be French, and Scotland still remembers that France was once her auld and kind alley. The women in their white mutches wondered a little, it is true, at the little old Italian's capless head, and knot of scanty hair; but her kind little brown face, and her clever rapid ways, took them by storm. When she spoke Italian to her mistress they gathered round her in admiration. 'Losh! did you ever hear the like o' that?' they cried, with hearty laughs, half restrained by politeness—though half of them spoke Gaelic, and saw nothing wonderful in that achievement.

Ombra, the discontented and unhappy, had never in her life before been so gentle and so sweet. She was not happy still, but for the moment she was penitent, and subdued and at peace, and the admiration and the interest of their humble neighbours pleased her. Mrs. Anderson had given a description of her daughter to the kind landlady of the little inn, which did not tally with the circumstances which the reader knows; but probably she had her own reasons for that, and the tale was such as filled everybody with sympathy. 'You maunna be doon-hearted, my bonnie lamb,' the old woman would say to her; and Ombra would blush with painful emotion, and yet would be in her heart touched and consoled by the homely sympathy. Ah! if those kind people had but known how much harder her burden really was! But yet to know how kindly all these poor stranger folk felt towards them was pleasant to the two women, and they clung together closer than ever in the enforced quiet. They were very anxious, restless, and miserable, and yet for a little while they were as nearly happy as two women could be. This is a paradox which some women will understand, but which I cannot pause to explain.

Things were going on in this quiet way, and it was the end of May, a season when as yet few even of the fishers who frequent that spot by nature, and none of the wise wanderers who have discovered Loch Arroch had begun to arrive, when one evening a very tall man, strong and heavy, trudged round the corner into the village, with his knapsack over his shoulders. He was walking through the Highlands alone at this early period of the year. He put his knapsack down on the bench outside the door, and came into the little hall, decorated with glazed cases, in which stuffed trout of gigantic proportions still seemed to swim among the green, green river weeds, to ask kind Mrs. Macdonald, the landlady, if she could put him up. He was 'a soft-spoken gentleman,' courteous, such as Highlanders love, and there was a look of sadness about him which moved the mistress of the 'Macdonald Arms.' But all at once, while he was talking to her, he started wildly, made a dart at the stair, which Francesca at that moment was leisurely ascending, and upset, as he passed, little Duncan, Mrs. Macdonald's favourite grandchild.

'The man's gane gyte!' said the landlady.

Francesca for her part took no notice of the stranger. If she saw him, she either did not recognise him, or thought it expedient to ignore him. She went on, carrying high in front of her a tray full of newly-ironed fine linen, her own work, which she was carrying from the kitchen. The stranger stood at the foot of the stairs and watched her, with his face lifted to the light, which streamed from a long window opposite. There was an expression in his countenance (Mrs. Macdonald said afterwards) which was like a picture. He had found what he sought!

'That is old Francesca,' he said, coming back to her, 'Mrs. Anderson's maid. Then, of course, Mrs. Anderson is here.'

'Ou ay, sir, the leddies are here,' said Mrs. Macdonald—'maybe they are expecting you? There was something said a while ago about a gentleman—a brother, or some near friend to the young goodman.'

'The young goodman?'

'Ou ay, sir—him that's in India, puir gentleman!—at sic a time, too, when he would far rather be at hame. But ye'll gang up the stair? Kath'rin, take the gentleman up the stair—he's come to visit the leddies—and put him into No. 10 next door. Being so near the leddies, I never put no man there that I dinna ken something aboot. You'll find Loch Arroch air, sir, has done the young mistress good.'

The stranger followed upstairs, with a startled sense of other wonders to come; and thus it happened that, without warning, Mr. Sugden suddenly walked into the room where Ombra lay on a sofa by the fireside, with her mother sitting by. Both the ladies started up in dismay. They were so bewildered that neither could speak for a moment. The blood rushed to Ombra's face in an overpowering blush. He thought he had never seen her look so beautiful, so strange—he did not know how; and her look of bewildered inquiry and suspicion suddenly showed him what he had never thought of till that moment—that he had no right to pry into their privacy—to hunt her, as it were, into a corner—to pursue her here.

'Mr. Sugden!' Mrs. Anderson cried in dismay; and then she recovered her prudence, and held out her hand to him, coming between him and Ombra. 'What a very curious meeting this is!—what an unexpected pleasure! Of all places in the world, to meet a Shanklin friend at Loch Arroch! Ombra, do not disturb yourself, dear; we need not stand on ceremony with such an old friend as Mr. Sugden. My poor child has a dreadful cold.'

And then he took her hand into his own—Ombra's hand—which he used to sit and watch as she worked—the whitest, softest hand. It felt so small now, like a shadow, and the flush, had gone from her face. He seemed to see nothing but those eyes, watching him with fear and suspicion—eyes which distrusted him, and reminded him that he had no business here.

And he sat down by the sofa, and talked ordinary talk, and told them of Shanklin, which he had left. He had been making a pedestrian tour in Scotland. Yes, it was early, but he did not mind the weather, and the time suited him. It was a surprise to him to see Francesca, but he had heard that Mrs. Anderson had left Langton-Courtenay—

'Yes,' she said, briefly, without explanation; and added—'We were travelling, like you, when Ombra fell in love with this place. You must have seen it to perfection if you walked down the glen to-day—the Glencoe Hills were glorious to-day. Which is your next stage? I am afraid Mrs. Macdonald has scarcely room—'

'Oh! yes, she has given me a room for to-night,' he said; and he saw the mother and daughter look at each other, and said to himself, in an agony of humiliation, what a fool he had been—what an intrusive, impertinent fool!

When he took his leave, Mrs. Anderson went after him to the door; she asked, with trepidation in her voice, how long he meant to stay. This was too much for the poor fellow; he led the way along the passage to the staircase window, lest Ombra should hear through the half-open door.

'Mrs. Anderson,' he said hoarsely, 'once you promised me if she should ever want a brother's help or a brother's care—not that it is what I could have wished—'

'Mr. Sugden, this is ridiculous; I can take care of my own child. You have no right to come and hunt us out, when you know—when you can see that we wish—to be private.' Then, with a sudden change, she added—'Oh, you are very good—I am sure you are very good, but she wants for nothing. Dear Mr. Sugden, if you care for her or me, go away.

'I will go away to-morrow,' he said, with a deep sigh of disappointment and resignation.

She looked out anxiously at the sky. It was clouding over; night was coming on—there was no possibility of sending him away that night.

'Mr. Sugden,' she said, wringing her hands, 'when a gentleman thrusts himself into anyone's secrets he is bound not to betray them. You will hear news here, which I did not wish to be known at present—Ombra is married.'

'Married!' he said, with a groan, which he could not restrain.

'Yes, her husband is not able to be with her. We are waiting till he can join us—till he can make it public. You have found this out against our will; you must give me your word not to betray us '

'Why should I betray you?' he said; 'to whom? I came, not knowing. Since ever I knew her I have been her slave, you know. I will be so now. Is she—happy, at least?'

'She is very happy,' said Mrs. Anderson; and then her courage failed her, and she cried. She did not burst into tears—such an expression does not apply to women of her age. The tears which were, somehow, near the surface, fell suddenly, leaving no traces. 'Everything is not so—comfortable as might be wished,' she said, 'but, so far as that goes, she is happy.'

'May I come again?' he said. His face had grown very long and pale; he looked like a man who had just come back from a funeral. 'Or would you rather I went away at once?'

She gave another look at the sky, which had cleared; night was more distant than it had seemed ten minutes ago. And Mrs. Anderson did not think that it was selfishness on her part to think of her daughter first. She gave him her hand and pressed his, and said—

'You are the kindest, the best friend. Oh, for her sake, go!'

And he went away with a heavy heart, striding over the dark unknown hills. It was long past midnight before he got shelter—but what did that matter? He would have done much more joyfully for her sake. But his last hope seemed gone as he went along that mountain way. He had hoped always to serve her sometime or other, and now he could serve her no more!

CHAPTER LXIII

This was the reason why Kate heard no more from Mr. Sugden. He knew, and yet he did not know. That which had been told him was very different from what he had expected to hear. He had gone to seek a deserted maiden, and he had found a wife. He had gone with some wild hope of being able to interpose on her behalf, 'as her brother would have done,' and bring her false lover back to her—when, lo! he found that he was intruding upon sacred domestic ground, upon the retreat of a wife whose husband was somewhere ready, no doubt, to defend her from all intrusion. This confounded him for the first moment. He went away, as we have said, without a word, asking no explanation. What right had he to any explanation? Probably Ombra herself, had she known what his mission and what his thoughts were, would have been furious at the impertinence. But her mother judged him more gently, and he, poor fellow, knew in his own soul how different his motives were from those of intrusion or impertinence.

When he came to the homely, lonely little house, where he found shelter in the midst of the night, he stopped there in utter languor, still confused by his discovery and his failure. But when he came to himself he was not satisfied. Next day, in the silence and loneliness of the mountains, he mused and pondered on this subject, which was never absent from his mind ten minutes together. He walked on and on upon the road he had traversed in the dark the night before, till he came to the point where it commanded the glen below, and where the descent to Loch Arroch began. He saw at his feet the silvery water gleaming, the loch, the far lines of the withdrawing village roofs, and that one under which she was. At the sight the Curate's mournful heart yearned over the woman he loved. Why was she there alone, with only her mother, and she a wife? What was there that was not 'exactly comfortable,' as Mrs. Anderson had said?

The result of his musing was that he stayed in the little mountain change-house for some time. There was a desolate little loch near, lying, as in a nook, up at the foot of great Schehallion. And there he pretended to fish, and in the intervals of his sport, which was dreary enough, took long walks about the country, and, without being seen by them, found out a great deal about the two ladies. They were alone. The young lady's husband was said to be 'in foreign pairts.' The good people had not heard what he was, but that business detained him somewhere, though it was hoped he would be back before the Autumn. 'And I wish he may, for yon bonnie young creature's sake!' the friendly wife added, who told him this tale.

The name they told him she was called by was not a name he knew, which perplexed him. But when he remembered his own observations, and Kate's story, he could not believe that any other lover could have come in. When Mr. Sugden had fully satisfied himself, and discovered all that was discoverable, he went back to England with the heat of a sudden purpose. He went to London, and he sought out Bertie Hardwick's rooms. Bertie himself was whistling audibly as Mr. Sugden knocked at his door. He was packing his portmanteau, and stopped now and then to utter a mild oath over the things which would not pack in as they ought. He was going on a journey. Perhaps to her, Mr. Sugden thought; and, as he heard his whistle, and saw his levity, his blood boiled in his veins.

'What, Sugden!' cried Bertie. 'Come in, old fellow, I am glad to see you. Why, you've been and left Shanklin! What did you do that for? The old place will not look like itself without you.'

'There are other vacant places that will be felt more than mine,' said the Curate, in a funereal voice, putting himself sadly on the nearest chair.

'Oh! the ladies at the Cottage! To be sure, you are quite right. They must be a dreadful loss,' said Bertie.

Mr. Sugden felt that he flushed and faltered, and these signs of guilt made it doubly clear.

'It is odd enough,' he said, with double meaning, 'that we should talk of that, for I have just come from Scotland, from the Highlands, where, of all people in the world, I met suddenly with Miss Anderson and her mother.'

Bertie faced round upon him in the middle of his packing, which he had resumed, and said, 'Well!' in a querulous voice—a voice which already sounded like that of a man put on his defence.

'Well!' said the Curate—'I don't think it is well. She is not Miss Anderson now. But I see you know that. Mr. Hardwick, if you know anything of her husband, I think you should urge him not to leave her alone there. She looks—not very well. Poor Ombra!' cried the Curate, warming into eloquence. 'I have no right to call her by her name, but that I—I was fond of her too. I would have given my life for her! And she is like her name—she is like a shadow, that is ready to flit away.'

Bertie Hardwick listened with an agitated countenance—he grew red and pale, and began to pace about the room; but he made no answer—he was confused and startled by what his visitor said.

'I daresay my confession does not interest you much,' Mr. Sugden resumed. 'I make it to show I have some right—to take an interest, at least. That woman for whom I would give my life, Mr. Hardwick, is pining there for a man who leaves her to pine—a man who must be neglecting her shamefully, for it cannot be long since he married her—a man who—'

'And pray, Mr. Sugden,' said Bertie, choking with apparent anger and agitation, 'where did you obtain your knowledge of this man?'

'Not from her,' said the Curate; 'but by chance—by the inquiries I made in my surprise. Mr. Hardwick, if you know who it is who is so happy, and so negligent of his happiness—'

'Well?'

'He has no right to stay away from her after this warning,' cried the Curate, rising to his feet. 'Do you understand what a thing it is for me to come and say so?—to one who is throwing away what I would give my life for? But she is above all. If he stays away from her, he will reproach himself for it all his life!'

And with these words he turned to go. He had said enough—his own eyes were beginning to burn and blaze. He felt that he might seize this false lover by the throat if he stayed longer. And he had at least done all he could for Ombra. He had said enough to move any man who was a man. He made a stride towards the door in his indignation; but Bertie Hardwick interrupted him, with his hand on his arm.

'Sugden,' he said, with a voice full of emotion, 'I am not so bad as you think me; but I am not so good as you are. The man you speak of shall hear your warning. But there is one thing I have a right to ask. What you learnt by chance, you will not make any use of—not to her cousin, for instance, who knows nothing. You will respect her secret there?'

'I do not know that I ought to do so, but I promised her mother,' said the Curate, sternly. 'Good morning, Mr. Hardwick. I hope you will act at once on what you have heard.'

'Won't you shake hands?' said Bertie.

The Curate was deeply prejudiced against him—hated him in his levity and carelessness, amusing himself while she was suffering. But when he looked into Bertie's face, his enmity melted. Was this the man who had done her—and him—so much wrong? He put out his hand with reluctance, moved against his will.

'Do you deserve it?' he said, in his deep voice.

'Yes—so far as honesty goes,' said the young man, with a broken, agitated laugh.

The Curate went away, wondering and unhappy. Was he so guilty, that open-faced youth, who seemed yet too near boyhood to be an accomplished deceiver?—or was there still more in the mystery than met the eye?

This was how Kate got no news. She looked for it for many a day. As the Summer ripened and went on, a hungry thirst for information of one kind or another possessed her. Her aunt's birthday letter had been a few tender words only—words which were humble, too, and sad. 'Poor Ombra,' she had said, 'was pretty well.' Poor Ombra!—why poor Ombra? Kate asked herself the question with sudden fits of anxiety, which she could not explain to herself; and she began to watch for the post with almost feverish eagerness. But the suspense lasted so long, that the keenness of the edge wore off again, and no news ever came.

In July, however, Lady Caryisfort came, having lingered on her way from Italy till it became too late to keep the engagement she had made with Mr. Courtenay for Kate's first season in town. She was so kind as to go to Langton-Courtenay instead, on what she called a long visit.

'Your uncle has to find out, like other people, that he will only find aid ready made to his hand when he doesn't want it,' she said—'that is the moment when everything becomes easy. I might have been of use to him, I know, two months ago, and accordingly my private affairs detained me, and it is only now, you see, that I am here.'

'I don't see why you should have hurried for my uncle,' said Kate; 'he has never come to see me, though he has promised twenty times. But you are welcome always, whenever you please.'

'Thanks, dear,' said Lady Caryisfort, who was languid after her journey. 'He will come now, when you don't want him. And so the aunt and the cousin are gone, Kate? You must tell me why. I heard, after you left Florence, that Miss Anderson had flirted abominably with both these young men—behind your back, my poor darling, when you were with me, I suppose; though I always thought that young Eldridge would have suited you precisely—two nice properties, nice families—everything that was nice. But an ideal match like that never comes to pass. They tell me she was called la demoiselle à deux cavaliers. Don't look shocked. Of course, it could only be a flirtation; there could be nothing wrong in it. But, you dear little innocent, is this all new to you?'

'Mr. Hardwick and Mr. Eldridge used to go with us to a great many places; they were old friends,' said Kate, with her cheeks and forehead dyed crimson in a moment; 'but why people should say such disagreeable things—'

'People always say disagreeable things,' said Lady Caryisfort; 'it is the only occupation which is pursued anywhere. But as you did not hear about your cousin, I am glad to think you cannot have heard of me.'

'Of you!' Kate's consternation was extreme.

'They were so good as to say I was going to marry Antonio Buoncompagni,' said Lady Caryisfort, calmly, smoothing away an invisible wrinkle from her glove. But she did not look up, and Kate's renewed blush and start were lost upon her—or perhaps not quite lost. There was a silence for a minute after; for the tone, as well as the announcement, took Kate altogether by surprise.

'And are you?' she asked, in a low tone, after that pause.

'I don't think it,' said Lady Caryisfort, slowly. 'The worst is, that he took it into his head himself—why, heaven knows! for I am—let me see—three, four, five years, at least, older than he is. I think he felt that you had jilted him, Kate. No, it would be too much of a bore. He is very good-natured, to be sure, and too polite to interfere; but still, I don't think—Besides, you know, it would be utterly ridiculous. How could I call Elena Strozzi aunt? In the meantime, my Kate—my little heiress—I think I had better stay here and marry you.'

'But I don't want to be married,' cried Kate.

'The very reason why you will be,' said her new guardian, laughing. But the girl stole shyly away, and got a book, and prepared to read to Lady Caryisfort. She was fond of being read to, and Kate shrank with a repugnance shared by many girls from this sort of talk; and, indeed, I am not sure that she was pleased with the news. It helped to reproduce that impression in her mind which so many other incidents had led to. She had always remembered with a certain amount of gratitude poor Antonio's last appearance at the railway, with the violets in his coat, and the tender, respectful farewell he waved to her. And all the time he had been thinking of Lady Caryisfort! What a strange world it was, in which everything went on in this bewildering, treacherous way! Was there nobody living who was quite true, quite real, meaning all he or she said? She began to think not, and her very brain reeled under the discovery. Her path was full of shadows, which threatened and circled round her. Oh! Ombra, shadow of shadows, where was she? and where had disappeared with her all that tender, bright life, in which Kate believed everybody, and dreamt of nothing but sincerity and truth? It seemed to have gone for ever, to return no more.

CHAPTER LXIV

All that Summer Mr. Sugden wandered about the world like a soul in pain. He went everywhere, unable to settle in one place. Some obliging friend had died, and left him a little money, and this was how he disposed of it. His people at home disapproved much. They thought he ought to have been happy in the other curacy which they had found him quite close to his own parish, and should have invested his legacy, and perhaps looked out for some nice girl with money, and married as soon as a handy living fell vacant. This routine, however, did not commend itself to his mind. He tore himself away from mothers'-meetings, and clothing-clubs, and daily services; he went wandering, dissatisfied and unhappy, through the world. He had been crossed in love. It is a thing people do not own to readily, but still it is nothing to be ashamed of. And not only was it the restlessness of unhappiness that moved him; a lingering hope was yet in his mind that he might be of use to Ombra still. He went over the route which the party had taken only a year before; he went to the Swiss village where they had passed so long, and was easily able to glean some information about the English ladies, and the one who was fond of the Church. He went there after her, and knelt upon the white flags and wondered what she had been thinking of, and prayed for her with his face towards Madonna on the altar, with her gilt crown, and all her tall artificial lilies.

Poor honest, broken-hearted lover! If she had been happy he would have been half cured by this time; but she was not happy—or, at least, he thought so, and his heart burned over her with regretful love and anguish. Oh, if Providence had but given her to him, though unworthy, how he would have shielded and kept her from all evil! He wandered on to Florence, where he stayed for some time, with the same vain idol-worship. He remained until the Autumn flood of tourists began to arrive, and the English Church was opened. And it was here he acquired the information which changed all his plans. The same young clergyman who was a friend of Bertie Eldridge's, and had known the party in Florence, returned again that Winter, and officiated once more in the Conventicle of the English visitors. And Mr. Sugden had known him, too, at school or college; the two young clergymen grew intimate, and, one day, all at once, without warning, the Curate had a secret confided to him, which thrilled him through and through from head to heel. His friend told him of all the importunities he had been subjected to, to induce him to celebrate a marriage, and how he had consented, and how his conscience had been uneasy ever since. 'Was I wrong?' he asked his friend. 'The young lady's mother was there and consenting, and the man—you know him—was of full age, and able to judge for himself; the only thing was the secrecy—do you think I was wrong?'

Mr. Sugden gave no answer. He scarcely heard the words that were addressed to him; a revolution had taken place in all his ideas. He had not spent more than half his legacy, and he had half the Winter before him, yet immediately he made up his mind to go home.

Two days after he started, and in a week was making his way down to Langton-Courtenay, for no very intelligible reason. What his plea would have been, had he been forced to give it, we cannot tell, but he did not explain himself even to himself; he had a vague feeling that something new had come into the story, and that Kate ought to be informed—an idea quite vague, but obstinate. He went down, as he had gone before, to Westerton, and there engaged a fly to take him to Langton. But, when he arrived, he was startled to find the house lighted up, and all the appearance of company. He did not know what to do. There was a dinner-party, he was told, and he felt that he and his news, such as they were, could not be obtruded into the midst of it. He was possessed by his mission as by incipient madness. It seemed to him like a divine message, which he was bound to deliver. He went back to the little inn in the village, and dressed himself in evening clothes—for he had brought his portmanteau on with him all the way, not having wits enough left to leave it behind. And when it was late, he walked up the long avenue to the Hall. He knew Kate well enough, he thought, to take so much liberty with her—and then his news! What was it that made his news seem so important to him? He could not tell.

Mr. Courtenay was at Langton, and so was Lady Caryisfort. The lady, who should have been mentioned first, had stayed with Kate for a fortnight on her first visit, and then, leaving her alone all the Summer, had gone off upon other visits, promising a return in Autumn. It was October now, and Mr. Courtenay too had at last found it convenient to pay his niece a visit. He had brought with him some people for the shooting, men, chiefly, of respectable age, with wives and daughters. The party was highly respectable, but not very amusing, and, indeed, Lady Caryisfort found it tedious; but such as it was, it was the first party of guests which had ever been gathered under Kate's roof, and she was excited and anxious that everything should go off well. In six months more she would be her own mistress, and the undue delays which had taken place in her life were then to be all remedied.

'You ought to have been introduced to the world at least two years ago,' said Lady Caryisfort. 'But never mind, my dear; it does not matter for you, and next season will make up for everything. You have the bloom of sixteen still, and you have Langton-Courtenay,' the lady added, kissing her.

To Kate there was little pleasure in this speech; but she swallowed it, as she had learned to swallow a great many things.

'I have Langton-Courtenay,' she said to herself, with a smile of bitter indignation—'that makes up for everything. That I have nobody who cares for me does not matter in comparison.'

But yet she was excited about her first party, and hoped with all her heart it would go off well. There were several girls beside herself; but there were only two young men—one a wealthy and formal young diplomatist, the other a penniless cousin of Lady Caryisfort's—'too penniless and too foolish even to try for an heiress,' she had assured Mr. Courtenay. The rest were old bachelors—Mr. Courtenay's own contemporaries, or the respectable married men above described. A most safe party to surround an heiress, and not amusing, but still, as the first means of exercising her hospitality in her own house, exciting to Kate.

The dinner had gone off well enough. It was a good dinner, and even Uncle Courtenay had been tolerably satisfied. The only thing that had happened to discompose Kate was that she had seen Lady Caryisfort yawn twice. But that was a thing scarcely to be guarded against. When the ladies got back to the drawing-room she felt that the worst of her labours were over, and that she might rest; but her surprise was great when, half an hour later, she suddenly saw Mr. Sugden standing in a corner behind her. He had come there as if by magic—like a ghost starting up out of nothing. Kate rose to her feet suddenly with a little cry, and went to him. What a good thing that it was a dull, steady-going party, not curious, as livelier society is! She went up to him hurriedly, holding out her hand.

'Mr. Sugden! When did you come? I never saw you. Have you dropped through from the skies?'

'I ought to apologise,' said the Curate, growing red.

'Oh, never mind apologising! I know you have something to tell me!' cried Kate.

'But how can I tell you here? Yes, it is something—not bad news—oh, not bad news—don't think so. I came off at once without thinking. A letter might have done as well; but I get confused, and don't think till too late—'

'I am so sorry for you!' cried Kate impulsively, holding out her hand to him once more.

He took it, and then he dropped it, poor fellow! not knowing what else to do. Kate's hand was nothing to him, nor any woman's, except the one which was given into another man's keeping. He was still dazed with his journey, and all that had happened. His theory was that, as he had found it out another way, he was clear of his promise to Mrs. Anderson; and then he had to set a mistake right. How could he tell what harm that mistake might do?

'Your cousin—is married,' he said.

'Married!' cried Kate. A slight shiver ran over her, a thrill that went through her frame, and then died out, and left her quite steady and calm. But, somehow, in that moment her colour, the bloom of sixteen, as Lady Caryisfort called it, died away from her cheek. She stood with her hands clasped, and her face raised, looking up to him. Of course it was only what she felt must happen some day; she said to herself that she had known it. There was nothing to be surprised about.

'She was married last year, in Florence,' the Curate resumed. And then the thrill came back again, and so strongly that Kate shook as if with cold. In a moment there rose up before her the group which she had met at the doorway on the Lung-Arno, the group which moved so quickly, and kept so close together, Ombra leaning on her husband's arm. Yes, how blind she had been! That was the explanation—at a glance she saw it all. Oh! heaven and earth, how the universe reeled under her! He had looked at herself, spoken to her, touched her hand as only he had ever touched, and looked, and spoken—after that! The blood ebbed away from Kate's heart; but though the world spun and swam so in the uncertainty of space, that she feared every moment to fall, or rather to be dashed down by its swaying, she kept standing, to all appearance immovable, before the tall Curate, with her hands clasped, and a smile upon her pale face.

'Kate!' said some one behind her—'Kate!'

She turned round. It was Lady Caryisfort who had called her. And what was there more to be told? Now she knew all. Spigot was standing behind her, with a yellow envelope upon a silver tray. A telegram—the first one she had ever got in her life! No civility could hesitate before such a letter as that. But for the news which she had just heard she would have been frightened; but that preparation had steeled her. She tore it open and read it eagerly. Then she raised a bewildered look to Lady Caryisfort and Mr. Sugden, who were both close by her.

'I don't understand it,' she said. She held it up to him, because he was nearest. And then suddenly put up her hand to stop him, as he began to read aloud. 'Hush! Hush! Mrs. Hardwick is here,' she said.

'What is the matter?' said Lady Caryisfort, rising to shield this group, which began to attract the eyes of the party. 'Kate, what is your telegram about?'

Kate held it out to her without a word. The message it contained was this: "Sir Herbert Eldridge died here last night.'"

'Sir Herbert Eldridge?' repeated Lady Caryisfort. 'What is he to you, Kate? What does it mean? Child, are you ill? You are like a ghost!'

'He is nothing in the world to me,' said Kate, rousing herself. 'If I am like a ghost it is because—oh! I am so cold!—because—it is so strange! I never saw Sir Herbert Eldridge in my life. Mr. Sugden, what do you think it means?'

She looked up and looked round for the Curate. He was gone. She gazed all round her in consternation.

'Where is he?' she cried.

'The gentleman you were talking to went out a minute ago. Who is he? Kate, dear, don't look so strange. Who was this man, and what did he come to tell you about?'

'I don't know,' said the girl, faintly, her eyes still seeking for him round the room. 'I don't know where he came from, or where he has gone to. I think he must have been a ghost.'

'What was he telling you—you must know that at least?'

Kate made no reply. She pushed a chair towards the fireplace, and warmed her trembling fingers. She crushed up the big yellow envelope in her hand, under her laced handkerchief.

'"Sir Robert Eldridge died last night." What is that to me! What have I to do with it?' she said.

CHAPTER LXV

The reason of Kate's strange paleness and agitation was afterwards explained to be the fact that she had suddenly heard, no one knew how, of the death of Mrs. Hardwick's brother; while that lady was sitting by her, happy and undisturbed, and knowing nothing. This was the reason Lady Caryisfort gave to several of the ladies in the house, who remarked next morning on Miss Courtenay's looks.

'Poor Kate did not know what to do; and the feelings are strong at her age. I daresay Mrs. Hardwick, when she heard of it, took the news with perfect composure, said Lady Caryisfort; 'but then at twenty it is difficult to realise that.'

'Ah! now I understand,' said one of the ladies. 'It was told her, no doubt, by that tall young man, like a clergyman, who appeared in the drawing-room all of a sudden, after the gentlemen came downstairs, and disappeared again directly after.'

'Yes, you are quite right,' said Lady Caryisfort. She said so because she was aware that to have any appearance of mystery about Kate would be fatal to that brilliant début which she intended her to make; but in her own mind she was much disturbed about this tall young man like a clergyman. She had questioned Kate about him in vain.

'He is an old friend, from where we lived in the Isle of Wight,' the girl explained.

'But old friends from the Isle of Wight don't turn up everywhere like this. Did he come about Sir Herbert Eldridge?'

'He knows nothing about Sir Herbert Eldridge. He came to tell me about—my cousin.'

'Oh! your cousin! La demoiselle aux deux chevaliers,' said Lady Caryisfort. 'And did he bring you news of her?'

'A little,' said Kate, faintly, driven to her wit's end; but she was not a weak-minded young woman, to be driven to despair; and here she drew up and resisted. 'So little, that it is not worth repeating,' she added, firmly. 'I knew it almost all before, but he was not aware of that. He meant it very kindly.'

'Did he come on purpose, dear?'

'Yes, I suppose so, the good fellow,' said Kate, gracefully.

'My dear, he may be a very good fellow; but curates are like other men, and don't do such things without hope of reward,' said Lady Caryisfort, doubtfully. 'So I would not encourage him to go on secret missions—unless I meant to reward him,' she added.

'He does not want any of my rewards,' said Kate, with that half bitterness of still resentment which she occasionally showed at the suspicions which were so very ready to enter the minds of all about her. 'I at least have no occasion to think as they do,' she added to herself, with a feeling of sore humility. 'Of all the people I have ever known, no one has given me this experience—they have all preferred her, without thinking of me.'

It was with this thought in her mind that she withdrew herself from Lady Caryisfort's examination. She had nothing more to say, and she would not be made to say any more. But when she was in the sanctuary of her own room, she went over and over, with a heart which beat heavily within her breast, Mr. Sugden's information. That Ombra should have married Bertie did not surprise her—that she had foreseen, she said to herself. But that they should have married so long ago, under her very eyes, as it were, gave her a strange thrill of pain through and through her. They had not told her even a thing so important as that. Her aunt and Ombra, her dearest friends, had lived with her afterwards, and kissed her night and morning, and at last had broken away from her, and given her up, and yet had never told her. The one seemed to Kate as wonderful as the other. Not in their constant companionship, not when that companionship came to a breach—neither at one time nor the other did they do her so much justice. And Bertie!—that was worst of all. Had his look of gladness to see her at the brook in the park, when they last met, been all simulation?—or had it been worse than simulation?—a horrible disrespect, a feeling that she did not deserve the same observance as men were forced to show to other girls! When she came to this question her brain swam so with wrath and a sense of wrong that she became unable to discriminate. Poor Kate!—and nothing of this did she dare to confide to a creature round her. She who had been so outspoken, so ready to disclose her thoughts—she had to lock them up in her own bosom, and never breathe a word.

Unconnected with this, but still somehow connected with it, was the extraordinary message she had received. On examining it afterwards in her own room, she found it was sent to her by 'Bertie.' What did it mean? How did he dare to send such a message to her, and what had she to do with it? Had it been a mistake? Could it have been sent to her, instead of to the Rectory? But Kate ascertained that a similar telegram had been received by the Hardwicks the same night when they went home from her dinner-party. Minnie Hardwick stole up two days later to tell her about it. Minnie was very anxious to do her duty, and to feel sad, as a girl ought whose uncle has just died; but though the blinds were all down in the Rectory, and the village dress-maker and Mrs. Hardwick's maid were labouring night and day at 'the mourning,' Minnie found it hard to be so heart-broken as she thought necessary.

'It is so strange to think that one of one's own relations has gone away to—to the Better Land,' said Minnie, with a very solemn face. 'I know I ought not to have come out, but I wanted so to see you; and when we are sorrowful, it is then our friends are dearest to us. Don't you think so, dear Kate?'

'Were you very fond of your uncle, Minnie?'

'I—I never saw much of him. He has been thought to be going to die for ever so long,' said Minnie. 'He was very stout, and had not a very good temper. Oh! how wicked it is to remember that now! And he did not like girls; so that we never met. Mamma is very, very unhappy, of course.'

'Yes, it is of course,' Kate said to herself, with again that tinge of bitterness which was beginning to rise in her mind; 'even when a man dies, it is of course that people are sorry. If I were to die they would try how sorrowful they could look, and say how sad it was, and care as little about me as they do now.' This thought crossed her mind as she sat and talked to Minnie, who was turning her innocent little countenance as near as possible into the expression of a mute at a funeral, but who, no doubt, in reality, cared much more for her new mourning than for her old uncle—a man who had neither kindness to herself nor general goodness to commend him. It was she who told Kate of the telegram which had been found waiting at the Rectory when they went home, and how she had remembered that Kate had got one too, and how strange such a coincidence was (but Minnie knew nothing of the news contained in Kate's), and how frightened she always was at telegrams.

'They always bring bad news,' said Minnie, squeezing one innocent little tear into the corner of her eye. Her father had gone off immediately, and Bertie was already with his cousin. 'It is he who will be Sir Herbert now,' Minnie said, with awe; 'and oh! Kate, I am so much afraid he will not be very sorry! His father was not very kind to him. They used to quarrel sometimes—I ought not to say so, but I am sure you will never, never tell anyone. Uncle Herbert used to get into dreadful passions whenever Bertie was silly, and did anything wrong. Uncle Herbert used to storm so; and then it would bring on fits. Oh! Kate, shouldn't we be thankful to Providence that we have such a dear, kind papa!'

Thus this incident, which she had no connection with, affected Kate's life, and gave a certain colour to her thoughts. She lived, as it were, for several days within the shadow of the blinds, which were drawn down at the Rectory, and the new mourning that was being made, and her own private trouble, which was kept carefully hidden in her heart of hearts. This gave her such abundant food for thought, that the society of her guests was too much for her, and especially Lady Caryisfort's lively observations. She had to attend to them, and to look as cheerful as she could in the evenings; but they all remarked what depression had stolen over her. 'She does not look the same creature,' the other ladies said to Lady Caryisfort; and that lively person, who had thought Kate's amusing company her only indemnification for putting up with all this respectability, yawned half her time away, and felt furious with Mr. Courtenay for having deluded her into paying this visit at this particular time. It does not do, she reflected, to put off one's engagements. Had she kept her tryst in Spring, and brought Kate out, and done all she had promised to do for her, probably she would have been married by this time, and the trouble of taking care of her thrown on other shoulders. Whereas, if she went and threw away her good looks, and settled into pale quietness and dulness, as she seemed about to do, there was no telling what a burden she might be on her friends. With these feelings in her mind, she told Mr. Courtenay that she thought that he had been very unwise in letting the Andersons slip through his fingers. 'They were exactly what she wanted; people who were amenable to advice; who would do what you wished, and would take themselves off when you were done with them—they were the very people for Kate, with her variable temper. It was a weakness which I did not expect in you, Mr. Courtenay, who know the world.'

'I never saw any signs of variable temper in Kate,' said Mr. Courtenay, who felt it necessary to keep his temper when he was talking to Lady Caryisfort.

'Look at me now!' said that dissatisfied woman. And she added to herself that it was vain to tell her that Kate knew nothing about Sir Herbert Eldridge, or that the strange appearance for half an hour, in the drawing-room, of the young man who was like a clergyman had no connection with the change of demeanour which followed it. This was an absurd attempt to hoodwink her, a woman who had much experience in society and was not easily deceived. And, by way of showing her sense of the importance of the subject, she began to talk to Kate of Bertie Eldridge, who had always been her favourite of the two cousins.

'Now his father is dead, he is worth your consideration,' she said. 'His father was an ill-tempered wretch, I have always heard; but the young man is very well, as young men go, and has a very nice estate. I have always thought nothing could be more suitable. For my own part, I always liked him best—why? I don't know, except, perhaps, because most people preferred his cousin. I should think, by the way, that after knocking about the world with Bertie Eldridge, that young man will hardly be very much disposed to drop into the Rectory here, like his father before him, which, I suppose, is his natural fate.'

At that moment there came over Kate's mind a recollection of the time when she had gravely decided to oppose Mr. Hardwick in the parish, and not to give his son the living. The idea brought an uneasy blush to her cheek.

'Mr. Bertie Hardwick is not going into the Church; he is reading for the bar,' she said.

'Well, I suppose the one will need as much work as the other,' said Lady Caryisfort. 'Reading for the bar!—that sounds profitable; but, Kate, if I were you, I would seriously consider the question about Bertie Eldridge. He is not bad-looking, and, unless that old tyrant has been wicked as well as disagreeable, he ought to be very well off. The title is not much, but still it is something; and it is a thoroughly good old family—as good as your own. I would not throw such a chance away.'

'But I never had the chance, as you call it, Lady Caryisfort,' said Kate, with indignation, 'and I don't want to have it; and I would not accept it, if it was offered to me. Bertie Eldridge is nothing to me. I don't even care for him as an acquaintance, and never did.'

'Well, my love, you know what a good authority has said—"that a little aversion is a very good thing to begin upon,"' said Lady Caryisfort, laughing; but in her heart she did not believe these protestations. Why should Kate have got that telegram if Sir Herbert was nothing to her? Thus, over-wisdom led the woman of the world astray.

Before long, Kate had forgotten all about Sir Herbert Eldridge. It was not half so important to her as the other news which nobody knew of—indeed, it was simply of no interest at all in comparison. Where was Ombra now?—and how must Bertie have deceived his family, who trusted in him; as much as his—wife—was that the word?—his wife had deceived herself. Where were they living? or were they together, or what had become of these two women? Then Kate's heart melted, and she cried within herself—What had become of them? An unacknowledged wife!—a woman who had to hide herself, and bear a name and assume a character which was not hers! In all the multitude of her thoughts, she at last stopped short upon the ground of deep pity for her cousin, who had so sinned against her. Where was she?—under what name?—in what appearance? The thought of her position, after all this long interval, with no attempt made to own her or set her right with the world, made Kate's heart sick with compassion in the midst of her anger. And how was she to find Ombra out?—and when she had found her out, what was she to do?

CHAPTER LXVI

It is hard to be oppressed with private anxiety and care in the midst of a great house full of people, who expect to be amused, and to have all their different wants attended to, both as regards personal comfort and social gratification. Kate had entered upon the undertaking with great zeal and pleasure, but had been suddenly chilled in the midst of her labours by the strange accidents which disturbed her first dinner-party. She had been so excited and confused at the moment, that it had not occurred to her to remember that Mr. Sugden's information was quite fragmentary, and that he did not tell her where to find her cousin, or give her any real aid in the matter. His appearance, and disappearance too, were equally sudden and mysterious. She ascertained from Spigot when he had come, and it was sufficiently easy to comprehend the noiseless way he had chosen to appear before her, and convey his news; but why had he disappeared when he saw the telegram? Why had he said so little? Why, oh! why had they all conspired to leave her thus, with painful scraps of information, but no real knowledge—alone among strangers, who took no interest in her perplexities, and, indeed, had never learned Ombra's name? She could not confide in Mrs. Hardwick, for many reasons, and there was no one else whom she could possibly confide in.

She got so unhappy at last that the idea of consulting Lady Caryisfort entered her mind more and more strongly. Lady Caryisfort was a woman of the world. She would not be so shocked as good Mrs. Hardwick would be; and then she could have no prejudice in the matter, and no temptation to betray poor Ombra's secret. Poor Ombra! Kate was not one of those people who can dismiss an offender out of their mind as soon as his sin is proved. All kinds of relentings, and movements of pity, and impulses to help, came whispering about her after the first shock. To be sure Ombra had her mother to protect and care for her, and how could Kate interfere, a young girl? What could she do in the matter? But yet she felt that if she were known to stand by her cousin, it would be more difficult for the husband to keep her in obscurity. And there was in her mind a longing that Bertie should learn that she knew, and know what her opinion was, of the concealment and secresy. She did as women, people say, are not apt to do. She threw all the blame on him. Her cousin had concealed it from her—but nothing more than that. He had done something more—he had insulted herself in the midst of the concealment. If Kate had followed her own first impulse, she would have rushed forth to find Ombra, she would have brought her home, she would have done what her husband had failed to do—acknowledged, and put her in her right place. All these things Kate pondered and mused over, till sometimes the impulse to action was almost too much for her; and it was in these moments that she felt a longing and a necessity to consult some one, to relieve the pent-up anxieties in her own heart.

It happened one afternoon that she was alone with Lady Caryisfort, in that room which had been her sitting-room under Mrs. Anderson's sway. That very fact always filled her with recollections. Now that the great drawing-room and all the house was open, this had become a refuge for people who had 'headaches,' or any of the ethereal ailments common in highly-refined circles. The ladies of the party were almost all out on this particular afternoon. Some had gone into Westerton on a shopping expedition; some had driven to see a ruined abbey, one of the sights of the neighbourhood; and some had gone to the covert-side, with luncheon for the sportsmen, and had not yet returned. Kate had excused herself under the pretext of a cold, to remedy which she was seated close by the fire, in a very low and comfortable easy-chair. Lady Caryisfort reclined upon a sofa opposite. She had made no pretence at all to get rid of the rest of the party. She was very pettish and discontented, reading a French novel, and wishing herself anywhere but there. There had been at least half an hour of profound silence. Kate was doing nothing but thinking; her head ached with it, and so did her heart. And when a girl of twenty, with a secret on her mind, is thus shut up with an elder woman whom she likes, with no one else within hearing, and after half an hour's profound silence, that is the very moment in which a confidential disclosure is sure to come.

'Lady Caryisfort,' said Kate, faltering, 'I wonder if I might tell you something which I have very much at heart?'

'Certainly you may,' said Lady Caryisfort, yawning, and closing her book. 'To tell you the truth, Kate, I was just going to put a similar question.'

'You have something on your mind too!' cried Kate, clasping her hands.

'Naturally—a great deal more than you can possibly have,' said her friend, laughing. 'But, come, Kate, you have the pas. Proceed—your secret has the right of priority; and then I will tell you mine—perhaps—if it is not too great a bore.'

'Mine is not about myself,' said Kate. 'If it had been about myself, I should have told you long ago—it is about—Ombra.'

'Oh! about Ombra!' Lady Caryisfort shrugged her shoulders, and the languid interest which she had been preparing to show suddenly failed her. 'You think a great deal more about Ombra than she deserves.'

'You will not think so when you have heard her story,' said Kate, with some timidity, for she was quickly discouraged on this point. While they were speaking, a carriage was heard to roll up the avenue. 'Oh!' she exclaimed, 'I thought we were safe. I thought I was sure of you for an hour. And here are those tiresome people come back!'

'An hour—all about Ombra!' Lady Caryisfort ejaculated, half within herself; and then she added aloud, 'Perhaps somebody has come to call. Heaven send us some one amusing! for I think you and I, Kate, must go and hang ourselves if this lasts.'

'Oh! no; it must be the Wedderburns come back from Westerton,' said Kate, disconsolate. There were sounds of an arrival, without doubt. 'They will come straight up here,' she said, in despair. 'Since that day when we had afternoon tea here, we have never been safe.'

It was a terrible reward for her hospitality; but certainly the visitors were coming up. The sound of the great hall-door rang through the house; and then Spigot's voice, advancing, made it certain that there had been an arrival. The new-comers must be strangers, then, as Spigot was conducting them; and what stranger would take the liberty to come here?

Kate turned herself round in the chair. She was a little flushed with the fire, and she was in that state of mind when people think that anything may happen—nay, that it is contrary to the order of Nature when something does not happen, to change the aspect of the world. Lady Caryisfort turned away with a little shrug, which was half impatience, half admiration of the girl's readiness to be moved by anything new. She opened her book again, and went nearer the window. The light was beginning to fade, for it was now late in October, and Winter might almost be said to have begun. The door opened slowly. The young mistress of the house stood like one spell-bound. Already her heart forecasted who her visitors were. And it was not Spigot's hand which opened that door. There was a hesitation, a fumbling and doubtfulness—and then—

How dim the evening was! Who were the two people who were standing there looking at her? Kate's heart gave a leap, and then seemed to stand still.

'Come in,' she said, doubtful, and faltering. And just then the fire gave a sudden blaze up, and threw a ruddy light upon the new-comers. Of course, she had known who it must be all along. But they did not advance; and she stood in an icy stupor, feeling as if she were not able to move.

'Kate,' said Ombra, from the door, 'I have been like an evil spirit to you. I will not come in again, unless you will give me your hand and say I am to come.'

She put herself in motion then, languidly. How different a real moment of excitement always is from the visionary one which you go over and over in your own mind, and to which you get used in all its details! Somehow all at once she bethought herself of Geraldine lifted over the threshold by innocent Christabel. She went and held out her hand. Her heart was beating fast, but dull, as if at a long distance off. There stood the husband and wife—two against one. She quickened her steps, and resolved to spare herself as much as she could.

'Ombra,' she said, as well as her quick breath would let her, 'come in. I know. I have heard about it. I am glad to receive you, and—and your husband.'

'Thanks, Kate,' said Ombra, with strange confusion. She had thought—I don't know why—that she would be received with enthusiasm corresponding to her own feelings. She came into the room, leaning upon him, as was natural, with her hand within his arm. He had the grace to be modest—not to put himself forward—or so, at least, Kate thought. But how much worse this moment was than she had supposed it would be! She felt herself tremble and tingle from head to heel. She forgot Lady Caryisfort, who was standing up against the light of the window, roused and inquisitive; she turned her back upon the new-comers, even, and poked the fire violently, making the room full of light. The ruddy blaze shot up into the twilight; it sprang up, quivering and burning into the big mirror. Kate saw the whole scene reflected there—the two figures standing behind her, and Ombra's black dress; black!—why was she in black, and she a bride? And, good heaven!—

She turned round breathless; she was pricked to the quick with anger and shame. 'Ombra,' she said, facing round upon her cousin, 'I told you I knew everything. Why do you come here thus with anybody but your husband? This is Mr. Eldridge. Did anyone dare to suppose—Why is it Mr. Eldridge, and not him, who has brought you here?'

Ombra's ice melted as when a flood comes in Spring. She rushed to the reluctant, angry girl, and kissed her, and clung to her, and wept over her. 'Oh! Kate don't turn from me!—Bertie Eldridge is my husband—no one else—and who else should bring me back?'

No one but Ombra ever knew that Kate would have fallen but for the strenuous grasp that held her up—no one but Ombra guessed what the convulsion of the moment meant. Ombra felt her cousin's arms clutch at her with the instinct of self-preservation—she felt Kate's head drop quite passive on her shoulder, and, with a new-born sympathy, she concealed the crisis which she dimly guessed. She kept whispering into her cousin's ear, holding her fast, kissing her, terrified at the extent of the emotion which had been so carefully and so long concealed.

'Now let Kate shake hands at least with me,' said Bertie, behind, 'and forgive me, if she can. It was all my fault. Ombra yielded to me because I would not give her any peace, and we dared not make it known. Kate, she has been breaking her heart over it, thinking you could never forgive her. Won't you forgive me too?'

Bertie Eldridge was a careless, light-hearted soul—one of the men who run all kind of risks of ruin, and whom other people suffer for, but who always come out safe at the end. At the sound of his ordinary easy, untragical voice, Kate roused herself in a moment. What had all this exaggerated feeling to do with him?

'Yes,' she said, holding out her hand, 'Bertie, I will forgive you; but I would not have done so half an hour ago, if I had known. Oh! and here is Lady Caryisfort in the dark, while we are all making fools of ourselves. Ombra, keep here; don't go away from me,' she whispered. 'I feel as if I could not stand.'

'Kate, mamma is in your room: and one secret more,' whispered Ombra. 'Oh! Kate, it is not half told!—Lady Caryisfort will forgive us—I could not stay away a day—an hour longer than I could help.'

'I will forgive you with all my heart, and I will take myself out of the way,' said Lady Caryisfort. 'I daresay you have a great deal to say to each other, and I congratulate you, at the same time, Lady Eldridge; one must take time for that.'

'Lady Eldridge!' cried Kate. Oh! how thankful she was to drop out of Ombra's supporting arm into a seat, and to laugh, in order that she might not cry. 'Then that was why I had the telegram, and that was why poor Mr. Sugden disappeared, that you might tell me yourself? Oh! Ombra, are you sure it is true, and not a dream? Are you back again, and all the shadows flown away, and things come right?'

'Except the one shadow, which must never flee away,' said Bertie, putting his arm round his wife's waist. He was the fondest, the most demonstrative of husbands, though only a fortnight ago—But it is needless to enlarge on what was past.

'But, Kate, come to your room,' said Ombra, 'where mamma is waiting; and one secret more—'

Mrs. Anderson was waiting in Kate's room, when Maryanne, sympathetic, weeping, and delighted, introduced her carefully. 'Oh, mayn't I carry it, ma'am?' she cried, longing; and when that might not be, drew a chair to the fire—the most comfortable chair—and placed a footstool, and lingered by in adoring admiration. What was it that this foolish maiden wanted so much to go down upon her knees before and do fetish worship to? Mrs. Anderson sat and pondered over this one remaining secret, with a heart that was partly joyful and partly heavy. This woman was a compound of worldliness and of something better. In her worldly part she was happy and triumphant, but in her higher part she was more humbled, almost more sad, than when she went away in what she had felt to be shame from Langton-Courtenay. She felt for the shock that this discovery would give to Kate's spotless maiden imagination, unaware of the possibility of such mysteries. She felt more for Kate than for her own child, who was happy and victorious. She sent Maryanne away to watch, and waited very nervously, with a tremble in her frame. How would Kate take it? How would she take this, which lay upon Mrs. Anderson's knee? She would not have the candles lighted. The dark, which half concealed and half revealed her, was kinder, and would keep her secret best. A film seemed to come over her eyes when she saw the two young women come into the room together. The first thing she was sure of was Kate's arms, which crept round her, and Kate's voice in her ear crying, 'Oh! auntie, how could you leave me—oh! how could you leave me? I have wanted you so!'

'Take it!' cried Mrs. Anderson, with sudden energy; and when the white bundle had been removed from her knee, she clasped her second child in her arms. It is not often that a mother gets to love an adopted child in competition with her own; but during all this past year, Kate had appeared before her many a day, in the sweet docility and submission of her youth, when Ombra was fretful, and exacting, and dissatisfied. The poor mother had not acknowledged it to herself but she wanted those arms round her—she wanted her other child.

'Oh!' she said, but in a whisper, 'my darling! I can never, never tell you how I have wanted you!'

'Here it is!' cried Ombra, gaily. 'Mamma, let her look at him; you can kiss her after. Kate, here is my other secret. Light the candles, Maryanne—quick, that your mistress may see my boy.'

'Yes, my lady,' cried Maryanne, full of awe.

A little laugh of unbounded happiness and exultation came from Ombra's lips. To come back thus triumphant, vindicated from all reproaches; to have the delight of showing her child; to be reconciled, and at last at liberty to love her cousin without any jealousy or painful sense of contrast; and, finally, to hear herself called my lady—all combined to fill up the measure of her content.

Up to this moment it had not occurred to Kate what the other secret was. Mrs. Anderson felt the girl's arms tighten round her, felt the sudden leap of her heart. Who will not understand what that movement of shame meant? It silenced Kate's very heart for the moment. This shock was greater than the first shock. She blushed crimson on her aunt's shoulder, where happily no one saw her. Her thoughts wandered back over the past, and she felt as if there was something shameful in it. This was absurd, of course; but it was some moments before she could so far overcome herself as to raise her head in answer to her cousin's repeated demands.

'Look at him, Kate!—look at him! Mamma will keep—you can have her afterwards. Look at my boy!'

Ombra was disinterring the baby out of cloaks and veils and shawls, in which it was lost. Her cheeks were sparkling, her eyes glowing with happiness. In her heart there was no sense of shame.

But we need not linger over this scene. Kate was glad, very glad, to get free from her duties that evening—to escape from the dinner and the people, as well as from the baby, and get time to think of it all. What were her feelings when she sat down alone, after all this flood of new emotions, and realised what had happened? The shock was over. The tingling of wonder, of pleasure, of pain, and even of shame, which had confused her senses, was over. She could look at everything, and see it as it was. And as the past rose out of the mists elucidated by the present, of course it became apparent to her that she ought to have seen the true state of affairs all the time. She ought to have seen that there was no affinity between Bertie Hardwick and her cousin, no natural fitness, no likelihood, even, that they could choose each other. Of course she ought to have seen that he had been made a victim of, as she herself had been made a victim of, though in a less degree. She ought to have known that Bertie, he whom she had once called her Bertie, in girlish, innocent freedom (though she blushed to recall it), could not have been disrespectful to herself, nor treacherous, nor anything but what he was. She owed him an apology, she said to herself, with cheeks which glowed with generous shame. She owed him an apology, and she would make it, whenever it should be in her power.

As for all the other wonderful events, they gradually stole off into the background, compared with this central fact that she owed an apology to Bertie. She fell asleep with this thought in her mind, and, waking in the morning, felt so happy that she asked herself instinctively what it was. And the answer was, 'I must make an apology to Bertie!' Ombra and her mysteries, and her new grandeur, and even her baby, faded off into nothing in comparison with this. Somehow that double secret seemed to be almost a hundred years old. The revelation of Bertie Hardwick's blamelessness, and the wrong she had done him, was the only thing that was new.

Sir Herbert and Lady Eldridge stayed at Langton-Courtenay for about a week before they went home, and all the minor steps in the matter were explained by degrees. He had rushed down to Loch Arroch, where she had been all this time, to fetch his wife, as soon as his father's death set him free. With so much depending on that event, Bertie Eldridge could scarcely, with a good grace, pretend to be sorry for his father; but the fact that Sir Herbert's death had been a triumph, and not a sorrow to him, was chiefly known away from home, and when he went back he went in full pomp of mourning. The baby even wore a black ribbon round its unconscious waist, for the grandpapa who would have disinherited it had he known of its existence. Probably nobody made much comment upon 'the Eldridges.' They were accepted, all things having come right, without much censure, if with a great deal of surprise. It was bitter for Mrs. Hardwick to realise that 'that insignificant Miss Anderson' was the wife of the head of her house, the mistress of all the honours and riches of the Eldridges; but she had to swallow it, as bitter pills must always be swallowed.

'Heaven be praised, my Bertie did not fall into her snares! Though I always said his taste was too good for such a piece of folly!' she said, taking the best piece of comfort which remained to her.

Bertie Hardwick came down to spend Christmas with his family, and it was not an uncheerful one, though they were all in mourning. It was not he, but his cousin, who had sent the telegram to Kate, in the confusion of the moment, not remembering that to her it would convey no information. But when the little party who had been together in Florence met again now, they talked of every subject on earth but that. Instinctively they avoided the recollection of these confused months, which had brought so much suffering in their train. The true history came to Kate in confidential interviews with her aunt, and was revealed little by little. It was to shield Bertie Eldridge from the possibility of discovery that Bertie Hardwick had been forced to make one of their party continually, and to devote himself, in appearance, to Ombra as much as her real lover did. He had yielded to his cousin's pleadings, having up to that time had no thought nor desire which the other Bertie had not shared. But this service which had been exacted from him had broken his bonds. He had separated from his cousin immediately on their return, and begun his independent life, though he had still continued to be, when it was not safe for them to meet, the mode of communication between Ombra and her husband.

All this Kate learned, partly from Mrs. Anderson, partly at a later period. She did not learn, however, what a dreary time had passed between the flight of the two ladies from Langton-Courtenay and their return. Her aunt did not tell her what wretched doubts had beset them, what sense of neglect, what terrors for the future. Bertie Eldridge had not been so anxious to shield his wife from the consequences of their imprudence as he ought to have been. But all is well that ends well. His father had died in the nick of time, and in Ombra's society he was the best of young husbands—proud, and fond, and happy. There was no fault to be found in him now.

When 'the Eldridges' went to their house, in great pomp and state, they left Mrs. Anderson with Kate; and to Kate, after they were gone, the whole seemed like a dream. She could scarcely believe that they had been there—that all the strange story was true. But she had perfectly recovered of her cold, and of her despondency, and was in such bloom, when she took leave of her departing guests, that all sorts of compliments were paid to her.

'Your niece has blossomed into absolute beauty,' said one of the old fogies to Mr. Courtenay. 'You have shut her up a great deal too long. What a sensation she will make with her fortune, and with that face!'

Mr. Courtenay shrugged his shoulders, and made a grimace.

'I don't see what good that face can do her,' he said, gruffly. He was suspicious, though he scarcely knew what he was suspicious of. There seemed to him something more than met the eye in this Eldridge business. Why the deuce had not that girl with the ridiculous name married young Hardwick, as she ought to have done? He was the first who had troubled Mr. Courtenay's mind with previsions of annoyance respecting his niece. And, lo! the fellow was coming back again, within reach, and Kate was almost her own mistress, qualified to execute any folly that might come into her head.

There was, however, a lull in all proceedings till Christmas, when, as we have prematurely announced, but as was very natural, Bertie Hardwick came home. Mr. Courtenay, too, being suspicious, came again to Langton-Courtenay, feeling it necessary to be on the spot. It was a very quiet Christmas, and nothing occurred to alarm anyone until the evening of Twelfth Day, when there was a Christmas-tree in the school-room for the school-children. It had been all planned before Sir Herbert's death; and Mrs. Hardwick decided that it was not right the children should suffer 'for our affliction—with such an object in view I hope I can keep my feelings in check,' she said. And indeed the affliction of the Rectory was kept very properly in check, and did not appear at all in the school-room. Kate enjoyed this humble festivity, with the most thorough relish. She was a child among the children. Her spirits were overflowing. To be sure, she was not even in mourning; and when all was over, she declared her intention of walking home up the avenue, which, all in its Winter leaflessness, was beautiful in the moonlight. It was a very clear, still Winter night—hard frost and moonlight, and air which was sharp and keen as ice, and a great deal more exhilarating than champagne to those whose lungs were sound, and their hearts light. Bertie walked with her, after she had been wrapped up by his sisters. Her heart beat fast, but she was glad of the opportunity. No appropriate moment had occurred before; she would make her apology now.

They had gone through the village side by side, talking of the school-children and their delight; but as they entered the avenue they grew more silent. 'Now is my time!' cried Kate to herself; and, though her heart leaped to her mouth, she began bravely.

'Mr. Bertie, there is something I have wished to say to you ever since Ombra came back. I did you a great deal of injustice. I want to make an apology.'

'An apology!—to me!'

'Yes, to you. I don't know that I ever did anybody so much wrong. I do not want to blame Bertie Eldridge. It is all right now, I suppose; but I thought once that you were her—'

Bertie Hardwick turned quickly round upon her, as if in resentment; his gesture felt like a moral blow. Wounded surprise and resentment—was it resentment? And somehow, though the white moonlight did not show it, Kate felt that she blushed.

'Please don't be angry. I am confessing that I was wrong; and I never felt that you could have done it,' said Kate, in a low voice. 'I believed it, and yet I did not believe it. That was the sting. To think you could have so little faith in me—could have deceived me, when we are such old friends!'

'And was that all?' he said. 'Was it only the concealment you thought me incapable of?'

'The concealment was the only thing wicked about it, I suppose,' said Kate, 'now that it has turned out all right.'

Bertie took no notice of the unconscious humour of this definition. He turned to her again with a certain vehemence, which seemed to have some anger in it.

'Nay,' he said, almost sharply, 'there was more than that. You knew I did not love Ombra—you knew she was nothing to me.'

'I did not—know—anything about it,' faltered Kate.

'How can you say so? Do you mean that you have ever doubted for a moment—that you have not known—every day we have been together since that day at the brook-side? Bah! you want to make a fool of me. You tempt me to put things into words that ought not to be spoken.'

'But, Mr. Bertie,' said Kate, after a pause to make sure that he had stopped—and her voice was child-like in its simplicity—'I like things to be put into words—I don't like people to break off in the middle. You were saying since that day by the brook-side?'

He turned to her with a short, agitated laugh. 'Perhaps you don't remember about it,' he said. 'I do—everything that happened—every word that was said—every one of the tears. You don't cry now as you used to do, or open your heart.'

'I don't cry when people can see me,' said Kate. 'I have cried enough, if you had been in the way to perceive it, this last year.'

'My poor, sweet—' Here he stopped; his voice had melted and changed. But all of a sudden he stopped short, with quite a different kind of alteration. 'Should you be afraid to go the rest of the way alone?' he said, abruptly. 'I will stand here till I see you on the steps, and you can call to me if you are afraid.'

'I am not in the least afraid,' said Kate, proudly. 'I was quite able to walk up the avenue by myself, if that was all.' And then she laughed. 'Mr. Bertie,' she said, demurely, 'it is you who are afraid, not I.'

'I suppose you are right,' he said. 'Well, then, as you are strong, be merciful—don't tempt me. If you like to know that there is some one to be dragged at your chariot wheels, it would be easy to give you that satisfaction. Perhaps, indeed, as we have begun upon this subject, it is better to have it out.'

'Much better, I think,' said Kate, with a glibness and ease which surprised herself. Was it because she was heartless? The fact was rather that she was happy, which is a demoralising circumstance in some cases.

'Well,' he said, with a hard breath, 'since you prefer to have it in plain words, Miss Courtenay, you may as well know, once for all, that since that day at the brook-side I have thought of no one but you. I don't suppose it is likely I shall ever think of anyone else all my life in that way. It can be no pleasure to me to speak, or to you to hear, of any such hopeless and insane notion. It is more your fault than mine, after all; for if you had not cried, I should not have leaped over the hedge, and trespassed, and—'

'What would you do?' said Kate, softly, 'if you saw the same sight again now?'

'Do?' he said, with an unsteady laugh—'make an utter fool of myself, I suppose—as, indeed, I have done all along. I am such a fool still, that I can't bear to be cross-examined about my folly. Don't say any more about it, please.'

'But, if I were you, I would say a great deal more about it,' said Kate, growing breathless with her resolution. 'Look here, Bertie—don't start like that—of course I have always called you Bertie within myself. I wonder how the Queen felt, when—I am very, very much ashamed of myself; but you can't see me, which is one good thing. Is it because I am rich you are afraid? For if that is all—'

'What then?—what then, Kate?'

Half an hour after, Kate walked into the little drawing-room, where so many things had happened, where her aunt was sitting alone, waiting for her return. Her eyes were like two stars, and blazed in the light which dazzled them, and filled them with moisture. A red scarf, which had been wrapped round her throat, hung loosely over her shoulders. Her face was all aglow with the clear, keen night air. She came in quietly, and came up to Mrs. Anderson, and knelt down by her side in front of the fire. 'Aunt,' she said, 'don't be angry. I have been doing a very strange thing. I hope you will not think it wicked. I have proposed to Bertie Hardwick.'

'Kate, my darling, are you mad?—are you out of your senses?'

'No,' said the girl, quietly, and with a sigh. 'But I am a kind of a princess. What can I do? He gave me encouragement, auntie, or I would not have done it; and I think he has accepted me,' she said, with a laugh; then, putting down her crimsoned face upon the lap of the woman who had been a mother to her, burst into a tempest of tears.

CHAPTER LXVIII

There is nothing perfect in this world. If Bertie Hardwick had been like his cousin, a great county potentate, on the same level as Miss Courtenay of Langton-Courtenay, they would both have been happier in their betrothal. Royal marriages are sometimes very happy, but it must be hard upon a Queen to be obliged to take the initiative in such a matter; and it was hard upon Kate, notwithstanding that she did it bravely, putting away all false pride. And though Bertie Hardwick went home floating, as it were, through the wintry air, in one sense, in a flood of delicious and unimaginable happiness; yet, in another sense, he walked very prosaically along a flinty, frost-bound road, and knocked his feet against stones and frozen cart-ruts, as he took the short way home to the Rectory. Cold as it was, he walked about the garden half the night, and smoked out many cigars, half thinking of Kate's loveliness and sweetness, half of the poor figure he would cut—not even a briefless barrister, a poor Templar reading for the law—as the husband of the great heiress. Why had not she been Ombra, and Ombra the heiress? But, in that case, of course, they could not have married, or dreamt of marrying at all. He thought it over till his head ached, till his brain swam. Ought he to give up such a hope? ought he to wound her and destroy all his own hopes of happiness, and perhaps hers, because she was rich and he was poor?—or should he accept this happiness which was put into his hands, which he had never hoped for, never dared to do anything to gain?

His mother waking, and hearing steps, rushed to the window in the cold, and looking out saw the red glow of his cigar curving round and round, and out and in among the trees. What could be the matter with the boy? She opened the window, and put out her head, though it was so cold, and called to him that he would get his death; that he would be frost-bitten; that he was mad to expose himself so. 'My dear boy, for heaven's sake, go to bed!' she cried; and her voice rung out into the deep night and stillness so that it was heard in the sexton's cottage, where it was supposed to be a cry for help against robbers. Old John drew the bed-clothes over his old nose at the sound, and breathed a sigh for his Rector, who, he thought, was probably being smothered in his bed at that moment—but it was too cold to interfere.

Next morning, Bertie had a long conversation with his father, and the two together proceeded to the Hall, where they had a still longer interview with Mr. Courtenay. It was not a pleasant interview. Kate had already seen her uncle, as in duty bound seeing the part which she had taken upon herself in the transaction, and Mr. Courtenay had foamed at the mouth with disgust and rage.

'Is it for this I have watched over you so carefully?' he cried, half frantic.

'Have you watched over me, so carefully?' said Kate, looking at him with her bright eyes.

And what could he reply? She would be of age in six months, and then it would matter very little what objections, or difficulties he might choose to make. It was, with the full consciousness of this that all parties discussed the question. Had the heiress been eighteen, things would have borne a very different aspect; but as she was nearly twenty-one, with the shadow of her coming independence upon her, she had a right to her own opinion. Her guardian did all a man could do in the circumstances to make himself disagreeable, but that could not, of course, last.

And when it was all over, the news went somehow like an electric shock through the whole neighbourhood. The Rectory received it first, and lay for ten minutes or so as if stunned by the blow; and then gradually, no one could tell how, it spread itself abroad. It had been fully determined that Bertie should return to town two days after Twelfth Night; but now he did not return to town—what was the use? 'If I must be Prince Consort,' he said, with a sigh that was half real and half fictitious, 'I had better make up my mind to it, and go in for my new duties.' These duties, however, consisted, in the meantime, in hanging about Kate, and following her everywhere. They were heavy enough, for she teased him, as it was in her nature to do; but he did not feel them hard. They made a pilgrimage to the brook-side, where, as Kate said, 'it was all settled' six years ago. They talked over a thousand recollections, half of which would never have occurred to them but for this sweet leisure, and the new light under which the past glowed, and shone. They did a great many foolish things, as was to be expected; and they were as happy as most other young people in the same foolish circumstances. It was only when he was away from her that Bertie ever grew red at the thought of the contrast of fortune. He called himself Prince Consort in Kate's company; but then the title did not hurt. It did—a little—when he was alone, and had time to think. But, after all, even when there is a sting like this in it, it is easy to content one's self with happiness, and to find a score of excellent reasons why that, and nothing else, should be one's lot.

Lady Caryisfort had gone away a week before. She came back, when she heard of it, in consternation, to remonstrate, if that was possible. But when she arrived at Langton-Courtenay, and saw how things were, Lady Caryisfort was much too sensible a woman to make herself disagreeable. She said, on the contrary, that she had divined how it would be from the beginning, and had been quite certain since the marriage of 'the Eldridges' had been made known to the world. I hope what she said was true; but it was not to say this that she had come all the way from Dorsetshire. She remained only two days, and took a very affectionate leave of Kate, and sent her a charming present when she married; but it was a long time before they met again. It was disappointing not to have an heiress to present to the world, to carry about in her train; but then it was her own fault. Had she not lingered in Italy till the last season was over, how different things might have been! She had no good answer to give to Mr. Courtenay when he taunted her with this. She knew very well herself why she lingered, and probably so did he; and it had come to nothing after all. However, we may say, for the satisfaction of the reader, that it did not end in nothing. Lady Caryisfort continued her independent, and, as people said, enjoyable life for some years more. Then it suddenly occurred to her all at once that to go every year from London to Paris, and from Paris to Italy, and from Italy back to London, with a quantity of dull visits between, was an unprofitable way of spending one's life; so she went to Florence early one season, and married Antonio Buoncompagni after all. I hope she was very comfortable, and liked it; but, at all events, so far as this story is concerned, there was an end of her.

Mrs. Anderson stayed with her niece for a very long time; naturally her presence was necessary till Kate married—and then she returned to receive the pair when they came back after their honeymoon. But when the honeymoon was long over Mrs. Anderson still stayed, and was more firmly established at Langton-Courtenay than in her daughter's great house, where old Lady Eldridge lived with the young people, and where sometimes there were shadows visible, even on the clear sky of prosperity and well-doing. Ombra was Ombra still, even when she was happy—a nature often sweet, and never intentionally unkind, but apt to become self-absorbed, and disposed to be cloudy. Her mother never uttered a word of complaint, and was very happy to pay her a visit now and then; but her home gradually became fixed with her adopted child. She and old Francesca faded and grew old together—that is to say, Mrs. Anderson grew older, while Francesca bloomed perennial, no more aged at seventy, to all appearance, than she had been at fifty. Never was such an invaluable old woman in a house. She was the joy of all the young generation for twenty years, and her stories grew more full of detail and more lavishly decorated with circumstances every day.

There is not much more to add. If we went further on in the history, should we not have new threads to take up, perhaps new complications to unravel, new incidents with every new hour? For life does not sit still and fold its hands in happiness any more than in sorrow—something must always be happening; and when Providence does not send events, we take care to make them. But Providence happily provided the events in the house of Kate and Bertie. He made an admirable Prince Consort. He went into Parliament, and took up politics warmly, and finally got up to a secondary seat in the Cabinet, which Kate was infinitely proud of. She made him rich and important—which, after all, as she said, were things which any cheese-monger's daughter could have done, who had money enough. But he made her, what few people could have done, the wife of a Cabinet Minister. When the Right Honourable H. Hardwick came down to Westerton, the town took off its hat to him, and considered itself honoured as no Mr. Courtenay of Langton-Courtenay had ever honoured it. Thus things went well with those who aimed well, which does not always happen, though sometimes it is permitted us for the consolation of the race.

Margaret Oliphant – A Short Biography

Margaret Oliphant Wilson was born on April 4th, 1828 to Francis W. Wilson, a clerk, and Margaret Oliphant, at Wallyford, near Musselburgh, East Lothian.

She spent her childhood at Lasswade, near Dalkeith, Glasgow before moving to Liverpool.

Her youth was spent in establishing a writing style so much so that, in 1849, she had her first novel published: Passages in the Life of Mrs. Margaret Maitland based on the Scottish Free Church movement. It met with some success and was a good start to her career.

Two years later, in 1851, her third book Caleb Field was published. It was also now that she met the publisher William Blackwood in Edinburgh and was asked to contribute to his well-received Blackwood's Magazine. It was to be a lifetimes endeavor. Over the course of the relationship she would have well over 100 articles published.

In May 1852, Margaret married her cousin, Frank Wilson Oliphant, at Birkenhead, and they settled at Harrington Square, Camden, London. He was an artist working primarily in stained glass. With the marriage she became Margaret Oliphant Wilson Oliphant.

Their marriage produced six children but three tragically died in infancy.

When her husband developed signs of the dreaded consumption (tuberculosis) they moved, on the advice of doctors, to warmer climes. In January 1859 it was to Florence, and then to Rome where, sadly, he died.

Margaret was naturally devastated but was also now left without support and only her income from her writing. She returned to England and took up the task of supporting her three remaining children by her literary activity.

By now she was being published both as an established novelist and regularly in Blackwood's Magazine, amongst others. Her incredible and prolific work rate increased both her commercial reputation and the size of her reading audience.

Against this her domestic life continued to be tragic, full of sorrow and disappointment.

In January 1864 her only remaining daughter Maggie died and was buried in her father's grave in Rome. Her brother, who had emigrated to Canada, was shortly afterwards involved in financial ruin. Margaret generously offered a home to him and his children, adding another demand to her already heavy responsibilities.

In 1866 she settled at Windsor to be closer to her sons, who were being educated at near-by Eton School. That year, her second cousin, Annie Louisa Walker, came to live with her as a companion-housekeeper. Windsor was now to be her home for the rest of her life.

Her literary career for three decades was one of constant delivery and success. Whether she wrote historical works or across several genres in fiction: domestic realism, historical, romance or supernatural she was successful.

For more than thirty years she pursued a varied literary career but family life continued to bring problems.

The literary ambitions she wished for her sons were unfulfilled. Cyril Francis, the eldest, died in 1890, leaving a Life of Alfred de Musset, incorporated in his mother's Foreign Classics for English Readers. The younger, Francis, who she nicknamed 'Cecco', collaborated with her in the Victorian Age of English Literature and won a position at the British Museum, but was rejected by Sir Andrew Clark, a famous physician. Cecco died in 1894.

With the last of her children now lost to her, she had but little further interest in life. Her health steadily and inexorably declined.

Margaret Oliphant Wilson Oliphant died at the age of 69 in Wimbledon on 20th June 1897. She is buried in Eton beside her sons.

At her death, Margaret was still working on Annals of a Publishing House, a record of Blackwood's Magazine with which she had enjoyed such a successful relationship.

Her Autobiography and Letters, which present a thoughtful picture of her domestic anxieties, was published in 1899. Only parts were written with a wider audience in mind: she had originally intended the Autobiography for her son, but he died before she could finish it.

Opinions on Oliphant's work are split, with some critics seeing her as a 'domestic novelist', while others recognize her work as influential and important to the Victorian literature canon. Critical reception from her contemporaries is also divided. John Skelton took the view that Oliphant wrote too much and too quickly. Writing a Blackwood's article called 'A Little Chat About Mrs. Oliphant', he asked, "Had Mrs. Oliphant concentrated her powers, what might she not have done? We might have had another Charlotte Brontë or another George Eliot." However not all of the contemporary reception was negative. The esteemed M. R. James admired Oliphant's supernatural fiction, concluding that "the religious ghost story, as it may be called, was never done better than by Mrs. Oliphant in 'The Open Door' and 'A Beleaguered City'. Mary Butts lavished praise on Oliphant's ghost story 'The Library Window', describing it as "one masterpiece of sober loveliness".

More modern critics of Oliphant's work include Virginia Woolf, who asked in Three Guineas whether Oliphant's autobiography does not lead the reader "to deplore the fact that Mrs. Oliphant sold her brain, her very admirable brain, prostituted her culture and enslaved her intellectual liberty in order that she might earn her living and educate her children."

Whatever the merits of their cases Margaret Oliphant has been shamefully neglected in modern years. She is now becoming more widely recognised as a leading writer of her day.

Margaret Oliphant – A Concise Bibliography

A canon of more than 120 works, including novels, travel books, histories, and volumes of literary criticism.

Novels

Margaret Maitland (1849)
Merkland (1850)
Caleb Field (1851)
John Drayton (1851)
Adam Graeme (1852)
The Melvilles (1852)
Katie Stewart (1852)
Harry Muir (1853)
Ailieford (1853)
The Quiet Heart (1854)
Magdalen Hepburn (1854)
Zaidee (1855)
Lilliesleaf (1855)

Christian Melville (1855)
The Athelings (1857)
The Days of My Life (1857)
Orphans (1858)
The Laird of Norlaw (1858)
Agnes Hopetoun's Schools and Holidays (1859)
Lucy Crofton (1860)
The House on the Moor (1861)
The Last of the Mortimers (1862)
Heart and Cross (1863)
Salem Chapel (1863)
The Rector (1863)
Doctor's Family (1863)
The Perpetual Curate (1864)
Miss Marjoribanks (1866)
Phoebe Junior (1876)
A Son of the Soil (1865)
Agnes (1866)
Madonna Mary (1867)
Brownlows (1868)
The Minister's Wife (1869)
The Three Brothers (1870)
John: A Love Story (1870)
Squire Arden (1871)
At his Gates (1872)
Ombra (1872
May (1873)
Innocent (1873)
The Story of Valentine and his Brother (1875)
A Rose in June (1874)
For Love and Life (1874)
Whiteladies (1875)
An Odd Couple (1875)
The Curate in Charge (1876)
Carità (1877)
Young Musgrave (1877)
Mrs. Arthur (1877)
The Primrose Path (1878)
Within the Precincts (1879)
The Fugitives (1879)
A Beleaguered City (1879)
The Greatest Heiress in England (1880)
He That Will Not When He May (1880)
In Trust (1881)
Harry Joscelyn (1881)
Lady Jane (1882)
A Little Pilgrim in the Unseen (1882)
The Lady Lindores (1883)

Sir Tom (1883)
Hester (1883)
It Was a Lover and his Lass (1883)
The Lady's Walk (1883)
The Wizard's Son (1884)
Madam (1884)
The Prodigals and their Inheritance (1885)
Oliver's Bride (1885)
A Country Gentleman and his Family (1886)
A House Divided Against Itself (1886)
Effie Ogilvie (1886)
A Poor Gentleman (1886)
The Son of his Father (1886)
Joyce (1888)
Cousin Mary (1888)
The Land of Darkness (1888)
Lady Car (1889)
Kirsteen (1890)
The Mystery of Mrs. Biencarrow (1890)
Sons and Daughters (1890)
The Railway Man and his Children (1891)
The Heir Presumptive and the Heir Apparent (1891)
The Marriage of Elinor (1891)
Janet (1891)
The Cuckoo in the Nest (1892)
Diana Trelawny (1892)
The Sorceress (1893)
A House in Bloomsbury (1894)
Sir Robert's Fortune (1894)
Who Was Lost and is Found (1894)
Lady William (1894)
Two Strangers (1895)
Old Mr. Tredgold (1895)
The Unjust Steward (1896)
The Ways of Life (1897)

Short stories
Neighbours on the Green (1889)
A Widow's Tale and Other Stories (1898)
That Little Cutty (1898)
The Open Door (1918)

Selected Articles

Mary Russel Mitford (Blackwood's Magazine, Vol. 75, 1854)
Evelin and Pepys (Blackwood's Magazine, Vol. 76, 1854)

The Holy Land (Blackwood's Magazine, Vol. 76, 1854)
Mr. Thackeray and his Novels (Blackwood's Magazine, Vol. 77, 1855)
Bulwer (Blackwood's Magazine, Vol. 77, 1855)
Charles Dickens (Blackwood's Magazine, Vol. 77, 1855)
Modern Novelists—Great and Small (Blackwood's Magazine, Vol. 77, 1855)
Modern Light Literature: Poetry (Blackwood's Magazine, Vol. 79, 1856)
Religion in Common Life (Blackwood's Magazine, Vol. 79, 1856)
Sydney Smith (Blackwood's Magazine, Vol. 79, 1856)
The Laws Concerning Women (Blackwood's Magazine, Vol. 79, 1856)
The Art of Caviling (Blackwood's Magazine, Vol. 80, 1856)
Béranger (Blackwood's Magazine, Vol. 83, 1858)
The Condition of Women (Blackwood's Magazine, Vol. 83, 1858)
The Missionary Explorer (Blackwood's Magazine, Vol. 83, 1858)
Religious Memoirs (Blackwood's Magazine, Vol. 83, 1858)
Social Science (Blackwood's Magazine, Vol. 88, 1860)
Scotland and her Accusers (Blackwood's Magazine, Vol. 90, 1861)
The Chronicles of Carlingford (Blackwood's Magazine 1862–1865)
Girolamo Savonarola (Blackwood's Magazine, Vol. 93, 1863)
The Life of Jesus (Blackwood's Magazine, Vol. 96, 1864)
Giacomo Leopardi (Blackwood's Magazine, Vol. 98, 1865)
The Great Unrepresented (Blackwood's Magazine, Vol. 100, 1866)
Mill on the Subjection of Women (The Edinburgh Review, Vol. 130, 1869)
The Opium-Eater (Blackwood's Magazine, Vol. 122, 1877)
Russian and Nihilism in the Novels of I. Tourgeniéf (Blackwood's Magazine, Vol. 127, 1880)
School and College (Blackwood's Magazine, Vol. 128, 1880)
The Grievances of Women (Fraser's Magazine, New Series, Vol. 21, 1880)
Mrs. Carlyle (The Contemporary Review, Vol. 43, May 1883)
The Ethics of Biography (The Contemporary Review, July 1883)
Victor Hugo (The Contemporary Review, Vol. 48, July/December 1885)
A Venetian Dynasty (The Contemporary Review, Vol. 50, August 1886)
Laurence Oliphant (Blackwood's Magazine, Vol. 145, 1889)
Tennyson (Blackwood's Magazine, Vol. 152, 1892)
Addison, the Humorist (Century Magazine, Vol. 48, 1894)
The Anti-Marriage League (Blackwood's Magazine, Vol. 159, 1896)

Biographies

Edward Irving (1862)
Francis of Assisi (1871)
Count de Montalembert (1872)
Dante (1877)
Cervantes (1880)
Life of Sheridan in the English Men of Letters series (1883)
John Tulloch (1888)
Laurence Oliphant (1892)

Historical & Critical Works

Historical Sketches of the Reign of George II (1869)
The Makers of Florence (1876)
A Literary History of England from 1760 to 1825 (1882)
The Makers of Venice (1887)
Royal Edinburgh (1890)
Jerusalem (1891)
The Makers of Modern Rome (1895)
William Blackwood and his Sons (1897)
The Sisters Brontë. In: Women Novelists of Queen Victoria's Reign (1897)

www.ingramcontent.com/pod-product-compliance
Lightning Source LLC
Chambersburg PA
CBHW052025020726
47501CB00004B/1245